THE LOST SUMMERS OF NEWPORT

Also by

Beatriz Williams, Lauren Willig, and Karen White

All the Ways We Said Goodbye
The Glass Ocean
The Forgotten Room

Beatriz Williams

Our Woman in Moscow
Her Last Flight
The Golden Hour
The Summer Wives
A Certain Age
Along the Infinite Sea
The Secret Life of Violet Grant
A Hundred Summers
The Wicked City series

Lauren Willig

Band of Sisters
The Summer Country
The English Wife
The Other Daughter
That Summer
The Ashford Affair
The Pink Carnation Series

Karen White

The Last Night in London
Dreams of Falling
The Night the Lights Went Out
Flight Patterns
The Sound of Glass
A Long Time Gone
The Tradd Street Series

THE LOST SUMMERS of NEWPORT

A Novel

BEATRIZ WILLIAMS,
LAUREN WILLIG,
AND KAREN WHITE

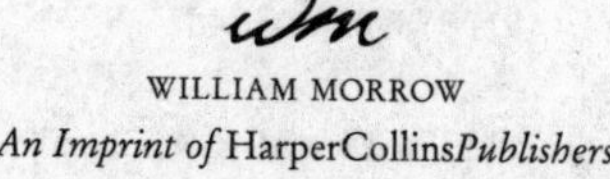

WILLIAM MORROW
An Imprint of HarperCollins*Publishers*

This is a work of fiction. Names, characters, places, and incidents are products of the authors' imagination or are used fictitiously and are not to be construed as real. Any resemblance to actual events, locales, organizations, or persons, living or dead, is entirely coincidental.

P.S.™ is a trademark of HarperCollins Publishers.

A hardcover edition of this book was published in 2022 by William Morrow, an imprint of HarperCollins Publishers.

FIRST WILLIAM MORROW PAPERBACK EDITION PUBLISHED 2023.

Library of Congress Cataloging-in-Publication Data

Names: Williams, Beatriz, author. | Willig, Lauren, author. | White, Karen (Karen S.), author.
Title: The lost summers of Newport : a novel / Beatriz Williams, Lauren Willig, Karen White.
Description: First edition. | New York, NY : William Morrow, [2022]
Identifiers: LCCN 2021049081 | ISBN 9780063040748 (hardback) | ISBN 9780063040762 (ebook)
Subjects: LCGFT: Thrillers (Fiction). | Novels.
Classification: LCC PS3623.I55643 L67 2022 | DDC 813/.6—dc23/eng/20211105
LC record available at https://lccn.loc.gov/2021049081

ISBN 978-0-06-304075-5

23 24 25 26 27 LBC 5 4 3 2 1

CHAPTER ONE

Andie

Newport, Rhode Island
September 2019

BY THE TIME my ancient Honda Civic and I made it across the Newport Bridge over the East Passage of Narragansett Bay and past the bars and tired neighborhoods nearest the harbor, it was clear I'd traveled more than just the thirty-three miles separating my hometown of Cranston, Rhode Island, from the coastal resort town of Newport. As soon as I turned left on Ruggles Avenue and into the historic neighborhood of Old Newport, it was as if I'd been dropped into another world; the three-bedroom split-level where I'd grown up with my parents and sister—and where I'd lived even after my mother had decamped for parts unknown—seemed a distant memory from another life. I found myself holding my breath, as if unwilling to allow the rarified air of this place to taint me. I'd seen it happen.

I slowed as I reached Bellevue Avenue and took another left, deciding at the last minute to take a brief tour to admire the palatial summer cottages. The novelist Henry James had nicknamed the houses and called Newport itself a breeding ground for White Elephants. He wasn't wrong. First impressions showed the grand scale of the sloping lawns and expansive views of both the water and the town, the monoliths of stone and marble towering above the sea cliffs like Zeus on Mount Olympus, protected by hedges and iron fences. But with my trained eye as an architectural historian, I spotted the signs of decay, of chipped paint and sagging porticos, and sympathized with the burden of general maintenance and leaky roofs.

The opulent Chateau-Sur-Mer dominated a corner lot, its mishmash of architectural styles ranging from its original Italian Renaissance to Second Empire French jarring to those of us who knew better, but nonetheless stunningly gorgeous to the less informed. It had been my mother's favorite of all the Newport mansions, as she'd point out during our frequent driving tours where she'd want to live if she ever had the money.

I detoured onto Narragansett to reach Ochre Point Avenue and glimpsed the famed Vanderbilt mansion, The Breakers. I was reminded of the oft-quoted F. Scott Fitzgerald, who'd once said, "The rich are different from us." Hemingway's famous reply had been, "Yes. They have more money." But even I knew it wasn't that simple.

Heading back to Bellevue, I inched my way down the street, glad that Labor Day weekend and the throngs of tourists were both gone so I was able to take my time without anyone honking behind me. I had been told that the driveway I was looking for would be hard to find, tucked between Marble House and Rosecliff, toward a less significant house perched near a small curve of coast with the improbable name of Sheep Point Cove.

I glanced down at the paper in my lap, the directions scrawled in my nearly indecipherable handwriting from an earlier phone call with my mentor and producer of *Makeover Mansion*, Marc Albertson. I frowned at the irony of how my handwriting matched his slurred words, recalling the number of times I'd had to ask him to repeat himself as I'd scribbled my notes.

I drove past the driveway twice. Judging from the sparse peppering of small, dark stones strewn over a mostly dirt drive, it was unsurprising that I'd missed it. I made the turn, unsure of what I would find on the other side of the open gates, now rusted in place and adorned with overgrown hedges and vines that brushed the roof and sides of my car as I passed through.

The sight of work vans and the film crew milling around, unloading equipment and unraveling cords, told me I was in the right place. As if the missing gray slate roof tiles and chipped pilasters wouldn't have been enough. A late-model Volvo station wagon with Connecticut plates and a dusty old Porsche 911 were parked on the lawn, but I instinctively knew that my Civic didn't belong next to them. Instead, I stopped my car at the end of the drive beneath a drooping porte cochere, where I was greeted by the headless statue of a well-endowed Roman god. Even his fig leaf had been worn away by time, in seeming solidarity with the crumbling mansion.

The house whimpered from gentle neglect, which was always better than the howling heard from houses with no hope of resurrection. A good friend from grad school had once told me that old houses were like holding a piece of history in one's hand. I knew she was right, which is why I'd devoted my career to saving them.

I exited my car and stepped out onto the weed-choked lawn, filling my nostrils with the salty tang of ocean air and stretching my neck to see above the third floor and count the number of chimneys. Viewers of *Makeover Mansion* always wanted to know that little factoid, as if it had anything to do with the importance of historic preservation or the perceived value of the structure. Not that the attitude surprised me. Going into our second season, I'd received enough email from viewers—and network heads—to understand that the general population was less interested in historic paint colors and authentic wood floor refinishing and more about modernizing kitchens and bathrooms for today's living. And the proverbial family skeletons hiding in musty closets. I found it all more than a little bewildering.

I walked toward a cluster of crew people, looking for Marc and then checking my phone again to see if he'd called. Except for three missed calls from a number I didn't recognize, there was nothing. Not even a voicemail. Ignoring the spam calls, I dialed Marc's number and let it ring ten times before giving up. I shoved the phone in the back pocket of my jeans and approached one of the men, a cameraman I knew from the first season of *Makeover Mansion,* George Chirona. He was older than me—midthirties—with muscled forearms and shoulders from hauling camera equipment all day. He gave me a bear hug in greeting.

"Andie! Good to see you. Any idea where Marc is? We've been waiting on him to get started."

"I was about to ask you the same thing. I spoke with him last night and he promised to be here before the crew to talk with the family to go over the ground rules, and to get a preliminary tour. That should have been more than an hour ago." Our eyes met in mutual understanding. "Let me see what I can do. Marc's been the only liaison with the family, but maybe they'll be okay dealing with me in his absence."

With a faked smile of confidence, I walked around to the front of the house, my steps slowing as I realized the sheer size of the home and tried to recall what little Marc had told me about the Sprague family. They'd purchased the mansion from the original owners in 1899, around the same time they'd changed the spelling of their last name from Spragg to the more high-brow Sprague. They'd seized the opportunity after a huge scandal resulted in a quick sale and renamed it Sprague Hall. Marc believed that sharing only sparse details about each project made for more interesting viewing as everything was as much a surprise to me as it was for the viewer—even though it left me looking like an unprepared amateur. I'd been tempted to Google, but a misplaced sense of loyalty to Marc always held me back.

I'd been tasked with the renovation of three major rooms in the Italian Renaissance mansion for a network how-to reality show. All that Marc had told me about the house's history was that it had been built in 1884 for a short-lived robber baron who had lost all his money less than a decade after he made it and who shot himself in shame. The house had been picked up by the Van Duyvils, an old-money Knickerbocker family who couldn't see their way to building one of the tacky new mansions but didn't mind picking one up cheap. But they'd had their own dramatic meltdown (Marc had said something about murder and suicide, not at this house, but at one of the Van Duyvils' others, which meant that, thank goodness, I wouldn't have to deal with them on the program) and that was when the house had fallen into the hands of the Sprague family. The Spragues were new money and desperate to disguise it behind the facade of a Newport mansion built to impress. Apparently Sprague senior had been pretty pissed about Rosecliff being built next door, overshadowing his comparatively modest palace (only thirty bedrooms). Mr. Sprague had accused the Nevada silver heiress and her husband who had built Rosecliff of knocking off Sprague Hall, just on a grander scale, even though, by all opinions, the Oelrichs were not in the least aware of the existence of Mr. Sprague, or his inferior mansion. As if there could be such a thing in Newport.

I climbed wide, narrow steps toward the front terrace adorned with a colonnade on three sides, then passed beneath three sweeping arches. Away from the bright sunlight, I blinked in the relative dim shade of the entranceway and found myself staring at two massive carved oak doors. I attempted to determine which was the *main* door and looked for a doorbell before giving up and knocking on the one on the right.

Four large holes in the door made me wonder if there had once been a door knocker at some point that had either fallen off or been stolen. Or been removed and sold. Looking up at empty chains suspended over the arch above me where an enormous lantern had undoubtedly once hung, I'd bet on the latter.

While I waited, I noted more signs of decay and the inevitable passage of time all structures were forced to endure, especially those in which the cost of upkeep overtook the funds needed to pay for it. Marc had explained that the elderly and reclusive Lucia "Lucky" Sprague had agreed to a season of *Makeover Mansion* to be filmed in her house for this sole reason, but from his inability to meet my gaze when he told me so, I'd been left to wonder otherwise.

Rosecliff and Kingscote, another white elephant, had been bequeathed to the Preservation Society of Newport County in the early seventies, complete with an income from a maintenance trust. I wondered why Sprague Hall had not been similarly blessed. My thoughts dwelled on the long list of tragedies that had plagued the estate and the families who'd lived in it since it was built in 1884. I saw the chipping and sagging ruin of this once graceful dame as one of the biggest tragedies of all.

I knocked again, the sound swallowed within the thick wood of the door. I imagined most visitors gave up and left after finding neither a doorbell to ring nor the staff to answer a knock. If I didn't need my job or the money it offered, I would have done the same. Instead, I took a deep breath, and turned the brass door handle, not all that surprised to feel it give and the door swing open on protesting hinges.

"Hello?" I called out.

The first thing I noticed was the heaviness of the air, an atmosphere of neglect and abandonment like the opening of an ancient crypt. I left the door open, hoping the crisp ocean breezes would dilute the oppressiveness and allow any restless spirits roaming among the dust motes to depart.

The second thing I noticed was the sheer magnitude of the space, the soaring fifty-foot ceilings and Caen limestone walls, the heavy cornices of plaster and gilt. The painted ceiling, depicting what might have been Poseidon taking control of the sea from Zeus, but whose once vibrant colors had faded, had great patches missing, presumably having long since taken a suicidal plunge to the marble floor below.

While working on my historic preservation degree and in my job as architectural historian, I'd seen plenty of large houses. But this was on a scale of Newport proportions: bloated, gilded, and overelaborate. Considering it had been built to mimic the Renaissance palaces of Turin and Genoa, it wasn't a complete surprise. The total absence of furniture and accessories was.

"Hello?" I called again, hearing the echo of my words and the faint cadence of voices coming from somewhere deep in the house. I followed the sound through the great hall, passing rooms whose uses had long since gone extinct from modern houses, but which pulled to me with a nostalgia felt only by those like me who loved old houses and all their quirks.

By the time I reached the unadorned back hallways, I knew I'd found the area of the servants' domain and possibly the kitchen—one of the rooms I'd been tasked with renovating.

As I approached a brightly lit room at the end of a hallway, the voices of a man and a woman got louder. Even though their voices weren't raised, it was clear by their clipped words that seemed to get shorter and shorter that they were arguing.

"Really, Luke," the woman's voice carried down the hall. "You need to exercise your power of attorney now before this ridiculous TV show is allowed to happen. It's not too late. You simply have to convince Lucky that she needs to sell this albatross to some Russian oligarch or tech millionaire—they're the only ones who can afford a place like this anymore. It's ridiculous to hold on to it and continue to live in it while it collapses around her—especially when she never even leaves her rooms! I will be more than happy to find a gorgeous retirement community for her."

"No," came the male voice, presumably Luke's. "She signed the contract and is mentally competent. As her power of attorney, it's my job to make sure that we abide by her wishes—not ours."

I stopped in the doorway of a bright kitchen taken straight from a fifties home-décor magazine, complete with black-and-white-check laminate floors, turquoise cabinets, and Formica countertops. Large windows framed the room, explaining the brightness, leaving me at a momentary disadvantage as the two occupants were backlit from the sunshine, the light aimed directly at me as if I were in an interrogation.

I took a step into the room, unwilling to accept the disadvantage.

The woman spoke, her accent polished New England, her bobbed hair Grace Kelly–blond, her clothes undoubtedly designer. "I'm Hadley Sprague-Armstrong. Who are you?" Her icy pale blue eyes swept over me, quickly taking in my dark hair, olive skin, crew neck cotton sweater from Target, and the Sperry Top-Siders I'd found at a garage sale while in college. Telling her my name would simply cement her snap first impression: not WASP and lacking funds. Both of which were correct.

"I'm Andrea Figuero, the show host for *Makeover Mansion*. The producer, Marc Albertson, and the crew call me Andie." I knew better than to offer a hand to shake. My gaze traveled between Hadley and Luke, their remarkable physical similarities identifying them as siblings, as I attempted to determine which of them was in charge. Luke appeared to be around the same age as his sister, about thirty, with sun-streaked light brown hair. His khaki shorts and button-down oxford cloth shirt with rolled-up sleeves exposing tanned forearms was a uniform I knew all too well. The fact that he wore sunglasses inside and reeked of stale beer made me dismiss him out of hand. Turning back to Hadley, I said, "Speaking of Marc, have you seen him?"

Her lips tightened. "No, we haven't. My brother and I were just discussing the show. Since our grandmother has changed her mind . . ."

"No, she hasn't," Luke said, wearily pulling off his sunglasses, revealing blue eyes the same icy shade as his sister's. Except his were bloodshot and his cheek wore a smear of lipstick, making me dislike him even more. "But Marc isn't here. I got up early to meet with him so I'm more than a little annoyed. He didn't say anything about sending an underling."

I bristled at his dismissive tone, but knew I had to hold on to my temper. I needed this job too badly. Forcing a neutral expression, I said,

"Since Marc's not here, I'd like to go ahead and do a quick tour of the three rooms scheduled for the renovation. I want to get the crew inside to film preliminary before shots so we can get started on that today."

Luke was already walking toward a back door. Over his shoulder, he said, "Hadley, I'm sure you can handle that. I'm meeting friends at the club. It's too nice a day to be wasting time indoors instead of out on the water."

He belonged to a yacht club. Of course. As if I needed yet another reason to dislike him.

"I really don't think . . . ," Hadley began to protest.

He opened the door just as Hadley's phone rang. She held up her hand to prevent Luke from leaving as she answered the call. After a short conversation, she tossed her phone into her large bag. "Sorry to disappoint, but I've got to go. The stationers have completely messed up Emmeline's fourth birthday party invitations. The font is not at all what I wanted and they can't seem to understand the problem. It's hopeless. I've got to go straighten it out. You're on your own, Brother." She let her cool gaze slip to me. "Goodbye, Adrienne. I doubt I'll be seeing you again. Despite what my brother thinks, this arrangement is not going to work."

"We'll talk later," Luke said through gritted teeth as he held the door open for his sister.

"It's Andrea," I called to her departing back, unwilling to let her have the last word.

Luke's mouth slanted upward in a reluctant and fleeting smile. "I guess I'm stuck with you." He glanced at his watch. "If we hurry, I can still make it. Hope you can walk fast. Just stay close so you don't get lost."

At an almost run, I followed him through opulent rooms redolent of their former glory with sculpted fireplaces, faded and peeling wall murals, missing chandeliers, and threadbare rugs. Yet the scope and elegance remained, a ghost of a curious past I was eager to uncover.

And perhaps help to regain its lost beauty and relevance. It's why I'd been attracted to historic preservation in the first place.

I followed Luke through back passageways I knew I'd never find again to the ballroom, the wall murals showing empty spots and loose wires where sconces should have hung. A threadbare sofa sat in one corner, the cushions sagging in the middle. "Where is all the furniture—" I began, interrupted by my phone ringing.

"Excuse me," I said, still running behind Luke as I spoke. "This must be Marc." I answered it without looking at the screen, not wanting to trip or lose sight of Luke and be lost forever. "Where are you?" I hissed.

"Miss Figuero? I was about to ask you the same thing. I've been trying to reach you all morning."

I didn't recognize the woman's voice but recalled the multiple phone calls from the same number I'd seen on my screen earlier and had assumed were spam. "I'm sorry, who is this?"

"This is Roberta Montemurno, Petey's first grade teacher. You were signed up to bring the snack for today. Can I hope it will be here within the next hour?"

Shit. "Yes. Of course. I'm so sorry. I don't know how I forgot. . . ."

"No worries. As long as they get here in time. I'm sure you can imagine what fifteen disappointed first graders can be like."

"Not really, but—"

"Thank you, Miss Figuero." She clicked off.

Luke, having finally paused, looked at me with annoyance. "One minute," I said, already dialing my dad. He picked up on the first ring.

"Dad, I need you to run to Price Right and pick up two dozen cupcakes from the bakery section and take them to Petey's school. Nut and gluten free. I completely forgot."

His heavy sigh rumbled through the phone. "All right. I'll take care of it. But it's going to cost you."

"Gin rummy or pinochle?"

"Your pick."

I heard his grin through his words. "Done. See you when you get home."

"Thanks, Dad. You're the best."

"I know."

I hung up, my smile fading as I looked at Luke, who didn't bother to hide his impatience. "If you're done chatting, can we continue the tour?"

I wanted to correct him and say that making me chase him at breakneck speed through a sixty-thousand-square-foot mansion was more like a marathon than a tour but bit my tongue. I followed him through another maze of passageways until I found myself crossing the great hall from another direction, then heading up the main staircase to the second-floor gallery. Its bronze and wrought iron railings were still intact as was the stained-glass skylight overhead. A faded spot on the wall indicated where a tapestry might have once hung. I wanted to ask Luke what had happened to it and all of the other missing pieces in the house, but I was afraid I already knew. I would ask Marc.

We walked down a long hallway over patched and frayed formerly red carpet to a doorway near the end. Luke turned the handle and stepped back, allowing me to go first. "Maybelle's bedroom. I believe this is the third room in addition to the kitchen and ballroom in our contract."

"Yes," I said, curious as to who Maybelle was, and why the décor in this particular room was at odds with that in the rest of the house. Before I had time to study it or ask questions, I was dragged back down the main staircase and out through the front door from which I'd arrived.

I was out of breath from the running, and it took me two attempts to speak. "Do you have a floor plan? I need to direct the crew, but I have no idea if I can find those rooms again."

"You'll figure it out." He glanced at his watch again. "I've got to go." He began walking toward the parked 911 as I jogged along beside him, my legs no match for his long strides. Luke continued: "In case Marc hasn't drilled this into you already, there are three stipulations for allowing the filming here. The first is that no one attempts to speak with our grandmother, Lucia Sprague. Her rooms are on the third floor and very private. She prefers to keep them that way. No one is to go up there. The second is that absolutely no filming is to be allowed in or around the boathouse."

"But . . ." I wanted him to slow down, to tell me why. I'd never been the sort of person to blindly follow directions. I always wanted to have a reason.

"Those are the rules. Break them, and the deal is off." He opened the driver's door and slid in.

"What's the third rule?"

"No one from the family is to be in any camera shot, including me. I live here, and I don't want to be disturbed." He shut the door before I could suggest he invest in a pair of earplugs because shooting started at eight A.M. The engine rumbled as he put the car into gear, then he sped away, churning up dirt and what little loose gravel was left on the drive.

I took a deep breath, trying unsuccessfully to calm my anger, and found myself looking down the lawn in the direction of the water, where the boathouse would be located. Luke had said we couldn't *film* there. But he hadn't said I couldn't actually *go* there. Still smarting at being so easily dismissed, I made the quick decision just to take a peek at the forbidden boathouse. After telling George and the rest of the crew that I'd be right back and to be on the lookout for Marc, I began walking briskly toward the water.

I'd barely gone twenty feet before the hairs on the back of my neck stood up as the inescapable feeling of being watched swept over me. I wheeled around, wondering if Luke had returned. The drive was empty. My gaze traveled up the Indiana limestone wall of the house to the row of third-floor windows. I squinted, wondering if the shadow of a woman was a figment of my fertile imagination. It was too far for me to see details, but I felt sure that dark, piercing eyes were staring down at me. I blinked, and the shadow disappeared, leaving only the slight movement of a curtain.

A cloud briefly obscured the sun. I didn't believe in omens or portents of doom, but I felt strongly that I was being urged to retrace my steps and return to the crew. I walked quickly, the surety of a direct gaze aimed at my back following me until I turned the corner.

CHAPTER TWO

Ellen

Newport, Rhode Island
June 1899

SOMEONE WAS WATCHING from the gallery above.

"Caen marble," Ellen's new employer was saying, his voice uneven with the effort of moving and talking. "The brasses are from France."

Upstairs, something moved behind the ornate railings of the gallery that ran across three sides of the room. A trick of the light, Ellen told herself, an illusion created by the glare of electric light on gold leaf, dazzling the eyes. Ellen squinted, craning her neck to try to peer through the elaborately curved metal to whatever lay beyond, but the railings overhead seemed to move and twist like something out of a nightmare.

Which was ridiculous. Those railings were solid iron or brass or whatever it was they were made of. Mr. Sprague had probably told her, and she simply hadn't heard it. Ellen had been terrified that he would quiz her on her background, that he would peer at her face and know her to be a fraud, but all he'd done since the moment she'd appeared at the door, carpetbag in hand, was conduct an itemized inventory of the wonders of his new home.

And it was wondrous. Wondrous and overwrought. Gold leaf piled upon gold leaf; marble clashed with marble. Deities writhed across the ceiling, something sea-themed, in honor of the ocean just outside the house. Ellen could spot nymphs simpering on shells and a bearded man with a toga and a triton, scowling fiercely at them all, scowling at Ellen as though he could suss out her secrets.

Whatever it was—whoever it was—on the balcony moved again, moving when Ellen and Mr. Sprague moved, keeping pace with them. Not a trick of the light, then. Ellen could feel the fear starting, the prickle at the back of her neck, the cold sweat beneath her stays. Someone was up there. Watching her.

"Magnificent, isn't it?" said Mr. Sprague, and Ellen realized he'd stopped, smack in the middle of the great hall. He was looking at her smugly, both his chins wobbling above his stiff collar, an absurd collar for summer at the seaside, starched and formal.

"Yes, yes," said Ellen hastily, her hands gripping the handles of her carpetbag a little too tightly. She forced herself to look at Mr. Sprague, to stop staring up at the railings. It was most likely a servant, eager to see the new addition to the household. Or her charge, Maybelle.

Yes, that was it. It must have been Maybelle, peering through the railings like any naughty child. That was all. They wouldn't have found her here, couldn't have found her here.

Not yet.

But she couldn't help herself staring up again, all the same.

Mr. Sprague peered at her through his slightly bulging blue eyes, as if he'd sensed something wrong in her response. "I'm surprised to see you gawping like that. You did say you'd worked for the Van Duyvils."

The Van Duyvils. Last winter's tragedy. Splashed all over the papers from New York to Boston. Murder and suicide or possibly murder and murder, and two small children left behind. This had been their house, one of their many houses, before death and scandal had struck.

Ellen knew Mrs. Bayard Van Duyvil as a grainy picture in the *New*

York World. As a name on a reference written in haste, a desperate attempt to start again.

"Only in New York," Ellen said, hoping the tremble in her voice would be taken for awe, and not fear. She'd never been a good liar. "They never came here when I was with them. Their house in New York was nothing to this. This is . . . something remarkable."

Mr. Sprague nodded, satisfied, and Ellen felt her breath releasing, just a little. "Isn't it? It cost a fortune to build. Based on an Italian prince's palace."

"It's fit for royalty, sir." It was fit for the madhouse, but Ellen would praise this riot of excess to the skies if it meant a place to hide. No one looked at a music teacher, not here, not in Newport. Here, she was simply another servant, one of the vast entourage of the great.

Or the hangers-on of the great, which was even better. No one was going to notice a second-rate social climber's music teacher. No one would think to look for her here. Ellen risked another glance at the gallery. No one.

"You understand what you're here for?" Mr. Sprague moved so close that his thigh nudged Ellen's carpetbag.

The smell of hair oil and sweat overwhelmed her. Ellen forced herself not to take a step back, not to show her revulsion. "To teach music, sir."

"To my sister. Maybelle." Mr. Sprague spoke the name slowly, holding it on his tongue. Abruptly, he clasped his hands behind his back and started moving through the room. "You won't have heard. It's not public knowledge yet. We've an Italian prince coming here. The Prince di Conti. His family goes back to . . . well, back to something."

Ellen nodded, trying to act as though this were news to her. She could hear Hildie, in the stuffy confines of the dressing room at the Hibernia, one leg up on a chair, rolling her stocking up her thigh. *And he's that excited about it, little Johnny-Boy. Gonna show all them Vanderbilts what's what with a real Your Highness, Your Highness.*

Hildie, with her brassy curls and her throaty alto voice, showing off the bracelet Mr. Sprague had given her—Johnny-Boy, she called him. *Poor man, all alone with the swells, trying to look like he belongs.*

The Spragues were new money, mining money, from somewhere out west. Sprague's mother had run an inn. *The sort that rents rooms that are already occupied*, Hildie had said with a wink. That, of course, had been before Sprague senior had hit copper. A great deal of copper. All that copper had turned rapidly to gold, and here he was, the boy raised in a bawdy house about to entertain an Italian prince—and hook a title for his sister.

That's what Hildie had said. Hildie, passing the time between shows, with her mimic's gift for mockery.

She'd never imagined that Ellen might take the information and run.

"It's very impressive, sir," Ellen said politely. Her carpetbag, with all her worldly goods, hung heavy in her hand. She'd abandoned most of her belongings, taking only the essentials of life, but her mother's music books—she couldn't leave those. They were all she had of her mother, of the life before.

"Italian, of course. There's that. But a prince is a prince. And he's coming here. To Sprague Hall." Mr. Sprague brooded a moment, before adding, darkly, "The prince likes music."

He made it sound like a deviant pastime.

"Many people do, sir," said Ellen politely. That was, after all, why she was here. Because the prince liked music. Because Mr. Sprague had placed an advertisement looking for a music teacher for his sister, Maybelle.

Sprague looked at her slyly. "The prince likes *singers*. If you know what I mean."

Ellen held herself a little straighter, feeling her face stiffening, as though she were the young lady of good family in reduced circumstances she claimed to be. "Sir?"

Sprague flapped a well-manicured hand at her. "Got to make sure that Maybelle's . . . how do you folk say it? In voice. Sweeten the pot, you see. The girl can sing in tune, but she needs . . . whatever you musical types do. Trills and whatnot. Make it look good. Like that Swedish Nightingale."

No amount of singing scales was going to turn a debutante into Jenny Lind in two weeks.

"I can teach Miss Sprague arias and ballads appropriate to sing in company, sir," Ellen said primly.

Sprague peered at her, as though she were a basket of cabbages he suspected of having worms. Ellen had met his type before, men who prided themselves on their shrewdness and missed that they were being robbed blind. Men who never enjoyed what they had because they were always convinced that everyone was out to cheat them. Possibly because they spent their time cheating others. "Arias and ballads, eh?"

"As are sung in all the best drawing rooms," Ellen said firmly.

Not that she'd know. The Hibernia was known for off-color jokes, bawdy songs, and bared knees. Although now and again, they'd do a respectable turn, something to keep the audience surprised, to change the mood. Dermot had asked Ellen if she'd consider it: stand up there in a ladylike dress with a lace collar up to her chin and her own gold broach and sing "Annie Laurie," "Make them think of their girl, or the girl they'd like to have."

Ellen had demurred. One didn't refuse with Dermot, not right out. But one could demur. He'd liked it, that show of ladylike modesty, the dropped chin, the hesitant shake of the head. Never knowing how hard she was shaking underneath, how afraid that he'd press her on it. Knowing that she survived on his sufferance, on the residual goodwill that came of being Aidan O'Donnell's girl.

But there were some refusals that weren't acceptable, some decisions that couldn't be erased by being Aidan O'Donnell's girl. She'd crossed that line. And now she was someone else, someone else entirely, Ellen Daniels, a music teacher, respectable and poor.

Well, the poor bit was true. Her father had been everyone's friend, everyone's odd job man (and it was best, after her mother and siblings had died, not to look at some of those jobs too closely), but he'd been as open-handed as he was friendly. Money, when he had it, slipped through his fingers. And why be after worrying? he'd asked. There'd always be friends to look after them.

Friends like Dermot. Friends who expected something of you in return.

Ellen swallowed hard. She shouldn't be thinking of Dermot. Dermot had been Eileen's problem. Eileen O'Donnell. She was Ellen Daniels now.

Simple, honest Ellen.

The sort of woman who knew what was sung in all the best drawing rooms. Annabelle Van Duyvil's music teacher.

Ellen spared a moment of gratitude for Annabelle Van Duyvil, that unknown woman who had been so considerate as to make herself a recluse from society before she disappeared—or was murdered. One of the few things anyone had known about her for certain, that wasn't rumor or speculation or outright libel, was Annabelle Van Duyvil's love of music.

There was no one, now, who would know whether Annabelle Van Duyvil had had a music teacher or not. At least, Ellen hoped not. All she had to do was carry this off, train this Maybelle Sprague, make her presentable for her prince—and then she'd have a real reference to carry her on to the next position. A reference from a princess. The Principessa di Conti. Every job, every reference, would take her farther away from the music hall, Hibernia. And Dermot. And all the things she wasn't meant to know but did.

"Can you do it?" Sprague was asking her. "Can you do it in two weeks?"

"By the end of two weeks, your sister will have several pieces fit for company," Ellen said, with more confidence than she felt.

"You may think that, but . . ." Mr. Sprague frowned down at her, pressing his lower chin into his collar. "You need to understand about Maybelle. She's . . . not like the other girls you've taught."

Ellen presumed not. Her acquaintance had been mostly chorus girls.

"She's . . . I guess you could say she's, er, unspoiled." Mr. Sprague pulled at his collar. Sweat dripped down the side of his face, bringing a sheen of hair oil with it. "Lacks polish."

"As any sheltered young girl of good family would," said Ellen tactfully, trying not to let her apprehension show. Maybe this was why the job had been so easy to obtain with her forged reference. Maybe Maybelle Sprague was a hoyden, a virago, the sort who ate governesses for lunch and spat out music teachers after tea.

"Er, yes. Quite. Exactly." Sprague preened at that "good family." Ellen hated herself just a bit. But you did what you had to do to survive. Within limits. There were lines one crossed and others one didn't, but a bit of false flattery fell in that gray area in between. "It's her father's fault. Er, our father's fault. He spoiled her. Kept her wrapped in cotton wool. Didn't push her forward. If he'd listened to me—"

"Has she a governess?" Ellen asked tentatively. Or a minder, from the sound of it. She was beginning to picture her charge as a cross between the maiden and the minotaur, chained slavering to a post and thrown the occasional chunk of red meat.

"Oh, governesses." Sprague shrugged that aside. "Useless, the lot of them. Dried up spinsters full of bookish nonsense. Well, if the prince takes her she'll be his problem, not mine. They're all Italians over there, anyway. But she has to sing, do you understand? It's crucial that she sing."

Ellen could only hope that the sister wasn't as tone deaf as the brother. She could hear it in his voice, that flatness, the lack of variation in the cadences. It did not bode well. "She will."

"Good." Sprague yanked on a cord half-hidden behind a tapestry.

To the maid who appeared, he barked, "You. Bridget. Take Miss Daniels to her room and then to Miss Maybelle."

And that was it. He hadn't asked a thing about Ellen.

She'd had it all prepared. Her name, her background, how long she had been with the Van Duyvils. Nothing that would stand up to too much scrutiny, but enough, she hoped, to pass muster. She'd practiced it again and again in the little scrap of mirror in the hired room in Providence, said it often enough that she didn't stutter on the names and her eyes wouldn't shift sideways as she lied.

But it had been for nothing after all. All John Sprague cared about was that she could teach his sister to sing.

And she could, she *could,* Ellen told herself fiercely, as she followed the maid up the great stair to the gallery above. She'd coaxed chorus girls chosen more for their legs than their tone into tune. It didn't matter how coarse Maybelle Sprague might be, how rude; she'd train her into song enough to sweeten the pot for the prince and get Ellen a respectable reference.

Ellen Daniels. Honest, insignificant Ellen.

She saw the way the maid's eyes glanced off her, glanced off her gray dress with its white collar and cuffs, the lace good but plain, the cut Quaker in its simplicity. Not a colleague, to be gossiped with; not a guest to be gossiped about; but in that murky in-between, a hireling, but of the sort that had "miss" appended to her name—and therefore entirely uninteresting to everyone both above- and belowstairs.

Good. That was exactly how Ellen wanted it.

She wondered if she was to eat with the servants or with the family, and who it was, here, who made those sorts of decisions. Not Mr. Sprague, she imagined. He didn't seem the sort to care whether anyone other than himself ate at all.

There was a Mrs. Sprague. Hildie had told her as much. But Mrs. Sprague was taking the waters in Switzerland. Mrs. Sprague appeared to be perpetually taking the waters in Switzerland. The household, from what Ellen had been able to ascertain, consisted entirely of Mr. Sprague and his sister, Maybelle.

The maid took her, not, as Ellen had expected, to the upper regions, but to a room off the great gallery itself, the area where the principal bedrooms were located.

"Are you sure?" Ellen had had an image of a little attic room, a Spartan space with a bed frame and washbasin where she could close the door and hide, like a dormouse curled in its hole, just another bit of dust in the corners of this great house.

This room wasn't large, but it was luxuriously appointed, the walls paneled in lightly gilded wood, the bed draped in blue velvet. And it had a direct view over the gardens that cascaded down the back of the house to the very edge of the cliff, where a treacherous path twisted down to the water itself.

"This can't be right."

"Mr. Sprague's orders." The maid set Ellen's carpetbag down. It looked particularly shabby on the rich Axminster carpet. "Shall I unpack for you?"

"No, no." There was nothing in there to give her away. At least she didn't think there was. But Ellen moved to block the bag all the same. "Thank you."

The maid didn't shrug. She was well enough trained for that. But she gave the impression of a shrug. Ellen wasn't a proper guest; she wasn't going to leave a tip or elegant cast-off clothing. In short, she wasn't worth the bother.

"Miss Maybelle's through here." Not giving Ellen time to take off her hat or splash water on her face, the maid pushed open a door set into the paneling.

On the other side lay a floral fantasy. It was all the rose gardens of the world jammed together. Roses on the walls, roses on the carpet. A great, gilded bed on a dais, draped with layers and layers and layers of ruched pink silk. Watteau shepherdesses simpered from the walls;

naked Cupids shot arrows from the corners of the ceiling. The simpering sweetness didn't go at all with the frenzied formality of the rest of the house. It was opulent, yes, but in a way that spoke of spring and sunshine and a young girl's dreams. A corner appeared to have been set aside as a sort of nook, the part of the room truly lived in, with books tumbled around a chaise longue, writing paper spilling out of an escritoire, slippers lying any which way on the carpet.

And on the chaise itself lay the most remarkable collection of flounces. Pink flounces, layer upon layer of them, and a little pair of matching pink slippers sticking out below. The flounces were so overwhelming that it took Ellen a moment to realize there was a woman within them, reclining with a book and an apple.

"Music teacher's here," said the maid laconically.

There was a flurry of lace-edged petticoats and the woman on the chaise lurched to her feet, dropping the apple, lunging for it, and finally righting herself. Not a woman—a girl, red-faced and flustered, her pink bow untied and her fair hair any which way about her face.

"Oh, hello. You must be Miss . . . Miss . . ."

"Daniels," said Ellen, feeling thoroughly discomfited.

The girl winced. "Miss Daniels! Yes, that's it. I'm so terribly sorry. I'd meant to remember; I'd even written it down."

"It's no matter," said Ellen slowly. Unspoiled, yes. But not in the way she'd imagined. Maybelle Sprague seemed far younger than her seventeen years, with the awkward posture of a schoolgirl, shifting from one foot to the other and shoving her hands behind her back in a futile attempt to get the apple out of the way.

"If that'll be all?" said the maid. Ellen hadn't been in many great houses, but even she didn't think that maids were meant to speak to their employers that way.

But Maybelle didn't seem to think anything of it. "Yes, thank you, Meg."

Meg, not Bridget. Ellen suppressed a grimace. It shouldn't surprise her that Mr. Sprague was the sort to call all his maids Bridget, even if they weren't. If he knew that she was an Eileen rather than an Ellen, she'd be a Bridget to him, too.

Maybelle turned back to Ellen, twisting her hands together nervously at her waist. "Oh, dear, what I ought to have said was welcome to Sprague Hall." She assumed the mantle of adulthood with great seriousness, like a child playing dress-up in her mother's clothes. "Have they made you comfortable?"

"Very." Ellen was gritty with dust from having walked down the road; her chemise was clinging to her with sweat; and her throat was dry with thirst, but she would never in a million years have said anything otherwise to Maybelle, who was looking at her anxiously, desperate to please. "I understand we're to be neighbors."

"Neighbors . . . oh, you mean the room! Yes. I hope you don't mind terribly? Not being in a real room, I mean. That used to be the dressing room, but I have quite enough room for my dresses. . . . It was—it was John's idea. He thought it might be nice for me to have another woman about. Lysette—Mrs. Sprague—my sister-in-law—she's away for her health. In Switzerland. Or maybe Baden-Baden? It's somewhere where they have waters. Special waters, I mean. And my mother died when I was a baby, so . . ."

She trailed off in an excess of awkwardness.

"It's a lovely room," said Ellen firmly, eager to stave off any more confidences. "I understand I'm to teach you to sing."

"Oh yes! My brother . . . well, he's not my brother, really. He's my stepbrother. My father married his mother, you see, when I was two, and John was fourteen. That was back in Colorado, you see, and my father . . ." Maybelle paused, her hands twisted in the expensive material of her dress. "But there's only the two of us now. John is the only family I have."

"I'm the only family I have," said Ellen before she could think better of it.

Maybe it was something about the way Maybelle was looking at her, the mute appeal in her face. She reminded Ellen painfully of her little sister. Clodagh, only six years old when she died, holding that rag doll she loved. Clodagh, who just wanted to make everyone happy.

Maybelle's face lit. "Are you? Then you know, you know how alone one feels, how it hurts to lose—"

Oh Lord, it hurt. It hurt so much.

Ellen stood there, her face frozen, unable to bring herself to respond. Clodagh and Niamh and Saiorise and Aislynn. And Mam. Lying there, thin white hands still on her wedding coverlet. She hadn't thought of them, she hadn't let herself think of them, not in the years of keeping house for her father, scolding him when he came home a little the worse for wear, trying not to think too much of what he'd been doing, trying not to see too much or hear too much, and then, later, at the Hibernia, just struggling to survive, to keep her place, to keep her dignity. Cold inside, dead inside, always afraid.

Always alone, even in a crowd.

Maybelle dropped her head, taking Ellen's silence for rebuke. "I shouldn't complain. I'm very fortunate to have John to look after me; he always tells me so."

Ellen was sure he did.

She's the one with the money. The kid. He just manages it. Manages it away, if you know what I mean. Hildie had twisted the bracelet on her wrist, scowling at the small stones sparkling in the light of the gas lamps. *At least I got something out of it while the pickings were good.*

Ellen hadn't paid attention at the time. She hadn't thought of it. But now—here with Maybelle—she remembered, and the words took on a whole new significance.

And what of it? Ellen pushed down the memories, pushed down the image of Clodagh, her blond hair in braids. Maybelle Sprague was nothing to do with Clodagh or any of it; they were worlds apart. She'd no call to be feeling sorry for an heiress, whose sugary confection of a dress cost more than Ellen could hope to earn in a year. The family relationships of the Spragues were none of her concern. As long as her salary was paid.

"You're lucky to have a brother to look after you," was all Ellen said.

Maybelle bit her lip. It was odd; they were much the same height, but Maybelle gave the impression of looking up at Ellen. It might have been the way she ducked her head before she spoke, as though apologizing for making a sound. "I hope—I hope you won't feel alone here."

"You're very kind, Miss Sprague," said Ellen quietly. Too kind. She'd latch on to Ellen if Ellen let her. She wasn't sure she had the strength to carry anyone else right now. She had barely the strength to carry herself.

"Maybelle." The girl looked up at Ellen with big, eager blue eyes. "Please, call me Maybelle."

"Maybelle." Ellen felt something twist in her chest, frustration and grief. The girl was too innocent to be left alone by herself. Like Ellen had been, once. Before. Back when her mother was still alive, before her father had sunk deeper and deeper into associations that could only bring them pain. "I understand you're to perform at a recital in two weeks' time."

Maybelle's eyes dropped. "Yes. For the prince."

Ellen looked at her quizzically. "It's a great honor to sing for a prince."

"I know." The girl didn't look honored; she looked terrified. Ellen wondered if John Sprague had pushed her too hard, made too clear what was expected of her: that she, this innocent little girl out of the schoolroom, attract an aristocratic man of the world.

Briskly, Ellen said, "We have our work cut out for us, but I'm sure you'll do splendidly. You have a beautiful speaking voice."

"I do?" Maybelle looked at her so hopefully that Ellen felt another inconvenient stab of emotion.

"You do," said Ellen firmly. "You can always tell from the speaking voice. If you'll direct me to the music room, we can get started."

Ellen desperately wanted to take off her hat, to wash her face, to turn around her strange new room and acclimate to her surroundings, but Maybelle needed her, even if it was only to play a few scales and tell her she had promise. Ellen found herself determined that Maybelle would sing for the prince—not like the Swedish Nightingale, perhaps, but good enough that any praise would be more than flattery. Not for the sake of the reference Mr. Sprague would give her, but for Maybelle.

Ellen straightened her spine, trying to ignore how damp and limp her collar was in the heat, how dusty the hem of her dress. "You can sing for me what you know—a song, or scales, anything you like—and I can see where we need to go from there."

"Thank you," said Maybelle with feeling. "I'll do my best, I promise I will. I only hope I'm not a disappoint— Ack!"

The doors of an armoire slammed open and a creature barreled out, laughing maniacally. "Got you, got you, got you!"

"Dudley!" Maybelle had dropped the apple she'd been holding.

The boy—because it was a boy, a stocky boy in short pants and high socks—snatched the apple up and took a big chomp out of it. "You should have seen your face! Gaping like a fish! Fish face, fish face, Maybelle has a fish face!"

Maybelle's mouth trembled, but she made a noble effort to control her feelings. "Miss Daniels, this is my nephew, Dudley."

"That's Master Dudley," said the boy, sizing Ellen up insolently. He took another large bite of the apple. "I'm going to be master here someday and you'll all have to do what I say."

He tossed the apple at Ellen, laughing as she fumbled to catch it, and disappeared down the hall, his shoes clumping on the marble.

"I hope—I hope you won't mind Dudley," said Maybelle uncertainly. "He doesn't mean it, he's only little."

Not that little. And Ellen was sure he did mean it. But that, again, was none of her concern. She was here only for the summer. Just long enough for Maybelle to catch her prince. And Ellen was suddenly quite, quite determined that Maybelle would catch her prince.

Anything had to be better than the Spragues.

"Come," Ellen said, with feigned cheerfulness, holding out an arm to her pupil. "Let's make a start, shall we? We have a great deal to do and very little time."

CHAPTER THREE

Lucky

Newport, Rhode Island
July 1957

LUCKY ALWAYS THOUGHT they had too much time on their hands. That was the real trouble with this crowd, wasn't it? Idle hands did the devil's work.

Well, the devil must be awfully busy here in the august rooms of the yacht club, Lucky figured. As you lurched from room to room, acquaintance to acquaintance, balancing your champagne or martini or gin and tonic in one hand and your cigarette in the other, trying to think of clever things to say about nothing, you might instead be doing something worthwhile. You might be stitching lace for a christening gown, for example, or walking out a colicky horse, or fixing dinner for your kids, or playing the piano for somebody's amusement. Except around here, those were all things you paid somebody else to do for you. So you gained all this luxurious time to fill any way you liked, and what did you fill it with? Gin and cigarettes and gossip. Civilized yet essentially pointless pursuits like . . . well, yachting. And sex—sex, of course!—when you could find someone interesting to do it with.

Speaking of which, where was Stuy?

Lucky hadn't seen her husband for at least an hour, not since he went back to the bar for his third scotch and soda. Or was it his fourth? Stuyvesant Sprague always did consider it his duty to follow in the fine family tradition of drinking himself to death. That was how they'd ended up married to begin with, wasn't it? He'd had too much scotch, she'd had too much champagne. (Well, it *was* her own debutante party, after all! She was *supposed* to get high on champagne and youth and the bright happy future!) Anyway, one drink led to another, and more things had come out that night than nineteen-year-old Lucia di Conti. Now here she was, eight years into her bright happy future, drinking more champagne and wondering where her husband had wandered off to.

And with whom.

Lucky sidled between a pair of chattering women—nod, smile, see you at the committee meeting tomorrow!—and took census of the likely suspects. Bunny Drummond was sitting on the wicker sofa near the French doors, though Stuy hadn't slept with her in years, at least so far as Lucky knew. Lucky had her suspicions about Lou Dumont, but Lou seemed happy enough flirting with one of the Grayson twins, Lucky wasn't sure which. Then there was Minty Appleton—

"Lucky, darling! *There* you are!"

"Minty, how funny! I was *just* wondering where you were *this exact second.*"

They traded kisses in the air. Minty wanted to know how the party plans were going, how excited Lucky must be. Between the two of them, Minty thought it was the *best thing going* in Newport all *summer,* the Tiffany Ball. And so generous of the Princes to open up Marble House itself for the occasion! It was going to be a swell night, an absolutely smashing party!

"And of *course* it's such a worthy *cause,*" she added, as an afterthought. "Historic preservation and everything."

"The committee meets again tomorrow," Lucky said. "You're welcome to help out."

"Oh, I *wish* I could, *really* I do. But it's the same time as the Junior

League garden committee. And you *know* my mother." Minty grimaced. "She and Mrs. Prince can't stand each other. She'd *kill* me if I switched sides. But we'll be there for the party, never fear! Tom's already bought the tickets."

"I'm so delighted."

Minty leaned forward. "Is it true about the *diamond*? The Tiffany Diamond? One of the committee members gets to wear it to the ball?"

"That's what they tell me."

"Well? *Who*?"

Lucky smiled. "If we knew the answer to *that*, we'd lose half our committee on the spot. The Tiffany people are taking their own sweet time deciding whose bosom to lay their precious yellow diamond on, believe me."

"I don't know how you can stand the suspense. Old Prunella Potts says it's a hundred and fifty carats."

"A hundred and twenty-eight, to be exact."

"*Well*." Minty looked crushed. "Anyway, I was *just* looking for your darling husband. Tom thinks he might buy some old yacht off Harry Grayson, and he wants Stuy's opinion first."

Lucky caught sight of someone at the bar, and for a precious instant she didn't care one whit about her husband's whereabouts. "Stuy? My goodness, haven't seen him in ages. If you catch him, tell him hello from me."

Minty laughed. "You're such a *hoot*. I always tell Tom, we should be more like Stuy and Lucky. You make it look *easy*."

"You're sweet. Look, I must go have a word with Teddy over there. Committee business."

"Oh, good *luck*. Just don't get him started about churches. *You* know." Minty rolled her eyes.

"I know. Ta ta, darling." Lucky kissed the air next to Minty's cheek and Minty did the same to Lucky, as if they actually *were* dear friends who enjoyed each other's company. When Lucky reached the bar and slung her dainty pocketbook on the counter next to Teddy Winthrop, he complimented her on her performance. Teddy was the only person in Newport who knew what Lucky really thought of Minty Appleton.

"Why, thank you. I thought it was pretty convincing, myself." Lucky pushed her champagne glass a few inches forward and lifted her eyebrows at the bartender. "She warned me not to get you started on churches."

"I could tell you things about aediculae that would make your toes curl."

"Teddy, *when* are we going to run off to Italy together? I'll take you around to all the ancient di Conti palaces to dig up all those missing paintings. It'll take you years to uncover and draw and catalog everything and by then we'll have had ten children and neither of our spouses will want us back. We'll grow old together sipping red wine on some hillside covered with olive trees, listening to the church bells in the village."

Teddy took her hand and kissed the fingertips. "Just say the word, my darling. You know I've been wanting to get my hands on those lost di Conti treasures for years."

Lucky laughed and drew her hand back to take the brimming glass of champagne from the bartender. She and Teddy flirted outrageously whenever they turned up together at one of these parties; it was the only feature of the evening—or the luncheon or garden party or polo match, for that matter—that made it bearable. It was like a pact between them. Lucky could remember the exact moment that pact was made, six years ago at the grand reopening of the Museum of Fine Arts. Teddy had chaired the renovation committee, had spent years overseeing the exact reconstruction of the original Greek Revival structure, the interiors, the gardens; he had curated an innovative exhibition of Italian Renaissance art for the grand reopening, cajoling the Uffizi and the Borghese and the Vatican to loan important works; he had given a witty and brilliant lecture to introduce it all to the summer people in their ballgowns and tuxedos.

Lucky was dazzled.

She'd known Teddy for years, of course—ever since she arrived in Newport with her grandmother, just off the boat from Italy, where her father had been imprisoned and later executed for sedition. Little Lucia was nine years old and lost and spoke hardly any English at all, and fifteen-year-old Theodore Winthrop was the only one who didn't make fun of her that summer—who actually spoke to her *in Italian* and asked her questions about home. Of course, the summer eventually ended and Teddy went away to Exeter and then to war, came home and went to Harvard and married Alice Peabody, went to Italy to study architecture and came back home again to start his own firm, while Lucky went to Miss Porter's and studied how to be an exact replica of a New England aristocrat, got drunk and got pregnant and married Stuy.

During that time she and Teddy didn't see much of each other, like a pair of stars drifting along in the same galaxy. But she always had a soft spot for him because he had been so kind to her when no ordinary fifteen-year-old boy would have been kind to an orphan refugee kid, and as she watched him deliver that lecture at the art museum six years ago, his spectacles nearly fogged over with excitement over Italian art and architecture—well, she just *knew* he must be a kindred spirit. Everyone else stampeded to the bar after the lecture was over, except Lucky. She came up to Teddy as he was wiping his glasses with a handkerchief and said she thought his lecture was just *wonderful*, and it took her right back to Italy when she was a child, and he said ruefully that it was a smashing success, obviously, couldn't you tell by the way people hung on his words? Don't worry about the philistines, she said, and their eyes and smiles connected and they became friends for life.

Each time they met after that, they would silently and mutually arrange for some moment together, even if it was only a minute or two—a moment of connection. Like stopping at a desert oasis for a drink of pure, sweet water. They could flirt outrageously because nothing would ever come of it; Teddy was such a devoted husband to poor Alice and his feelings for Lucky were naturally those of a beloved friend, nothing more, so it was all harmless fun.

Harmless fun, Lucky reminded herself, sipping her champagne. Her fingers still buzzed from the touch of Teddy's lips. He wore his navy yacht club jacket, like all the men there, over a crisp white shirt and yacht club tie. Neat light brown hair, thinning a little at the temples. Blue eyes crinkling mischievously behind his glasses as he spoke of the di Conti treasures. "I do mean it, though," she said. "Next time you're in Italy, you must let me write to my cousins. The buildings are mostly shambles, but they'd be happy to show you around. I know you'd fall in love. And you never know—you might be the one who discovers all the lost paintings."

"Now you're just teasing me. It's plain the Nazis must have looted it all."

"Then why hasn't a single one of those paintings turned up since? That Caravaggio *alone,* Teddy. It could make your hair curl, it's not going to hang around unnoticed on somebody's wall. No, I've told you before, I'm positive my grandfather hid them around the old villa somewhere. I'd go myself, but . . ."

"But what? What's stopping you?"

Teddy's voice turned serious. Sometimes he did that—pivoted in an instant from delicious mischief to that quiet, forceful intellect of his, which had first dazzled her six years ago. That sympathy between them that couldn't be named or defined, simply existed all by itself.

"Everything," Lucky said wearily.

Teddy laid his hand over hers atop the bar.

"Mrs. Sprague?"

Lucky jumped and turned, splashing champagne over Teddy's hand and hers. The club manager stood before her in his exemplary jacket and see-no-evil expression. God knew he'd had enough practice around here.

"I'm sorry to disturb you, Mrs. Sprague, but there's a telephone call for Mr. Sprague. It's from the hospital."

"And I suppose my husband's nowhere to be found?"

"The call seemed urgent, Mrs. Sprague. I thought perhaps you'd want to take it yourself?"

"Yes, of course. Teddy, you'll excuse me, won't you?"

Teddy made a little bow of his head. "Of course. I hope it's nothing serious."

LUCKY TOOK HER glass with her into the manager's office. She'd found it was useful to have booze on hand when taking calls from the hospital where her father-in-law lay in the final throes of liver disease, which had only made him even more unpleasant and vulgar than in the good old days when he was simply drinking himself to death. The irony of this did not escape her. Still, she brought the champagne. She could always stop drinking after he was dead and she no longer needed it.

As luck would have it, the voice on the other end belonged to Nurse Silva, who was the least pleasant of the nurses who tended to Dudley Sprague, probably because she'd been doing it the longest. "He's having another attack, I'm afraid," Nurse Silva informed her.

"What kind of attack?"

"His blood pressure is sky-high, his kidneys are failing. Fever of a hundred and one and climbing. He's been calling for Mr. Sprague this past hour."

"And how urgently is Mr. Sprague's presence actually required, do you think?"

"That depends, of course," Nurse Silva said caustically, "on how important your party is."

Lucky lifted her glass and swilled down the last of the champagne. "We'll be over as soon as possible."

SHE DID NOT ask for help looking for Stuy. He might be smoking cigars on the deck with the other husbands, of course.

Then again, he might not.

She passed through the cardroom, the ballroom. Looped past the bar again and saw that Teddy had struck up a conversation with that nice girl who had married Gray Pendleton, what was her name. Dottie or Darcy or something. She was from out west and tried to hug you—it was awful. Lucky went out through the French doors onto the wooden deck that ran all along the back of the club, overlooking the three docks. Saw the boats bobbing at their moorings, drenched in moonlight. The air was warm and humid and smelled of cigars. Three or four men clustered by the railing, smoking and laughing. She paused to peer at them, but Stuy's familiar golden head didn't tower above. Always easy to spot, her other half. Tommy Appleton caught Lucky's gaze for an instant and looked swiftly away. *Guilty,* she thought.

She walked down the length of the deck and around the corner. Saw a dark shape leaning over the rail, in the shadow near the kitchen entrance. "Stuy?" she called out softly. The figure stirred. Lucky came closer and called out Stuy's name again, a little louder, and the shape broke apart into two shapes. One of them dashed into the kitchen, straightening its dress in frantic movements. The other one disappeared around the corner of the building.

Lucky vaulted into a run. "Stuy! Don't you slink off! It's your father!"

She whipped around the corner. Stuy stood the other way, fixing his trousers. The moonlight gleamed on his hair. She crossed her arms and waited politely until he finished and turned to face her.

The worst thing was he looked so handsome. Honestly, why on earth would a just God waste so much beauty on a man like Stuyvesant Sprague? Even sheepish and guilty, his blue eyes charmed you. You could hang your washing from his cheekbones. The moon caught the dimple in his chin. How she hated his face, his broad shoulders, the white shirt hastily tucked into his trousers. How she wanted to tear that shirt out again and—do what? Kill him?

Or pull him against the railing and screw him herself?

"Your father's having another attack," she said. "He's asking for you."

Stuy's expression went from sheepish to stricken. "How bad is it?"

"It's your father, who knows? But Nurse Silva seemed to think we should head over there, just in case. To the hospital."

He tore a hand through his hair and swore. "All right, let's go."

EVERYTHING ABOUT THE Newport Hospital made Lucky's spirits sink, from the sluggish swish of the revolving door to the cheap and determinedly cheerful yellow chairs in the waiting room to the smell of cigarettes and Lysol and chicken broth that hung around everywhere you went. That nice receptionist was on duty, the cute brunette whose white cap always cocked endearingly to one side, and who addressed herself to Lucky because Stuy's good looks made her stammer. "Oh, Mrs. Sprague, there you are!" she said, as if Stuy wasn't even there. Lucky wanted to hug her for it. "Nurse Silva told me to send you right up. They've moved him to Ward B, room"— she looked down at her desk—"room 322. Dr. Goldberg's on duty."

"Thank you, Miss . . . Hancock." Lucky remembered her name just in time.

Stuy leaned forward and gave the woman his smokiest gaze. "Thank you *so much*, Miss Hancock."

Miss Hancock turned bright pink and reached for her telephone, even though it wasn't actually ringing.

Lucky grabbed Stuy's hand and tugged him toward the elevators. "Your father's dying, for God's sake," she whispered fiercely. "Can't you leave it off just *once*?"

"Leave what off?"

"Oh, never mind."

The elevator doors staggered open. They got inside and Lucky pressed 3. Up they went in silence, staring numbly at the dial as it crawled from 1 to 2 to 3 and stopped with a ding. Usually they turned left, to Ward A, but Miss Hancock said Sprague had been moved to Ward B, for acute patients. Sprague went there every month or so, when he was dying. They would gather anxiously around his bedside, confer with the doctors outside his door, wait and wait for his last breath. Lucky would cross her fingers and pray. Not for him to *die*, exactly—that would be unchristian. Just that he would pass as painfully as possible, please God, make him suffer and repent and all that, take him to Your merciful bosom and give him a good goddamn shaking. Sprague's breath would rasp in his lungs, the nurses would frown over his blood pressure and his protein levels and colostomy bag and everything. The doctors would shake their heads and prescribe something for the pain. Any minute now. And then, miraculously, right there hovering on the brink of death, he would pull back. His vital signs would tick back up, digit by digit. His color would improve. He would open his mouth and complain about something—usually Lucky. And a week later they would wheel him back to Ward A to start all over again.

So Lucky turned right and tried not to get her hopes up.

Stuy walked along beside her, his hands shoved in his pockets, shortening his long stride to match hers. "Say, Lucky," he said. "About what you saw at the club. It really wasn't what—"

"Oh, save it. I don't really care anymore."

"But you know I don't—"

"I said save it, all right? Dr. Goldberg!"

The doctor was still halfway down the hallway, but Lucky called to him anyway, just to keep Stuy from muddling on with his usual apology about how none of these larks really *meant* anything, it wasn't what it *looked like*, only a little harmless kissing. Dr. Goldberg turned around—he was talking with Nurse Silva—and waited for them to reach him. His face was grave. He looked at Stuy and said, "I'm glad we were able to find you, Mr. Sprague. Why don't we go inside. Mrs. Sprague?"

Lucky always had the feeling Dr. Goldberg didn't like her. She found this off-putting, because Dr. Goldberg was the head of the acute care department and absolutely *radiated* brains—well, he probably *did* radiate brains from time to time, come to think of it, but what she meant was that he was visibly intelligent, extremely so, and she figured *he* figured she was merely some brainless socialite, with her blond hair and slim figure and icy green eyes. She wanted to tell him she'd been accepted to *Smith,* for God's sake, she'd been one week away from leaving for college to study chemistry when she found out she was pregnant with Stuyesant Sprague's baby. But she never did. She simply put on an expression of sincere grief and allowed Dr. Goldberg to wave her into the room first.

Her father-in-law lay propped on the bed. A nurse was taking his pulse and his blood pressure. A bag of serum or something stood on a pole next to the bed, connected to his arm by a clear plastic tube that disappeared beneath a white bandage on his wrist. His eyes were closed. Lucky thought she was used to his jaundiced color by now, but the yellowness of his skin actually shocked her. "My goodness," she exclaimed, without thinking.

"Mrs. Sprague, if you can't keep your composure, I must ask you to leave the room," said Dr. Goldberg.

"Oh, she's all right," said Stuy. He marched up to the bed and took his father's hand. "How are you, Dad?"

Sprague's eyes flashed open. The whites of his eyes were the color of hay. "Where the hell have you been?"

"I'm sorry, Dad. We were at the club. Didn't get the message until now."

"Ha. Knocking some waitress, I'll bet. Right, Lucky?"

Dr. Goldberg coughed. Lucky stepped forward. "Dudley. How are you feeling? Have they made you comfortable?"

"Comfortable? I'm dying, for Christ's sake. Goldberg? Where is that Jew? Tell them I'm dying, Goldberg."

Dr. Goldberg cleared his throat. "Mr. Sprague's condition worsened during the day, so he's been moved here so we can keep closer watch."

"What he's trying to say is I'm dying," said Sprague.

"Dad, come on. Don't say that."

"You heard him."

"We'd like to put your father on an experimental medication," Dr. Goldberg said to Stuy. "It's showing some promise. We'll need your permission, of course, but—"

"What about *my* permission? Don't I have a say in this?"

"Dudley, you granted medical power of attorney to Stuy last autumn, when you had that attack—"

"Shut up, Lucky. I don't want some experimental medication. It'll kill me."

"Didn't you just say you were already dying?" Lucky asked.

Dr. Goldberg made a choking noise and said quickly, "We can discuss all the risks and the potential benefits, Mr. Sprague. If you don't mind coming to my office?"

"Sure. Absolutely. Honey? You okay with Dad for a bit?"

"Stuy, I really—"

"Great. Be back in a bit." Stuy kissed her cheek and hurried out of the room. He hated sickness, hated seeing his father jaundiced and helpless in a hospital bed. Lucky figured it was because he was such a heavy drinker himself. Certainly not because there was much love lost between father and son.

"Don't you let him bamboozle you!" Sprague called after them. "These Jew doctors, they're crafty bastards! Smart as hell, but crafty! Goddamn it. There they go." He looked at Lucky, then at the nurse, who gathered up her equipment and left the room to the two of them.

Lucky dragged over the chair from the corner and sat in it, just out of reach. "You seem in good spirits, for a man who's supposed to be dying."

"Don't want to give you the satisfaction, that's why."

She shrugged. "You're in God's hands, not mine."

"Catholics." He snorted. "Anyway, I'm holding out until your grandmother dies. She oughta go first, she's older."

"But you've drunk more. A lot more."

"At least I'm still in my right mind. Not wandering around the place at midnight in my nightgown."

"She does *not* wander in her nightgown."

"Because you lock her up at night, that's why. Poor old Maybelle. Never had all that much upstairs to begin with." He tapped his temple. "Not like *our* side of the family."

Lucky checked her watch. "I wonder what's keeping them."

"Maybe Stuy's found a pretty nurse on the way back."

"If you're trying to hurt me, it won't work. I don't give a damn where Stuy gets off to in his spare time. I have far more important things on my mind."

"Liar. Well, it's a shame you can't keep him interested, a pretty girl like you. I told him when you got married, I said, Stuy, you're making a mistake. She's an ice queen. Frigid as a goddamn Popsicle, I can just tell. You'll be tired of her in a month. And guess what? I was right."

"No you weren't," said Lucky. "You were off by ten whole months."

Sprague barked out a laugh that turned into a phlegmy cough. "Waited until after Joanie was born, did he? Well, he's a gentleman, after all."

"Unlike his father."

The coughing stopped. Sprague stared at her like he might kill her if he had the strength to reach out his two hands and close them around her throat. Lucky held her ground, just barely. *Just barely*, she kept her hands in place on her lap, her back straight, her legs crossed. Exactly as she had learned to do, ever since she'd arrived at Sprague Hall as a young girl and realized that she was no longer living in a household of eccentric aristocrats and passionate artists and radical idealists, raised by an adoring father and grandfather and a grandmother ever so slightly off her rocker.

She stared at Dudley Sprague's cold, yellowed eyes and tried not to wish he were already dead. *In God's hands*, she reminded herself. Not for *you* to lift that tempting pillow and place it over his face and just . . . and just . . . *shut him up*.

As if he could read her mind, he turned his head away and smiled at the ceiling. "Can't do it, can you? Don't have the nerve. Like you don't have the nerve to leave Stuy."

"Don't tempt me."

"What, leave all this money and high society? You couldn't do it."

Lucky uncrossed her legs and gripped the edges of her chair. How she hated him. She hated this hateful room, this hospital, this marriage. She hated Newport. She hated them all, except Joanie. Darling Joanie. And Teddy, whom she couldn't have. My God, if *only* she could have Teddy!

That was all she needed. One good reason.

She leaned forward. "Leave? I think you've got it all wrong, Dudley dear. It's not *me* who has to leave, it's Stuy. My grandmother's the one who owns the place, remember? It's *her* money, her house. If I wanted to, I could kick you both to the curb."

"No you couldn't."

"Watch me."

Sprague looked back at her. His face was thin and hollow, like a death mask of the man he'd been when Lucky first saw him: large, florid, bombastic. His wife cowering at his every word. *Don't you ever forget how we took you in*, he told her grandmother. *Don't you ever forget.* At the time, Lucky hadn't understood the English words, but she had understood his meaning, even at nine years old. *Ha*, her grandmother said later. *He knows it all belongs to me. He can't do a thing, don't worry.* But she hadn't quite convinced Lucky. Some peculiar fear made her grandmother's voice a little too brave, a little too defiant.

"You listen to me, you little Italian brat," Sprague said. "I could finish you off in a second, if I wanted. You put a foot wrong, you think for *even one second* you can take all this for yourself, you'll find out just how mistaken you are."

"You're a bully, Dudley Sprague. I'm not afraid of you."

"You should be, though." He tapped his finger against his temple. "You should be."

"I don't know what you're talking about."

"Maybe you should ask your grandmother. Crazy old Maybelle. Ask her for me and see what she says. Ask her about—"

"Excuse me," said Lucky. "I'm going to get some air."

Gracefully Lucky rose from the chair and walked out of the room. From the nurse's station, Nurse Silva looked up and stared at her.

"Mrs. Sprague?" she said. "Are you all right?"

"Quite all right, thank you."

Lucky opened her pocketbook and hunted around for the emergency cigarette she kept there, for occasions like this. Then she remembered she had already smoked it hours ago, on the way to the yacht club, because Stuy had called to say he was tied up and would meet her there, and she had hung up the phone and wondered what he meant by that. Whether he was *literally* tied up—God knew he'd try anything—or just busy.

She snapped her pocketbook shut. That was the trouble with this family, wasn't it?

Like Sprague Hall itself, you never knew what kind of rot lay behind the facade.

CHAPTER FOUR

Andie

Newport, Rhode Island
September 2019

"LOOKS LIKE THE entire column is rotted through." I scraped away flakes of crumbling wood on one of the Corinthian columns holding up the side portico. I looked up at George, confirming the red light on his camera meant that we were recording. Straightening, I said, "These were originally made of stone taken from the cliff's edge. But when the Spragues bought the estate in 1899, they had them replaced with untreated pine then painted and capped with Corinthian columns for a grander facade. Unfortunately, wood—especially untreated—in this climate is tough to maintain, but the Spragues at that time seemed more interested in impressing their neighbors."

"What sort of monster would do such a thing?" Meghan Black, my best friend from grad school in Charleston and newly hired technical consultant for the show, wore an expression that most people would reserve for car wrecks and air disasters. Her manicured hand flew to her neck and the ubiquitous set of pearls that she wore whether exercising or going out to dinner. "You'd think someone spending this kind of money on a replica of an Italian palace would have used solid marble columns. I mean, what a cheap way to save a dollar."

I looked up at George. "Do we need to reshoot that or can you edit out her comments? You'll have to excuse Meghan for her dramatic excesses. She's from Georgia."

Meghan sent me a withering glare, which usually preceded one of her famous quips, but we were interrupted by a sudden flash of movement on the weed-bedecked lawn.

"Meghan, Meghan—look what I found!" Six-year-old Petey ran toward Meghan, his index finger extended in front of him like a wand.

"That's not a booger, is it?" Meghan asked as Petey approached, swooping in like a plane coming in for a landing.

I smirked. "Anything's a possibility, but boogers were last year's fascination. This year it's insects."

Meghan, who was not only my best friend but Petey's surrogate aunt, feigned left just in time, catching the little boy from behind in case a creepy-crawly might be clinging to his outstretched digit.

Petey looked down at his empty finger and frowned. "I founded a worm."

I knelt in front of him, pushing aside the blond hair he'd managed to inherit from his father despite my family's dark Portuguese genes. "Mr. Worm probably wanted to go back to his house. I bet he loves school and didn't want to miss the school bus."

Petey nodded solemnly as I ruffled his hair, then sent a worried glance toward the house. Despite feeling sure that Luke was probably sleeping off a bender and wouldn't emerge until well past noon, I didn't want him to see Petey. I usually didn't bring him to work with me, but it was a teacher in-service day, meaning a day off from school, and my dad had been called in by a friend to do the final finishes on a yacht for a demanding client. His own boatbuilding business having long since gone under, he'd jumped at the chance to revisit his dream, if only for a few days.

And we needed the money. The furnace had finally breathed its last and with winter coming, replacing it later wasn't an option. I'd had no choice. I'd brought a backpack full of contraband items of processed food and an iPad full of games ready to blackmail a six-year-old boy into staying put.

A member of the crew emerged from one of the vans parked on the drive and headed toward the front steps, studio lights on collapsed tripods in each hand and ropes of electrical cords draped around his shoulders.

I turned to George. "Have you heard from Marc? He said he'd be here first thing."

The cameraman shook his head. "Nope. Haven't seen him. Didn't really expect to. He was still at the Landing when me and the guys left around midnight. Looks like you're in charge again."

With a grim smile I nodded. I'd like nothing better than to be in charge of the entire project, especially since that was what had interested me in doing *Makeover Mansion* in the first place. Well, that and working with my mentor. When Marc had first approached me with the job as host for the first season, dangling a Dutch Renaissance Revival mansion in Providence as bait, I was flattered. Even though it promised more money than I was currently making at the Rhode Island Historic Preservation and Heritage Commission, my practical self had made sure he understood that I was a historic preservationist, not a Pat Sajak. My interest—and what I had assumed Marc's was, too—was all about the careful restoration of our collective past that was held in trust by old buildings. It was our sworn *duty* to make sure they saw at least another century intact. And I'd seen the show as an excellent opportunity to inform viewers of this responsibility and to perhaps encourage them to open their wallets in their own communities to support historic preservation.

But after the first season's disastrous ratings and threats to cancel the show, Marc had pulled in every last favor he'd saved up from his lauded past as an author, lecturer, and expert in the field, and convinced the network execs to give us another chance. They'd agreed—but only with new stipulations. The execs had forbidden me from doing anything more than point at wood rot and mold while keeping up a rambling stream of salacious details about the families and any skeletons that might be lurking in the corners. And if I couldn't find any, it was understood that I should use my imagination and create some. It was a wonder a lightning bolt hadn't struck me as I'd signed the contract for the second season.

"Seriously, Andie." Meghan slid on a pair of bright yellow Kate Spade sunglasses. "Why are you focusing on basically redecorating three interior rooms when judging from what I can see on the outside it would be prudent to start here to at least preserve the integrity of the existing structure?"

I swallowed back an annoying knot in my throat that held the words I really wanted to say. "Because that's not what *Makeover Mansion* is all about." I stepped back as two crew members walked between us carrying a ladder and more lighting equipment followed by another wearing a heavily laden tool belt. I waved, recognizing the muscles behind the makeover, Mike Brantley. He'd be the one doing the sledgehammer removal of walls and sawing through plaster and beams while I smiled prettily as I discussed paint color options and the benefits of quartz countertops.

Marc had said something about scripted arguments I was to have with Mike about the pros and cons of an open concept in a historic home, but I'd hung up on him midsentence with the excuse that Petey needed me. I wished I could tell Marc and Meghan that I was above all of this ridiculousness and quit. But principles didn't pay the bills.

"Then why am I here?" Meghan asked, her tone understandably petulant.

I shrugged, not sure I really knew why. "I don't know—moral support? Maybe to sneak you on camera often enough that you can question the historical integrity of our renovations? I'm desperate. It's bad enough to be a sellout, but it's awful to be demonstrating to what degree on national television." I rubbed the heels of my hands into my eyes, gritty from lack of sleep. "I'm sorry if I misled you. When you said your company was sending you to take a few classes on historic property documentation at Salve Regina I jumped at the chance to work with you. I didn't even have to beg Marc to allow you on as a consultant." I gave her a conciliatory smile. "I know it's not a lot of money, but your name will be listed in the credits."

She screwed up her face like I'd asked her to demo the Trevi Fountain. "No thank you. I thought your goal was to introduce viewers to the concept of arrested decay. You know, like at Drayton Hall in Charleston. You did your entire thesis on it. With Marc as your mentor and advisor. How did this happen?"

"Yes, well, trust me, the viewers of *Makeover Mansion* would think I was talking about a skincare line if I said 'arrested decay.'" I watched with a wary eye as Petey ran in circles, his arms outstretched like the wings of a plane, appropriate zooming noises buzzing from his mouth. I drew a deep breath. "His last asthma attack put him in the hospital for a week. I'm still trying to pay those bills, and his medication isn't cheap. His doctor says he'll grow out of it eventually, but for now . . ." I shrugged again to hide the skip in my voice.

Meghan squeezed my arm. "I get it. I do. And I'm sorry." She looked up at the crumbling plaster of the column, frowning at the exposed, moist wood beneath. It made me think of my once lofty dreams of following in Marc's footsteps—the ones before they'd fallen off his path completely—and becoming an acclaimed advocate and respected authority on the relevance and importance of historic buildings. Everything eventually turned to rot no matter how hard you tried to reverse the inevitable.

Meghan continued. "I promise to do what I can to inject any sort of professionalism into this show." She grinned. "But please, for the love of God, don't put my name in the credits. I've got a reputation to uphold." Her big brown eyes sparkled, but I knew she wasn't entirely joking.

Sheila Evans, the grip operator, stomped toward me in her black combat boots and carrying a metal pole and a tripod. "Sorry to interrupt, ladies, but I don't have a clue where Maybelle's room is. I know you showed us all yesterday, but, well, Marc said he'd be here early this morning to give us a more thorough tour so we could get a feel for the place."

"Yeah, he told me the same thing." I didn't say anything else, tired of making excuses for Marc. I reached into the pocket of my multi-pocketed painter's pants—more functional than fashionable—and pulled out a folded stack of papers. I'd stayed up way too late the previous night drawing a color-coded map to the three locations and taping maps to all of the major doors along each route to the various rooms. I'd also made extras to hand out to any lost souls wandering the maze of hallways.

"Here," I said, peeling off the top sheet and handing it to Sheila.

She studied it, her eyebrows raised. "Wow. It's even color coded. Impressive. Nice to know reality show hosts have other talents."

She'd said it lightly, but it still stung. "I have a graduate degree in historic preservation, you know!" I shouted after her as she walked away.

Meghan took one of the maps. "My friend in Charleston, Melanie, would really appreciate this."

"The one who sees dead people?"

Meghan nodded. "You know, if you really want to give this show a spin—"

"No." I cut her off. "It's bad enough how low I've stooped already for this project. I'm embarrassed to admit that I have an entire file folder full of newspaper clippings from the last seventy years showing all the scandals and salacious details of the Spragues that Marc wants me to sprinkle into each episode."

"That's pretty bad," Meghan agreed.

"It gets worse. The number one rule dictated by the family is that

I'm not supposed to approach the matriarch, Lucky Sprague, or even acknowledge her presence, but I know I will be forced to break that rule sooner rather than later if I'm going to keep this job. It's what the network heads want. My conscience is already keeping me up at night over that alone. It's practically guaranteed that I'll never sleep again if I also manufacture ghosts for ratings."

"But what if—"

"Petey!"

He was still soaring in wide circles, his arms bobbing up and down like a plane stuck in a downdraft, his focus consumed by his erratic pattern, and apparently oblivious to Luke emerging down the front steps, studying a piece of paper in his hand, also unaware of the approaching collision.

I began running, but Luke was faster, quickly sidestepping the little boy, using the momentum to swing a gleefully shouting Petey in a wide circle before setting him down. Both of them were laughing, which I found unnerving because I didn't like Luke and I didn't want to believe that he knew how to make a small child laugh.

I grabbed Petey and lifted him on my hip. Even though he had told me many times he was too old to be carried, he was small for his age and I sometimes—like now—found it worked to my advantage.

"Mommy, put me down!" He struggled to escape, but I held him tight.

"I'm sorry," I said to Luke. "I know he shouldn't be here but it's only for today. I promise to keep him out of trouble."

I kept a serene smile on my face as I put Petey down while keeping a firm hand on his shoulder and waited for Luke to cancel the shooting for the day or something equally asinine.

"Just tell him to be careful."

I was so surprised by his response that I was barely aware of Meghan taking Petey by the hand and introducing herself to Luke. He even smiled at her.

Luke held up one of my maps, the tape still attached. "Is this really necessary?"

"Yes. Unless you want the crew stumbling through the house looking for the right rooms, I suggest putting that back where you found it. Maybe you'd prefer that we use bread crumbs?"

The corner of his mouth quirked, but he immediately stilled it as he caught sight of the catering truck pulling into position on the lawn. If I thought they'd be ruining the grass, I would tell them to move. Apparently, Luke agreed since he didn't complain.

Turning back to me, he said, "There's one more rule I forgot to tell you yesterday."

I braced myself, wondering if whoever had been watching me from the window had ratted on me and I was about to be banned altogether from the boathouse. "The filming has to be done by four thirty sharp and the house vacated by all crew. No exceptions."

"Four thirty? That's really not enough time. . . ."

"No exceptions."

"But—" My protests were cut off by the blaring of a car horn.

An ancient Cadillac meandered toward us, frequently slipping off the drive and flattening the Muppet hair–like grass that edged the side. We watched as Marc stopped in the middle of the drive, either unaware that there were more appropriate parking spots or simply not caring. He sat for a moment, seeming to struggle with something in the passenger seat. I hurried over and opened his door, wanting to be helpful without pressing home the point that he needed help.

"Marc, I'm so glad you're here." I failed completely to keep the annoyance out of my voice, but he didn't seem to notice. His gray eyes appeared foggy behind his glasses, and I wanted to believe it was because the lenses were dirty. He wore a slightly rumpled suit that carried the funk of stale cigarettes and cheap bourbon and his signature bow tie sat at an odd angle, like a stalled propeller. As I leaned in to kiss his cheek in greeting, a large patch of gray stubble missed during his morning shave brushed my skin. My annoyance faded into something more resembling pity.

"Can you go around to the other side? I brought something that Christiana wants you to wear whenever you're on camera."

A plain brown grocery bag sat on the passenger seat, and I knew whatever was inside was something I wouldn't want. Christiana McMorris was the executive producer and liaison between Marc and the network. It was a rocky marriage between an overly ambitious millennial and a man well past his prime who was trying desperately to cling to his former glory. Which, if I thought about it, was a lot like trying to restore an old home whose roof had already caved in.

I banished the ungrateful thought and sucked in my breath, preparing for what my dad always called the sucker punch. I helped Marc out of the car before reaching over and grabbing the bag and looking inside.

"No. Absolutely not."

"What is it?" Petey bounded over to me, trying to grab the bag out of my hands.

"Yeah, what is it?" Meghan asked. She, along with Petey and Luke, had followed me to the car. And, if Petey had his way, they were all about to witness the biggest embarrassment of my life.

"No," I said again to Marc, holding the bag high so Petey couldn't reach.

At least Marc had the decency to avoid my eyes. "I'm sorry. I really am. But we have to be as accommodating to Christiana and the network as we can if we want this show to continue into another season. We're already treading on thin ice as it is. If you say no, we might as well call it quits now and be done with it."

I dropped my hand so Petey could pull out the pink construction hat and equally hued tool belt. The only tools on it, a hammer and a flathead screwdriver, had matching pink handles. I'd never been a fan of that particular color—possibly because it was my mother's favorite—but I'd never quite hated it as much as I hated it now.

"Eww," Petey said, dropping both on the ground. "It's pink."

"That it is," Luke said. I could see he was trying hard not to laugh. If I hadn't been so humiliated, I might have found the effort admirable.

Luke cleared his throat. "Glad you're here, Marc. We've got a lot to go over. It's important to Lucky that we're all on the same page."

Marc seemed relieved to be leaving the scene of the crime that right now looked like purged Pepto-Bismol on the barren lawn. He began following Luke in the direction of the water, not even bothering with a backward glance. My former pity evaporated in a lavalike stream of anger.

"I have a graduate degree in historic preservation along with three years of experience working for the Rhode Island Historic Preservation and Heritage Commission! There is *no way* I'm going to wear those. It's demeaning."

Marc pretended he hadn't heard me.

Pinching the pink articles between her thumb and forefinger, Meghan replaced them in the bag before tightly twisting the top like a doggie poop bag. "I wish I could drop these in the ocean and say they were stolen, but I have a feeling they'd send more."

Petey had returned to his airplane buzzing and swooping, happily unaware of my black mood.

"You okay?" Meghan asked.

I let out a long breath. "Not really."

"I'm sorry. Pardon my French, but this really sucks. At least you get to spend time with that hottie Luke. Wow. I'd say it's almost worth having to wear the hat and belt if only to be in the same room with him."

"Not to borrow a word from a six-year-old, but eww. Luke Sprague is just another sailor boy with a trust fund. And you know how I feel about them."

"Yes, I do. And why. But I think you're being unfair. You don't even know him."

I grabbed the bag from her and began marching toward the house.

"I don't need to. I'm already aware of the type and I know to stay away. Case closed. Let's get started on Maybelle's room. Most of the renovation has already been scripted by the writers, but I'd like to get your technical expertise to interject when possible. To add some sort of depth to what we're doing here."

"It'll be like papering over the cracks—especially if you're wearing a pink construction hat and belt—but it's worth a try." Meghan grinned, but I couldn't reciprocate.

I headed up the front steps, pausing beneath the capped electrical wires above us. "There's so much to be done here—much more than three rooms. I do wonder why Lucky Sprague won't sell and move on. It's not like she was raised here or anything, and from what I've read she didn't have a happy marriage while living here, either."

"Maybe she simply loves old houses and it's blinded her to reason. It's been known to happen." We shared a glance and started laughing until I suddenly cut mine short.

"Where's Petey?"

We simultaneously became aware of the absence of buzzing noises. We hurried down the steps to the lawn, calling his name more and more loudly. He hadn't run past us and into the house, so he had to be outside. As if our thoughts were moving in tandem, we turned in the direction of the water. We began to run across the sloping lawn, vaguely aware of the overgrown trail that might have once been a carefully groomed footpath, past shriveled vines hanging from a derelict arbor, and over the ghostly humps of terraces that had long since been allowed to go to seed. The slope tapered off before the rocky cliff path, allowing us to pause and catch our breaths.

"Petey!" I shouted as I spotted the roof of what might be the forbidden boathouse perched on the rocks on the opposite side of the cliff path from the house. The squat, angular building was missing roof shingles and had weathered clapboards the color of a rain-soaked sky that showed decades of bearing the brunt of blowing nor'easters.

I clambered down the precarious rock steps leading to the cliff path before coming to an abrupt stop, Meghan nearly colliding into me. Beside the boathouse, and built alongside an outcropping of rocks protruding from the water and large enough to stand on, sat a long dock comprised of splintery mismatched two-by-fours. Petey and Luke casually sat on the edge with their bare feet hanging over the side, watching the white-tipped surf wash over the rocks.

Petey turned to me with excitement, holding up a wooden toy sailboat with cloth sails. "Look what Luke gave me, Mommy! He found it in that little house and said I could keep it. He says he can teach me to sail!"

"What are you doing?" I shouted at Luke, wanting to run and rescue Petey, but eyeing the boards suspiciously. "He's not supposed to leave my side."

Luke stood, then lifted Petey to his feet. "He followed us down here and wanted to stay with me when Marc left." Even though I didn't hear an accusatory note in his voice, I knew what he must be thinking about a woman who brought her child onto a job site and then left him to his own devices. It made me even more unreasonably angry than I already was.

I put a foot on the dock, then hesitated.

"Don't worry," Luke said. "It's safe. I keep it in good repair myself."

Not only did I not trust him, but I didn't want Petey to spend another minute in his company. I reached Petey in four very wide steps and picked him up, swinging him onto my hip again. "Give Luke his boat back, Petey."

Petey responded by clutching the toy to his chest. "But Luke said I could keep it. That it was mine."

Luke's eyes grew cold. "I did. The boat is his."

"Give it back, Petey. Now, please."

Petey twisted away from me, and I realized that I was immersed in a battle I couldn't win.

Using as much force as I could without hurting the little boy, I wrenched the boat from his hands, breaking one of the sails in the process. Without a word, I handed the toy back to Luke. "I'll keep Petey by my side for as long as he's here, and I promise he won't come back again."

I stomped off the dock with a screaming child in my arms, my best friend looking at me as if I'd just grown horns, and feeling the glare of Luke Sprague on my back. I wasn't sure what made me angrier: the debasing and undignified costume I was expected to wear to keep my job, or the man on the dock who reminded me too much of someone else I'd spent years trying to eradicate from my memory.

CHAPTER FIVE

Ellen

Newport, Rhode Island
June 1899

"YOU'LL REMEMBER TO tell them about the trumpet fanfare?"

"Yes, sir." Ellen didn't write it down. It had been said so many times it was chiseled into her memory.

The Prince di Conti was to arrive today and John Sprague was determined that there be a greeting fit for a prince, complete with a trumpet fanfare. Ellen had only persuaded him not to release doves by pointing out that it would make a very poor impression if one were to crap on the princely head. But she hadn't been able to talk him out of the musicians, a group from Providence hired for the occasion.

"In livery. The musicians must remember to wear the livery." John Sprague glared suddenly at one of the men adding the final touches to the false pillars that had been added to the front hall. "What are you doing! This was meant to be done yesterday! The guests are arriving within the hour!"

The workman wobbled on his ladder, his brush leaving a streak that Ellen hoped would be attributed to irregularities of marble. "The first coat had to dry before they could apply the second. Sir."

She didn't add that it was Mr. Sprague's fault in the first place for deciding on the spur of the moment that his entry hall was insufficiently supplied with columns. Just as he had decided they needed more stuffed swans on the menu, more topiary in the formal garden, more everything. The household plunged into chaos as rooms were haphazardly turned out to receive the guests invited for the house party, boxes hastily moved out of attic rooms to serve as accommodation for visiting ladies' maids and valets, additional footmen—temporary footmen—hired, and ill-fitting liveries cobbled together out of silk and velvet and far too much gold braid. The past week had been a nightmare of maids colliding carrying linens, workmen spilling paint, and John Sprague barking at everyone to work harder, work faster, stop wasting his money.

At first, Ellen had heard the bustle only from the safety of the music room, as she took Maybelle again and again through her voice exercises, through the pieces carefully selected to display the best of her sweet, high voice, which lacked depth but had an almost surprising clarity. There was no scraping or sliding; Maybelle hit the notes cleanly and plainly. Ellen had been surprised and pleased, and Maybelle pathetically grateful for her praise.

Ellen wondered what the girl's upbringing had been like, to make her so delighted by the slightest approbation, but then remembered that she had been handed over young to a stepmother, John Sprague's mother, and decided that if the mother were anything like the son, it wasn't the least bit surprising that Maybelle was starved for a kindly word. There were framed daguerreotypes of the second Mrs. Sprague in one of the smaller drawing rooms, taken sometime after the money had begun to come in; her eyes were as hard as the diamonds around her neck and wrists. John Sprague spoke of his mother with a combination of reverence and fear. Maybelle didn't speak of her at all. And given that Maybelle spoke about most things, artlessly and at length, it told Ellen more than she needed to know about Maybelle's childhood at the hands of her stepmother.

But whatever the detriment to Maybelle, it made her absurdly easy as a pupil, eager to please, delighted by a kind word, apologizing for infractions she had never committed. Ellen worried about what would become of Maybelle out in the world. She hoped this Italian prince had a kind heart as well as an empty bank account. All Maybelle needed, really, was someone to be decent to her; having never known romance, she wouldn't demand it—only kindness.

Ellen wasn't sure whether that made her sentimental or cynical or a bit of both. But she felt herself, as the days passed, increasingly responsible for Maybelle, who clearly saw her as less of a teacher and more of a companion. An older sister. The thought made Ellen wince.

She'd had her own siblings. To think of Maybelle as a sister, even a temporary sort of one, felt like a betrayal.

A cousin, then. Ellen an older, poorer relation turned hired companion. That was how Maybelle treated her, as a blood relative—although perhaps, Ellen thought, that was because Maybelle no longer had blood relatives of her own, only a stepfamily exemplified by Mr. Sprague, his sickly wife, and his loathsome offspring. If Ellen had expected to be condescended to by a spoiled debutante, the reality was quite the contrary; Maybelle looked up to her, deferred to her, relied on her. And Ellen, who had successfully kept to herself since her father's death, or, at least, as much as one could in a place like the Hibernia, found herself, increasingly, reluctantly, concerned with her new charge.

They breakfasted together in the little round breakfast room paneled in boiseries torn from a French château before retiring to the music room for lessons. After lunch, they walked together in the gardens—and Ellen never once had the heart to tell Maybelle how much she would have preferred to walk alone, how she longed to explore the long path down to the ocean, or sit alone, entirely alone, in the rose arbor, gathering her thoughts around her, in this strange new calm. In the afternoons, Maybelle read or wrote letters, and that was Ellen's one time to herself, to sit by herself in her velvet jewel box of a room before joining Maybelle in the great dining room that seemed absurd when tenanted by only two—three, when they were joined by Dudley's tutor, Mr. Whitmarsh.

Of course, that was only when Mr. Sprague was dining out. On those nights he dined at home, the meal was richer, the lights brighter, and Maybelle dressed in a fearful profusion of satins and trim that engulfed her small form before setting off, shrinkingly, to dine in state with her brother.

On those nights, Ellen got her tray, but she paid for it later, when the latch on her door would rattle in the night and she would open it to find Maybelle in her nightdress, her eyes wide and unseeing. Ellen would guide her back to bed, soothe her, and hold her cold hand until she slept.

But other than those nights, the nights when Maybelle walked, the house by the sea was calm. Strangely calm.

It shouldn't have been. It was a terrible, ill-run household. Even Ellen, who didn't know anything about great houses, could tell that Sprague Hall was woefully understaffed. What staff there were shirked their work and pocketed what they could. The maids were slatternly, the footmen insolent, and the butler considered it beneath him to do anything other than polish the silver and guard the good wine from the depredations of the footmen. Not that Ellen blamed them. Mr. Sprague's particular mix of bullying and penny-pinching was practically an invitation to pilfer.

But despite it all—or perhaps because of it, because everyone in the house was in it for what they could get, and no one cared in the least about the honor of a family that had no honor—it was easy to sink into the disorderly household, just another quiet figure moving through the quiet house, occasionally colliding with Dudley's harassed tutor as he darted off after his infuriating charge. Maybelle had no visitors, no friends; when John Sprague entertained business associates, he did so elsewhere, in New York or Boston. They received no invitations from the other denizens of Newport to their balls or picnics or breakfasts, not even from their nearest neighbors, the William Vanderbilts of Marble House. The house felt like an island, isolated from the world, half asleep in the shadow of the sea.

For the first time in a very long time, Ellen slept without a hand on the knife beneath her pillow.

But the house was awake now, awake with a vengeance. The prince's visit was upon them. There were twenty guests expected, such hangers-on at the edges of society as John Sprague had been able to cadge and cajole in the hopes of impressing a prince with the company they kept: Vanderbilt cousins and lesser Livingstons, society women who hadn't quite made it into Mrs. Astor's Four Hundred, fortune hunters, and the would-be fashionable.

John Sprague fizzled with nervous energy. "Make sure Cook follows the menu. No skimping, no changing my choices. She's to follow it exactly, do you understand? Exactly."

"Yes, sir." If only Cook didn't leave. The housekeeper had already decamped, taking with her a ruby bracelet and what cash she could carry. It was one thing to suddenly be called upon to be housekeeper as well as music teacher, but Ellen drew the line at cooking, too.

What he ought to have done was hired a French chef for the occasion, but Ellen was beginning to learn that the glitter of the Sprague household was all for show: wood pillars where there were meant to be marble and a music teacher doing the work of the housekeeper.

They just had to get through the next two weeks, Ellen told herself—and wondered what would happen after.

Perhaps Maybelle would like to keep her on as companion. Italy was a long way away. She might like to keep someone of her own with her. And the demons that chased Ellen might follow her from Boston to Newport, but she couldn't imagine they would ever find her in Italy.

If Maybelle married the prince. If Maybelle took Ellen away with her.

It didn't bear thinking about, Ellen told herself firmly. The only thing to do was make the visit a success. She would think about what might happen after that later.

There was the sound of wheels crunching on gravel, a carriage turning up the drive, beneath the porte cochere.

Sprague stopped barking instructions at Ellen. His round face went pale. "They're here. They're early. Go, damn you! Go!" he shouted at the man with the paint, who nearly dropped it in his haste.

Ellen grabbed it for him just in time, handing it back with a smile and a nod.

John Sprague glared at the footmen. "You! What are you doing loafing about! Stand up straight! Look lively!"

The footmen, hired for the occasion, looked sideways at each other, slouching toward the door, uncomfortable in their ill-fitting livery.

"Where's that damned butler?" Sprague was sweating heavily, pulling at his collar as he peered out the window at the crest on the carriage. "Not the prince yet. Thank God. It's the Schuyler woman. Prunella Pratt Schuyler. The Pratts are nearly as new as we are, but the Schuylers . . . they're an old family. Very old. It's good she's taken an interest in Maybelle—teach her how to get on—"

He seemed to have forgotten that he was talking to Ellen, speaking more to himself than her. Ignoring everyone, the butler, alerted by his own spy system in the servants' hall, emerged from his green baize door and proceeded at a stately pace through the great hall to the door.

The butler's presence seemed to snap Sprague out of his trance. Coming to himself, he said brusquely to Ellen, "Take Mrs. Schuyler to Maybelle. Somewhere away from the smell of paint. And make sure you find those musicians and get them into their livery! I don't care what it takes. Just do it. Mrs. Schuyler! Welcome!"

"*What* is that smell?" A fashion plate come to life bustled through the entryway. Her tightly fitted jacket was of startling crimson, the wide lapels patterned in a dizzying geometric arrangement of black velvet zigzags on white satin, both contrasting with a sleek and sweeping emerald-green skirt lavishly trimmed in black scrollwork.

The enormous hall seemed a great deal smaller as Prunella Pratt Schuyler came to a stop in the center of the room, ignoring the butler, ignoring the footmen, ignoring Mr. Sprague as she lifted her ostrich-feather adorned head to sniff audibly, a pose which also had the effect of showing off the elaborately arranged golden curls of her hair to best advantage.

"Er, gold leaf . . . some repairs . . . so difficult getting good help," babbled Mr. Sprague.

"Well, if you must buy someone else's house rather than having one built for you . . ." Mrs. Schuyler smiled sweetly at Mr. Sprague, beautiful in her scorn.

Never mind that Mrs. Schuyler hadn't a Newport house of her own. Never mind that she was a guest here. Mr. Sprague went red, then pale, then red again, muttered a few words about the press of business and fled, leaving Mrs. Schuyler to Ellen.

If he was this intimidated by one society woman, Ellen didn't like to think what would happen when the prince arrived. Perhaps she had best have smelling salts on hand, although who would need them more, the prince or Mr. Sprague, she wasn't quite sure.

Resignedly, Ellen approached the first houseguest. "Mrs. Schuyler? Mr. Sprague asked that I show you to—"

"I'm in need of a maid," said Mrs. Schuyler without preamble. "Mine left this morning, I can't think why. There's really no finding good servants these days."

"Mmm," said Ellen, not quite sure how a servant ought to respond to that. Although she wasn't quite a servant. She was neither here nor there.

"Just a few little late nights—and, really, hauling those milk jugs was good for her. And I don't see why being kicked by one cow should upset her so. But no. I'm too good to milk cows, she told me. As if no one keeps a cow in their yard for milk to bathe in!"

Ellen could only stare. There was something quite mesmerizing about that black and white pattern on Mrs. Schuyler's lapels. The woman was tiny, under five feet, but she seemed to expand to fill the whole room.

"Milk . . . for bathing?" she said tentatively.

"Oh yes, that reminds me." Mrs. Schuyler turned in a swish of emerald-green skirt, revealing exceedingly smart buttoned boots. "I require a milk bath. It must be new milk, do you understand? It only works if it's fresh. I will not be put off with rancid milk fit only for swine."

"No, of course not." A milk bath? Like every other household in Newport, the Spragues didn't keep their own cows, but acquired their milk from a creamery. The kitchens used a great deal of milk, to be sure, but hardly enough to fill a bath.

"For the complexion. It keeps the skin soft and supple." Mrs. Schuyler smiled sweetly at her, her pale blue eyes as clear as a china doll's and as lifelike. "I don't imagine you'd know. Who are you?"

Belatedly, Ellen got about to introducing herself. She had rather been hoping that she wouldn't have to, that she could disappear unobtrusively into the paneling. "My name is Ellen Daniels. I teach music—"

Mrs. Schuyler straightened, giving her feathers a shake, like a bird preening itself. "Oh, the *music* teacher. I have a music teacher, too, you know. My darling husband said a gift such as mine shouldn't be left to wither on the vine. Isn't that sweet? Of course, I shan't be singing this weekend—unless someone absolutely *begs* me to do so. I shouldn't want to put darling Maybelle in the shade. This is her night, after all. Have the servants taken my things to my room?"

The servants were staggering under enough trunks to stock an Arctic expedition for a month. Livingston had gone off to find the source of the Nile with less.

"Prunella?" Maybelle paused on the landing of the broad staircase, like a little girl not sure whether she might come to a grown-up party.

"Maybelle! You dear little thing!" Mrs. Schuyler was at least a head shorter than Maybelle, and her sleek traveling outfit was half the width of Maybelle's flounces, but somehow Maybelle did look little. Or, at least, very young. Mrs. Schuyler waited for Maybelle to come to her before swishing her cheek with ostrich feathers in lieu of an embrace. "It's been an age! Frank sends his very *warmest* regards."

The tips of Maybelle's ears turned as pink as her dress. "That's very kind of Mr. Pratt."

"Oh, Frank has the kindest heart in the world. I'm so terribly blessed in my cousins. There's no one dearer than darling Frank. Do you know he's to come to Newport?" Mrs. Schuyler waved an imperious hand at Maybelle. "Come, you can sit with me while I repair the ravages of travel, and I'll tell you *everything* that's occurred since your departure from town."

Maybelle trotted obediently after her as though Mrs. Schuyler were mistress of the house and she the guest. Ellen watched them go rather uneasily. Maybelle wasn't supposed to be watching Mrs. Schuyler change, she was meant to be greeting her guests.

And who was Frank?

Not the prince, that was for certain. The prince whom Maybelle was meant to be greeting in—Ellen checked the modest watch pinned to her shirtwaist—three hours.

There was no time to fret. Mrs. Schuyler was only the first of the wave of guests, tumbling out of carriages, complaining about the roads, about the train from New York, servants bickering over precedence, ladies' maids clutching jewel cases and eyeing footmen askance, Mr. Sprague appearing to greet some of his guests only to disappear into his study on a very important matter of business. That business appeared to be peering through binoculars at the new mansion going up next door, a summer palace for Nevada silver heiress Tessie Oelrichs. Bringing the neighborhood down, Sprague complained, as though his sister weren't a copper heiress, insistently aligning himself with the old guard even as they just as insistently refused to deign to notice him.

Ellen excused herself from the fray long enough to grab the liveries that had been hastily run up for the hired musicians. She tracked them down in the kitchen, where they were sitting at a corner of the long table, getting in the way of Cook's dinner preparations, and eating bread and drippings.

"Signor Rinaldo?" Ellen tried to count heads. There were meant to be eight musicians, four to a side for the trumpet fanfare, after which they would break up in groups to play in the various rooms of the house throughout the evening. "I have your liveries for you."

"Liveries?" Signor Rinaldo sounded about as Italian as she was. Ellen was pretty sure that Signor Rinaldo was more likely a Mr. O'Reilly when he was at home, and his Italian accent was about as convincing as the French accent of Maybelle's lady's maid.

"The clothes you and your troupe are to wear tonight," said Ellen tiredly. It had been a very long day, and it wasn't even three yet.

Signor Rinaldo lost any pretense of an accent as he stared at the garment Ellen was holding out to him. "Tights? You expect us to wear tights?"

Not just tights. Yellow tights cross-gartered with crimson ribbons. And pantaloons with great puffs. John Sprague's idea of the sort of clothes the retinue of an Italian potentate might have worn in the time of the Medici.

"It isn't my wish, but Mr. Sprague's," said Ellen firmly, thrusting the pile of clothes into Signor Rinaldo's arms. She'd love to tell herself that it was Signor Rinaldo's problem now, but it wasn't, not really. If something went wrong, John Sprague would blame her. "When the prince's carriage arrives, you will line up on either side of the drive to deliver a trumpet fanfare, followed by madrigals in the front hall."

Signor Rinaldo mustered one last attempt at protest. "He didn't say anything about no fancy dress."

Ellen abandoned any attempt at diplomacy. She'd already been condescended to by Prunella Schuyler and pinched by one of Mr. Sprague's business associates. "You want to get paid, don't you? If you want to get paid, you wear these. It's as simple as that. The front hall. Four o'clock. Be there. In these."

Needing air, she let herself out through the kitchen garden, almost colliding with a harried Mr. Whitmarsh, who appeared to be hunting for something behind the rosemary and parsley.

"Miss Daniels," he said thankfully. His hands were visibly shaking. Ellen felt quite sorry for the poor man. He had probably been quite a decent schoolmaster before being sacrificed to Dudley. "The very person. You haven't seen Master Dudley about, have you?"

"No, I'm afraid not," said Ellen.

Mr. Whitmarsh smiled tiredly at her. "You might say, *no, thank goodness*, and be honest about it."

Ellen couldn't help smiling back at him. Over the past month, they'd become friends, of sorts. Comrades in misfortune, as Mr. Whitmarsh called it, not realizing that Ellen felt very fortunate, indeed, to have found any refuge, even one such as Sprague Hall.

Mr. Whitmarsh liked, when he had the odd moment, to sit with Ellen and discuss Latin translations and modern poetry. Ellen had no interest in either ancient Romans or living poets, but she felt it was little enough to do for Mr. Whitmarsh, whose job was far more trying than hers. Better to have recourse to Romans than to the bottle.

Shy one, shy one, shy one of my heart, Mr. Whitmarsh had read to her only last night, a modern poet, an Irish poet, and she had wondered a little uneasily if there was something more to it than poetry.

Mr. Whitmarsh was a dear man, and not unhandsome, in a thin, fine-boned, nervous sort of way. If she were who she claimed to be—a poor young lady of good family—it would still make no sense, Ellen told herself firmly.

Ellen looked sympathetically at Mr. Whitmarsh. "What has he done this time?"

No need to specify who. If there was one person in the household known only as "he," uttered with a combination of dread and loathing, that person was Dudley Sprague, a terror in short pants.

Mr. Whitmarsh tried to smile, but it came out as a grimace. "Stole a bucket of paint and wrote rude sayings all across one wall of the schoolroom. I might have minded less if they'd been better spelled."

Ellen walked with him out of the kitchen garden. On one side, paths led down to the more utilitarian bits of the estate, to greenhouses and cutting gardens, arranged to be carefully out of sight. On the other, a paved walk led back around toward the front of the great house, around acres of marble balustrades and pillars. "Could you make him correct them? Or translate them to Latin, perhaps?"

"I don't want to encourage him."

"Breathing encourages him," said Ellen frankly.

"Yes, but stopping his breath would be murder, and I'm not sure I'm quite as far along as that," said Mr. Whitmarsh ruefully. "Although there are times when the prospect of hanging feels like a blessed release."

"He's not worth it. Don't let him torment the life out of you." Pausing in the shadow of an ornamental loggia thick with pillars, Ellen looked at Mr. Whitmarsh with genuine concern. "Don't you think you might do better elsewhere? Surely even a school would be better than this."

"With twenty beasts to my care instead of one?" He tried to make a joke of it, but Ellen could see the despair beneath it. She knew something of men and despair. And what they might do in the grips of it.

"A whole menagerie would wreak less havoc than one Dudley." John Sprague was weak and venal, a petty bully, robbing his sister and stinting his servants. But Dudley—there was something else there entirely. Something missing. Something wrong.

These weren't just schoolboy pranks. His was the sort of malice that delighted in pain, any pain, so long as it wasn't his own.

Ellen rubbed her hands up and down her arms, suddenly cold, even in the afternoon sun. "You could work at a school in the winter and have the summer holidays to write your poetry. Or even better, find a family who needs a tutor to take their son to Europe on the grand tour. You could wallow in Roman ruins and good wine."

"Thank you, Miss Daniels. You make me feel like there's still hope in the world." Mr. Whitmarsh took her hand, squeezing it warmly. "When Pandora opened the box and all the ills of the world flew out, the one fugitive virtue left—the only consolation—was hope. That's what you are here, in this house."

"A fugitive virtue?" "Fugitive" was close enough. A little too close.

Ellen glanced over her shoulder, and saw, for the first time, that their loggia already had an occupant, a man leaning against a pillar, enjoying a cigarette, and watching them.

Ellen yanked her hand away from Mr. Whitmarsh, saying quickly, "Speaking of fugitives, it looks like I have one right there. I've been trying to round up musicians, but it's worse than herding cats. I thought I had them all corralled in the kitchen, but . . ."

"Of course," said Mr. Whitmarsh awkwardly. "I mustn't keep you. Thank you."

Ellen looked back at him, not wanting to encourage him, but not quite able to leave it. "You'll be all right?"

"As the indifferent children of the earth."

Ellen let out a breath of relief. If he was back to poetry, he was back to himself. Until the next time Dudley did something appalling.

Ellen concentrated her annoyance on the man beneath the loggia, who was smoking and regarding her progress with detached amusement.

She imagined he must have come out the same way she had, through the kitchen garden and around the side of the house. Guests wouldn't have come this way. They would have been directed through the house to the series of descending terraces, formal garden upon formal garden, leveling out right before the edge of the cliff, with its view of the sea.

He watched her as if she were one of the acts at the Hibernia, there entirely for his entertainment, which was rather rich, considering that he was the entertainment.

"A pretty scene," he said, in an accent that was far more convincing than Signor Rinaldo's.

Ellen frowned at him. "Has Signor Rinaldo given you your livery?"

The man didn't bother to unfold himself from his supporting pillar. "My . . . livery?"

Ellen wondered what sort of musician he was. His voice was a beautiful, well-modulated tenor, but with his long, elegant fingers, he might equally have been a flautist or a pianist. Whatever he was, he clearly had an ego to match. "It's Mr. Sprague's orders that everyone be in livery in anticipation of the prince's arrival."

The man regarded her thoughtfully over his cigarette. "The prince?"

"Yes, the Prince di Conti. The man whom you are to serenade." She had guests to see to and Dudley to catch and Maybelle to get away from that Mrs. Schuyler and a prince to prepare for. She didn't have time for this. "Perhaps if you had been with your troupe instead of tainting your voice with that foul stuff you might be better informed."

"Perhaps the prince has no desire for a serenade."

He was getting one whether he liked it or not. "That's not for you to say. Or for me," she added. "Do you need me to escort you back to your people?"

"Need, no," said the man, and Ellen felt he was laughing at her. She would have left him there but Mr. Sprague had been quite insistent. Matched musicians. In livery. There had been, she thought, seven at the table. This man made eight.

Perhaps they could do it with six, three to a side?

No. Mr. Sprague had paid for eight musicians. He would expect eight musicians. And it would be Ellen's fault if he had fewer. If this man, this loathsome, conceited, dawdling man, threw off Mr. Sprague's precious arrangements.

"Are you coming or not?" Ellen demanded.

"Always a question," murmured the man.

It had been a simple request, not a philosophical debate. "Do you always question the wishes of your employers? If so, I'm not surprised you were available on such short notice," said Ellen, frustrated. "And so cheap."

The plume of smoke trailed away as the man lowered his cigarette. He wasn't smiling anymore. "You would be surprised at my price, *mia bella*." He looked at someone behind Ellen's shoulder. "Ah, Mr. Sprague. You have discovered me, I see."

John Sprague was staring from the lost musician to Ellen with raw horror. "Your nobleness . . . my lord . . . er—"

"My lord?" Ellen looked from her employer to the man in the shadows, feeling her stomach do something very uncomfortable beneath her chemise.

"The correct form is 'Your Excellency.'" The man flicked his cigarette away, unfolding himself easily from his pillar. "But as we are in the land of democracy, you may call me Don Sebastiano."

Ellen felt sick to her stomach. All this time, the prince. Her tongue tasted like the leavings of the prince's cigarette. Her job—her dreams of accompanying Maybelle to Italy—all ash on the floor of the loggia. "I shouldn't wish to presume."

The prince stepped forward, out of the shadow, looking her directly in the eye. He was older than she'd realized; his face had a cynical cast to it. "You may presume all you like—so long as you don't make me wear livery."

Mr. Sprague bumbled in between them. "Your lordship—I mean, Your Excellency—I assure you, no offense was meant. This girl—"

"This woman," the prince corrected pleasantly, but there was something in his voice that made Mr. Sprague stop and swallow hard.

"This woman . . . she's new to my employ . . . just a music teacher . . . my Maybelle . . . she's very musical, you see—"

The prince ignored him. "Do you have a name, music teacher?"

"Daniels," said Ellen, just wanting the game, whatever it was, to end, so John Sprague could sack her, and get it over with. She wondered if she could get her room back at the boardinghouse in Providence, or if it might be safer to go elsewhere. Where would Dermot never think she might go? South, perhaps. Or west. She could go to California. And do what? Prospect for gold? "Ellen Daniels."

"Miss Daniels." Her borrowed name was something exotic on the prince's tongue. "It has been a pleasure."

"For you, perhaps." Ellen bit down hard on her lip. She hadn't meant to say that out loud. She'd been so good all those years at hiding her feelings, at staying quiet and calm. And now, well, she'd hoist her own petard anyway. What was the use?

Mr. Sprague's face was gray. "I apologize for the girl's—er, Miss Daniels's—insolence. I assure you, her behavior—"

"Has enlivened a dull afternoon." Ellen wasn't sure how he did it, but the prince seemed to distance himself, even though he still stood exactly where he had been. He had cloaked himself in majesty, looking at John Sprague in a way that reduced him to the crawling underling he was. The prince's tone forbade any disagreement. "If all in your employ are as . . . original as this one, I am sure I shall be well entertained, indeed."

"I suppose . . . if you say—" John Sprague floundered, desperately wanting to wring Ellen's neck but unable to gainsay the prince.

And the prince knew it. The wretch knew it.

The prince turned to Ellen and did the unthinkable. He bowed to her. As though she were his equal and not a music teacher. "Miss Daniels. I look forward to furthering our acquaintance."

"Your Excellency," murmured Ellen, feeling two spots of red burning in her cheeks. She bobbed a belated curtsy.

He honored her, she knew, not out of any regard for her but for the entirely understandable purpose of annoying John Sprague. Which was all very well for the prince, but it was she who would pay the price. Soon, if the look in Sprague's eyes was anything to go by.

At the moment, Ellen impartially hated them both. The prince for compromising her position and Sprague for being the loathsome toad he was.

She'd been happy here. Well, maybe not happy here, but at least peaceful here. And now . . .

"If Your Excellency would care to come in by the front way?" John Sprague said stiffly.

"For my serenade? Indeed." With one last nod to Ellen, the prince clasped his hands behind his back and strolled down the loggia toward the front of the house without looking to see if his host was behind him.

Mr. Sprague cast Ellen a look of barely concealed rage. "I'll talk to you later," he hissed, and then hurried away after the prince.

CHAPTER SIX

Lucky

Newport, Rhode Island
July 1957

LUCKY HAD SPENT most of her American life learning how to conceal her rage. Back in Italy, if you felt a thing, you expressed it; here in New England, a lady wasn't supposed to *feel* anything so vulgar as anger, and even if she did—*well*! She had better not raise her voice, for God's sake. Cool as a cucumber, that was the American Lucky. An ice queen, veins frozen solid.

Except sometimes. Sometimes the anger boiled over, and the ice melted.

You never knew what might set it off, either. So much accumulated rage this evening, from Stuy and his waitress to Dudley Sprague and his bullying. When they walked out of the hospital into the muggy night air, they crossed the parking lot to the car, Stuy's pride and joy, a dashing little MG convertible imported from England with the steering wheel on the right-hand side. Lucky slid into the passenger seat and felt a lump she hadn't noticed earlier, so she dug her fingers into the crack between seat back and seat and came out with an opera-length glove that was not her own.

She threw it in Stuy's face.

Well, she was *mad*!

But he was just turning out of the parking lot into the road, so he didn't take it well. Swerved all over the road, swearing and trying to peel the tenacious black lace—oh yes, the glove was *black lace*!—from his famous cheekbones. And it all went downhill from there, as they drove down Bellevue Avenue to Sprague Hall through the hazy July moonlight. They'd both drunk too much, they were both too tired and nervy to argue with logic.

It was a doozy, all right.

"For God's sake, if I can't get it at home, what do you expect?"

"I expect you to take care of these things somewhere I won't be *sitting*!"

"You don't even care!"

"Sure, I care! I care about *hygiene*!"

"You are the goddamn coldest woman I ever met, Lucky Sprague!"

"I wasn't so cold at my debutante party! Christ, if *only* I'd been cold then!"

"You're saying you wish we didn't have Joanie?"

"I'm saying I wish I had Joanie with somebody else! Somebody who isn't spreading himself thin all over the Eastern seaboard the second I take my eyes off him."

"Like Teddy Winthrop, maybe?"

"What's Teddy got to do with it?"

"Why don't *you* tell *me* what he's got to do with you?"

"I wish he did have something to do with me! But he's not like you, Stuy. He loves his wife enough to keep his tool in his belt!"

"So you admit it!"

"Admit what?"

"You and Winthrop!"

"Oh, that's rich. You screw some waitress against the railing at the club, anybody could see you, and then accuse me of—"

"That doesn't mean anything! You know it doesn't!"

"Oh? Then why do you do it so much?"

"It may surprise you to know that a man has *needs*!"

"So does a *woman*, it may surprise you to know!"

"You coulda fooled *me*!"

"Oh, am I supposed to jump right into bed with you while you're still stiff from somebody else? You might give me a five-minute window once in a while, in between all that stuff that doesn't *mean anything*!"

"What for?"

"What *for*? For our marriage! Our child!"

Stuy turned the car into the Sprague Hall drive in a screech of burning tires. "You just said you wished she wasn't mine!"

"Maybe I don't!"

"Are you trying to tell me something, Lucky? Are you?"

"I'm sick of it, that's all! The cheating and the flirting and all of it!"

"Maybe if *my own wife* flirted with me once in a while!"

"Is that what you want? A flirt?"

The car banged to a stop. Stuy leapt out and swung around the hood to jerk open her door, because even in the middle of a knock-down, drag-out fight you had to observe the niceties.

"I want a *wife*, that's all! Not an ice statue!"

"Oh, so you're taking cues from your father, now?"

"Don't talk about Dad that way!"

"I'll talk about him any way I like! He's a bastard, a bastard to *you* and a bastard to *me*, and I wish to God he would just die and leave us in peace!"

"Oh, is *that* how it is?"

"You know you want it just as much as I do!"

"I just want a little peace and quiet around here, that's all! A wife who appreciates me!"

"Well, maybe I want things, too!"

"Like *what*?"

"Like a husband who doesn't run around on me! A father-in-law who doesn't insult me! Maybe I want a real marriage—"

"That's up to *you*, cupcake—"

"—another baby, which I'm not going to get around here, that's obvious—"

"*WHAT*?"

"Oh, go to hell!"

Lucky marched toward the door. Stuy caught up and grabbed her arm.

"*What* did you say?"

"Nothing!"

"Do not—*do not* tell me you want to get pregnant by Teddy *Winthrop*!"

"I want to get pregnant by *you*, you idiot! You're my *husband*! But you're busy fertilizing the willing soil of New England's finest—"

"That's not true!"

"Oh, you think I didn't hear? You think I didn't know about her?"

They came to a stop on the wide front portico and faced each other. The moonlight spilled over Stuy's hair and cast deep, symmetrical shadows beneath his cheekbones. His eyes were wide and pained. So were hers, probably. She felt like all the world's tears ached behind her eyeballs.

"About who?" he rasped. "What did you hear?"

"That girl in Fall River. The one you paid to get an abortion."

"Who told you that?"

"I see you don't deny it!"

"I don't admit a thing! I want to know who told you that!"

Lucky turned away and flung open the door.

"Mommy?"

A little girl stood in the doorway. Long white nightgown. Big, scared eyes. Dark entrance hall behind her, shadowy pale pillars, like a girl in a novel from a hundred years ago.

"Joanie," Lucky whispered.

Joanie looked from Lucky to Stuy and back again. Tears brimmed in her wide blue-green eyes. "Are you going to get a divorce?"

Stuy lurched forward. "Of course we aren't, darling. Never in a million years." He swooped her up in his arms and staggered.

"For God's sake, put her down!" Lucky whispered fiercely. "You're too drunk!"

"I'm not . . . too drunk . . . to carry my own daughter!"

Lucky ran in front of them and pulled Joanie from his arms. "That's enough," she said, setting Joanie on her feet. Taking her small hand. "Let's go upstairs, sweetie. Mommy will put you back to bed."

"If she *is* mine," Stuy muttered.

Lucky whirled around. Her hand flew up to smack him. Stopped just in time, but only because of Joanie. Joanie, who stood there choking her sobs back, so brave and terrified by that monumental staircase in her white nightgown. Darling Joanie.

Lucky leaned in to whisper right next to his ear. "How *dare* you. When I only *married* you because of her. When I wrecked my *life* because she was yours."

Then she turned and walked to the stairs, Joanie's hand firmly inside her own.

OF COURSE SHE'D once had a terrible crush on Stuyvesant Sprague. How could she not? He was six years older than she was, had just finished his first year at Choate when she arrived from Italy, and already he was an Adonis. Like a handsome, dashing older brother, living in the same house every summer, except he wasn't her brother at all so she was free to worship him.

How she worshipped him.

The way he sauntered confidently into a room, the competent way he sailed his sleek little sloop around Narragansett Bay and sometimes out to sea, just everything about him. He never learned a word of Italian, but he taught her some English words when he could be bothered. Once he told Lucky her accent was cute and she practiced her rusty Italian vowels for weeks, but that autumn she left for Miss Porter's, where the teachers ironed them scrupulously out of her. Another time he took her out sailing for the day. The wind whipped his golden hair around his face; his eyes were the color of the sea under the sunshine, only *brighter, alive*. He had just enough brains to go on to Princeton with the help of the remnants of the Sprague fortune and Newport connections, and he'd graduated and begun working at some Wall Street investment bank when he came to Newport at the end of May for her debutante party.

Oh, she could still remember the look on his face when he glanced up from some conversation and saw her on the stairs, dressed like a fashion model in a gown of iridescent white chiffon, her shoulders bare and gleaming, her golden hair done up properly by a real hairdresser, her icy green eyes rimmed by long black lashes and set off by Helena Rubenstein Red Velvet lipstick, carefully blotted and reapplied so it would last through a couple of glasses of champagne at least. It was like in the movies, when the man forgets everything else and walks dreamlike (in his tuxedo, his hair slicked back, his shoes polished) up the stairs to the sound of some swelling orchestra (yes, there was an orchestra) to kiss the hand of the swan who's finally shed her duckling feathers. *My God, kid,* he'd said, truly awed, *who would've thought you'd turn out to be such a stunner?*

In retrospect, it was not the compliment of Lucky's dreams. But it was enough. They danced and drank and eventually stole away to the cliffs near the boathouse, where the water reflected the moon in dazzling shapes on the rocks and the wooden walls, and Stuy told her he'd fallen in love with her, just like that. *I'm on my knees, kid,* he told her, his skin turned to silver in the moonlight, his hair glinting. *I'm a goner.* He had kissed her very gently, and she had put her arms around his neck and they had kissed less gently, and somehow she had ended up in the grass, luminous chiffon dress wadded around her waist, Stuy telling her he couldn't stop, was it okay, he couldn't stop, she was so beautiful, he loved her. And she was drunk on champagne, drunk on kisses and everything, on the brand-new electricity between them, and she told him it wasn't just *okay*, it was everything she ever wanted.

In the morning, he was awfully remorseful, brought her a dozen roses and a pretty gold bracelet, and the next time they did it in her bedroom and he wore a rubber. But by then it was too late for such precautions. Joanie already existed.

BY THE TIME Lucky tucked the blankets around Joanie's small body, the remorse had already spilled in terrible waves over her heart and stomach, almost drenching her. What an awful, terrible thing to say. To her own husband! No wonder he slept with other women. No wonder he didn't love her. No wonder—

"Mommy?"

"Yes, honey?"

"Could you go with us tomorrow? When Daddy takes me sailing?"

Lucky leaned forward to kiss her forehead. "Maybe, sweetheart. I've got lots to do with the ball coming up."

"Oh, that's right. I forgot."

Joanie looked up at her from the white pillowcase, dotted with tiny blue flowers. Joanie had never liked pink. Her bedroom was decorated in blues and yellows, to the extent it was decorated at all. Lucky did not believe in interior decoration. She thought rooms should grow naturally over time, curtains here and rugs there, as you found things that delighted you. Anyway, here was her daughter in her nest of blue and yellow, gazing up longingly with her eyes that were an eerily exact replica of her father's eyes, except that the color was an unfathomable blend of the two of them, Stuy and Lucky, merged together for a drunken moment eight years ago to create this perfect creature. Maybe Stuy had looked into Lucky's eyes at the moment of release, the instant of conception, and that was how Joanie's eyes became that marvelous shade of blue green. Lucky honestly couldn't remember. She'd been too drunk, and sort of stunned by the unfamiliar mechanics of intercourse.

But it was a nice story, wasn't it?

"I'll see what I can do, darling. You know I'm not fond of sailing."

"I *love* sailing."

Lucky kissed her warm forehead again. "You're Daddy's little girl, aren't you?"

"Mommy?"

"Yes?"

"Why don't I have a brother or sister? Everyone else has them."

Lucky ran her hand along the blanket, as if to smooth it. "Not everyone."

"Patty's going to get one for Christmas."

"Oh, is that so?"

"She told me today."

Lucky lifted her hand and stroked the wisps of gold hair at Joanie's temple. Felt the soft warmth of her daughter's skin under her fingertips. Her eyes ached, her heart ached. Where had it come from, this longing? Out of nowhere, it seemed. Just *surged over her* during the past year, like a tide that wouldn't go out. She saw babies everywhere, sweet creamy-skinned round-cheeked fuzzy-haired babies, and she wanted one so badly she couldn't breathe. She couldn't even open Joanie's bottom drawer anymore, the tiny baby clothes tenderly folded away in case of siblings, the smell of Joanie's babyhood. Maybe that was why it hurt so much, the sight of Stuy buttoning his trousers on the yacht club terrace. Like some steel knife was butchering her through the middle. What should be *hers* was inside some waitress, some girl dazzled by Stuy's movie-star looks, as Lucky herself had once been dazzled.

Now, whenever she went to the club she would wonder *which one*. Which girl had tangled against the railing with Lucky's husband?

"I have an idea," Lucky said. "My grandmother once told me that sometimes when we close our eyes and pray very hard, very *sincerely* for the thing we most want in all the world, the Virgin Mary will give it to us."

Joanie squinted her eyes shut. Lucky kissed her forehead a third and final time.

"Are you praying?"

Joanie's head nodded frantically. Lucky reached for the lamp and clicked it off.

OUTSIDE JOANIE'S DOOR, Lucky paused. The hallway ran the width of the house, ending in a window that overlooked the ocean. To the left of the window lay her bedroom. Stuy's bedroom was around the corner.

It was like that now.

There was no sign of Stuy. He was probably downstairs in the library, pouring out single malt whisky from the liquor cabinet and drinking it neat. Lucky walked down the hall toward the dark window overlooking the sea. In that quiet house, when the wind was right, you could sometimes hear the crash of waves on the cliffs and beach through all the glass and wood. Lucky didn't enjoy sailing—the wild, unpredictable ocean frightened her, to tell the truth—but she did love watching the sea from a place of safety.

She stopped at the window and looked out. The few lights from the house didn't penetrate the darkness much, and the crescent moon made a pitiful light through the summer haze. Down the lawn, the boathouse lay in deepest shadow, not even visible. Somewhere on the lawn not far from that boathouse, in the shelter of the hydrangea, her fate had been sealed. Sometimes she wondered. She played with *what if.* What if she *hadn't* said it was okay? Would he have stopped? He'd said he *couldn't* stop, but surely he *would* have, if she told him to. Right? Anyway, it didn't matter. She didn't want a world in which Joanie didn't exist. She only wanted her world to be a bit different than it was.

As Lucky turned away from the window to put her hand on the doorknob of her bedroom, a glimmer of movement caught her eye. She peered back out through the glass and swore.

THE TEMPERATURE HAD dropped enough—and the air was humid enough—that Lucky's shoes were soaked with dew by the time she reached her grandmother. She called out softly to the ghostly white nightgown.

"Nonna!"

The woman in the nightgown turned and frowned at her. A mist of moonlit white hair surrounded her face. "Lucia? Is that you?"

"Yes, Nonna. It's bedtime."

"I have to find her first."

"There's nobody there, Nonna. It's the middle of the night. You're out walking again."

"But I have to find her."

"She's already gone inside. She's asleep in bed, like you should be."

"Is she? Really? That's strange. She said . . . she said . . ."

"You'll see her in the morning," Lucky said.

She took Nonna gently by the elbow and urged her toward the house. Behind them, the water washed against the dock. Nonna had always been a little—well, not quite *all there,* as people said, even back in Italy. Lucky had never known her mother, who had died when she was born, so she was mostly raised by her grandparents, and Nonno had always seemed like the one person who anchored Nonna to earth. Her father—when he was around, and not off with his political friends—said it was because of some terrible thing that had happened when they were first married, which neither of them would talk about, and when Nonno went it was like Nonna had lost her moorings. Sometimes it seemed to Lucky that Nonna's mind—never one to keep to a strict path, anyway—had begun to wander back down to that time long ago, when she first met Nonno. Had they been happy together? What was this terrible thing? Lucky never wanted to ask, especially now that she knew how badly a marriage could go wrong. What terrible things two people who were supposed to be in love could still inflict on each other.

Nonna started to sing. She had a beautiful singing voice, high and clear and remarkably in tune, for a woman of seventy-nine. Lucky didn't know the song. The words were English, the tune old-fashioned and waltzy, the kind of thing you might hear in a music hall. They reached the terrace and the French doors.

"That's right," Lucky said. "In we go."

Nonna stopped singing and gripped Lucky by the elbows. Her eyes took on a fierce glow. "She didn't deserve it, you know."

"Who?"

"She didn't deserve it. She was so kind to me."

"Nonna, what's the matter? Didn't deserve what?"

Nonna's hands dropped away. The light died in her eyes.

"Never mind," she said. "You wouldn't understand."

AT LAST LUCKY settled Nonna in her room. For years now, she and Stuy had debated whether to lock Nonna in her bedroom at night, and Lucky had resisted. But maybe now it was time. Maybe they could install some kind of house telephone in there, so Nonna could call them if she was distressed or something. Or maybe Nonna could move into the room next to Lucky's.

No. Nonna would never want that. She liked her room where it was.

Lucky arrived at her own room and opened the door. Reached for the nearest lamp and switched it on.

"Lucky?"

She was so startled she had to grab the edge of the bureau so she wouldn't stumble. Stuy stood next to the window, holding his glass of neat whisky. His eyes were red, his face hollow and pale.

"Sorry. Didn't mean to surprise you."

"I'd say that's exactly what you meant to do. What the hell are you doing here?"

"I just came to apologize."

Lucky kicked off her wet shoes and tossed them in the wardrobe. Of course she should wipe them dry and stuff her old linens inside to save the leather, but she was beyond caring about her damn shoes anymore. "What for?"

"Everything, I guess. You're right. I'm a rotten husband, done nothing but made you miserable. You're a saint, patient and beautiful and marvelous, and the better you are the worse it makes me. The worse I behave. You're right about all of it. I should just do the decent thing and offer you a divorce. God knows you have plenty of grounds."

Lucky straightened away from the wardrobe and stared at him. How stricken he looked, how remorseful. He'd discarded his jacket and tie somewhere and stood in his white shirtsleeves, his trim trousers over his flat stomach. His knuckles were white where they gripped the lowball glass, half full of whisky. His hair was the color of candlelight and looked as if he'd gone outside in a hurricane.

What *was* it about apologies? They sapped the wind from your sails. All your powerful, righteous anger. How could you remain furious at so much honest remorse?

"Did you do it with her?"

"What?"

"That waitress tonight. Or did I interrupt too soon?"

"No. I mean yes. I mean . . . God, Lucky. No, I didn't. I wasn't really going to—not like *that*—we were just fooling around and . . . *hell*." He turned back to the window. "Sometimes you look at me like you loathe me. And this nice pretty girl comes up and she looks at me like I'm some kind of god, and I just—"

"You just can't resist."

Stuy lifted the whisky glass and slung back the rest. "Dad once told me—you know that voice of his—he said, *It's a damn good thing you're such a good-looking son of a bitch, because there isn't a damn thing else you're good for.*" He paused. "Except he didn't say *damn*."

"That's not true. You can sail."

"I can sail. That's right." He turned to her and spread out his arms. "The man you married, Lucky. A good-looking son of a bitch who can sail."

"And you're a good father."

"When I'm not drunk."

"And you're good in bed. Also when you're not drunk."

"I'm drunk now, I'm afraid."

How long had it been since they last went to bed together? Months. But it was always like that. They would go weeks and weeks in some kind of Paleolithic deep freeze, hardly speaking except to argue, and then suddenly and without warning the ice melted, the permafrost thawed, and they would fall in bed and do it twice a day for weeks, the old electricity, the raw sex connection that brought them together in the first place. For a little while, everything would be terrific again, until it wasn't.

Lucky closed her eyes. She thought of Teddy, but only for an instant—slipping like a ghost through her brain, like Nonna in her nightgown, not quite real. Another thought took hold, a memory, the scene outside the yacht club. The dark shapes tangle and separate against the railing, the girl bolts for the kitchen, Stuy fumbles at his trousers. *Much* more real. Anger bubbled in Lucky's stomach. But it wasn't just anger, either. Sometimes you couldn't quite tell what it was that made your belly hot, your skin flush, your hair tingle.

"Lucky," Stuy whispered. "Beautiful kid. You know I'm crazy about you. You know it kills me to hurt you."

"Then stop hurting me."

Her eyes were still closed. She heard the faint click of his whisky glass landing on the lamp table. She didn't want to see him approach her, his glorious face, his shoulders and arms. She didn't want to see his hands touching her arms. His lips at the hollow of her throat, climbing ever so carefully to her jaw, her chin, finally her mouth. She tried to summon her fury—the waitress, the woman in Fall River, all the rest of them, *Stuy kissing other women, having intercourse with other women!*—but her animal blood took that kindling and burned hotter. She must be sick, some kind of pervert, now the whisky of Stuy's breath sent her up in flame.

CHAPTER SEVEN

Andie

Newport, Rhode Island
September 2019

"This room needs a flamethrower, not a renovation."

Only the red light on George's camera stopped me from verbally and wholeheartedly agreeing with Devon, the boom operator. His main job consisted of operating and placing microphones on lengthy boom poles and keeping them out of camera shot, but his unofficial capacity was that of offering background commentary. Despite his heavily muscled arms—presumably from holding boom poles for extended lengths of time—he looked barely old enough to be shaving, yet he had the cynicism and brutal honesty of a seasoned reality star exec.

He was right, of course. Maybelle Sprague's childhood bedroom would have been more suited to Vlad the Impaler's Transylvanian castle than the private retreat of a virginal heiress. The first time I'd seen it, I'd suggested to Marc that if the Spragues were that hard up for money, they might make a mint renting out this room for low-budget horror movie sets instead of going through a renovation. He'd regarded me with unfocused eyes before patting my shoulder and telling me to do what I thought best.

I'd pretended he was just having an off day and brushed it aside. Because if he really wanted me to do what was best for this old palace, it wouldn't be a simple matter of fixing up three rooms for a reality show. After seeing the condition of most of the house, simply redecorating three rooms was going to be like sticking a Band-Aid on a ruptured artery.

Limp paper sagged from the walls, like tears of exhaustion caused from the sheer strength it took to cling to the old plaster. Chunks of the ceiling dusted the faded Aubusson rug, and we'd learned to avoid bumping the heavy draperies due to the risk of being attacked by a swarm of moths or choking on the layer of dust covering the heavy Gothic furniture and crimson-and-gold brocade fabric.

With a pointed stare at Devon, I continued. "The rather large and exuberant gasolier in the middle of the room was never converted to electricity and will be replaced with something more contemporary—with chrome and glass to add more light." I cringed inside but kept speaking. "We will also be installing can lights, with dimmer switches to control the intensity and to highlight the new faux-wood laminate flooring we will be installing over the existing oak floors to give the room a fresher, lighter feel."

Feeling thoroughly nauseated at the proposed defamation of the room, I dropped the color palette I'd been holding up to a stark swath of plaster where the red brocade wallpaper had given up and lay curdled on the floor. I motioned to George to turn off the camera and then glanced at my Timex watch. It had been a wedding gift from my father to my mother, and in all of my recollections of her she wore it. In the end it had been just one more thing she'd left behind.

I cleared my throat. "It's a wrap for today. And please hurry—we're pushing our four-thirty deadline to be out of here." I pulled off my pink construction hat and tossed it harder than necessary on the floor. "We'll meet back here tomorrow morning at eight and pick up where we left off. I think the budget is way off for this room, so we're going to have to condense the original plan to a smaller area. I'll work on it tonight so we're ready to go first thing."

Meghan tugged on a strip of wallpaper, ripping it cleanly from the wall. "Maybe we'll be lucky and find platinum wall panels under all of this brocade—like they did at The Breakers. Nobody could figure out why the metal panels weren't tarnishing until they figured out they were platinum and worth a fortune. That would solve the Spragues' money problems for sure."

"I don't think the families who lived here were the kind of people to splurge on platinum walls. The Vanderbilts, yes. The Spragues, not so much."

"Fair point," Meghan said, rolling up the wallpaper into a ball and letting it drop to the floor.

I pulled out my phone and sent a quick text to Marc asking him to clear my plan with Christiana. His role in this production had been reduced to the single function of playing liaison between me and the executive producer. There had once been a time when I wouldn't have made any decisions regarding a project without consulting with Marc first. Not because I wasn't confident, but because he was the most knowledgeable person I knew in the field and I always learned something from him.

I couldn't pinpoint the exact time our relationship had changed, only recalling in hindsight it had been around the time of tabloid gossip of a personal loss, a loss he didn't share with me and I didn't ask out of respect for his privacy. Our professional relationship didn't warrant such confidences. But I'd been sure I would've known if the rumors were true because I would have seen it. As if a person's internal crisis would be a sudden flash of light or blare of a trumpet. Even after the academic world had discarded him like yesterday's fish, and the phone had stopped ringing for the consulting jobs that had become his bread and butter, we still pretended—at least with each other—that nothing had changed. In my twenty-nine years, knowing how to pretend like an Oscar winner had elbowed its way to the top of my skill set.

"I think this area surrounding the bay window would be perfect," Meghan said, walking toward an alcove out of the line of sight of the bedroom door. "It doesn't even look like it belongs in this room, much less the rest of the house."

While the crew began shutting off lights and wrapping cords, I moved to stand next to her. The small alcove was the single nod to cozy elegance in the entire mansion, a welcome contrast to the gaudy and over-the-top filigreed opulence found in the rest of the room and the entirety of Sprague Hall. Like a dainty rowboat moored alongside testosterone-dripping superyachts, it was floral fabric and needlepoint rugs to faux marble and second-rate tapestries. A chaise longue festooned in faded and threadbare pink-and-white chintz rosebuds was the first realistic nod to a former occupant that I'd seen. Matching panels hung at the floor-to-ceiling windows facing the chaise.

Because it had been left out of the script, I'd ignored the alcove, unwilling to become attached to anything that was destined for the Dumpster. Out of curiosity, I held my breath and moved the curtains aside, waiting a moment for the dust to settle before looking out the window. From the chaise, the occupant had a stunning view of what had once been extravagant gardens and, presumably, anyone outside. And beyond that, a narrow view of the ocean and the shards of reflective light bouncing off the water. Whoever this Maybelle Sprague had been, she had the best view from any room. Except maybe from the third floor. Not that I'd know, since I'd been barred access to Lucia Sprague's rooms in my contract. But that didn't stop me from wondering.

I turned, catching sight of a low bookcase nudged close to the chaise for easy access. The books were crammed neatly on two shelves, the overflow stacked on top. I carefully pulled a volume from the pile, being careful not to dislodge the thick crusting of dust that hid the title. I slid my index finger down the spine to reveal embossed words. I held it up to Meghan. "Your favorite, *Pride and Prejudice*."

Meghan was already pulling out two more books and revealing their titles. "*Jane Eyre* and *Wuthering Heights*. I hope these weren't her only introductions to romantic relationships. Jane Austen, yes, but the other two might have left her with a warped sense of true love."

I was leaning over to select another book when the top row shifted, toppling the stacked books onto the floor with a loud clatter and a cloud of dust. Devon appeared in the alcove, his eyes wide. "Was that the ghost?"

I rolled my eyes. "No. Just some books shifting because we'd removed a few. No ghosts."

Meghan sent me a sidelong glance. "You do know this place is supposed to be haunted, right? Something about a lady in white. I read it in one of the articles you collected. She's been spotted wandering outside on the lawn."

Devon nodded enthusiastically. "Oh, yeah—there's something spooky here for reals. In a lot of the photos I've been taking with my phone, I swear there are orbs all over them."

I didn't bother to hide my sigh. "It's dust, Devon. In case you haven't noticed, this room hasn't been cleaned in years."

He frowned. "But how do you explain George's missing lunch bag? And the lightbulbs that had all been unscrewed when we showed up this morning?"

That got my attention. My pink hammer had disappeared after I'd used it to smack a protruding nail. Not that I was upset I had the opportunity now to replace it with a normal one, but it was certainly something that would stand out and be hard to miss. I assumed someone was playing a prank. There had also been creaks I'd heard in the hallway when I'd been left alone upstairs while the crew went outside for lunch. But old houses always creaked and moaned—it was part of their charm. And some of those creaks and moans sounded like footsteps, which is what I'd kept reminding myself as I continued stripping the brocade wallpaper while making sure my back was never turned toward the doorway leading into the hallway.

Before I could think of a plausible explanation, Meghan perked up.

"I know someone who talks to dead people. In Charleston. I could call her—"

I cut her off. "No. There are no ghosts. No need to stage an intervention."

"An intervention?"

I looked up to see Luke leaning casually against the archway to the alcove. He wore boat shoes and an untucked oxford cloth button-down that looked like it had been slept in. A pair of aviator sunglasses hung from the breast pocket. I hadn't seen him since the horrible scene on the dock with Petey and his appearance now brought back all the irrational fear and anger that had nothing to do with Luke. He'd simply made a likely target and at some point I needed to apologize. But not now, as he regarded me with bloodshot eyes and looking like the stereotype I'd pegged him to be.

Before I could say anything, Meghan piped up. "She meant a cleansing. For the ghost."

Luke's expression remained impassive. "The white lady, you mean?"

Meghan nodded eagerly. "Yes. Nobody's seen her, but we have orbs that may or may not be dust motes. In photos. And things keep disappearing."

"Because of the ghost." Luke's voice had an edge that Meghan didn't seem to notice.

"Yes! Have you seen her?"

Luke pushed himself off the wall. "No. Because she doesn't exist." He lifted his wrist and pointedly examined his watch—something big and bright with lots of dials and buttons. I didn't have to see the face to know it was most likely a Rolex Yacht-Master, a uniform requirement for a sailor boy and costing more than my father made in a year. "It's four twenty. You and your crew have ten minutes to be gone."

"Give me a minute," Meghan said, heading toward Devon, presumably to look at his photographs of dust motes.

I noted with satisfaction that the crew had left, leaving cords and other equipment sitting neatly stacked against the walls like compliant students, the large floodlights switched off with lightbulbs intact. "There," I said, unable to resist swiping my hands together. "Just as you asked. Although I will say that we could have worked for at least three more hours. This whole early deadline thing is only going to prolong the entire shoot. You know, if the whole idea is so that you can take a nap before heading out to party all night, maybe you should rethink your life choices." I wanted to make a grand exit, but he was blocking me and the only way to get out of the alcove would be to brush against him so I remained where I was, waiting for him to either make some angry retort or move. He did neither.

"I'm sorry," he said.

It took me a moment to register his words and to remember that he knew nothing about my past. "For what?"

"For yesterday. I should have brought Petey right to you. I can only imagine your panic to find your son missing. You had every right to be angry and upset."

His blue eyes regarded me as my jaw worked up and down like that of a beached fish. His words were so unexpected that anything I'd planned to say knotted my tongue. Luke Sprague wasn't supposed to be nice or thoughtful or care about anything except sailing and girls. Stereotypes existed for a reason.

"I, uh, I'm sorry about the toy sailboat," I finally stammered.

"No worries. I can fix it. And if you allow it, I can show Petey how to sail it. The sails actually work."

"Please, don't bother. I won't be bringing Petey back to Sprague Hall."

He was about to say something but was interrupted by a tinny-sounding horn outside the casement window. Meghan returned and joined us at the window. We all stared out at the sleek antique coupe idling on the drive, its red-and-black paint shiny and new. For a moment I wondered if it might be self-driving until I spotted two hands clutching the top of the steering wheel and the rear brim of an old-fashioned fedora last seen on men's heads prior to the Kennedy era crouched in the driver's seat.

"What kind of car is that?" I asked, pressing my forehead against the glass. Cars rarely interested me except as a means of transportation, but the little roadster outside reminded me a bit of historic houses—unique, skillfully made, and expensive to maintain.

"That is a Bugatti Type 101 C Antem Coupé. Only eight of them were made in the early fifties. I believe that particular one is the last in existence." Luke turned from the window and moved to stand under the alcove archway. "It's time for you to go." His voice carried an edge of something that sounded a lot like worry. As if he might be in trouble if anyone was in the house past four thirty and the arrival of this particular visitor.

The driver's door of the Bugatti swung open and I stared as an old man pulled himself up using the door as leverage, then took his time retrieving a walking cane. I could almost hear him grunt as he laboriously closed the door. He looked up at the house, his glasses reflecting the sky above him and obliterating his eyes.

"Who is that?" I asked Luke, intrigued by the car and its occupant. And the fact that the visitor had arrived at four thirty on the dot.

"That's my grandmother's . . . friend."

Meghan sucked in her breath. "That looks like—"

"Out," Luke said. "And use the servants' stairs and the kitchen exit, please, so you don't run into my grandmother's guest."

I wanted to protest that I would have to walk around the house now to get to my car, but I held back, remembering that he'd said he was sorry. And that he would fix the sailboat for Petey. "Fine," I said, slinging my backpack over my shoulder.

I took one step then found myself flying forward as I tripped over a loose floorboard, barely managing to hang on to my balance and dignity by going down only on one knee before miraculously righting myself. I turned to glare at the errant board, surprised to find that the entire board had lifted out of the floor like the piece of a jigsaw puzzle.

Luke's look of concern made me raise my hand. "I'm fine. And we're leaving."

"Hang on a minute." Meghan squatted in front of the exposed hole in the floor and lifted something out. "It's a trinket box."

She held it toward me so I could see the initials *MSG* inlaid in gold atop a pale blue enamel box the size of a brick. An elaborate golden clasp on the front latched the lid closed. "Maybelle Sprague, I assume," I said. "I wonder why she left it here."

"We should put it back," Meghan said. "Maybe Maybelle wanted it to stay here."

"You're right. We should put it back. Because then George can film me discovering it and opening it. That's the sort of thing Marc says the viewers want." I grimaced, hating myself for even thinking it.

"Actually, I'll take that." Luke held his hand out and Meghan placed the box in his outstretched palm. "This is private and has nothing to do with renovation and isn't part of the show."

I wanted to argue, to tell him how much I needed something like a hidden trinket box to help with the ratings, but despite the pink tool belt I wore, I still had my pride. "Fine," I said. "We'll see you tomorrow."

We left Maybelle's room and I led Meghan through the maze of hallways—she had a horrible sense of direction—toward the kitchen.

"So, who was that in the Bugatti?" I asked.

Meghan's eyes widened. "Teddy Winthrop! The famous author and historian!"

I rolled my eyes. "I know who Teddy Winthrop is, Meghan. You even borrowed my copy of his *Atlas of Italian Renaissance Architecture* for so long that I had to buy another copy. But I thought he'd moved to Italy."

"Apparently not," Meghan said, still fangirling. "If he's Lucky Sprague's good friend, I wonder if we can find a way to meet him. I've had the most amazing crush on him since he came to speak at one of my undergrad classes. He signed my book and gave me the sweetest smile."

"Don't even think about it. Pretend you didn't see him, all right? We are *not* to speak to Lucky under any circumstances or I could lose my job. All right?"

"Whatever," she said, looking completely deflated.

As soon as I opened the back door, thunder shook the leaden sky, quickly followed by an electrifying streak of lightning. I swore under my breath, taking in the thick air saturated with the smell of rain. "I have to pick up Petey from his after-school program so I'm going to try and make it to my car before the deluge hits."

"Be my guest," Meghan said, already scrolling through her phone, apparently prepared to wait. "Just be careful—I read that the ghost likes to wander in the rain."

I rolled my eyes before dashing out the door. I'd made it halfway to my car when the sky opened and the rain came down in sheets, covering me in a liquid world of silver and gray. By the time I'd reached my car and shut the door behind me, my waterlogged hair and clothes stuck to my skin like wet cheese. I waited a moment to catch my breath and wipe the water out of my eyes before starting the engine, wishing I had more time so I could drive to the front door and give Luke a piece of my mind for sending me out in the rain.

Making a U-turn in the muddy gravel, my almost-bald tires spun before gaining traction and propelling my old car down the drive. I glanced at myself in the rearview mirror if only to confirm that I looked as bad as I imagined, catching sight of a flash of movement behind the car. I braked hard before twisting in my seat. Despite the gooseflesh creeping down my back, I forced myself to think that Meghan might have changed her mind and run out into the rain. But no matter where I looked or how hard I squinted my eyes, I saw only the torrential rain hitting old columns and weedy grass.

The windshield wipers thumped back and forth, squeaking their rhythm across the glass as I returned my gaze to the front of the car, telling myself that I hadn't seen anything at all. That was the thing about pretending. It wasn't always meant to mislead others.

I drove slowly over the bumpy drive, keeping my attention focused on the road ahead, thinking of Teddy Winthrop and red brocade wallpaper and anything else except a flash of something moving right outside my field of vision.

CHAPTER EIGHT

Ellen

Newport, Rhode Island
June 1899

ELLEN WALKED THROUGH the chaos in the hall without seeing any of it.

She started, by habit, to head to the grand staircase and then checked, remembering. She wasn't to be taking the main stairs while the guests were here. Mr. Sprague had been quite clear about that. She was to take the servants' stairs, like the servant she was. The soon-to-be-unemployed servant she was.

The prince. She had sassed the prince.

Everything, everything Ellen had hoped for, planned for these past few weeks, was crumbling around her. There would be no trip to Italy, no position as Maybelle's companion in her new life abroad. There would be no glowing letter of reference, no finding another job as a music teacher, tucked away into someone else's household. Instead, she would have to sink back into the slums, trying to make a living as best she could, praying that her past wouldn't find her.

She'd felt safe here, heaven help her. Too safe. How could she have been so colossally stupid?

But it wasn't entirely her fault. As she let herself into her room, Ellen felt a tiny spark of anger burning through the cold panic. The prince wasn't supposed to be lounging in the loggia. If he'd done what he was meant to do, arrived properly in a carriage with his coat of arms painted on the side, strode regally through the front door, instead of—Ellen grasped for the right word—instead of *skulking* like a ruffian, none of this would have happened.

What was she meant to think?

And he had enjoyed it, blast him. He had stood there and laughed at her. Laughed at poor Mr. Whitmarsh holding her hand and calling her a fugitive hope, as though they were the prince's own private commedia dell'arte. Laughed at her confusion. Laughed at Mr. Sprague's obvious embarrassment.

The only *decent* thing to have done would have been to declare himself at once and let her get on with curtsying and apologizing and showing him to where he was *meant* to be.

But what did it matter now? It didn't matter what the prince ought to have done, only what he had done. He was a prince. He could get away with what he liked. But as for those lesser mortals so unlucky as to be in his path . . .

He would never know, never care, that he'd ruined a life with a casual flick of his cigarette.

Like Dermot. Safe in his fortress at the Hibernia. Ordering executions as another man might squash a fly.

They might occupy different worlds, Dermot and the prince, but they had the same lordly disregard for anyone else's humanity.

What was she, after all? Just a bit of human flotsam, without family, without friends. Expendable.

I'm your family now, she could hear Dermot saying, as he put a hand on her shoulder at her father's wake, a physical indication to all present that she was under his protection, untouchable. *I'll stand friend to you.*

But at what cost? Only her soul.

Ellen gave a little shiver. "Stop being an idiot," she told herself, and her voice sounded strange in the empty room, wobbly and uncertain, a little girl's voice.

She grimaced at herself in the looking glass, making faces the way she used to for her little sisters, hideous faces, to make them laugh. Mr. Sprague might mean—clearly did mean—to give her notice at the first opportunity, but there was still tonight to get through. Ellen owed it to Maybelle to see her safely settled before Mr. Sprague booted Ellen out.

If a timid creature like Maybelle could be safely settled with a man such as the prince.

Ellen bit down her misgivings. Even if the man looked—and behaved—like a rogue, better a rogue who knew what he was doing than a clumsy bully like John Sprague. And wasn't it true that in novels it was always the innocent girl who won the heart of the cynical old roué? Look at Jane and Mr. Rochester. Look at Samuel Richardson's *Pamela*. Maybelle would adore being the heroine of one of her favorite novels. In fact, it would never occur to her that it might be otherwise. The books she read had only happy endings.

"Maybelle?" Ellen knocked gently at the door between their rooms, opening it without waiting for a response. "Maybelle, it's Ellen."

Maybelle rolled to her feet in an agitation of ruffles, stuffing a piece of paper into the treasure box that sat on the top of the bookshelf next to her chaise longue.

"Oh, Ellen! You surprised me! I was miles away, reading!" Maybelle grabbed at *Jane Eyre,* which had been lying abandoned on the chaise longue. She waved it in the air, looking anxiously at Ellen.

Maybelle had been reading something, but not *Jane Eyre*. Ellen wondered what it was that had been on that piece of paper she had shoved so hastily away.

It was on the tip of Ellen's tongue to ask her about it, but Maybelle looked at her so pleadingly that Ellen said, instead, "I had thought you would be dressed already."

Maybelle darted a glance at her treasure box. "I know, but it's so hard once you're immersed in a book. . . . And I had such a lovely long visit with Mrs. Schuyler. She's very kind to me."

"Hardly kind to keep you from your toilette on such a night as this." Before Maybelle could launch into a slew of excuses for her friend, Ellen added, "I met your prince."

"You did?" Maybelle looked at Ellen wide-eyed. "Not that he's mine. He's not mine, really. John just thinks . . . well, you know. Did he seem . . . pleasant?"

Her voice cracked a little on the last word, and Ellen felt her chest contract with pity. Strange to pity Maybelle, the heiress, but . . . it was Maybelle. Some heiresses might stomach a marriage of convenience, might even connive at one. But that wasn't Maybelle. She wasn't the simpleton her brother had claimed, but she was a romantic, a dreamer. To some a prince was a goal. For Maybelle, it was a terrifying thing to be sold in marriage to a stranger, shipped abroad for the sake of her stepbrother's social aspirations.

You would be surprised at my price, mia bella.

Ellen could see the twist of his lip as he said it, hear his voice. That beautiful, mocking voice. A voice fit for the stage, flexible, clear, conveying all sorts of unholy insinuations and innuendoes. It was a voice one could lose oneself in as one would a dark wood full of promise and terror and dangerous pleasures.

Maybelle was more a sunlit garden sort of creature.

Ellen had accounted herself worldly after her years in the Hibernia, but she had been aware, immediately, that the prince inhabited a level of sophistication and privilege beyond anything she had known—a world in which a man might be so jaded that he could find pleasure in playing with the feelings of a servant.

The thought left a nasty taste in her mouth. If he would toy with a nobody, what might he do to poor Maybelle, so helpless, so easily led?

But it was her duty to promote this marriage, her duty to see Maybelle wed to a prince. If she didn't, Sprague's repercussions—not to her, to his sister—would be swift and terrible.

It wasn't a case of the tiger or the lady. In this case, both doors concealed tigers. It was simply a question of which tiger was the more dreadful.

"The prince went out of his way to pay notice to a mere music teacher," said Ellen, hating herself a bit for lying in spirit, if not in fact. It was all true as far as it went, but his attitude had been less noblesse oblige and more cat with mouse.

"That was kind, wasn't it?" Maybelle looked beseechingly at Ellen, all her fears and doubts written on her face. "It says something, how people treat servants. Not that you're a servant! You're really more one of the family. Not a servant at all! I'm sure that if people saw us together, they would take us for sisters! Don't you think we look alike?"

No, she didn't. They were of similar height and both had fair hair and light eyes, but that was where any resemblance ended. Even there, Ellen's hair was straight where Maybelle's curled, her eyes grayish-green to Maybelle's blue. And their features were nothing alike at all. Maybelle's face still boasted the roundness of youth, where Ellen's had been whittled to sharpness by grief and care. They were both female and fair, but that was the extent of it.

But Ellen knew why Maybelle had said it, even if it was palpably untrue. It was to make up for calling Ellen a servant.

And so she smiled, feeling like Judas, and said only, "Would you like to rehearse one last time before your performance tonight?"

Maybelle ducked her head. "Do you think I might perform tomorrow instead? You have such a way of putting things. If you spoke to my brother—"

"No," said Ellen a little too abruptly. Softening her voice, she added, "Your brother wishes you to make a strong impression upon the prince. I don't think anything short of a volcanic eruption would make him change his mind, and possibly not even that."

Maybelle clutched the cameo at her throat. "Yes, but to be in front of all those people . . . when I haven't even met most of them yet . . ."

Maybelle wasn't to sing after dinner, in the gentle confines of the drawing room, when other women might also take their turn at the piano and dilute her triumph. Oh no. She was to wait until the whole party had been assembled and seated at the great table in the dining room. Alone, Maybelle was to make her grand entrance between the double doors of the dining room, contrary to all protocol, to all tradition. She would wait until all eyes were upon her and then . . . sing.

It was the worst possible way to introduce Maybelle to the company. But that was John Sprague for you. He wasn't one for subtlety. Instead of realizing that his sister had the sort of gentle charm that showed best gradually, in a domestic setting, he was intent on flinging her onstage to show her wares, as if she were Hildie doing high kicks at the Hibernia.

"'Allo, 'allo! It eez zee time to make you magnifique, mamzelle!" Maybelle's maid breezed into the room, holding Maybelle's jewelry case in both hands. As far as Ellen could tell, Delphine came from Paris by way of Schenectady, but she did a lovely job with Maybelle's fine, light hair. "I 'ave zee gown glorieuse pressed parfaitment and zee jewelry to make mamzelle shine."

Maybelle clutched the cameo at her breast. "I'd like to wear my mother's cameo tonight."

"That little thing? Er, I mean, zat petite nothing?" Delphine thrust the jewelry box at her mistress. "Monsieur Sprague, 'ee wishes that you wear zee diamond spray."

Maybelle looked like a cornered mouse, hunched into her reading nook, darting anxious glances back and forth from Delphine to Ellen. "Yes, but it's not *his* debut. I don't *like* the diamond spray."

"Eet eez made of zee diamonds." Delphine waggled the bauble at Maybelle.

"But it wasn't my mother's." Maybelle's eyes misted with tears. "If my mother were still alive . . . if my mother were here . . . when I wear it, I can almost imagine—"

"Wear the cameo," said Ellen abruptly. She could only lose her job once, and she'd already done that, hadn't she? She might as well give Maybelle what comfort she could in the hours remaining to her.

Delphine was staring at her as though she'd gone mad. "But Monsieur Sprague . . ."

Ellen ignored her. "You'll sing better if you feel comfortable with yourself. Wear the cameo."

"Do you mean it? Really?" Maybelle stared up at Ellen as though she'd just given her the moon. Never mind that Maybelle was the mistress of the house and her money paid for Ellen and everything in it. Her brother had her convinced she was nothing, deserved nothing.

"There's no need for you to be tarted up like a prize pony," Ellen said, and Maybelle gave a watery giggle. Delphine gave Ellen a look of outrage. Sidestepping the maid, Ellen gave Maybelle's hand a gentle squeeze. "I'll be in my room if you need me."

Back in her own room, Ellen wondered vaguely if she ought to pack. She should, she knew. It was best to be prepared. The thought made her very, very tired. She'd come to like this strange, opulent room in this strange, opulent house, and the thought of leaving again, of going out into the unknown, made her weary down to her toes, with the sort of dragging exhaustion that blunted movement and muffled thought.

Later. She would pack later. First there was Maybelle's performance to get through.

Slowly, Ellen removed her new dress from the wardrobe, a simple, high-collared affair of gray so dark it was nearly black, the perfect clothing for someone blending into the background.

Maybelle had insisted that Ellen be there when she sang, but there was, as far as Mr. Sprague was concerned, no need for Ellen to actually be visible. In this, as in everything else, Mr. Sprague had been quite explicit in his instructions. She wasn't to stay for dinner, not in such exalted company. Instead, she was to accompany Maybelle downstairs, cue the musicians, offer such aid and support as Maybelle needed, and then disappear.

Which suited Ellen just as well. Back to a tray in her room—possibly her last tray in this room, her last night in this room.

Well, she'd always known it couldn't last forever, hadn't she?

When Ellen met her charge to bring her downstairs, Maybelle had been cinched into a gown of pale pink satin. Satin flowers edged the deep neckline, and at the center of each winked a diamond, or a very good facsimile thereof. A ruffle of antique lace bristled out beneath the flowers and gathered at the shoulders to provide the briefest of sleeves.

Maybelle's mother's cameo, Ellen saw, had been placed at the center of her décolletage, in the place where the diamond spray was meant to be.

The woman in the cameo had a worn, comforting sort of face. A motherly face.

Ellen held out a hand to Maybelle. "Nervous? You shouldn't be. You know this too well to worry."

Maybelle looked a bit green beneath an elaborate confection of golden curls, crowned with a small ostrich feather held by a diamond comb. "I feel like I can't remember a word. I'll open my mouth and nothing will come out."

"If you forget, I'll be there next to you whispering it all to you. And the musicians will be accompanying you, so you haven't a chance of forgetting the tune." In livery. The livery she had threatened to make the prince wear.

The thought made Ellen's cheeks burn.

"Come. Let's get this over with," she said, more curtly than she intended. Maybelle looked stricken. Ellen softened her voice. "I mean, it's not so bad as all that. Think of the actresses who go onstage every day! With footlights."

"Yes, but they're trained for it." Maybelle accompanied her with dragging steps down the stairs, although that might have been partially the effect of the short train she had forgotten to loop up.

Ellen leaned down, retrieved the trailing fabric, and tucked the loop securely around Maybelle's wrist. "You've trained for this. Every day for the past month. Don't worry, you'll be brilliant."

But even Ellen balked as they approached the dining room, where the guests had already been seated. This wasn't the simple scene she had imagined. The dining room by day, empty, was a very different thing from the dining room by night, lit with thousands of branches of candles, crammed with guests in all their finery.

Maybelle checked, staring wide-eyed at the assemblage. Ellen didn't blame her. The walls were painted with hunting scenes, and the images that, in the day, had been merely flat paint, leapt out at her with alarming clarity: a hunter driving his spear into the breast of a struggling boar, a pack of dogs ripping into the body of a fallen doe, the saliva glistening on their pointed teeth.

The guests took on a nightmare quality; Ellen could smell the strong reek of the women's French perfume, the pomade the men used to slick down their hair. Their voices were too loud, their jewels too bright, and as they opened their mouths to shout social niceties at each other, Ellen thought she could see the glinting fangs of the dogs between their painted lips.

At the head of that glittering, terrible company sat the prince.

In evening dress, with orders thick upon his breast, he was a different man from the creature smoking his cigarette in the loggia.

Or maybe not. As he lifted his eyes and noted them, Maybelle in her pink, shivering in the doorway, Ellen in the shadows behind her, urging her on, Ellen could have sworn she saw the same lazy amusement in his eyes.

John Sprague rose to his feet, clinking his crystal goblet with a gold-plated fork to gain the attention of the company. One by one, the chattering voices died out and the curled and feathered, bejeweled, and pomaded heads turned to look at their host.

The silence was, if anything, even more terrifying than their chatter had been.

Ellen had a fanciful image of Maybelle as the doe, shoved into the enclosure to run and die for their entertainment. She'd never had a chance of getting away, had she? The hunters had already closed around, ready to prod her into place.

John Sprague bounced on the balls of his feet, lifting himself as high as he could go without actually standing on a chair. "Your Excellency. Ladies and gentlemen. It is my great pleasure to introduce to you my sister."

Maybelle clutched Ellen's sleeve. "I—I can't."

"Shh," murmured Ellen, grateful that Mr. Sprague was busy expounding on the virtues of a Maybelle so unlike the original as to be entirely fictional, drawing attention away from the ashen-faced girl in the doorway. "Of course, you can. You've sung it a thousand times—and beautifully, too."

"I'm going to be sick."

"No you're not. Not in that dress." The dress, as Mr. Sprague was fond of reminding everyone, was a genuine Worth and had cost more than Ellen earned in a year. Possibly two years.

Ellen put a hand beneath Maybelle's elbow, helping her up onto the dais that had been brought in to give her extra height for her performance. The dais, however, was little more than a footstool, dwarfed by Maybelle's skirts. Ellen devoutly hoped she wouldn't fall off midstanza.

John Sprague waved a hand at the trembling girl. "I give you my sister, Maybelle!"

"Don't. Don't think of them," whispered Ellen. "Just think of the music. The music is your friend."

Stepping back, she nodded to the musicians concealed behind a painted screen. The formal, mannered notes of the eighteenth century sounded in the vast room, tinny against the crimson and velvet, the gilt and crystal.

Maybelle drew in a deep breath, or as deep a breath as she could with her waist cinched to nothingness. "Where'er you walk," her voice wobbled on the words, "cool gales shall fan the shade."

She cast Ellen a look of pure panic. It had been meant to be "glade," not "shade."

Ellen nodded as reassuringly as she could. "Trees where you sit," she mouthed.

Maybelle looked helplessly out at the prince across the long, vast table and sang, "Trees where you sit, shall crowd into a shade."

John Sprague was glaring at Ellen, his expression pure hatred and thwarted rage. If there hadn't been other people here, he would have been across the room by now, sticking out his chest and haranguing her. But he couldn't, not here, not with his guests all around him.

He had wanted Maybelle to sing in Italian, as a compliment to the prince. But singing in Italian had only made Maybelle more nervous, and the simple, well-known aria had seemed to suit both the occasion and Maybelle's high, sweet voice.

Ellen had thought it would give her confidence, would make it easier. And it had. During rehearsal.

Not here, not now, where what had been simple sounded strained. The music had been designed for an earlier era, a less excessive era, the age of reason, of classicism, not this mad abundance, where brilliant colors warred and flashed and one's eyes were dazzled with rubies, emeralds, and sapphires, great chunks of precious stones, flaunted with barbaric extravagance.

Maybelle stood frozen with panic as the musicians played a stanza, her breast rising and falling rapidly under her mother's cameo. Her eyes looked like glassy blue marbles in the candlelight.

It was all Ellen could do not to pull her down and bustle her away to the safety of her own rose-strewn boudoir. This was cruel; it was horrible. And it was her fault, at least some of it. She ought to have known that an eighteenth-century air wouldn't do for the dining room. For the drawing room, yes, as an after-dinner piece, but not this, not John Sprague's big performance, Maybelle's introduction to the company, her grand entrance.

She had thought it was a kindness, picking a piece suited to Maybelle's voice, her personality, trying to display the girl's innate goodness, to show the prince what she was, what a prize she was in herself behind the ruffles and lace.

But it was all wrong here. Ellen could see that Maybelle knew it, knew she was failing, could see her closing in on herself, frozen in fear of her brother's disapproval. They had lost the guests already. They had begun to turn to each other, to whisper and chatter again.

"Where'er you walk," Ellen whispered to Maybelle, hoping Maybelle wouldn't notice how her hands had twisted into claws at her sides, how close she was to despair. Maybelle always had trouble with that first high F after the intermezzo, even on a good day.

But she hit it perfectly, and Ellen could see the delight and relief show on her face, the way her hands loosened at her sides. Maybelle soared easily through the first set of trills, her voice rising and building in a way that almost made her earlier hesitation sound planned.

Ellen was so relieved she could have cried.

The guests were listening again, their rouged and powdered faces lifted to Maybelle, their conversations stilled.

"Where'er you walk, the blushing flowers shall rise!" There was a becoming flush on Maybelle's pale cheeks as she lifted her head and sang to the prince. Ellen could see the way his chin jerked up as Maybelle hit the F-sharp perfectly, how he looked at her as though he were first seeing her.

Growing in confidence, Maybelle spread her hands out in front of her, like a minor deity conferring blessing. "And all things flourish, and all things flourish, where'er you turn your eyes."

The prince's eyes were turned to Maybelle, regarding her with a sort of casual speculation. And Maybelle was certainly flourishing. There was an animation to her face and her voice that hadn't been there before as she sang the reprise, "Where'er you turn your eyes, where'er you turn your eyes."

The final note faded. Maybelle stood on her dais, pink-cheeked, triumphant, her chest rising and falling as she looked to Ellen for approval.

A clatter of spontaneous applause rose from the crowd. People were pushing back chairs, standing up, raising their glasses, turning to one another to exclaim over the performance, how wonderful, how surprising, how refreshing.

Ellen let out the breath she'd been holding, giddy with the relief of it. This was exactly what she'd wanted, exactly what she'd hoped for: Maybelle showing the very best of herself. Not the imaginary Maybelle her brother had so desperately attempted to conjure, but the real Maybelle, the girl who loved to surround herself with flowers and kindness, who wanted nothing more than for everyone to be happy and comfortable.

Prunella Schuyler's voice rose piercingly above everyone else's. "Of course, I would have handled those trills better, but it really wasn't at all bad for an amateur. With a great deal of practice, she might be nearly as good as I am someday, don't you think, Frank? It was really quite pretty."

"Er, yes, quite," said the man next to her, who appeared to be not entirely sober. He was very handsome in a chocolate box sort of way, with slicked back blond hair and a fresh complexion. Maybelle beamed at his words, glowing as though he had praised her in the most extravagant of terms.

The prince stood.

He didn't have to clink a glass to draw attention. He didn't have to utter a word. All he had to do was stand, and the company magically fell silent, obedient to his unspoken whim. It wasn't the medals that glittered on his breast. There were other guests who boasted more. It was the sheer magnetism of his personality. He commanded the room simply by being in it.

He lifted his glass in the direction of the doorway, his beautiful tenor voice carrying even more clearly than Maybelle's. "To the so-lovely Miss Sprague, who sings so sweetly."

But he wasn't looking at Maybelle. He was looking at Ellen. As she watched, he tipped his glass to her with a twist of the lips that in a lesser personage might have been termed a grin.

It was too hot, too bright; Ellen's high collar was too tight. She had the strangest urge to dive under the nearest piece of furniture, to flee.

She wasn't here. She wasn't meant to be here.

Maybelle didn't need her anymore. Maybelle, blushing, was being escorted to her seat beside the prince by a phalanx of admirers, all of them extravagantly complimenting her singing. The prince, meanwhile, simply sat there in his chair and waited for his bride to be brought to him. And all the while his eyes were on Ellen, as though there were something secret shared between them, something private and personal.

Ellen turned abruptly and blundered into one of the pillars that weren't meant to be there, one of the pillars made of wood painted to look like marble.

They'd had a hypnotist perform once at the Hibernia. He was nothing to the prince.

Perhaps it was a good thing, Ellen told herself. Perhaps he would so mesmerize Maybelle that she would go joyfully to Italy, grateful for her good fortune, rather than as a captive bride in a loveless marriage.

Not that Ellen would be here to see it.

As she changed out of the gray dress into her nightdress, listening to the sounds of revelry from the floors below, Ellen wondered dimly just how long it would take Sprague to get around to dismissing her.

Not long, it turned out. He found her just after breakfast, when she ventured downstairs to the music room to collect such personal belongings as she might have left there.

Sprague grabbed her by the arm as she walked inside, kicking the door shut behind him. "I've been looking for you."

Ellen retreated a few paces, to the safety of the piano. He would dismiss her, but he would humiliate her first. Politely, she said, "I am always at your service, sir."

Sprague seemed distracted, glancing over his shoulder, bouncing on the balls of his feet. "Ha! At my service, is it? I told you I wanted Maybelle to sing in Italian. What was that, last night? That wasn't Italian."

Ellen looked at him in surprise. She'd expected to be sacked straight out for her rudeness to the prince, not taken to task for the smaller of her infractions. "The prince hears Italian all the time at home, sir. This was his welcome to an American household." Never mind that the music had been written more than a hundred years ago by a German living in England. "Miss Sprague's Italian pronunciation, while proficient, is not yet as polished as one might like. It seemed safer to have her sing in English, rather than blundering into mistakes that might prejudice the prince's opinion of her."

"Hmm." Sprague's brows drew together. He jutted his chin at her. "And why isn't it that polished? It's your business to polish it."

She had never promised proficiency in Italian. Not that John Sprague would ever admit that. Ellen dipped her head, wishing he would just get it over with. "My apologies, sir. I believed Miss Sprague would be more confident in her performance if she were singing in her own tongue."

Sprague cleared his throat. Ellen couldn't understand why he seemed so jittery; he wasn't the one about to be tossed out without a reference. "She'll need a better song for the next one. A proper song. An Italian song."

Ellen lifted her head, thoroughly confused. "The next one?"

"Didn't I say? The prince has requested a musical evening." Sprague regarded Ellen with mingled dislike and jubilation. "He specifically complimented your tutelage."

"That was—that was very kind of him." Ellen's stomach twisted uneasily. She should be grateful, but . . . she remembered that toast last night, his expression as he looked at her. He was playing with her, she was sure of it. A diversion for the jaded.

He would tire of it. It was only that she'd been rude to him; that was the novelty of it. And in the meantime, she was saved from the streets. For the duration of the prince's visit, at least.

"The credit is all Maybelle's—I mean, Miss Sprague's," Ellen said unsteadily, trying not to think of the prince, of that cynical, clever face, that beautiful, cruel voice.

"So I told the prince, but he seemed to think you had something to do with it," grumbled Sprague. He pointed a finger sharply at Ellen. "You have one week to put together a program of performance."

"Sir," said Ellen, already turning over possibilities in her head, trying to think what might suit Maybelle. What might appeal to a prince.

In Italian.

"No more surprises. You follow instructions. Exactly." A flicker of something that might have been fear crossed Sprague's face. "You get this right, do you understand? There's more riding on this than someone like you could ever imagine."

CHAPTER NINE

Lucky

Newport, Rhode Island
July 1957

LUCKY OPENED HER eyes to some confused, exhausting idea that she'd been out riding a horse all night. Then she felt a heavy arm across her stomach, the noise of a man's contented breath near her ear, and she remembered it wasn't a horse at all.

She turned to look at the head that shared the pillow with hers. He was so close, she couldn't focus properly. His hair was matted with perspiration, tousled in a hundred different directions; his eyes were closed, lashes spread, cheekbone propped at its familiar angle. Lucky could just make out the smudges of lipstick along his jaw. Red Velvet, her loyal favorite. If it weren't for his arm pinning her to the mattress, she would lift her finger and touch the little marks of her possession. Of course, plenty of other women left their marks on Stuy—she'd wiped those off herself, more than once, and shown him the pink-stained handkerchief in accusation—but these went deeper than skin, she knew. For all his faults, for all he lent himself out generously to others, Stuy was *hers*.

The curtains were drawn, the room dim but not dark. At this time of year, the sun was long up. She and Stuy had made love twice, the second time just before dawn, and they hadn't gone easy on each other.

Had fallen deep asleep after the last one—what *had* she been dreaming about? Whatever it was, it had made her uneasy. Restless. She turned her head in the opposite direction, toward the bedside table, and squinted at the clock.

Half past *eight*?

Joanie.

Lucky threw off Stuy's arm and sat upright. Each muscle released its own individual howl of protest. My God, what had they *done* to each other? She remembered how fiercely they came together, how desperate. And all the while, at the back of her mind, the tiny, dirty hope—maybe he would make her pregnant this time.

Now she shook her head as if to shake off a dream. Stuy stirred and lifted his head and groaned. Fell back on the pillow. Threw his arm back around her waist and tried to draw her down with him.

"Stuy, I can't. It's half past eight."

"Mmm, sounds early to me."

"Your daughter's been up for hours already."

He tugged again. "Angela will get her breakfast. C'mon."

"Haven't you had enough already?" she snapped.

Stuy opened his eyes. "Say, what's the matter?"

"Nothing. It's late, that's all. I have a committee meeting this morning."

"Tell them you have a headache. Tell them your husband has a headache—terrible, awful sick headache—and you have to tend to him, like a wife should." His voice was gravelly and cajoling, thick with sex appeal and hangover. She had a feeling he wasn't kidding about the headache, and that sex was supposed to be the cure. Like always.

"It's the *ball* committee, Stuy. The Tiffany Ball? Next week?"

"Aw, who cares about an old party? Just some ladies all dolled up in puffy dresses, their poor old husbands drinking out back."

"For God's sake, Stuy. It's not any old party. It's the biggest thing to happen to this town in years, and it's all going to save these white elephants we're living in from the wrecking ball. It's *vital*."

"All the more reason to make sure you're looking your best." He sat up to nuzzle her neck. Lucky exhaled an exasperated sigh and swung her legs over the side of the bed.

He sat up behind her and kissed her shoulder. "Thought you said you wanted another baby, kid. Far as I know, this is the best way to make one."

Lucky pulled away and stood up. The world tilted for an instant, her head spun, and she realized she was hungover, too. Not a benign hangover, either. The sick kind. "I guess you would know," she snapped.

"Oh, so we're back to *that*, are we? I thought we'd kissed and made up, just now."

Lucky didn't dare look back at her husband as she crossed the rug to the bathroom door. He would look handsome and winsome and tousled, like a gorgeous overgrown puppy, and she would be tempted to go back to him and kiss his warm skin and forgive him for everything, everything. Transform back into that shameless woman who'd mated so ferociously with him in the night.

"We had a good time, that's all," she said, over her shoulder. "Now I'm going to take a shower."

Ten minutes later, when Lucky got out of the shower and dried herself, she saw a pink smear on the white towel and closed her eyes to do some arithmetic, although she already knew the answer.

The tiny spark of hope went out, if she'd even felt it to begin with.

In the humid midmorning sunlight, Marble House seemed to float atop the horizon. Lucky paused along the cliff path to gaze at the dreaming walls, the slate peaks of rooftop against the hazy sky, and for an instant she was back in Italy, a small child, and the mist was lifting from the vineyard on the slope opposite the crumbling old villa where they lived. Her grandfather was up early, nursing a cup of hot coffee with lots of fresh milk. He would join her in the garden and tuck her against his warm chest that smelled of coffee and clean linen and of Nonna, who was still in bed. He would call her his beautiful child and tell her about her ancestors, about some ancient Principessa di Conti who used to hitch up her robes and help with the grape harvest each year. She said it made her fruitful, and sure enough she had a new baby every year at the beginning of summer, Nonno said solemnly, so for the longest time—almost embarrassing, really—Lucky had thought that drinking wine made a woman have a baby.

Although that wasn't altogether far from the truth, when you thought about it.

"Nickel for your thoughts," said a warm voice at her shoulder, and Lucky was so startled she nearly fell forward. Only Teddy Winthrop's quick hand at her elbow saved her. He apologized and said he didn't mean to interrupt.

"Oh, don't be silly. You can interrupt me anytime. I was lost for a moment there."

"Lost? Where?"

She laughed. "Italy, if you can believe it. The haze took me right back."

"Ah, that morning mist on the slopes of the hills. Long rows of grapevines waking up to the sun."

Lucky turned her head to gaze at him. "It's as if you can read my mind."

Teddy waggled his eyebrows above his glasses. "Perhaps I can. One of my many talents. And it seems to me you're feeling—let me see—a little out of sorts this morning?"

"Oh! Does it show?"

"Only to your humble admirers."

She squinted at him. "You're not looking so well rested yourself, if you don't mind my saying so. Is everything all right?"

"Everything's fine." Teddy glanced at the water and back again with a new expression, careworn. "Alice had a bad night, that's all."

Lucky touched his elbow. "Oh, I'm so sorry, Teddy. Is there anything I can do?"

But was she? Sorry? She was sorry for *Teddy*, of course. But Alice—poor, exhausted Alice, never quite recovered after her last bout of illness a few years ago. Was Lucky really sorry that Alice wasn't . . . well, everything a wife should be to Teddy?

Not as sorry as Lucky *should* be, anyway. God forgive her.

Teddy shook his head and offered a small, grateful smile. "Some nights are like that. The doctor's with her now." He held out his elbow. "Shall we brave the dragons together, milady?"

ALL THE BEST ladies in Newport were on the ball committee, which was why Lucky looked forward to meetings about as much as she looked forward to piano recitals when she was a kid. Maybe more! After all, now she had all the grown-up fun of knowing that possibly half the members had slept with—or *almost* slept with—Lucky's husband, at some point in their lives.

Teddy Winthrop, on the other hand, seemed to enjoy himself—maybe because he was the only man on the committee, the fox in the henhouse, or maybe because he only attended the meetings in his role as an advisor on matters of historical architecture and its preservation. He sat at one end of the table in the Marble House dining room—where, in another age, Consuelo Vanderbilt used to eat her luncheon under the exacting eye of her mother, speaking in French—and arranged his face in a grave expression. Only Lucky knew that the graver his expression, the more he was fighting the impulse to laugh. In fact, she'd learned to keep her face averted from his throughout the meeting. One instant of eye contact might prove fatal to her composure.

Instead she tilted her head and concentrated on Mrs. Potts.

Prunella Pratt Schuyler Potts was a Gilded Age relic who'd begun reappearing in Newport in recent summers thanks to an advantageous marriage to Edwin Potts (known to his friends as *Stinky*)—the so-called Fixtures King from somewhere down south and as stinking rich as his nickname suggested. Like a living museum tableau, Mrs. Potts still wore her hair in towering splendor and her figure in a flat-chested, hip-tilted S curve, to which it was permanently molded by the corsets of her heyday. She thought it was terribly crass to charge the guests for champagne.

"Fifty cents!" she said indignantly. "As if this were some kind of cheap night at the *pleasure garden*!"

Lucky cleared her throat. "We *are* trying to raise money for the society, Mrs. Potts. These beautiful old cottages are crumbling down around us. Every cent matters."

"In *my* day, people kept up their houses, or else they sold them to someone who could."

"But nobody's buying mansions anymore, except to tear them down. Nobody can afford that kind of upkeep, not with wages as high as they are, to say nothing of taxes. Why do you think we started the preservation society to begin with?"

Prunella's mouth screwed into a snug little rictus. "Well, perhaps in *Italy* they do these things differently. Perhaps in *Italy* your host charges you for champagne inside his own home. Here in *America* we don't expect our guests to carry cash to a ball."

Quietly Lucky said, "This isn't the kind of ball you used to have in the old Newport. It's a charity ball. The point of a charity ball is to raise money, Mrs. Potts. I think everyone who attends will understand that."

"Oh, *naturally*. When you charge twenty-five dollars for a ticket and fifty cents for a glass of champagne, I guess you'll attract all kinds of people who are ignorant of the customs of entertaining among the upper classes."

A delicate silence descended over the committee table. Around them, the lamps glowed on the walls of rosy marble, the gilded moldings, the portraits of European nobility. Against Mrs. Potts's skeletal shoulders, the faded red upholstery of the reproduction Louis XIV chair was like a caricature of opulence.

"When we formed this committee," Lucky said, "and indeed, when the Preservation Society of Newport County itself came into being, we drew purposefully on the democratic traditions of the United States of America. We thought that if we were going to preserve these extraordinary buildings for future generations, we should make them open to everybody. Everybody should feel as if he has a stake in the architectural heritage of Newport. Everybody should feel as if he can contribute. Art and beauty belong to humanity."

"How nice," said Mrs. Potts. "I always thought that art belonged to people who have the taste to appreciate it."

Lucky smiled. "Money and taste don't necessarily go hand in hand, Mrs. Potts."

At the other end of the table, somebody clattered her teacup into a saucer.

Teddy roused himself and cleared his throat. "Mrs. Prince," he said, "how do you feel about charging for champagne inside your own home?"

"Oh, I say we stick them for every cent," Mrs. Prince said coolly, from her seat at the head of the table. "For the *cause*, of course. Anything's better than standing by while another damned developer tears down one of the grand old cottages and puts up another hideous apartment block."

Prunella's voice took on a petulant whine. "And what about this diamond of theirs? It's *my* belief these Tiffany people are just stringing us along for the free publicity. My goodness, how long does it *take* to decide which committee member has the style and the pedigree to carry off a gem of that size?"

Somebody tittered at the other end of the table. Teddy made a strangled cough and turned swiftly to the small notepad in front of him, on which he scribbled a few words with his ballpoint pen.

"Tiffany's been enormously generous to us, from the beginning, Mrs. Potts," said Mrs. Prince. "The silver service will be delivered tomorrow, and I'm sure it will look magnificent on the supper table."

Lucky felt something nudge her knee. She slipped her hand underneath the table, where Teddy's fingers met hers, urging a slip of paper.

"How nice," said Mrs. Potts. "Of course, *some* of us can remember the ball the William Vanderbilts threw for the Duke of Marlborough, right here in Marble House. The decorations, the *footmen*! All dressed in *livery*! You don't see livery *today*, that's for sure. No notion of separation between master and servant. There were three orchestras, so you never stopped dancing." She sighed. "Dear Alva. *She* knew how to throw a party."

"That was sixty years ago, Mrs. Potts," Mrs. Prince said crisply. "Times have changed."

Mrs. Potts sniffed. "More's the pity. Still, I'm sure the Tiffany people are delighted to have—in *me*, that is—a living link to the glorious times of yesteryear. It will add such an air of authenticity and glamour to the occasion. I should be delighted, for example, to speak about my experiences during the final voyage of the *Lusitania*, which I survived by clinging to a fragment of wreckage from the first-class salon. Alas, my dear friend and cousin perished in the tragedy. Marjorie Schuyler. I expect you've heard of her. She was a pillar of society."

Lucky discreetly unfolded the paper. *See Mary smirk*, it said.

Lucky looked at Mary Whitehouse across the table and three chairs to the left. She was doodling on her notepad with a fine lacquered pen, leaning her cheek into her palm. A smile curved one side of her small, red mouth.

Well, why not? Who better to display the magnificent Tiffany Yellow Diamond—mined in South Africa in 1878, masterfully cut into a cushion-shaped brilliant, mounted on a necklace of smaller white diamonds and never before worn in public—than Mrs. Sheldon Whitehouse? You couldn't ask for a bluer-blooded, older-monied family than the Whitehouses, chock-full of diplomats and senators and Episcopalian bishops and the occasional English aristocrat. Pillars of the Newport summer season, the Whitehouses, and when September arrived they moved back into their apartment at the fabled 1040 Park Avenue, along with the rest of society's hereditary rulers.

No, if anyone could carry off a legendary jewel like it had grown right there on her bosom, it was Mrs. Sheldon Whitehouse.

Poor Prunella Potts hadn't stood a chance, had she?

Lucky folded up the note and slipped it into her pocket. "Frankly," she said, "I don't give a damn who wears the diamond. It makes for good publicity, of course, but a jewel that ostentatious seems to me awfully out of touch with modern sensibilities."

"Do you know something, Mrs. Prince?" Prunella Potts smiled a wide, stiff smile at their hostess. "I find that women who claim to think diamonds are vulgar are the very women who can't afford jewelry of their own. You know, the kind of woman whose house is mortgaged to the hilt, who doesn't have a penny in the bank? Who stays in her summer house all year round because she can't afford a place in the city? That type of woman."

Lucky rose to her feet. "If you'll excuse me, I'm going to get a breath of fresh air. It's funny how things get a little stuffy, no matter how big the room is."

USUALLY LUCKY MARCHED straight home after the weekly Tiffany Ball committee meeting to pour herself a drink, and Teddy usually happened to join her for the walk along the cliff path and into the sunroom of Sprague Hall for a Bloody Mary or two that inevitably slid into lunch. *Oh look, noon already*, she'd say, and *Guess we might as well have a bite to eat*, he'd reply. But today, though she badly wanted a drink, Lucky scrambled down the rocks to sit by the ocean's edge, where she blotted her eyes carefully with a handkerchief from her pocket.

What was *wrong* with her? Lucky never cried. And today of all days! She and Stuy had just shared a night of glorious passion, had reconciled like they always did. She was supposed to feel like she'd fallen in love all over again—everything was wonderful and electric once more—

determined that *this time* they would hold on to this magical physical connection between them, the way she always felt when she and Stuy fell back into bed together.

So why did she feel that her world was spinning off its axis, crashing off into the unknown reaches of the universe? Why did she feel so desperate? At the end of her rope? Capable of some terrible, shocking act, like dunking Prunella Potts's head into one of her husband's toilet fixtures and flushing it?

Maybe because this time, she was older and wiser. She understood that falling into bed with Stuy didn't mean a new beginning, didn't transform him into a faithful, happy husband. Falling into bed just started the cycle all over again, each agonizing turn of the wheel the same as before, as predictable as sunrise and sunset.

Nothing in the world could start things all over again between Lucky and Stuy.

The only way to make a fresh start was to smash the wheel altogether. To end her marriage once and for all. And she could never, ever do that. There was Joanie. There was Nonna, and Sprague Hall. Everything she loved, everything that was home to her.

There was Dudley Sprague.

Lucky stuffed the handkerchief back in her pocket. In her head, she heard a voice snarl, *I could finish you off in a second, if I wanted.*

Ridiculous. Dudley Sprague would be dead within a week. No fancy experimental medication could save him now, whatever that Dr. Goldberg said. Anyway, what did *he* know? Sprague Hall belonged to her grandmother. Nonna was the rightful and only heiress of the great fortune that had built the place, even if that fortune *was* mostly spent. And Lucky was the rightful and only heiress to Nonna.

Wasn't she?

A woman whose house is mortgaged to the hilt . . .

"Lucky? That you?"

Lucky sprang to her feet and spun around, wavering dangerously on the damp rock for a second or two. A man stood on the cliff's edge, staring anxiously down at her.

"Teddy!" she exclaimed.

"Need some company down there?" he asked.

Lucky didn't know how it happened. She didn't *mean* to scramble up the rocks and launch herself at Teddy Winthrop, to throw herself on his chest and sob like a child. But once she was there, she had the peculiar feeling that she'd existed in this place always, tucked into Teddy's arms, safe and adored.

Adored. Teddy adored her. She felt it, she *knew* it.

"I'm sorry," she gasped, into the lapel of his navy blazer.

He stroked her hair. "Shh. It's all right."

"No, it's not." With terrible effort, she pulled away. But that was a mistake, because now she was looking into Teddy's face, handsome and wise and drawn with—no, not sympathy. *Empathy*. Understanding. From behind the sheen of his eyeglasses, his gentle gaze met hers.

Lucky thought of Alice—wan, delicate, lovely Alice, who stayed indoors out of the sun, lay on a chaise longue and flipped through fashion magazines while the light dragged from one window to another to darkness and back again, day after day. A terrible cycle of their own.

You know she can't *anymore*, someone had whispered to Lucky once.

Or won't, someone else had giggled.

Lucky wasn't sure whether Alice's malady was mental or physical, or some combination of both—she never dared ask Teddy, because she didn't want to seem as if she was angling for something—but whatever it was, this trouble gave them something in common, she and Teddy. The understanding pulled between them, until Lucky couldn't stand the truth of it anymore and leaned to rest against Teddy's chest. His arms folded around her.

Anyone could see them, right there on the cliff path where everybody walked, and she didn't care. It was worth the gossip, just to feel like this. Known. Beloved. As if her burdens were no longer burdens, exactly, but a sorrow she shared with Teddy.

"I don't know what to do," she whispered.

"Neither do I," he replied.

Over the crest of Teddy's firm shoulder, where the roof of the Sprague Hall boathouse poked against the horizon, Lucky thought she saw a shiny gold head turn in her direction and flash in the sunlight.

The next instant, it was gone.

CHAPTER TEN

Andie

Newport, Rhode Island
September 2019

IT WAS GONE. My notebook containing the script with all of my mark-ups and notes—essentially my production bible—had vanished. In our haste to leave the previous day, I had forgotten to put it in my backpack. I was positive I'd left it on the Louis XIV escritoire in the bedroom, even recalled the scratches in the marquetry made by careless writers with sharp nibs as I'd placed my notebook carefully on the surface. But it wasn't there or on the bed or the chaise or the dressing table or anywhere else. Not that it should be somewhere else because I had definitely left it on the escritoire.

I'd arrived early with the new plan and script changes I'd worked on the night before to insert into the notebook and had now wasted a precious twenty minutes searching for it. Approaching tires on gravel heralded the arrival of the crew, the sound making me sweat. Being prepared and calm were the most important qualities I brought to this job, and both had just deserted me.

A floorboard creaked in the hallway outside the bedroom, turning my sweat cold. I stood, unmoving, waiting for someone to appear. A full minute passed before I could find my voice. "George?" The word squeaked through dried lips, the high pitch barely recognizable as my own voice.

The only reply was the light tap of retreating footsteps, the pace quickening as the unseen feet reached the stairs. *There is no such thing as ghosts.* I had to repeat that to myself twice before I took off at a swift run toward the servants' stairs. A door closed on the landing beneath and I propelled myself recklessly downward, throwing open the door that hadn't had time to fully latch.

I found myself standing in yet another back hallway of the house, this one unfamiliar to me. The space was deserted and I paused, wondering if I should go back to Maybelle's bedroom and continue looking for my notebook. A gentle *snap* at the end of the hallway had me running toward two facing doors. I yanked the first one open to find myself staring into a broom closet filled with ancient cleaning implements and an elaborate tapestry of spiderwebs. I slammed it shut and opened up the other door.

I paused, feeling a bit like Alice after she fell down the rabbit hole. The room I found myself in was as shabby and devoid of furniture as the rest of the house, the ceiling mural as faded and flaking, the woven rug as threadbare. But these walls were lined with tall dark wood shelves filled with row after row of dust-covered books. I remembered reading in my research that John Sprague had added a library to showcase a valuable collection of books he'd acquired from—depending on where one found the information—either an indebted friend, an estate sale, or gambling. Judging from what I'd learned so far about Mr. Sprague, I'd bet on the last.

A rolling ladder rested at one end, tempting me to climb up and examine the books more closely. Resisting the impulse, I pulled a book from a shelf, being careful not to dump the layer of dust on my shirt, and read the title on the leather cover: *Fall of the Roman Republic* by Plutarch. The spine wasn't creased—nor were the spines of the adjacent books, all volumes in Plutarch's *Parallel Lives* series. Despite the dust, it appeared the books had been placed in the library under false pretenses.

Looking down, I spotted a set of small footprints in the dust heading toward the large bay window at one end of the room. Subtle goose bumps pricked the skin at the back of my neck. As far as I knew ghosts didn't leave footprints. Or did they? I'd have to ask Meghan since she seemed to know a lot more about the subject than I did. A solitary writing table, an apparent recent addition to the house due to its lack of ornamentation or any style whatsoever, sat tucked inside the bay window, a lone book sitting on the surface. I didn't need to get closer to see that it was my missing notebook.

I quickly retrieved it, flipping through the pages to make sure it was all there, my relief almost overtaking the uneasiness tugging at me. What was it doing here? There was a logical explanation. There had to be. Because everyone knew that ghosts weren't real.

Looking at my watch, I realized I'd wasted too much valuable time. Hugging the notebook to my chest, I turned around, feeling disoriented. The servants' door from which I'd entered was apparently disguised on this side by a bookshelf—I just wasn't sure which one. The one thing I *was* sure of was that if I left through the main door, I'd never find my way back to Maybelle's bedroom.

A lone volume on a bottom shelf caught my attention if only because it seemed it might have more dust on it than any of the other volumes. As if it had been even less read than any of the other books. Despite my urgency, I slipped it from the shelf to read the title on the cover. *Prunella Pratt Schuyler Potts—Cultural Icon and Society Doyenne: Memoirs of a Great American Heroine and Survivor of the* Lusitania. Curious, I glanced at the author's name. *Prunella Pratt Schuyler Potts.* I raised my eyebrows as I quickly slid it back into its space, no longer wondering why I'd never heard of her. Even without opening the cover and creasing the spine, I had no doubt that Mrs. Potts, whoever she was or thought herself to be, had used a vanity press.

I looked down to see the familiar set of footprints—definitely a woman's—leading toward the dark and imposing double doors that sat under a broken pediment, the thick plaster scrolls no longer imposing. Dots of bare wood peered from underneath what I'd at first assumed was solid mahogany. Veneer, then.

Like the painted columns that were meant to appear marble, superficiality seemed to be the dominant architectural style of Sprague Hall. Despite my disdain for taking structural shortcuts in the same time period that the Vanderbilts were using platinum for wall panels, I found myself intrigued by the family that had called this place home for so long. For the first time, the folder of newspaper articles and Google searches about the Spragues that I had assembled but not read held at least some interest. Maybe even enough for me to actually crack it open and study. I knew sooner or later I'd have to mention something salacious enough to attract viewers, slip it in between architectural terms and try not to squirm in front of the camera. Yet I still held the distant hope that my passion for architecture and history would come through in the telling, alleviating any need to embellish the script.

Walking quickly, I retraced my footsteps and fumbled for only a moment to open the bookcase, finding myself in the back hallway. I took two wrong turns before I discovered the staircase and then followed the crew's voices to Maybelle's bedroom.

Pretending I wasn't late, I took out the copies of the changes I'd made and handed them to George, Devon, Sheila, and the impeccably dressed Meghan, who looked like she'd just stepped out of a J.Crew catalog. She handed me a Styrofoam cup from the catering truck, knowing it was for everybody's protection that I was supplied with a steady stream of coffee, unadulterated by sugar or creamer.

Without looking at the paper she said, "I have an idea."

Knowing that Meghan had been hired to function as technical advisor, I prepared to listen even though I knew what she'd say before she opened her mouth.

"It's about the wallpaper," she said. "I did some research and it's an actual Brunschwig & Fils paper—one of their earliest designs. I have a contact at the company, and I've already put in a call. I think that before we strip any more of it we should find out if they have ideas on how to arrest the decay, to leave what's already there to give a better idea of the historical context . . ."

"No." I sent her a warning look, aware that the crew was listening. "We've gone over this before, remember? Historical context is not what our audience wants." I considered my words, attempting to sound enthusiastic at least in front of the film crew. As host, I was responsible for their morale and excitement over the project. If there was one thing my mother had taught me, it was how to fake it as if you meant it. "The audience wants bright and light and modern—think how transformed and beautiful this space will be without all of that old wallpaper drooping all over the walls."

Meghan looked at me as if I'd just sprouted two more heads. In her usual dramatic fashion, she plastered herself against the wall like a mother bear protecting her cubs. "That's obscene! I can't believe you said that out loud."

Before I could respond, I was distracted by the sound of a woman's voice, the clipped words of a true New England Brahmin. She was speaking loudly, presumably into her phone, as her footsteps approached the doorway. "The cake frosting must *precisely* match the lavender of her party dress. Emmeline specifically selected that color as it's her favorite. I want you to visit the caterer in person with the dress to make sure it's the exact color and go ahead and order the custom napkins in the same shade. It's not every day a young lady turns four, so we need this to be . . ."

Luke's sister, Hadley, stopped in the doorway, a Kelly bag swinging on her arm, her gaze taking in my stacks of flooring, fabric, and paint samples, the bright lights, the cords, the crew, and—finally—Meghan hugging the wall. "I'll call you back," she said, then lowered her phone. Her icy gaze rested on me. "What is going on here?"

"We're making an episode of *Makeover Mansion.*" I waited for her to nod or say something, but only the flush of color in her pale cheeks indicated that she'd heard. I continued, wondering if she'd just forgotten. "We're restoring three rooms—"

"Renovating," Meghan interrupted. "Restoring is something other people who care about history do." Meghan crossed her arms, her gaze reluctantly settling on Hadley's purse. Even in times of crisis she always noticed the details, especially regarding fashion.

"I don't care what you call"—Hadley stuck out her phone like a fencing saber, swishing it in a slicing pattern—"this. I need you people to glue back that wallpaper, remove any evidence that you were ever here, and eradicate yourselves from the premises. We are not doing anything with this albatross except selling it." Before she'd finished speaking, she'd raised her phone and stabbed her finger on the screen, waited a moment for someone to answer, and then calmly—although at a higher decibel—said, "Get. Here. Now."

My phone pinged with a message from Marc.

Meet me at the yacht club ASAP. We need to talk.

I looked up to see George's red light on the camera, the lens pointed at me. I wondered how much he'd filmed and if it included Hadley's histrionics. "Turn that off," I said, but he'd already rotated the camera just in time to catch Luke strolling into the room wearing only running shorts and sneakers, a sweaty T-shirt hanging over his shoulders.

I heard Meghan's intake of breath, which hopefully covered my own. At the boatyard, hanging out and watching my dad do his restoration work, I'd seen lots of shirtless men. But most of those men had dad bods and the only six-packs were those in their coolers. Considering the dissipated life I felt fairly sure Luke Sprague led, I had to admit he had an admirable set of abs. And legs, if I was to be completely honest. Not that I was paying any attention to his body at all because

I was trying to listen to the heated conversation he was having with Hadley.

"It's a done deal, Hadley. Lucky wants this renovation because the money will allow her to live here a little while longer. She's an old woman and has had to deal with many losses over her long life. Do you want to take away the one thing that she has left?"

"Don't be ridiculous. This place is crumbling down around her. It's not safe for her to be living here. There are some lovely assisted-living places where she'd be much more comfortable—I've brought some brochures with me to show Lucky. And I'm sure we can find some idiot with more money than brains dying to get his hands on one of these crumbling piles of rock." She straightened her shoulders. "That's why I'm here. I've already contacted a real estate agent and I've come to tell Lucky that I've set up an appointment for the agent to have a walk-through to give us an estimate of what he might be able to get for Sprague Hall." She slid a derisive glance in our direction. "Because selling Sprague Hall would be better than having *strangers* in our *home*. Nosing into our *business*." I could almost see her internal shudder.

Luke followed her gaze, settling on George, who had been busy filming the entire interaction. "Hey, man, turn that camera off. Personal interactions are off-limits, do you understand?"

George made the mistake of looking at me for corroboration, giving Luke the opportunity to grab the camera so that they began to play tug-of-war with a very expensive piece of equipment that could quite possibly end my tenure in reality television if it got broken on my watch.

"Stop it," I said, moving between the two men and trying to keep my gaze focused on Luke above the neck. "Please put it down, George. We'll talk about this later, okay?"

"Whatever," he said, pulling the camera away from Luke and switching it off. "I'm just trying to do my job."

"I rest my case," Hadley said. "I'm going to speak with Lucky right now. You are welcome to join me, but you're not going to change my mind." She left the room with Luke following, and I had to force myself to not stare at his bare back as he exited.

I looked at my watch. "Okay, everybody. Please see the notes I just gave you and get set up so we can start filming at twelve thirty on the dot. I have to leave now so let's do an early lunch break. Just make sure you're back on time. The change has put us behind schedule and we'll have to hustle to catch up."

I grabbed my backpack—making sure that my notebook was tucked safely inside of it—and left, taking the servants' stairs so I wouldn't run into Hadley. Or Luke. Then I jumped in my Civic, crossing my fingers that it would start on the first try, and headed toward the yacht club.

I was nearly there when I realized that I might not be dressed properly to be admitted inside the club. Didn't these places usually have a dress code? My favorite pairs of jeans and grungy work pants were currently tumbling in my washing machine at home and I'd been forced to wear actual dress pants, so there was that. Beneath my Death Cab for Cutie sweatshirt I wore a plain white blouse that was at least clean and sported a collar. I also had a pair of black short heels in the back of my car. That was the second thing I'd learned from my mother.

When I reached the club and realized there was no self-parking and only valet, I felt grateful for the foresight that had made me pull onto the side of the road before I reached the club to take off my sweatshirt and change my shoes. I'd dug into my backpack for a brush then tamed my hair back with a rubber band I kept on the gear shift, and with a quick glance in the rearview mirror I'd decided I at least looked presentable if not particularly yacht club material. Not that I would ever want to be.

As I approached the club, I grudgingly admired the gray shingle walls and slate peaks of the rooftop, crisp like starched sheets against the blue of the water and sky behind it. Spiky masts from the harbored boats in the marina lazily nodded, reminding me of the well-dressed set at cocktail hour waiting for something exciting to happen.

The valet did a good job of not recoiling in horror at the sight of my car and took my key with a smile. I wasn't completely surprised when I was guided to the bar instead of the dining room. I told myself it was too early to be serving lunch, but a quick glance into the dining room with occupied tables told me I was once again pretending that everything was fine.

A half-empty tumbler of amber liquid sat on the polished surface of the Burmese teak bar in front of Marc, its resemblance to the deck of a yacht not an accident. I greeted Marc and sat on the stool next to him, ordering a soda water with lemon so it wouldn't appear that he was drinking alone.

He reeked of bourbon, and his bow tie hung diagonally at his neck, one end beginning to pull itself free of the knot. I wanted to reach across and fix it for him, but Marc's sloppy smile made me angry. It was only eleven thirty in the morning, yet he had clearly been drinking for a while. Or maybe he just hadn't stopped.

Without preamble, he said, "I had a long chat with Christiana last night. George has sent her everything you've done so far, and she had a lot to say." He didn't smile, telling me that none of what she'd said was good.

I straightened my shoulders, the equivalent of raising my defensive hackles. "Seriously? We're following the script that she approved, and of course what she's seen is the unedited version, so if she's critiquing, I'd say it's a bit premature. Was it about the changes I submitted yesterday?"

His response was to drain his glass and slide it across the bar before raising his finger to order another drink.

I squirmed in my seat, uncomfortable with his silence and desperate to defend myself before I even heard the charges. I couldn't lose this job. Too much depended on it. "Look, Marc. The reality here is that when I signed on it was to be the host and you the producer, guiding the production. Forgive me for pointing this out, but you've been pretty much missing in action. I appreciate your confidence in me, but I'm not qualified to be a producer—not yet, anyway—and I'm way over my head without your guidance. My only experience is from hosting that small production in grad school, which is hardly on the same level of what I'm doing here. I'll admit that I'm struggling to wear both hats. But I promise to do better. Maybe if you could just stop by for a few hours each day . . ."

I let my voice trail off, realizing he was more interested in sucking down his drink than listening to me. I took a sip from my own drink, waiting for him to say something. Finally, he sat back, sliding his glass away from him. Avoiding my eyes, he said, "They want it to be more about the personal stuff, and less about plastering techniques and flooring options. Just . . . sexier."

"Wait . . . what?" I swiveled my stool to face him, sure I'd misunderstood, although the pink ensemble that had been selected for me to wear should have been a warning. "Did you say 'sexier'? Are you sure you're talking about *Makeover Mansion* and not *The Bachelorette*? Because I can't say I've ever heard the words 'sexy' and 'renovation' in the same sentence."

I waited for him to laugh, to let me know that this was all some kind of a joke. Instead, he lifted his finger again to the bartender, then took another sip before answering.

"I'm sorry, Andie. I really am."

I could only sit and stare, wondering how this icon in the world of historic restoration and my mentor could have fallen so far. He'd once been the Robin Leach of his field, hosting two successful television series that had gone into syndication, the author of coffee table books and textbooks found on the shelves of socialites and academics alike. I recalled again the rumors about a great personal loss, and how I'd been too focused on my own family's crisis at the time to give them any credence. I should ask; I needed to ask, but now wasn't the time. Not when so much was hanging in the balance. With a burst of anger, I asked, "So, she means to make this show more a *Desperate Housewives* meets *Kardashian House Flip*?"

That at least elicited a grin. But if I thought he'd contradict me, I was wrong. "Yes, actually. I think that's exactly what she wants." He swayed on his stool and I reached to grab him, thinking he might slide off.

"But . . . how?" I hated how desperate my voice sounded.

He dropped his head down to his chin and held it there for so long that I thought he might have fallen asleep. "Marc?"

He jerked his head up. "Yes, sorry. I was thinking. You need to get Lucky on camera. Interview her if you can. Ask her about Stuy."

"Stuy?" I remembered vaguely thumbing through my research folder, seeing the name. Stuyvesant Sprague.

"Her husband," he mumbled.

I shook my head. "You know I can't. It's not allowed in the contract to have any contact with her. We'll get thrown out and then we all lose."

His head bobbed up and down, his eyes now like slits. "No worries. I'll get my people on it."

Hot, impotent anger raced through me, and I was too worried and too frustrated to hold it back. "'Your people'? Who do you think 'your people' are, Marc? I'm the only one you've got left. The only one who's stuck by you. The only one who's still here. You need to pull yourself together or we're both going to find ourselves thrown out on our asses."

Stinging regret pricked at the back of my throat as soon as the words had flown from my mouth. Especially when his lip quivered and I knew I'd hurt him. But my anger remained, the consequences of not solving this problem too dire. Lowering my voice, I said, "You've got to help me, Marc. You got me into this. How am I supposed to get to Lucky?"

His head sunk again, but he glanced up with bloodshot eyes. "Joanie. You need to talk to Joanie."

"Joanie? Who's Joanie?"

He answered with his once famous smile, then proceeded to slide off his stool like a stringless puppet, already snoring before he hit the floor.

CHAPTER ELEVEN

Ellen

Newport, Rhode Island
June 1899

THE GUESTS WERE still snoring when Ellen snuck out of the house.

Out of habit—it was strange how quickly one fell into habit—she peeked through the connecting door to Maybelle's room. The girl slept in her magnificent bed with one arm flung over her head, her fair curls tumbled around her face. The bedclothes were mounded up around her and Ellen had to resist the urge to slip in and tuck them up around Maybelle's chin as she used to do with her little sisters.

But this wasn't one of her sisters. This was Maybelle Sprague, heiress—and, if the last two nights were anything to go by, toast of Newport.

The success of that first song had been followed immediately by a rash of praise for Maybelle. A Vanderbilt cousin (best not to look too closely at the connection) had insisted on sitting beside Maybelle at breakfast. A distant relation of the Van Rensselaers had deigned to look over the latest fashion plates with Maybelle in the morning room. And Frank Pratt, the young man with the pomade in his hair, had favored Maybelle with the treat of a drive down Bellevue Avenue in his smashing new motorcar.

Ellen pulled her shawl a little closer around her as she turned to the back of the house, to the servants' stairs. She could remember that moment in the doorway of the dining room. It had been such a very close-run thing. Had the prince not praised Maybelle's performance, all of these elegant, refined people would have turned on her and torn her to shreds.

But the prince had raised his glass to her and so Maybelle Sprague was officially a success, to be praised and petted and feted.

Last night, there had been a dance—not a ball, there were quite strict rules about what constituted a ball—an impromptu dance in the ballroom, with Ellen dragged downstairs to play because John Sprague, in one of his many odd economies, had engaged the musicians to play only for the first night of the prince's visit.

Ellen had pounded out reels and waltzes until her fingers ached. Maybelle's delight had been wonderful to behold. She had galloped in and out of the figures of the dance with her ruffles flying and her cheeks pink, so painfully grateful to everyone for taking such an interest in her.

It hadn't escaped Ellen's notice that Frank Pratt had solicited Maybelle's hand again and again.

At a ball, a proper ball, there would have been dance cards, and a limit on the number of dances a girl could give to any one man—at least, according to the women whom Ellen had overheard gossiping. But at an informal occasion such as this . . . There had been so few young men there, Ellen told herself. That was all. Maybelle would have danced with anyone who had asked her and that was why she had gone turn and turn around the room with Frank Pratt, while the prince sat in his seat of honor, watching with detached amusement the cavorting of lesser mortals.

Ellen could feel his gaze on the back of her neck as she bent over her music, doing her best to be invisible.

But the prince wasn't here now. He was abed, like the rest of the elite. Soon, housemaids would begin to tiptoe through the house with breakfast trays, guests would begin their toilettes, the more adventurous might even step outside to take the air. But, for now, all was calm, and Ellen escaped gratefully out a door that was little more than a gap in the masonry. She hadn't realized quite how airless the atmosphere in the house had been until she was outside it, breathing deep breaths of the crisp morning air, the varied flowers of the gardens mingling their scents with the tang of the sea.

There were elaborate gardens, trompe l'oeil terraces progressing in a carefully choreographed series of spectacles, from formal parterres to mock wildernesses of wildflowers, a rose arbor, a grotto of tumbled rocks and violets with a little stream running through it, so that one might think one had escaped civilization—even though it was all entirely visible from the windows of the house.

But it wasn't the gardens Ellen was after. It was the path that led down to the sea, forty rickety steps pressed into the rocks and scrub, slick with spray toward the bottom. The guests didn't come down here and neither did the family. They did their bathing at Bailey's Beach. Someone—someone, like her, who wanted to hide—had carved this rough trail to the water, where she could sit on the rocks and feel the damp on her cheeks and the sea air in her hair and feel . . . free, as if she could lift her arms to the air and be carried on the sea spray.

Boston was by the water, but not water such as this. Those were docks clogged with shipping. Here was nothing but the wild, wild waves and the gulls and slick, jagged rocks, primitive and bare. It called to something in her.

Or maybe it was just that it was as far as one could get from Dermot and the stifling atmosphere of the Hibernia, all red velvet and flaking gilt. One couldn't imagine Dermot here. One couldn't imagine anyone here.

And then a man's head rose from the water.

Ellen skidded on the slick rocks, catching herself just in time. "Who's there?"

No one swam here. It was too dangerous, the tides unpredictable, the rocks sharp.

But someone was. She could see the head again now, clearly, a dark head, slick with wet, diving under and rising again, arms pulling against the waves. One hand grasped the rocks by her feet, and then another, and the prince hauled himself up out of the water in all his naked glory.

Well, not quite naked. He'd had the decency to wear his skivvies, but they were so soaked with water they did little to protect his modesty—or hers.

Ellen didn't mean to gawp. It was just that he looked like a statue in the morning light, all those muscles, glistening with wet, except that statues were static and the prince was all motion, every single one of those muscles in play as he shook off the water, shoving his hair out of his eyes.

"What do we have here?" he drawled, as though she were the one who had emerged naked from the spray.

"I might have asked you the same thing," snapped Ellen. This was her place, her private place. He had no business invading it. But he was the prince and she was meant to kowtow to him, like everyone else. Ellen tried to turn her annoyance into solicitude. "You might have drowned."

"I learned to swim in wilder waters than these." The prince stretched his arms over his head. Ellen looked hastily away. The prince laughed. "If you would spare your blushes, little music teacher, you oughtn't to wander so far."

Ellen bit down hard on all the things she might have said. "Do they not wear bathing costumes, then, in Italy?"

The prince's smile mocked her. "No, only tights and doublets. Cross-gartered. Hand me my dressing gown, won't you?"

Was she to be his body servant now? Ellen followed where he pointed and gathered up the pile of priceless brocade left carelessly wadded behind a pile of rocks. Handing it to him, she said primly, "I meant no disrespect, Your Excellency. I'd really no idea you weren't one of the musicians."

"Because all Italians must be performers?"

Ellen's cheeks flamed. It was a little too close to the truth. "You were expected to arrive the usual way."

The prince wrapped himself in crimson brocade, fastening the tie neatly at his waist. "Which was precisely why I didn't. Sometimes, one can learn a great deal by being where one isn't meant to be."

"And what did you learn?" Ellen asked shortly. She'd been where she wasn't meant to be once. Because of it she was here, now, dependent on the whims of a half-naked potentate instead of peacefully playing piano for scantily clad dancers.

The prince looked down his aristocratic nose at her. "That would be telling."

"I hope it was worth it," said Ellen bitterly, knowing she shouldn't, but goaded by his amusement. It was all a game to him. But not to her. It was deadly serious for her. "Knowledge isn't always a boon."

"The fruit of the serpent?" The prince regarded her with interest. His eyes, Ellen noticed, weren't the brown one would have expected, but as green as leaves reflected in water. "One imagines that life in Eden would have grown dull after a time."

Ellen wrapped her arms around herself, even though she wasn't the one half-dressed. "That's blasphemy."

"Is it? The Lord created both the garden and the apple. Why dangle it in front of us if he didn't mean us to eat it?"

The prince's voice was rich and seductive, promising forbidden pleasures.

"Is that what you tell all the girls?" Ellen asked tartly.

The prince burst into a laugh, a real one this time. "Only the ones who require persuading."

Ellen held up a hand to shield her eyes from the sun. "Well, there are some who might not desire persuading."

"Doesn't one of your poets say something about a woman who

protests too much? Hold, hold—I only tease you," he added, as Ellen turned away. He reached toward her, and then caught himself, holding his hands in the air, palms up. "I cannot speak in jest to any of the women of the house party. They would only take it in the wrong part."

He was standing with his back to the sun, and the light made rainbows at the corners of Ellen's eyes. She blinked hard. "The wrong part?"

"Too seriously," he said. "There are some who like to brag that they received the attentions of a prince."

It didn't sound like much of an excuse. "So you only flirt with servant girls. Who can't refuse you."

The prince's nostrils flared. "I only flirt with you because you do refuse me. Do you think I force myself on your kitchen maids?"

He wouldn't be the first. Ellen wasn't sure she bought his act of outraged dignity. "You might save the charm for your intended."

"Ah yes, my *intended*." His expression turned dark, before he said, with deliberate lightness, "But would she put me in my place so neatly? I think not."

Ellen looked reprovingly at the prince. "Miss Sprague wishes only to please."

The prince was silent a moment, his hands in his pockets. Then he said, slowly, "Miss Sprague does not seem so much to wish to please as to avoid displeasure. Those are not the same thing."

Ellen looked at the prince in surprise. She'd never thought of it that way, but he was completely right. Maybelle reminded her a bit of a mistreated animal, attempting to curry favor in an attempt to ward off more blows. But she didn't like that he made it sound as though it were Maybelle's fault, some lack in her character, almost a kind of falsehood, when it wasn't anything of the sort. If Maybelle was quick to appease, well, she had good reason for it.

"You would be afraid of displeasure, too, if you'd been raised as Miss Sprague was." Ellen might be poor, she might be an orphan, but at least she'd been loved. So loved. Even in his darkest times, she'd never doubted her father's devotion. What he'd done, misguided though it might have been, he'd done for love of her. "She's never had anyone to love her, truly love her for herself."

"Love," said the prince, as though the word were a quaint one. "A pretty notion perpetrated by poets."

Ellen looked at him in frustration. "Fondness, then, if you don't like the word 'love.' Can you imagine what it is to know that there isn't one person in the world who likes you for yourself? That you're simply tolerated for what you can provide?"

The prince had a strange expression on his face. "Oddly enough, yes. I am familiar with that notion."

Ellen caught up short. "Well, then. But you're a man, and a man of authority." The prince sketched an ironic bow. Ellen refused to be deterred. "Think what it would be to be a woman—a girl—entirely at the mercy of others. You can bark orders and be all princely and lordly, but Maybelle—Miss Sprague—her only defense is to try not to displease. It isn't fair to mock her for it."

The prince was staring at her, and Ellen couldn't entirely blame him. She felt a little silly for her outburst. "What has Miss Sprague done to command such loyalty?"

Ellen twisted her hands in the material of her skirt. "Miss Sprague . . . Miss Sprague is kind. Don't laugh! It's not such a common quality, kindness."

There was no laughter in the prince's face. "Has someone been unkind to you, little music teacher?"

If one counted attempted murder as unkind. Ellen shook her head, trying not to think of it. Dermot would say she'd brought it on herself. He'd been nothing but kind. Until she had betrayed him. And she had. There was no disputing it. "No. No one."

The prince looked at her closely. "No? Not even the ever-so-charming Mr. Sprague?"

"Mr. Sprague was justly put out by my rudeness to his guest." Ellen took a deep breath, trying to sound cool and detached, to put the distance back between them. "And he was right. I oughtn't to be speaking with you like this. Haven't you something princely to do?"

"Oh yes, a crown to polish—and village girls to despoil." The prince grinned as her cheeks reddened. "Have you ever considered that a prince might be merely a man with a superfluity of ancestors?"

"I haven't been in the way of meeting many princes. You're my first."

"Am I?" The prince raised a brow, as if laughing at a private joke. "We shall have to make the experience a pleasant one, then."

"The pleasantest experience would be to keep my position. Your Excellency." Ellen dropped a quick curtsy, meaning to go, but she couldn't stop herself turning and asking, "Why did you persuade Mr. Sprague to keep me on?"

"Perhaps I enjoy the novelty of being insulted." The prince's eyes met hers. "Or perhaps it is because I recognize a true musician when I see one."

His voice was level and grave, with no hint of mockery about it. "I'm only an accompanist."

"You do yourself too little credit." The prince didn't move, but there suddenly seemed to be a great space between them, as though he had stepped away from her. "I look forward to seeing what you produce for our musical evening."

That, Ellen could tell, had been undoubtedly a dismissal, prince to subject. He ought to have looked ridiculous, standing there at the shore in a brocade dressing gown, his bare legs showing beneath the hem. But he didn't. He looked ready to receive monarchs.

"Your Excellency," Ellen said, and this time when she left, she didn't look back.

She hadn't realized how long she had been there on the rocks with the prince. But by the time she struggled up the steps and made her way past the greenhouses and the outbuildings, the house had quite definitely come awake. She could see ladies taking the air on the terrace, gentlemen hiding in the loggia for a quick smoke.

As Ellen skirted the edges of the formal gardens, Prunella Pratt Schuyler's commanding voice carried all the way through the twining vines of the rose arbor. "It's horrid your brother subjecting you to that. What was he thinking?"

"I would be a princess," said Maybelle tentatively, as Ellen drew closer, moving very softly until she was separated from them only by a screen of petals and thorns. "It would be nice to be a princess. I think."

"Yes, but princess of *what*? Put a title on a cur and it's still a cur," said Mrs. Schuyler firmly. "Animals, all of them."

"Curs?" Maybelle sounded justly confused.

"Italians," Mrs. Schuyler corrected. "It's the hot weather that does it. It gives them terrible carnal appetites."

She sounded like she rather relished the thought.

"No, my dear," said Mrs. Schuyler, and Ellen could see her briskly patting Maybelle's hand. "It won't do at all. You can do *much* better than that."

"Than a prince?" Maybelle sounded uncertain, but ready to be convinced.

"What's a prince these days? Oh, they're all very well for fairy tales, but they hardly matter now, do they? I mean, unless you really *want* to have crowns embroidered all over your underthings."

She made it sound the height of absurdity. Ellen frowned at the screening vines. She had no doubt Mrs. Schuyler would adore crowns embroidered on her underthings. And that, if the prince had so much as nodded at her, she would have been the first to boast of it.

For the first time, she appreciated the prince's complaint about his inability to speak lightly with the women of the party.

Perhaps that was why, Ellen thought, he had chosen to sit and gaze loftily at everyone rather than joining the dancing. She had thought it hauteur. It might have been simple self-preservation. Or a bit of both.

"I—I have no ambition to wear a crown," Maybelle began.

"A coronet," Mrs. Schuyler broke in authoritatively. "The monarch wears a crown. Lesser titles wear coronets."

"That's just the problem. I don't know any of the things I ought to know," Maybelle said miserably. "But my brother feels—"

"Brothers," said Mrs. Schuyler dismissively. "What's in a brother? I have two of them and they're both utterly useless. Worse than useless. One had the poor manners to disappear and the other got himself killed in a drunken brawl."

"Oh dear," said Maybelle. "I'm so sorry."

"It was most inconsiderate of them. But what can one expect from brothers? So, really, you ought to allow yourself to be guided by me. There's nothing like the advice of an older woman of consequence." Mrs. Schuyler thought for a moment. "Not that much older. Just a bit older. It's really not about the *age*, so much as one's experience of society."

"I don't have any experience of society," Maybelle confessed.

"You poor, dear thing." Mrs. Schuyler sighed heartily. "You're just a lamb among the wolves. Now, if what I've heard about that prince is true . . ."

Ellen decided to intervene before Mrs. Schuyler could poison Maybelle's mind with more rumor and innuendo. She stepped around the edge of the arbor, surprising the two women at their bench, Maybelle in a morning dress of printed silk in which stripes of pale pink dots on a dark pink background alternated with stripes of deep pink roses on a pale pink background, creating a highly floral and headache-producing effect, Mrs. Schuyler in a dashing ensemble of rose pink embroidered all over in swirling designs of jet beads, which must have taken weeks to complete and cost more than Ellen's salary for a year.

"Miss Sprague?"

"Ellen!" Maybelle half rose from her seat. "I'm so terribly sorry. Am I late? Have you been looking for me?"

Before Ellen could reply, Mrs. Schuyler tugged Maybelle back into her seat. "Do sit back down." She waved an imperious hand at Ellen, her jet beads jangling. "It's far too early in the day for a music lesson. Go away, she doesn't want you now."

Ellen ignored her. "May—Miss Sprague?"

Maybelle looked anxiously from Ellen to Mrs. Schuyler in an agony of indecision. "I might . . . I might just sit a little longer."

Ellen looked at Mrs. Schuyler and then back at Maybelle, not wanting to leave her, but without the power to protest. There was something corrosive about Mrs. Schuyler, a cloying kind of poison at odds with the porcelain loveliness of her face. "If you're quite sure . . ."

"Of course, she's sure! Now go away." Mrs. Schuyler made shooing motions at Ellen. "Heavens, it's maddening dealing with menials."

Ellen's lips set hard. She looked at Maybelle. "I'll be in the music room when you're ready."

Maybelle looked at her with anguished eyes, terrified of disappointing anyone. "I'll be by presently. I just—it's such a lovely morning."

"Too lovely a morning to be cooped up with a piano like a paid performer." Mrs. Schuyler pointedly turned her back, cutting Ellen out of the conversation. "But that's beside the point. You needn't explain yourself to the help. No wonder the creature is getting above herself!"

As she backed out of the arbor, Ellen could hear Maybelle saying faintly, "She's not a creature, she's Ellen."

"It doesn't do to think of them by their names," said Mrs. Schuyler seriously. "I call all my maids by the same name. It saves a great deal of trouble."

"But don't they mind it?"

"Mind? Why should they mind? They have a roof over their heads, haven't they? You mustn't make the mistake of thinking of servants as people."

"But they are," said Maybelle daringly. "Just the same as you or I."

"Oh, my dear." Through the vines Ellen could see Mrs. Schuyler patting Maybelle's hand, her voice rich with pity. "You have so much to learn."

From her spot behind the arbor, Ellen could see Mrs. Schuyler's cousin coming down the path from the house. She moved a bit more out of the way as he paused, smoothing his hair and checking his pocket watch before sauntering into the arbor, saying heartily, "Thought I heard a familiar voice in here!"

Mrs. Schuyler's voice rose to levels of ear-shattering sweetness. "Oh, Frank, what a lovely surprise! Doesn't Maybelle look charming among the roses?"

"Charming," said Mr. Pratt flatly.

"I do think they bring out the pink in her complexion, don't you? Such a lovely, fresh, *unspoiled* complexion." There was a great deal of innuendo in that one word. Ellen wasn't quite sure what Mrs. Schuyler was getting at, but whatever it was, Ellen didn't like it, not one bit.

"Lovely," echoed Mr. Pratt, with a poor attempt at enthusiasm.

"*Do* come sit here, Frank, next to Miss Sprague. Now, my dear, isn't it nice to be with a proper American gentleman? *He* won't importune you, would you, Frank?"

Mr. Pratt rose to the occasion. "Wouldn't even dream of it."

"*Frank*." Mrs. Schuyler must have poked him with something, because Ellen heard a strangled yelp.

Mr. Pratt modified his statement. "Er, that is, might dream of it, but wouldn't think of taking liberties."

"A perfect gentleman," said Mrs. Schuyler. "Oh dear, I just remembered, I promised Mr. Schuyler faithfully that I would write today. No, no, there's no need for you to get up. I'll go write my letter while you enjoy the wonders of nature."

A jangling of jet heralded Mrs. Schuyler's imminent departure. Ellen hastily removed herself. Mr. Pratt might be too distracted to notice her lurking, but Mrs. Schuyler was made of sterner stuff.

Ellen beat a retreat in the direction of the kitchen, where she snagged a passing footman. "Miss Sprague is in the rose arbor. Would you tell her that Miss Van Rensselaer requires her presence in the morning room?"

She didn't think there was anything too compromising about Maybelle sitting in a garden with Frank Pratt at ten in the morning, but it didn't hurt to be sure. The entire scene in the arbor had left a nasty taste in her mouth. There was no doubt as to Mrs. Schuyler's intentions—or Frank Pratt's for that matter. An heiress was an heiress, and Ellen had no doubt that Mr. Pratt was in debt up to his expensively creamed hair. She'd seen plenty of his type at the Hibernia, do-nothings who thought the world was owed them, who'd sooner marry money than make it.

It was none of her business, Ellen knew that. She'd been hired to help Maybelle perform, that was all. But she wouldn't—she *couldn't*—let Maybelle marry Frank Pratt.

The prince might be dangerous and foreign and thoroughly maddening . . . but there was something about him that there wasn't in Frank Pratt.

Ellen found herself looking back, down the slope that led to the sea, wondering if the prince was still there, standing in his dressing gown by the edge of the water.

She and the prince, she thought heavily, were going to have to have a very long talk.

If only she could be sure he would listen!

CHAPTER TWELVE

Lucky

Newport, Rhode Island
July 1957

"AREN'T YOU *LISTENING*?" A small hand tugged at the sleeve of Lucky's dressing gown. "*Listen,* Mama!"

"What's that, sweetheart?"

"I said *listen*! You never *listen* to me!"

"I *am* listening."

"No, you're *not*!"

Lucky tore her gaze away from the newspaper and fastened on the small tanned face of her daughter, surrounded by tumbled blond curls. She smelled of ocean air and damp green grass. "Why, Joanie! Have you been outside?"

Joanie made a noise of exasperation such as only a seven-year-old could make. "That's what I'm trying to *tell* you, Mama! It's *Nonna*! She's down by the boathouse and she won't come in!"

THE AIR WAS still cool, the sun newly risen. Lucky raced over the wet turf, toward the public footpath to where the ground fell away to the ocean. The pale, fierce sunlight stung her eyes. Behind her, Joanie panted out some garbled explanation: how she'd seen Nonna pacing along the edge of the rocks from her bedroom window, had tried to wake Daddy, had raced outside herself but Nonna wouldn't speak, just kept humming some song to herself, shivering and pacing and sitting and pacing some more.

Lucky swore at herself. She should have noticed that Nonna hadn't come to the breakfast table, though she was usually the first one up. Instead, Lucky had chosen to savor these unexpected minutes to herself, nursing her coffee and newspaper, the house blissfully silent around her. Nobody asking for her, nobody needing her.

Except Nonna *had* needed her.

Her hair flew out of its curlers. Her slippers dripped with dew. She raced through the gap in the boxwoods, across the Cliff Walk to the narrow footpath leading down the rocky slope to the boathouse. Where was Nonna? Oh God. Lucky's wet slippers skidded on the pebbles. She reached out and caught herself on the corner of the building. A soft, keening voice rose from the rocks nearby, and for an instant Lucky was confused—she was back in Italy, she was at the seaside near Livorno with Nonna and the cousins, she lay exhausted on the sand while the sun baked her salty young skin to a nice crust, and somewhere a woman sang "*O mio babbino caro*" in a clear, carrying soprano—Lucky loved the part about the girl threatening to go to the Ponte Vecchio to throw herself into the Arno, it sounded so *exactly* like teenage love—and the beauty of life surrounded her like the heat shimmering down from the sun.

Then Lucky snapped to the present. The singer wasn't some long-ago young woman—it was Nonna, *Nonna's* clear soprano. Lucky scrambled around the back of the boathouse and there she was, sitting on a rock in her white nightgown hitched up to her knees, feet dangling in the surf, warbling Puccini in a voice that trembled to the rhythm of her shivering.

EVEN AS A child, Lucky had known that Nonna was different from everybody else. It wasn't just that she was American; it was something peculiar, some fey streak inside her. She liked to take walks and sing to herself; she would slip sometimes into a kind of trance while her lips moved like she was holding an earnest conversation with some invisible person. She would take sudden impulses—whims, Nonno called them, shaking his head with equal parts fondness and bemusement.

But for all that, she wasn't what you'd call crazy. Because Lucky's mother had died soon after Lucky was born, Nonna had been both grandmama and mama to her, and Lucky had never wanted for love or instruction or correction, when she required them. Nonna managed the estate ably—or as ably as she could, given how little money they had to keep the place running. She was expert at all the little economies, all the growing of vegetables and canning of fruit, the careful husbanding of the roast for soups and stews. When Nonno or Papa brought back duck or pheasant or goose from their shooting, she would pluck and dress those birds herself. Still, sometimes it seemed like she did all those things to keep herself busy, to keep her head and hands occupied with practical tasks in the here and now, so they wouldn't stray off on their own to heaven knew where.

What really held Nonna to earth was Nonno. They shared some unspoken bond that was more than love—it was like all the sorrow of the world, known only to them, borne by them together. Only Nonno could make Nonna laugh—really *laugh*, like she meant it—and sometimes Lucky would turn the corner into a room, or some section of garden, and discover them sitting close, or standing together, their arms circled around each other, not kissing or anything, just touching their foreheads together as if to transmit thoughts through bone and skin, instead of speaking them aloud. So when Nonno died in that terrible March of 1939—pneumonia that snuck up at the raw, cold end of winter and carried him off in a week—Nonna was like a sailboat that had somehow lost its moorings. Nobody knew what to do with her. She would wander the house and grounds at all hours, singing to herself.

All spring and summer it was like that. Lucky took over the running of the household, the chores. Then one morning at the beginning of September they sat in the kitchen and listened in horror to the news bulletins on the radio. Papa's face was heavy and grave. Nobody spoke. Nonna rose to make more coffee. When she returned to the table with the coffeepot, she announced in a calm, lucid voice, not to be argued with, that it was time Lucia went to America to visit her family, and Nonna would take her there by the first available steamship.

Only years later did Lucky learn that Papa had been actively supporting the opposition to Mussolini's government, that Nonna had taken her away because of the danger, and that in the summer of 1943 Lucky's father had been lined up against a stone wall in Florence and shot to death after the Gestapo had discovered the Jews hiding in the wine cellar at their villa outside the city.

BUT EVEN AT her worst, after Nonno died, Nonna had never acted like *this*. Wet and shivering, bathed in the light of the newborn sun, she sat on the rocks and sang. Lucky dropped next to her and gathered her close. The frail bones shocked her. *Nonna,* she whispered.

Her grandmother paid no attention. *Mi struggo e mi tormento,* she warbled. Joanie came up behind Lucky, panting a little.

"Help me get her up," Lucky said.

Joanie put her little hand on Nonna's arm and tugged. "Come on, Nonna," she said. "It's morning. Let's go get some breakfast."

Nonna broke off. "But we can't just leave her here," she said.

Lucky and Joanie traded glances. "Who, Nonna?" Joanie said. "Leave who here?"

"It was my fault," Nonna whispered. "It was all my fault. I don't deserve . . . don't deserve . . ."

"Nonna, please," said Lucky. "Come inside. It's all over now."

"But what if someone finds her?"

Lucky put her hands firmly under Nonna's shoulders and drew her up. "You're just dreaming, Nonna. It's just a dream. I'm here, Joanie's here. You're not alone."

"Lucia," said Nonna.

"That's right. Come on, now. One step at a time. Careful."

Joanie took Nonna's right arm. Lucky took the left. Step-by-step, they led her over the rocks and past the boathouse, where the rising tide had begun to rush at the pilings. The old boards creaked and groaned. When they reached the Cliff Walk, Nonna stopped, turned her head over her shoulder, and whispered into the breeze.

Lucky wasn't quite sure what she said, but it sounded like *Forgive me*.

WITH JOANIE'S HELP, Lucky bathed Nonna, slipped a fresh white nightgown over her head, and put her to bed. She gave Angela strict instructions to make sure Nonna napped until lunchtime. A quick glance inside Stuy's bedroom revealed him deeply asleep, the curtains drawn tight over the windows. Long, sputtering snores intruded the quiet, like the revving of a motorcycle. When Lucky had switched off the bedside lamp last night at eleven o'clock and tucked her book neatly on the nightstand, he still hadn't returned home from wherever he was.

Lucky checked her watch and saw it was only ten minutes past seven. She looked down at Joanie's anxious face and forced herself to smile.

"Let's get dressed and go for a walk to clear our heads, okay?"

They walked south along the cliff path, toward Bailey's Beach. Joanie skipped ahead, playing hopscotch with her shadow. Sometimes she stopped to examine a rock or a shell, maybe the remains of a crab dropped by a breakfasting seagull, and her inquisitive expression reminded Lucky of Nonna—so much, she caught her breath. And it was funny, because if you set their two faces next to each other, Maybelle di Conti and Joanie Sprague, you saw only the faintest fragments of resemblance lingering across the generations, great-grandmother to great-granddaughter.

Along this stretch of the Cliff Walk, the terrain flattened out and the path crumbled into shingles, and Lucky's sandals slipped and skidded on the rocks. The breeze was picking up now; the waves rolled in and slapped against the rocks with new urgency, reminding Lucky that she had work to do, a whole list of telephone calls and errands waiting for her back in her office. She had no right to be taking walks like this, only four days before the party!

Still, she went on. She followed Joanie's bright yellow dress as it bobbed along the edge of the shore and found the path again on the other side. Joanie turned and called out, *Come on, Mama!* and instead of calling Joanie back, telling her it was time to return home, Lucky hurried after her down the twists and bends, the tall hedges to her right protecting the privacy of the houses on Bellevue Avenue, until the path crumbled away again to a rocky beach and Lucky stopped. This house had no hedge, only a small line of shrubbery to mark out the boundary between private garden and public pathway. On the other side of the shrubbery you could see the terraced Italian-style garden and the elegant rear of the house itself—a house Lucky knew well, because it belonged to Teddy Winthrop and his wife, Alice.

Lucky stood a moment, shading her eyes although the sun was behind her. Not a creature stirred in the gardens or the house. The morning sunshine bathed the stone facade in warmth, so it seemed almost alive, blood pulsing beneath the surface. That was an illusion, of course. Houses didn't *live,* no matter how beautiful. A single green-and-white-striped umbrella interrupted the line of the terrace, matching the green-and-white-striped awnings that protected the windows from the sun's fierce glare. Underneath that umbrella sat a pair of wicker chairs, both empty.

"Well, what do we have here? A selkie? Right here on my own beach?"

Lucky whirled around just in time to hear Joanie's answering giggle as the owner of the house—dripping with salt water, wearing a pair of navy swim trunks and nothing else—lifted her daughter high in the air and whirled her around in a couple of flying circles.

"Teddy!" she exclaimed. "I didn't know—I'm so sorry—"

"Sorry for what?" He set down Joanie and reached for the towel that lay folded on a rock nearby. "It's a nice surprise, finding the two of you right here at the end of a long swim."

"Well, I didn't mean to—I forgot you like to swim in the morning—"

"Mama," Joanie said, "your face is all red."

"It's just the sun, darling."

"Joanie," said Teddy, "I've left my glasses on the garden table. D'you mind fetching them for me?"

Joanie ran off toward the lawn. Lucky turned to the ocean and stared across the twinkling morning water. Next to her, Teddy stood with his hands on his hips, towel draped over his wide, spare shoulders. There was not an ounce of extra weight on him. He was like a monk, she thought, eschewing all luxuries of the flesh. Mortifying himself with hard exercise and lean diet and long hours of study.

"Listen," he said softly. "About the other day."

"I shouldn't have—have flung myself at you like that. I've been meaning to apologize—"

"There's no need for apology between the two of us, Lucky. I know what things are like for you."

Lucky turned her head toward him and concentrated on his face, which was oddly naked without the glasses. Just the clean angles of cheekbone and jaw, his blue eyes narrowed against the sun, his hair wet against his skull. "Do you? Do you really?"

Teddy opened his mouth and hesitated. He glanced to the lawn, where Joanie skipped toward the garden table like a small yellow bird. "I've known Stuy most of my life, Lucky. He's not a bad fellow, not like his dad at all. But some people . . . well, it's like they say. Some people should never get married."

"Is that so? And what about *your* wife?"

The words popped out before she even realized she was thinking them. She started to take them back, but Teddy held up his hand.

"Alice and I . . ." He stopped and rubbed his forehead with one finger. "I love Alice very much. She's like a sister to me. I think you know that."

Lucky stared up the velvet lawn. As if watching an actor in a play, she saw Joanie lift the glasses triumphantly from the garden table and start back toward them. She cast desperately for something to say, anything at all, but her heart pounded too hard. She couldn't think.

Teddy said softly, "It seems to me you're in need of a friend, right now."

"What kind of friend do you mean?"

"Whatever kind you need me to be."

"What I *need* . . . I don't know. I don't know what I need. Everything's falling apart, don't you see? Everything's cracking, all at once. I don't know what to do."

He stepped closer. "Listen. I'm booked on the *Cristoforo Columbo* out of New York next Sunday, right after the party—"

"That soon?"

"Well, I can delay the trip, if you want. Or . . ."

"Or?"

"Or I can book another stateroom for you and Joanie."

The world seemed to whirl around her. "But—but what about Alice?"

"I'll speak to Alice. She'll understand."

"She'd understand the three of us running off to *Italy* together?"

At that instant, Joanie's voice sang out between them. "*Italy*? We're going to *Italy*?"

Lucky startled and looked down at her daughter, who had skipped near with Teddy's glasses and now stood staring up at the two of them, pink-faced.

Teddy crouched down and took the glasses from Joanie's hand.

"What do you say, scamp? Would you like to visit Italy and see the castle where your mama was born?"

"You were born in a *castle*, Mama?" Joanie shrieked.

"Not really—"

"What? Your mother hasn't told you she's a princess?"

"Oh, Teddy, *stop*."

"A *princess*, Mama?"

"Mr. Winthrop's just teasing, sweetheart. Now come along. We have to get back home before Daddy wakes up."

Joanie took her hand and tugged it. "*Can* we, Mama? Can we go to Italy with Mr. Winthrop?"

Lucky looked at Teddy. The water still trickled from his hair, down his temple to his jaw, where he brushed it away with the corner of his towel. One side of his mouth turned upward in a soft, abashed grin. Behind his glasses, slightly fogged, his eyes were as warm as the sun.

"Of course not," Lucky said. "Mr. Winthop is just being silly."

She turned and drew Joanie back up the path toward home.

LUCKY SAW THE trouble at once, as soon as she turned off the path into the Sprague Hall gardens. So did Joanie. "Oh, look, Mama! There's a car in the driveway!"

"I see it. And if I'm not mistaken, it's your aunt Louise and uncle Reggie."

Joanie wrinkled her nose. "Aunt Louise smells like rotten flowers."

"That's just her perfume, Joanie. And it's very expensive perfume, so you mustn't tell her you don't like it."

"Why not?"

Lucky paused. "You know what, gumdrop? That's a very good question. I'll let you decide."

By now they could hear Louise's voice, carrying from the open windows in staccato bursts. Stuy's replies came in cranky shouts. Probably his sister had rousted him out of bed, Lucky thought, with a tiny satisfaction that did nothing to dilute the dread of dealing with Louise, on top of everything else.

And just where is that wife of yours? Louise demanded, on cue.

Lucky drew a deep breath and swept through the French doors into the sunroom.

"Here I am!" she said cheerfully. "Just out for a morning walk with Joanie. How are you, Louise?"

"Simply *exhausted*." Louise kissed the air next to Lucky's cheek. "Drove up from Long Island this morning."

"Did you? But we weren't expecting you until Thursday."

Louise plucked off her white cotton gloves and smiled sweetly. "Daddy called and said we should come up today. He said you wouldn't mind. I mean, there's plenty of room in the old barn, isn't there?"

Lucky forced herself to smile. "Of course. I'll tell Angela to air the beds when she's finished with the cleaning."

"Can't she do it now? I was hoping to lie down for a bit. Tell her to send up a breakfast tray, too."

Lucky glanced at Stuy, who had happily relinquished the care and feeding of his sister to Lucky and now sprawled on a wicker sofa, lighting a cigarette. He still wore his dressing gown, belted carelessly around his waist—hair askew, eyes squinted against the morning sun, shadows bruising the skin beneath. The hand that lit the cigarette trembled a little.

"I'll do what I can," Lucky said, "but I'm sure you understand my time's not my own at the moment. The party's in four days and I'm just run off my feet."

"Don't worry about a thing. We'll make ourselves at home."

Louise's husband spoke up from the corner of the room, where he seemed to be mixing Bloody Marys at the liquor cabinet. "So how much time does the old man have left?"

"I beg your pardon?"

Reggie started across the room and handed Stuy a tall glass. "Here you are, old chap. Hair of the dog and all that. I mean the pater, of course. Lou seems to think he's at death's door at last." He propped himself on the arm of the wicker sofa, next to Stuy.

"Reggie, *really.*" Louise made a brittle laugh. "I said nothing of the *kind.*"

Reggie winked at Lucky. Louise had found him in London somewhere, not long after the war, and he'd been only too glad to marry her and leave England behind forever. Louise insisted he was the younger son of an earl or something. Reginald Pelham-Mayhew—how could you argue with a name like that? His accent had a curious habit of swinging between an exaggerated Mayfair drawl and—when he was drunk, anyway—a fluent and profane brogue. He also took a sharp interest in the fixtures and fittings of Sprague Hall. But he was handsome, all right, if you liked sleek dark hair and sharp-painted features, and Louise simply adored him. They spent their summers racketing between Sprague Hall and various friends in the Hamptons, and the rest of the year in Palm Beach, surviving mostly—so far as Lucky knew, because Reggie had no evident employment—on handouts from Dudley Sprague. The pater, as Reggie called him.

"Well?" he said. "Any word? Throwing off his mortal coil at last?"

"He had a bad attack last week," Lucky said, "but they're giving him some kind of experimental medication, and he seems to be getting along. Stuy's been visiting him."

Stuy blew out a cloud of smoke. "Jaundiced as a dandelion as of yesterday afternoon. Might last a week, might last another month or two."

"Damned tough little bugger, isn't he?" said Reggie.

"Reggie, *please.*" Lucky tilted her head toward Joanie, who sat on the wicker chair across from Stuy and Reggie, swinging her legs and eyeing the grown-ups with the silent, intelligent curiosity of an only child.

"Oh, righto." Reggie zipped his lips. "Anyway, Louise wanted to scamper on up before he finishes this business with the will."

"What business with the will?" asked Lucky.

"Why, didn't your husband tell you?" Reggie elbowed Stuy in the shoulder. "The pater's decided to rewrite the whole thing, top to bottom."

"LOOK," STUY SAID, lighting another cigarette, "I didn't think it was that important. What's to change? There's not much money left, after all. And the house is yours. As you so frequently remind us."

"It's not mine, it's Nonna's."

He shrugged. "What's the difference? Nonna's off her rocker. Prob'ly kick off herself before long."

He sat in the overstuffed chintz chair in Lucky's small office, and without the flattering glow cast by the morning sun, his face looked even more gaunt than before. In his left hand, he held the remains of his second Bloody Mary. His right held the cigarette.

"You don't even care, do you?" Lucky said. "As long as the money keeps up."

"Why should I? Dad's always been a bastard. Your nonna—well, she's a harmless old bird, I guess, but she looks right through me, like I'm not even there."

"You know, I could demand an audit. All this time he's been playing ducks and drakes with Nonna's money—why, all the way back when I was a kid and we were just scraping by in Italy, and he was living like a prince here in America. I could demand an audit, I could probably have all of you put in jail—"

"But why?" Stuy gestured with his cigarette. "You have everything you want, don't you? Everything except old Teddy, I guess. Or maybe you're having him, too?"

Lucky gasped. "How *dare* you! I've never *once*—"

"Oh, spare me the maidenly protest. I saw the two of you on the cliffs the other day. Nice and cozy, there on the path where anybody could see you."

"We were just—it wasn't what you think—"

Stuy shrugged and tipped some ash into the vase on Lucky's desk. "Whatever you say, darling."

Lucky's fingers sizzled. Her face grew hot and tight. She thought of Teddy's warm, bashful, eager face, bathed in salt water and sunshine, just about *imploring* her to run away with him, her and Joanie, leave all this behind and travel with him to a distant land, and what had she said?

Of course not.

Of course not, Teddy—she couldn't possibly betray her husband, couldn't possibly break her marriage vows. She couldn't possibly take Joanie away from her father and live sinfully with a lover, oh no!

She was an idiot.

Lucky whispered, "Do you know what you are? You're vultures. Vultures, all of you. You take our money and our—our *innocence*! You take our love and loyalty and just—just *live* on them!"

"Oh, for God's sake—"

"It's true! *Vultures*!"

Stuy sprang to his feet, eyes blazing. "Why the hell don't you just go back to Italy? My God, everything was *fine* until the two of you came back! Just go back to goddamn Italy, why don't you!"

"Maybe I will!"

"Mommy?"

Lucky and Stuy spun to the door, where Joanie stood, white-faced.

"Mommy, is it true?" she whispered. "You're going to leave?"

Stuy cackled out a laugh and dropped his cigarette in the vase. "I should be so lucky," he said, and walked out of the room.

CHAPTER THIRTEEN

Andie

Newport, Rhode Island
September 2019

IF I HAD ever been the sort of person where luck stood a chance of gracing me with more than a glancing blow, I might have left the yacht club after the disastrous meeting with Marc and driven straight to a casino and gambled what little money I had so I'd have the freedom of walking away from Sprague Hall, *Makeover Mansion*, and what remained of my once lofty career aspirations.

Instead, I found myself rumbling down the rutted driveway of Sprague Hall, my car belching exhaust as I pulled in next to a familiar Volvo station wagon. I grimaced, hoping that there might be two identical vehicles belonging to separate entities who might have a reason for visiting the house today. But the Greenwich Country Day back window sticker confirmed my suspicions that any luck that I might have once claimed had run out.

Despite the pressing schedule, I took my time exiting the car, searching for any last reserves of determination and fortitude that might have survived my meeting with Marc. I stood facing the direction of the water and breathed deeply. Autumn had quickly shut the door on summer, the nip of cold wind pushing nickel-hued clouds across gray skies. The distant thunder of waves crashing on the sea cliff rocks below warned of approaching winter. Yet the wind carried the scent of salt and the memory of summers past when life had been far less complicated. When I'd felt loved and protected in the small circle of my family. When I'd felt as if I had choices.

Meghan met me at the front door. I needed to tell her about my meeting with Marc before I saw the film crew to save her the embarrassment of tears and the temptation of handcuffing herself to an antique curio. We'd been warned about the direction the show would be heading, but we'd both managed to keep wearing our rose-tinted glasses, hoping we could win over the show's producers with our knowledge and passion for historic preservation. I'd even conceded that we would have to remove wallpaper and gut the old kitchen—all while wearing a pink construction hat and tool belt. And until my chat with Marc, I'd believed that I could do all those things while promoting the importance of saving our collective pasts by using upcycled cabinets and restored fixtures. I had believed it until the words "*Desperate Housewives* meets *Kardashian House Flip*" had been uttered and then I knew that we were doomed. I should have known sooner. It certainly wouldn't be the first time that I'd been so completely naive.

"I have some bad news . . . ," I began.

Meghan grabbed my elbow. "It has to wait. You're not going to believe who's here." She led me across the reception room, our footsteps on the bare marble floors echoing in the stripped-down space.

I pulled my arm back, trying to get her to stop, but she was apparently too determined to listen, or she was exhibiting the results from the new kickboxing classes she'd been taking. "I just met with Marc. . . ."

She dragged me through a door into the back hallway leading to the kitchen, where I'd first seen Luke and his sister, Hadley, and overheard them arguing. Just like they were doing now. "This is really the craziest thing. Remember all those gossip magazine articles and newspaper clippings you collected but haven't read?"

"That's not true," I said, stumbling after her. "I've glanced at them enough to know that there's nothing there I want to use. . . ."

Meghan stopped, making me bump into her. She swung around so that she faced me and put her hands on my shoulders before giving me a little shake. "She's *here*. In the *kitchen*." She began leading me forward again.

"Who is?" I demanded, trying to dig in my feet. I strained my neck to see into the kitchen without Hadley spotting me.

"Luke and Hadley's *mother*," she hissed. "The woman who was married to Ted Mungo."

"Who?"

She rolled her eyes. "Ted *Mungo*. The lead singer of one of the biggest rock bands in history—Glass Eye."

When I still didn't register recognition, she rolled her eyes again. "'Rolling Heads'? The song they blast at the start of just about every football game across the country? It's a legendary rock anthem."

It did sound vaguely familiar, but I'd never been a football fan. My mother, when she'd lived with us, had banned football from the television, saying it was too uncouth. By the time she'd left, my father's interest had dwindled enough that his previous enthusiasm had never rekindled. Or maybe he still hadn't given up hope that she'd return.

Meghan hissed out a breath. "Honestly, Andie, you should have done your research."

She stepped back at my scathing look. "Sorry. You did all the right research. On the house, anyway. It kills me inside to say this, but there's a lot more to the history of this house than just the architecture."

I jerked back. "Who are you and what have you done to my friend?"

"Funny. If you'd read all those articles you'd know." Meghan took a deep breath then pulled me back against the hallway wall so we couldn't be seen. "In a nutshell so you won't make a fool out of yourself: Luke's mom ran away to San Francisco in 1969 when she was eighteen and had relationships with several high-profile rock stars, but she only married Ted. She had Luke and Hadley late in life, but they kept her last name because she divorced their dad when they were babies so they never really knew him. Their mom continued with her groupie lifestyle after the divorce so the kids were raised here by Lucky."

"Why should I care?" I know I sounded belligerent, but I was still smarting from my meeting with Marc and wasn't in the mood to witness my best friend turning to the dark side.

"Because she's *here*. Hadley asked her to come from California in order to help press her case to Lucky about selling the house. I ran into them coming back from lunch and I knew you'd want to know right away. So you can do . . . whatever it is you need to do to stop her."

"Trust me, Meghan. After my talk with Marc, it might be best that they sell—if only to spare us both from being kicked out of the preservation community. Unless you think our careers could survive having '*Desperate Housewives* meets *Kardashian House Flip*' on our resumes."

Her eyes widened. "That's"—a shudder went through her—"despicable."

"That's what I was trying to tell you when you started dragging me through the house. According to Marc, it's the only way to save the show. And in complete disregard of the contract, Christiana wants us to get Lucky on film talking about her husband."

"Stuy?" At my look of surprise, she said, "*I* actually read through your folder. And I may have Googled some stuff, too."

I shrugged. "Not that it matters. Marc said I needed to speak with someone named Joanie to get through to Lucky. I have no idea who that is—he passed out before he could tell me—and even if I did, I'd like to think I have enough integrity left to just walk away."

"Did you say 'Joanie'?"

I could only nod, transfixed by the odd expression on Meghan's face, something between resignation and excitement.

"Integrity won't put food on the table or a roof over your head. How badly do you need this job, Andie?"

"I signed a contract! Regardless of how dysfunctional this family and this entire production is, I can't—"

With a soft grunt of frustration, Meghan grabbed my arm and propelled me toward the kitchen. I managed to dislodge my arm but we'd already been spotted by the four people standing amid the ruins of what had once been the outdated yet oddly charming kitchen. The room in which I'd been hoping to rescue as many of the vintage details as I could to save this particular space from looking like every other kitchen remodel.

I paused in the doorway, aware that the arguing had stopped and that I had become the focus of attention. I blinked, hoping I had somehow stepped into the wrong room or that my eyes needed to become accustomed to the dimmer light of the unlit kitchen.

The previous day's shoot had shown me in all of my pink glory smashing a sledgehammer into a Formica countertop in this very room. Later, while I'd been upstairs filming the bedroom segment and arguing about wallpaper, the invisible construction crew—hired to do all the heavy lifting off camera—had pulled up the laminate flooring to reveal glue-stained and water-damaged wood floors, and managed to remove the rest of the cabinets. All that remained was the ancient breakfast table with the cracked Formica top and wide metal edge. Four yellow vinyl chairs had been pushed against a wall, white stuffing erupting like lava from the cracked seats. Strips of brilliant blue duct tape had been slapped across the tears like Band-Aids, their edges now curling in defeat.

I bit my lip to stifle a cry at seeing the cabinets gone, knowing there'd be no opportunity now to update them with paint and new knobs. Not that there had ever been the sliver of a chance to begin with, but until seeing the denuded kitchen, I'd held out hope. But hope, as I'd first learned as a young girl watching her mother enter a taxi without a glance back, was an empty basket full of holes.

Hadley stalked toward me, her phone clutched in her white-knuckled hand, her eyes icy. Her words came at me with the staccato notes of a machine gun. "What. Have. You. Done?"

I almost looked behind me, with the hope that Marc had miraculously appeared. Anyone, really. At some point I'd have to realize that I was alone on my raft. And sinking fast. I faced Hadley. "I'm assuming you're referring to the gutting of the kitchen. To be honest, I had no idea this was happening. . . ."

"I'm going for backup," Meghan whispered as she retreated out of the doorway, leaving me alone to face the lion.

Hadley's lips were nearly white. "I told you to take your film crew and leave. Why are you still here, and why are you destroying this house? We can't sell it without a kitchen!"

"Actually, Mrs. Sprague-Armstrong, it might be easier to sell with a renovated kitchen—"

The soft voice came from the corner of the kitchen, where a diminutive man wearing a navy-blue suit and bow tie had wedged himself into the small space between the old refrigerator and the back door as if trying not to be noticed. His graying hair and clean-shaven chin indicated that he was probably in his forties, but he had the stature of a prepubescent boy, all spindly arms and legs and a skinny neck with an Adam's apple that protruded awkwardly, bobbing up and down like a terrified gerbil.

Hadley cut him off. "You are mistaken, Mr. Callihan. *I* certainly wouldn't buy a house without a kitchen. I thought you, as a very highly recommended real estate agent, would know better."

The man seemed to shrink another inch. "Of course—" he began, but was cut off by the sound of jangling coming from the other side of the kitchen.

I turned to see a woman dislodge herself from the side of an angry-looking Luke and walk toward me with outstretched arms, each covered with a dozen or so bracelets—apparently the source of the jangling. Her long hair, almost to her waist, lying in one thick braid tossed over her shoulder, was heavily streaked with white, almost overtaking the original bright blond. She wore a crown of sorts, made of fresh flowers that were now dead or on their way, as if the wearer hadn't known they would wilt quickly. But, judging by the woman's calm and warm smile, she wasn't the type to care. The drooping petals might have even added to the overall impression of otherworldliness. Her long skirt swayed with the same rhythm as the withered petals, giving her the appearance of floating like a ghost without feet.

I looked to make sure, and saw a pair of slender, pale feet tucked inside thin-soled cork sandals, the toenails bare. I was fairly confident that those toenails had never seen a drop of polish.

"Oh, my poor dear," she said as she embraced me in a bear hug that smelled of flowers. I was too shocked to pull away but stood there with my arms dangling. The woman and I were the same height so I was able to see Hadley's and Luke's faces over her shoulder. Hadley's skin was a mottled puzzle of red and white blotches, but Luke's lips were tugging upward in a reluctant smile.

The woman pulled back, leaving her hands on my shoulders. Her light blue eyes—the same shade as Hadley's and Luke's—searched mine. "Your aura is gray. And there are definitely black spots." She shook her head sadly. "That means you are sad and unbalanced."

I wasn't sure if she wanted me to agree or argue so instead I held out my hand. "I'm Andie Figuero. With *Makeover Mansion*. I'm sorry about the kitchen."

Instead of shaking my hand, she cupped it between her own two and gave it a gentle squeeze. "No need to apologize." Her voice was as pleasant and calming as her physical appearance and I had the unexpected wish that she would hug me again.

"Mother, this is that horrid woman I was telling you about—the host of that appalling show that is intent on nosing into our family business and airing all of our laundry on a television show. She's—"

Luke stepped forward. "Cut it out, Hadley. It's bad enough that you dragged our mother across the country and hired a real estate agent—all against Lucky's wishes—but to attack Andie when she's done nothing except do the job she was hired to do is beneath even you."

Hadley sucked in her breath and opened her mouth, but nothing came out, her outrage temporarily paralyzing her vocal cords.

"Come on, Joanie," Luke said, reaching his hand toward his mother, "let's get you settled in and I'll take you to see Lucky."

Joanie? I stared at the woman, her name bringing the kitchen and its occupants into sharp focus. This was Lucky and Stuy's daughter. The person whom Marc had told me I needed to speak with to get to Lucky. The person who could help me do the one thing I was contractually, ethically, and professionally bound *not* to do. The one thing that might save my job.

Ignoring Hadley, Joanie smiled at me before dropping my hand and reaching for a small leather pouch tied around her waist. "I'm going to have my guru send you aura cleansing incense bricks." She opened the drawstring of the pouch and peered inside before extracting a smooth, dark, oval-shaped stone. "In the meantime, I want you to take this hematite crystal." She picked up my hand and carefully placed the stone into my opened palm. "It works to ground our energy and strengthen and seal the aura as well as offering protection and a stabilizing effect. It also helps us to work systematically through our responsibilities and choices."

I closed my fingers over the stone, the initial chill overtaken by an odd, radiating sensation I felt down in my toes. I was sure it was my imagination, wanting desperately to believe that something as simple as a crystal could help solve all of my ailments, the least of which being the ability to work through my conflicting responsibilities and choices.

"Thank you," I said, carefully placing the stone in my pocket.

"Mother!" Hadley's voice had risen at least a decibel, and Mr. Callihan now appeared to be actively searching for an escape route. "This is neither the time *nor* the place for this ridiculousness."

Hadley's phone rang. After plucking it from her Kelly bag, she stabbed her finger onto the screen and slid it across to answer. She turned her back and stepped away from us, but remained in the kitchen, every word audible despite her attempt to lower her voice. "Is anyone bleeding from the eyeballs? I told you not to call me for anything less. It's why I pay you the exorbitant rates you charge." She waited a moment, the sound of a disembodied voice mumbling on the other end. "I don't care if the afternoon nanny hasn't shown up. You can't just leave three children unattended. You'll simply have to reschedule your doctor's appointment. I'm tied up at the moment and can't come home. Wait until Rebecca shows up, and let me know when she does so I can dock her pay."

From the corner of my eye, I spotted George outside in the hallway, the camera light on. I had no idea how long he'd been there, or how much he'd recorded, but if Marc and Christiana were hoping to capture more drama than replastering a wall, we'd just succeeded. I wasn't sure if I was happy or disgusted that I was happy.

"What are you doing?" Hadley screeched, her gaze settling on the cameraman. She lunged in George's direction, but was held back by Luke, his jaw tense as if deciding on whose team he was supposed to be.

Luke continued his hold on his twin, his expression grim. I imagined that King Solomon wore the same expression when confronted with the two women claiming to be the mother of the same child. "Calm down, Hadley," he said through gritted teeth. "Lucky wants the filming." He glared at George. "But no footage of the family. It's in the contract so you need to stop now."

Joanie waved at George, who continued to film. "Come on in and pay no mind to our little family drama." Speaking into the camera, she said, "I welcome a camera within these walls. There is too much of our hidden past lurking in them, and it's darkening everyone's auras." She raised her arms, the gold bangles clinking together. "I say it's beyond time to open up about our past, to cleanse this house and this family of all of its secrets. I think we should look at this as a fabulous opportunity to refresh and renew." Joanie beamed at me. "Perhaps we should be thanking Andie instead of trying to fire her."

"Joanie," Luke began, his voice carrying a warning, "that is not what Lucky—"

"We'll see about that!" Hadley pulled away from Luke, then turned to the cowering agent. "Come on, Jeremy. I need to show you the rest of the house. Ignore the film crew. They won't be here for long." With a glowering look aimed at me, Hadley exited the room, Mr. Callihan scurrying behind her.

"She's always been a little dramatic. She gets that from her father." Joanie put her arm around me and gave a squeeze before locating two stray chairs for us. After sweeping construction dust off the seats with her hand, the movement sending her bangles into waves of euphoria, she sat down and patted the chair next to her. "Why don't you and I get to know each other a little better, Andie? Seeing as how we're going to be practically roommates for the next few weeks."

I thought about the rest of the crew upstairs, waiting for my direction, and the four-thirty curfew. But then I realized that I was somehow with the enigmatic Joanie through no machinations of my own. It was as if my luck had finally taken a turn for the better, and regardless of my conscience raising its hand to object, I sat down.

Luke marched over to George, his hand held up flat to block the lens. "Turn it off. Now. Unless Lucky says it's allowed, there can be no filming of the family."

George glanced over at me, and at my nod the red light flickered off and he lowered the camera. "Why don't you film some more 'before' footage of the ballroom—make sure you get a lot of close-ups of the ceiling murals. The plan is to cover them in shiplap, so we'll need to record them for posterity. And please tell Meghan I'll be up shortly. But don't tell her about the shiplap."

As George turned to leave, I added, "Oh, and please get some footage of the faded rectangles on the walls. I'd like to find photos of what used to be there to be included with the historical portion of the show." Assuming they'd allow it, but I had to at least try.

Joanie picked up her sandal-clad foot and pushed out another chair. "Why don't you sit down, Luke? I think you should get to know Andie, too."

Luke and I looked at each other in alarm as he sat down next to his mother. "But not for too long. Andie has to be gone by four thirty. Lucky's rules."

Joanie nodded slowly. "Ah. Teddy?"

Luke nodded.

I sat up. "Teddy Winthrop? We knew that was him in the Bugatti. When Meghan—my technical consultant—and I saw him yesterday. Is he a friend of Lucky's?"

"You could say that." A soft smile crossed Joanie's face. "I've known him all my life. He was like a second father to me. And after my own father left us, Teddy easily slid into the role permanently. I didn't know he was famous until I was much older and had moved away. To me he was always just Teddy."

I recalled something I'd read, something about her father that had resonated with me. Stuy. And I suddenly remembered why. "Your father left you and your mother. When you were just a little girl."

She nodded, studying me closely. "Your aura just darkened. As if you were there or know what it's like to be left behind. I think there's a story there."

There was something about Joanie Sprague, beyond the hippie accoutrements and crystals, something much more cerebral and authentic and . . . motherly. Or maybe it was just wishful thinking. Whatever it was, I felt the need to tell her the one thing I never talked about with anyone. Even Meghan hadn't known for three years before I'd shared the story with her.

"My mother left our family when I was twelve and my sister ten. She wanted more from life than a boatbuilder could give her. Melissa and I were just collateral damage. She lives in Los Angeles now with her new husband and is a designer for the stars. Which makes sense, I guess. She read all those design magazines like some people read the Bible, and had pages taped up all over the house, saying my dad needed encouragement to work harder so we could afford beautiful things. Until she realized that wasn't going to happen. So she left."

I felt Luke shift in his chair, but I was too ashamed to look at him. Joanie covered my hand with her own. "I know how painful that must have been for you and your sister. It's not something we get over easily."

I looked away at the mention of Melissa. But the way she'd said *we* warmed me to her, as if after all this time I'd somehow managed to find a kindred spirit.

Joanie patted my hand then sat back in her chair. "Some rumors say that Teddy killed my father because he was having an affair with my mother. Which is ridiculous, really. Teddy is the gentlest, kindest person I've ever met. Other rumors claimed that my father ran off with one of his many girlfriends. I grew up believing the latter until I became an adult and developed my own theory. Personally, I think he killed himself."

"Joanie . . ." Luke's voice carried a warning.

Ignoring him, Joanie continued. "They found his boat adrift with a good stockpile of empty liquor bottles. He was an expert sailor, but if a person is drunk enough—and I do believe he was a functioning alcoholic for most of his adult life—they're not capable of rational thought. Or maybe it was an accident." She shrugged, releasing a calming cloud of lavender. "Who knows. They never found his body. But he was obviously not mentally sound at the time of his disappearance. It's why I've chosen to devote my life to mental health issues and am on the board of several mental health charities back in California."

Luke slid back his chair and stood. "I think you've said enough, and Andie needs to get back to work. Don't you, Andie?"

I stood, but hesitated, remembering the ultimatum Marc had given me. Joanie's unexpected and calming presence emboldened me. "Joanie . . . ," I began, *Ms. Sprague* sounding too formal.

She looked at me expectantly.

I thought of Petey, and my father, and the broken furnace. And Melissa. Always Melissa. My pride and integrity would have to take a distant last place in my list of wants and needs. I took a deep breath. "I would like to speak with Lucky. To get her permission to film her—and you. To get your personal stories as they relate to the house. And I'd like to ask if we could film down by the water, at the boathouse. I've seen it and it's a wreck. I think it would be a fun and interesting addition to the show if we could fully renovate it—"

Joanie interrupted me with a surprisingly deep, throaty laugh. "Oh, my dear Andie. My mother hasn't even allowed *me* near the boathouse since my father disappeared. I think the whole theory that he may have drowned made her frightened of water. I don't think you have a chance at changing her mind about that. However, if you want her permission to interview us on camera, well, it won't work asking her directly."

"What do you mean?"

She stood and slid a couple of bangles off her wrist. "You need to go through Teddy. She's had an enormous soft spot where he's concerned for as long as I've known him. If you want her to say yes, you've got to get him to agree first."

"But . . . ," I began, watching as she placed the bangles on my arm.

"There! Now you look fully dressed." She stood on her tiptoes to kiss Luke on the cheek. "You look tired, dear. You both could benefit from meditation and yoga. I'll expect the two of you in the ballroom tomorrow morning at seven o'clock. I'll provide the mats. I'm going to go rest now." She patted Luke's cheek then gave me a hug before leaving.

I met Luke's gaze. "What just happened?"

"Welcome to my world."

"Seems like it's not a bad place to be." I tried to keep the reproach from my voice. My own mother's abandonment had nothing to do with him.

He stared at me as I raised my hand to tuck hair behind my ear. "You're jingling."

I surprised myself by laughing. "I suppose I am."

"Andie." He paused. "Why didn't you ask me about talking to Lucky?"

"Because I knew you'd say no. And I didn't really consider it a necessity until today. There have been . . . developments that make the matter more pressing."

He waited for me to say more. Instead, I looked at my watch. "I've got to go. I was actually hoping to close up shop a little early today—teacher conference at Petey's school. My dad said he'd go, but I really want to be there."

His eyes, identical in color to his sister's but with all the warmth Hadley's lacked, regarded me closely. "It must be hard. Being a single mom. I know it was for Joanie. And Lucky."

I shrugged, uncomfortable under his scrutiny. "It is what it is. We manage. He's a great kid so it makes it easier."

Luke nodded. "Does his father help in any way?"

I froze. Despite his look of genuine interest and the gentle tone of his voice, I reverted to my safety zone of distance and deflection. I couldn't lose sight of who Luke Sprague was, the yacht-club frat-boy type who looked at women with the same consideration they would at comparing teakwoods for a deck, and collected them like racing trophies.

I pretended to study my phone, acting as if I hadn't heard him. "So, what do you do when you're not running interference for your grandmother and sailing with your friends?"

The warmth in his eyes disappeared. He was silent so long I thought he wasn't going to answer. Almost reluctantly, he said, "I was working in Guatemala with Doctors Without Borders, but Lucky needed me so I came home."

It wasn't the answer I'd expected, but it didn't change my response. "Must be nice to only have to work when you want to."

He didn't flinch, but his eyes hardened, resembling his sister's more than I thought they could. "Well, then, don't let me stand in the way of real work." Without another word, he left the room, his footsteps echoing down the long hallway.

I waited until I'd heard the slam of a door before following but stopped when I caught sight of an object left on an upturned paint can behind where Luke had been standing. It was the toy sailboat I'd broken when I'd wrenched it out of Petey's hands, the one Luke said Petey could have. I picked it up, the miniature mast that had snapped in my hand now whole, the repair invisible as if it had been done by the hands of an expert surgeon. I put it down, feeling unworthy of his gift.

I walked quickly out of the room but stopped in the deserted hallway, the humming of the ancient refrigerator behind me the only sound. "I'm sorry," I said to no one, my words once again too late.

CHAPTER FOURTEEN

Ellen

Newport, Rhode Island
July 1899

I'M SORRY," ELLEN apologized for the fiftieth time, edging past a group of bathers as she searched for Dudley.

She had been saying that a great deal. In the twenty minutes since they had arrived at Bailey's Beach, Dudley had already managed to put a crab down someone's back and pink a fashionable matron in an unmentionable part of her anatomy with the mast of his toy sailboat. The sailboat had survived the experience. So had Dudley, but only barely. It had taken all of Ellen's ingenuity to keep Mrs. Rheinlander from boxing his ears.

Ordinarily, this wouldn't be Ellen's problem. But Dudley had finally done it; he'd driven Mr. Whitmarsh to take a position at Groton, on the grounds that forty brats couldn't be as much trouble as one. Ellen had hated to see him go—and not only because his departure meant that she'd been conscripted as nursemaid. Mr. Whitmarsh, like Ellen, had occupied that odd, intermediate ground between upstairs and downstairs. Without him, she felt entirely alone and left strangely bare.

Not to mention saddled with Dudley.

From music teacher to both housekeeper and nursemaid in one

month. What next? Ellen wondered irritably as she worked her way among the bathers. She swiped a lock of sweat-damp hair out of her eyes. Would she be expected to cook as well? Dust the downstairs rooms? Draw Mr. Sprague's bath?

Now there was a thought too dreadful to be contemplated.

A cry from the water drew her attention. Ellen hurried in that direction, but as she broke through a cluster of parasols, she saw it wasn't Dudley; it was Frank Pratt, holding Maybelle aloft as she clung to his neck and shrieked.

Ellen checked at the edge of the water, distracted from her search for Dudley by this new and entirely unwelcome spectacle.

"Mr. Pratt!" Maybelle's cheeks were becomingly flushed, her fair hair dampened around her face. "You know I can't swim."

"Don't worry. I wouldn't let you sink." Pratt winked over Maybelle's shoulder at one of his friends. He dipped her playfully toward the water. "Although that bathing costume does look awfully heavy. Once they start sucking up water—"

"Mr. Pratt!" Maybelle clutched at his shoulders in genuine alarm.

"Now, Frank," said Prunella Schuyler indulgently, wafting a handkerchief at her cousin. "You must remember that not everyone has your athletic prowess."

"Just a little dip." Ellen didn't at all like the way Pratt was holding Maybelle. Yes, things were different at the beach, but should she be allowing such liberties? "You can't come to Bailey's Beach and not bathe. It's against the rules."

"Is it, really?" Maybelle looked at Pratt wide-eyed, ready to be convinced of anything he said.

Ellen felt a surge of frustration, born of fear and powerlessness. Did Maybelle need to bare her breast for the slaughter like those beasts in the paintings on the dining room wall? She was all but inviting Pratt to take advantage of her ignorance and there was nothing Ellen could do about it.

This was all wrong. Maybelle desperately needed a chaperone, a proper chaperone, a mother or older sister, someone who could tell her what not to do and scare off the fortune hunters. What did Ellen know? She wasn't of this world. She wasn't even of the fringes of this world. It hadn't mattered when all she was meant to do was teach music. She knew music. What she didn't know was this. This world. These rules. Maybelle needed better.

But Maybelle didn't have better. Maybelle had her.

Ellen tried to edge her way past, to signal to Maybelle, but Mrs. Schuyler very deliberately planted her parasol in Ellen's path, blocking her way.

Mrs. Schuyler looked Ellen up and down from her sandy buttoned boots to the flowers trimming her one and only hat, drawling, "Aren't you meant to be minding that little beast with the boat? Really, it's just impossible to get decent help these days."

"Don't you worry," crooned Pratt to Maybelle. "You'll be swimming like a fish in no time."

Prunella Schuyler's attention was diverted. "You mean like a mermaid, Frank," she called impatiently, abandoning Ellen to mince her way to the edge of the surf. "Not a fish. Although some fish do have rather lovely iridescent scales. I wonder if my dressmaker could do something about that. . . ."

"Like a mermaid," repeated Frank Pratt, baring his teeth at his cousin in a fixed smile. He set Maybelle down on her feet in the surf. "You'll be swimming like a mermaid."

"What if—what if a wave knocks me over?"

"Then I'll catch you," said Pratt, a little too heartily, casting his cousin Prunella a self-righteous look. There was no doubt in Ellen's mind who was really running this courtship. Pratt was merely a puppet, Prunella Schuyler the puppeteer.

"Now all he wants is to tell her that she will rise like Venus from the waves," said a cynical voice in Ellen's ear.

Ellen started, turning so fast that her nose bumped the prince's chin. "You startled me," she protested, backing away as quickly as dignity and her long skirt would allow.

The prince didn't allow himself to be drawn into apologies. He eyed Ellen's gray wool dress, ridiculously inappropriate for the seaside. "You're not dressed for bathing."

"I'm not here to bathe. I'm here to watch Dudley." Oh, goodness. In her concern for Maybelle, she had lost track of Dudley. Again. Ellen craned her neck, looking for signs of mayhem. "You haven't seen him, have you?"

"That creature doesn't need a nursemaid. He needs a warder." The prince's voice changed, became serious. "It is a waste of your talents."

"Mr. Sprague believes his servants should be able to put their hands to anything."

"You're a musician, not a servant."

He said it as though he meant it, as though she mattered. "My employer would beg to disagree."

"Your employer is a man of no refinement and less sense."

"He pays me." Let the prince decide what that made her. Ellen flapped a hand at Maybelle and Pratt, who was now holding her hand as he coaxed her out into the surf. "Oughtn't you intervene?"

"Why? She's unlikely to come to harm in such shallow waters."

Ellen frowned at the prince, trying to decide whether he was speaking of more than the nature of the waves. "You do know he's trying to cut you out, don't you?"

The prince seemed amused by her concern. "But of course."

"You don't mind?"

The prince gazed meditatively out at the swimming lesson, Maybelle in her bulbous black wool bathing costume clutching at Pratt's arm, Pratt preening at her obvious partiality. "It is a minor annoyance at best. And possibly a boon. It saves me having to dance attendance and say sweet things."

Ellen looked uncertainly at the prince, a queasy feeling at the pit of her stomach. If the prince was only toying with the Spragues, if he didn't mean to marry Maybelle, what would become of Maybelle? What would become of Ellen?

"But—I had thought—don't you mean to marry her?"

"Most likely." The prince shrugged as though it were a matter of little concern.

"But . . . oughtn't you to feel more strongly about it than that?"

"Oh, but I do." The prince looked directly at her, the intensity of his gaze unnerving. It was like coming out from the shadows into strong sunlight. "I feel strongly about preserving what is mine. My heritage. It is only for that that I am here."

"I don't understand."

"My family have been lords in the north since man crawled out of caves. To us, the Sforza were nothing but mercenaries for hire, the Borgias Spanish upstarts, the Medici mere money counters. We have ruled—and we have endured. Sometimes, we have survived by the sword." The prince locked his hands behind his back, his eyes on Maybelle. "And other times, in the marriage bed. When a Medici became pope, we married one of his illegitimate daughters. When Bonaparte began his march through Italy, we saved our lands and our title by a convenient marriage to one of his wife's Creole cousins. And now . . . an American."

Ellen shook her head, trying to clear it. The effect of all those generations, one on top of the other, was dizzying. "You speak as though you married them all yourself."

The prince smiled without humor. "I might as well have. It is all in the blood. And the end is all the same. We carry on. Generation after generation we carry on."

Like felons chipping away at rock. "That sounds rather . . . grim."

The prince's lips twisted. "There are consolations. The cage is lined in the very finest velvet—and I may sport myself as I will."

Something about the way he said it made Ellen's skin tingle. A cage lined in the very finest velvet . . . she'd seen more than a maiden ought at the Hibernia. But none of it had made her tremble like this.

Well, he wasn't going to sport himself with her.

"That's all very well," said Ellen, rather more stridently than she intended. "But what about your future wife? What about you? Oughtn't either of you to have a say?"

"Spoken like a true daughter of the new world, where man is the measure of all things and you have no thought to anything but the present."

"You say that as though it's a bad thing," said Ellen, stung. "Perhaps most of us have pasts we don't care to think about."

"Do you have a past, little music teacher?"

Murder and betrayal, bodies in the harbor, and small rented rooms. "Doesn't everyone? But I can't sit there counting my ancestors. I have my bread to earn. I have no choice but to think of the present, however distasteful you may find it. If you'll pardon me—"

"Sheath your claws." The prince put up a hand. He didn't touch her, but the movement had the force of a royal command. "What did I say to make you flee?"

He wasn't the one who had made her flee. That was Dermot. Running and running, still, even now.

"You shouldn't be wasting your words on me, that's all," said Ellen smartly. "Say it to Miss Sprague. All she wants is a bit of attention. If you would only . . ."

"Recite poetry to her? Mouth sweet nothings?"

"Yes! Would that be so hard?"

The words burst out of her with all the heat and frustration of the day. If she could just make one thing right, one small thing, if she could make this prince, this strange, arrogant, fascinating man exert one iota of his charm on the woman he meant to make his wife, she could feel that she had accomplished something, made someone's life better. That there was some purpose to her existence.

The prince stared at her, struck by her vehemence.

"I find," he said slowly, "that while my honor will permit me to marry for gain, to pretend to an ardor I do not feel is another matter entirely."

Ellen tilted her head back to try to see his face better without the brim of her hat getting in the way. "A business contract, then. Is that how you see it?"

"It is cleaner so."

Ellen's heart ached for her friend, for Maybelle, who wanted so badly to be loved, even just a little. "For you, perhaps. But what about Maybelle? Is your honor worth more than her pride?"

He didn't answer that, not really. "Would you have me lie to her like that Pratt?"

"No." Ellen stared miserably at the stretch of sand between them, poking at a bit of seaweed with one booted toe. She looked up at him, trying to find a middle ground, a way that would spare both their feelings. "But couldn't you . . . mightn't you . . . isn't there the chance you might come to care? If you willed it so?"

The prince's eyes were very green in the sunlight. Ellen couldn't look away from them. "Cupid's arrow flies where it will. Or hadn't you heard?"

That was mere self-indulgence, that was what Ellen meant to tell him. But she couldn't seem to muster the words. They all dried on her tongue as the weak New England sun made halos around them, bathing the prince in gold, making her forget what she meant to say, making her forget herself.

"Gotcha!"

Ellen stumbled as she was yanked backward by her hat, hair tearing from her scalp with a searing pain that made her eyes water.

Thoroughly bewildered, she clapped her hands to her aching head. "My hat!"

The hat had been wrenched off her head. Her hair had been torn from its knot, wisps poking out any which way. Her hairpins lay scattered in the sand. Ellen's head ached, her eyes stung, and she could feel humiliation washing over her as she stood there bareheaded as Dudley took off down the beach, waving his prize in the air.

"Ha ha, can't catch me!" caroled Dudley joyfully.

Ellen would have gone after him, but the prince touched a hand to her arm. "Stay. It was my foolishness that distracted you. I shall retrieve your hat."

Numbly, Ellen put a hand over the spot the prince had touched as he sprinted after Dudley; she felt that the mark must show like a brand. She could feel it burning still. Foolishness. Ellen shook her head at herself, bending down to try to retrieve however many pins she could find. She felt shamed to the core, left bare and disheveled. She might be a servant, but she had some pride.

Maybe that was her mistake.

"Miss Daniels!" It was her employer, huffing and puffing, his figure not flattered by his black bathing costume.

"If it's about Dud—I mean, young Master Sprague—" Ellen began, hastily trying to reassemble her hair as best she could without a mirror.

Dudley turned to blow a raspberry at his pursuer, tripped over his own feet, and fell headlong into the sand before scrambling up, making straight for the water.

"Let the boy enjoy himself," said Mr. Sprague impatiently. "And stop that prinking. I don't pay you to beautify yourself. What are you doing letting Pratt make up to my sister?"

Letting? As if she had any other choice. "You told me to watch young Master Sprague. . . ."

Mr. Sprague took a moment to eye his offspring fondly. "Boys will be boys. Good lad, playing with the prince." Young Master Sprague was currently waving his battered trophy in a kind of strange victory dance. The prince took a flying leap at Dudley, just missing him as the boy feinted right and bumped into Prunella Schuyler, who spectacularly lost her balance, flailing with her parasol. "But keep that fortune hunter away from my sister! The man doesn't have a feather to fly with. I won't have it, you hear me?"

"Yes, sir, I understand."

Sprague turned his glare on Ellen. "As to that, what were *you* doing with His Highness?"

Ellen bit her lip, deciding honesty was the best policy. "Much the same thing you were just saying, sir. I suggested to him that Mr. Pratt might be trying to cut him out."

Sprague eyed Ellen, as though trying to discern whether she was telling the truth. "Good girl." He thrust his jowls in her general direction. "It is imperative that the prince come up to scratch. Do you understand me? Imperative."

"Yes, sir." Something about his urgency made Ellen uneasy. "I believe he could make Miss Sprague happy."

"Happy?" Sprague's brow wrinkled, as if trying to decipher a foreign tongue. "Right. Certainly. Naturally, my sister's happiness is my first concern. Just see that she finds that happiness with the prince and not that bootlicking hanger-on!"

As they both turned to look toward the ocean, Dudley elbowed the prince in the stomach, wrenching himself free. He spun Ellen's hat gleefully in the air before flinging it out to sea.

The prince gave Dudley a look that would have reduced a lesser mortal to mere ash. Then he took three running steps out into the waves and dove into the water, like one of the creatures Ellen's mother used to tell her stories of, part man, part seal. Never mind those college boys clowning in the shallows. The prince in the water was a thing of beauty, at one with the waves as he struck out in pursuit of Ellen's mistreated headgear, which appeared to be making rapidly for Greenland.

Mr. Sprague harrumphed loudly. "Miss Daniels! What are you doing standing there? I told you, you're to see Maybelle spends the rest of her time here with the prince. Retrieve him!"

"Yes, sir." Easier said than done. Ellen's feet sank into the damp sand as she held her hem as high as modesty would allow. The prince, invigorated, triumphant, waded out to meet her, holding aloft the sad remnants of her only hat.

The prince gave the hat an experimental shake, sending droplets of dye running down onto the sand. "I'm afraid your hat is somewhat the worse for its encounter with the ocean."

Numbly, Ellen put out a hand. The black felt wasn't black anymore, but a sort of streaky gray. The brim flopped loosely. The purple flowers that had once seemed so cheerful hung drunkenly off their stems, some broken off entirely, lost somewhere in the Atlantic.

The back of Ellen's throat itched. She blinked away silly tears, forcing herself to speak cheerfully. "It's no matter. It was just my only one."

"Take my hat," said the prince.

Ellen looked up abruptly from the ruin of her hat. "What? No. I couldn't."

The prince raised a hand as if to touch her cheek, stopping just short. "Your skin is too fair to be exposed to the elements."

"I'm not one of your fine ladies to be protected from life's harshness," Ellen said rapidly, not sure who she was trying to convince, the prince or herself. "Besides, this is Rhode Island, not Italy. Look, the sun's gone behind a cloud again."

"Even so . . . ," the prince began.

Ellen could feel Sprague watching them. Watching her.

"Really, I couldn't," she said urgently, crushing her ruined hat in her hands. "It would make me conspicuous. And one in my position can't afford to be conspicuous."

The prince's eyes searched her face. "All right," he said slowly. "But only because you ask it of me."

It was like something out of a fairy tale, to have a prince at her command. But she wasn't the princess; she was the serving maid. She had to remind herself of that. She had to remind the prince of that.

"Then I shall ask you something else," Ellen said, trying to make a jest of it, even though she didn't feel the least like laughing. "Won't you go wade with Maybelle?"

"What is it your poet says? 'I'll look to like, if looking liking move.'" The way he said it left no doubt of the prince's feelings, either about the Bard or the success of that particular strategy. He cocked a brow. "Would you like me to challenge young Pratt to a duel to show my devotion?"

Blood pooling on the floor of Dermot's office . . . Ellen could feel the blood draining from her face. She held up both hands. "No! No bloodshed."

"A romance, then, and not a tragedy." The prince affected a bow. Ellen looked over his shoulder, hoping no one had seen. A prince wasn't meant to bow to a music teacher. It wasn't the way things were done. "As you wish."

CHAPTER FIFTEEN

Lucky

Newport, Rhode Island
July 1957

LUCKY WISHED FOR a lot of things that Thursday morning—a cool breeze, a dozen extra pairs of hands, the world's largest gin and tonic—but most of all she wished the damn ball were over already.

The stage for the orchestra was now finished. The carpenters had just left, sweating from the terrible heat, and it looked pretty good, all things considered, covered by a giant striped awning so as to keep the musicians dry in the likely event of a summer squall. Lucky lifted her bangs from her brow and stared down the lawn to the Chinese teahouse and the blue ocean beyond, hanging motionless under the hot sky. To her left, chairs and tables were spread in stacks across the stone terrace, to be set up on the lawn at the last minute Saturday. To her right, Prunella Potts stood beneath a parasol and criticized the carpenters' work.

"In *my* day, tradesmen took *pride* in their craft. They certainly weren't in and out in a single *morning*." She paused to sniff the air like a beagle. "Is that *pine*?"

"It's only a temporary stage, Mrs. Potts. They're coming back to take it down on Sunday."

"*If* it doesn't tumble apart before then. And it's so bare and ugly, so unsuited to an elegant occasion like this."

"I couldn't agree more, Mrs. Potts. In fact, since you feel so strongly about it, perhaps you can help me fasten on the decorations. See those piles of pink chiffon? They're going in swags all around the edge of the stage, and then we can set the flower arrangements where the—"

"I'm afraid I don't understand," said Prunella. "Doesn't Mrs. Prince have *help* to do that kind of thing?"

"They're all busy getting the indoors spic-and-span."

"Well! In *my* day we hired enough people to do the cleaning *and* the decorations. It's really unseemly, the way these new matrons run their households. So devoid of style and taste. Really, as I've *often* said, if you can't afford the upkeep, you shouldn't buy the house to begin with." Prunella lowered her parasol and cast a critical eye over the endless marble walls and columns, the windows upon windows, everything gleaming in the sunshine. "Mortgaged to the hilt, I'm sure."

"I don't think it's a question of money, Mrs. Potts. People just don't live that way anymore, like princes. My God, who wants to be a servant these days? When you can make a decent wage and live in your own place."

Prunella turned to Lucky and stabbed her parasol into the air between them. "You see? *That's* the trouble, right there. The lower classes think they're too good for an honest day's labor."

Lucky sighed and made for one of the piles of pink chiffon. Her dress stuck to her back, her hair stuck to her face. "And when was the last time *you* did an honest day's labor, Prunella Potts?" she muttered.

"What's that? What did you say?"

"Nothing!" Lucky carried an armful of chiffon toward the stage and cast around for the tacks and the slender hammer she'd brought with her from Sprague Hall earlier that morning. A moment ago, the terrace had been practically swarming with members of the committee, chattering, brandishing their clipboards, sipping from tall, sweaty glasses of gin and tonic as they watched the men pound away with their hammers. Now everyone had scurried to the cool marble shelter indoors, leaving Lucky alone to tack up the pink chiffon bunting under the fierce sun.

She discovered the hammer under a pile of chiffon and the tacks in the pocket of her pink gingham sundress and started to work. A tune rose in her throat. That was the Italian in her, Stuy used to say—she'd grown up with music, her entire childhood had been set to a never-ending score of snatches of song. Actually, she didn't mind the task so much. Something about the hammering, the repetitive movement, the neat, even, pretty swags of pink chiffon that draped from her fingers, all combined to settle her fractious nerves. Without realizing it, she sang louder. There was nobody to hear her, after all—no Stuy, no Nonna, no Joanie, no crummy Dudley Sprague from his crummy vindictive deathbed, no sharp-eared members of the committee in their pastel dresses, no—

A flattened demicircle of shade slipped over her shoulder. "That tune," Prunella Potts said softly.

Lucky whirled and clapped her hand over her mouth, nearly bludgeoning herself with the hammer. "I'm sorry! I didn't realize you were still there!"

The fringes of the parasol shimmered around Prunella's head. A strange light flickered in her blue eyes, the color of Delft china. "I know that tune. Your grandmother used to sing it."

"I guess so. She sang a lot of things."

"No! I mean before you were born." Prunella snapped the parasol shut and stabbed the terrace with it. "Here in Newport. The summer your grandparents met."

"You were there? You knew them?"

"Of *course* I knew them. I knew *everybody*. I married a *Schuyler,* don't you know?" Prunella cackled. "*Everybody* wanted me. Not that they don't want me now, of course. But in *those* days, well. Nothing like this ramshackle society today. We had *real* money then. Real houses and real servants and the *parties*, oh! *This* is nothing." Prunella waved her arm to the stage, the stacks of chairs and tables.

"Well, times have changed," Lucky said. "They always do."

Prunella's voice turned almost dreamlike. "Did you know that at Alva Vanderbilt's ball for the Duke of Marlborough, Hodgkins created this—this bronze *fountain* in the main hall of *this very house*, with lotuses and water lilies and what have you all floating inside. *Hummingbirds*. And that was just the centerpiece. Oh, I can still picture it. The floral arrangements . . ." Prunella snapped back to Lucky. "That was before Sprague Hall was even built, of course. When the Spragues were still nobodies, and no one thought to marry off poor Maybelle to some Italian prince."

"As it happens," said Lucky, who'd heard the stories about the Marlborough ball a thousand times, "they were very happy together."

"Ha! That's what you think. Her first choice was my cousin Frank."

"Frank? Frank who?"

"Frank Pratt, of course! Oh, they were madly in love that summer. Everybody talked about it. Your grandfather was *wildly* jealous. He practically *kidnapped* poor Maybelle away. Ravished her, I'm sure. You know these Italians."

"That's ridiculous," Lucky said. "They were in love."

Prunella lifted her parasol and spread it out. A smirk turned the corners of her mouth. "I suppose she had no choice, being ravished by an Italian."

Lucky tried to imagine her grandfather ravishing anybody and shuddered. "I really think you're mistaken, Mrs. Potts. Nonna never mentioned anybody named Frank, and she certainly never loved anybody except my grandfather."

"Didn't she? She was supposed to elope with *Frank* that night, not the prince. Frank told me himself. Maybelle agreed to meet him at the boathouse and sail away together. I saw him before he left. He was so thrilled, so happy. So in love. And she jilted him."

Lucky set the hammer carefully on the stage. "Did you say the boathouse? They were supposed to meet at the *boathouse*?"

"Yes. Frank was an expert sailor, you know. He would have done anything for her." Prunella turned her head and stared out to sea. "Poor, poor Frank."

Lucky stuck her hands in her pockets so Prunella wouldn't see her fingers shaking. "Poor Frank? My goodness. What happened to him?"

Prunella looked back at her. Her blue eyes turned to ice. "Why don't you ask your grandmother? Although I *doubt* she remembers such inconsequential details as her *former lovers*."

Lucky was too astonished to speak. The venom in Prunella's voice struck her dumb. My God, where did it come from? What had Lucky ever done to Prunella Potts, other than consider her a silly, vain, old-fashioned woman—a fact she always kept scrupulously to herself.

Even Prunella seemed to realize she'd overstepped. Her hard expression softened; her icy eyes melted back into their usual vacant blue. She gave her parasol a sharp little twirl.

"Dear me, the time. I *must* go speak to Mrs. Prince about the—"

"Lucky! There you are. I should've known you'd be outside doing all the work."

Lucky turned in the direction of Teddy's voice, which emerged through the French doors—along with Teddy himself—in a gust of cool air from the marble halls. She grinned in relief.

"Am I glad to see *you*."

"Not half as glad as I am to see you. Say, you look like you could use a drink." From behind his back, Teddy produced two tall, clear, bubbling glasses, each topped with a delicate slice of lime.

Lucky clapped her hands together. "You *darling*!"

"If you'll *excuse* me," said Prunella, sweeping past, "it seems I am de trop."

Teddy craned his neck to watch her depart. "What was that about?"

"I don't know, to be honest. Some ridiculous fantasy about a love affair between my grandmother and a cousin of hers, sixty years ago." Lucky shrugged and clinked her glass against Teddy's. "You really *are* a darling. I've been dreaming about one of these for the past hour. Oops, hold on."

"What's the matter?"

Carefully Lucky slid the eyeglasses from the bridge of his nose and wiped away the fog from the lenses with the handkerchief from his jacket pocket. "Does this always happen to you when it's hot outside?"

"Only when I'm around you."

"You're awfully frisky today. Something in the air?" Lucky wriggled the glasses back on his face and lifted the drink to her lips. For some reason, her heart was hammering.

"You're going to get a terrible sunburn, working out here alone," Teddy said.

Lucky snapped her fingers. "All my committee members mysteriously vanished into thin air, as soon as the hammers came out."

"You're saying you could use a hand?"

"If it wouldn't wound your male vanity to hang swags of pink chiffon."

Teddy grinned his wolfish grin and set down his glass on the edge of the stage. "Hand me that hammer, will you? I guess my vanity can take a hit or two for a good cause."

IN LESS THAN an hour, the pink bunting hung in perfect swags all around the edge of the orchestra stage, and Lucky dripped with heat and exhaustion. Even Teddy wiped his brow with a linen handkerchief and folded it neatly back in his pocket. He looked at Lucky and lifted an eyebrow. "I could do with another cool drink."

"Me too."

"I'll tell you what. You head on over to the teahouse and put up those lovely feet of yours in the shade and the sea breeze, and I'll mix us something fresh to quench the flames. Have we got a deal?"

Lucky smiled at his damp, rosy face. "Deal."

Teddy picked up the empty glasses and disappeared through the French doors into the house. Humming to herself, Lucky gathered the hammers and the remaining tacks and dumped them back in her canvas bag. It was now past noon, and the air had taken on that heavy, sticky stillness that promised thunderstorms. She glanced at the sky—hazy blue, no sign yet of the familiar cumulonimbus bruising the horizon to the west.

But that was the trouble with thunderstorms. You never saw them coming.

Lucky slung the bag over her shoulder and crossed the lawn to the teahouse. She'd only once been inside it, when the Princes held a garden party the previous year. Or was it the year before? Socializing in Newport was such a blur, the same old parties summer after summer, the same faces, the same conversations. At least this ball would be different. Bigger, brighter, dazzling. They'd talk about this for years, wouldn't they, and every last chitchat would lead to it somehow—*It was the same summer as the Tiffany Ball*, or *That was a couple of years after the Tiffany Ball*. And as much as Lucky grumbled about the committee ladies and the endless logistics and the hammering of pink chiffon under a hot sun, it wasn't so bad to be part of something like this, was it? Not so bad to spend a few hours a day immersed in something other than her poisonous in-laws, her broken marriage, her Nonna slipping away bit by bit.

She hurried up the steps and under the shelter of the tiled roof with its snarling dragons. Inside, the air was blissfully cool. What slight breeze came off the ocean today seemed to channel through the open doors and windows and wash everything clean. Lucky drew in a deep breath and listened for voices. Only the faint crash of the ocean interrupted the stillness around her. She gazed out to sea for a moment, enjoying the peace, the anticipation of Teddy's arrival with a pair of gin and tonics. Maybe her stomach fluttered a little, who knew. She set down the bag on the dark wooden floor and sat on one of the benches set against the walls. Well. She only *meant* to sit, but as soon as she'd eased herself down, she couldn't help but swing up her legs and settle herself back, hands knit across her belly. The ocean whispered in her ear, the breeze whispered across her skin. Her eyelids fell.

"Working hard, I see?"

Lucky bolted upright. "Stuy! What are you doing here?"

Her husband stood right where the empty breeze had flown an instant ago—or was it a moment? Had she fallen asleep? Tall and glowering and puffy, his hair lank and tousled, his arms crossed over his chest. Because of the light streaming behind him, she couldn't see his face, but she felt his anger like a gust of hot wind.

"I was going to ask the same of you!" he snapped. "Woke up this morning to the house in uproar, Louise and Reggie complaining about some goddamn thing, breakfast gone cold or something, Joanie's screaming in my ear about Nonna. And that's another thing, that damn grandmother of yours, I've had it—"

Lucky stood. "Don't you say a *word* about Nonna—"

"You've got to face facts, Lucky—"

"We are *not* having this conversation!"

"She went down to the damn boathouse again, singing and muttering like a lunatic! It's *time*, Lucky, I can't take it anymore—"

"We are *not* putting Nonna in some *institution*! It would kill her!"

He threw out a fist against the thick wooden column. "Then you had damn well better stop lazing the day away in a damn pagoda and come back to your house and take care of her! *And* your daughter, *and* your houseguests. And while you're at it, you might think about taking care of your husband once in a while!"

"Take *care* of you? All I ever *do* is take care of you and Joanie! And whoever else drives in and sets up under our roof!"

"Are you talking about my sister? Your own sister-in-law?"

"She doesn't lift a finger while she's here, you *know* she doesn't, just moans and complains and makes work for poor Angela—"

"All the more reason you should come home and take charge of things."

"You might take charge of things *yourself* once in a while, you know! It's not like you have some big important job to do!"

"What does that mean? What are you saying? You're saying I'm some kind of bum?"

"I'm just saying you're not *helpless* without me. You don't need me taking care of you every single *minute*—"

"Well, if you're sick of it, just say so! Believe me, I don't want to hang around where I'm not wanted."

"Of *course* you're wanted. Of *course* I—oh, damn it, Stuy." Lucky ran a hand through her damp hair. "I've been working all morning in this awful heat, all alone—the committee members left on me—I'm hot and exhausted. I just took a single minute to lie down and cool off—"

But Stuy wasn't looking at her. He was looking over her shoulder, toward the entrance. Face slack with shock.

Lucky turned. Teddy stood in the doorway, holding a pair of tall glasses, topped with lime. He cleared his throat. "Stuy. Nice to see you. I was just bringing your wife a cool drink."

"So I see."

"It's a scorcher, all right. We've been working on the decorations—"

"Funny," said Stuy. "My wife told *me* she'd been working all alone."

"Well, she *was* working all alone, until I stumbled on her a little while ago. Helped her finish up before she wilted." Teddy held out one of the glasses. "Gin and tonic?"

"No, thanks." Stuy looked at Lucky, and the expression on his face struck her like a blow. "I'll just leave you two to get on with the decorating."

Lucky reached for his arm. "Stuy—"

"Don't bother." He shrugged her off. "What's good for the goose, right? Believe me, I'm not going to cry alone into a glass of milk."

"Stuy, wait—"

"When you're done in here, Lucky, you might want to go check on your nonna. Make sure she hasn't snuck off to the boathouse again and drowned herself."

"Damn it, Stuy!"

But he was already out the door, striding up the cliff path back toward Sprague Hall. Lucky stood there helplessly, watching him appear and disappear through the succession of doorways and windows, until he was gone.

"You should go after him," Teddy said quietly.

"Maybe I should."

Behind her came a deep sigh. "I'm sorry, Lucky. I'm a heel. Go after him, talk to him—"

"I don't want to go after him. I don't want to talk to him." Lucky turned. "I've gone after him enough. I've talked myself hoarse."

"He's your husband, and I'm in the way. It's not fair, what I'm doing."

"What are you doing, Teddy? Tell me. What are you doing with me?"

Teddy rubbed his thumb into the skin above his right elbow. The condensation from the glass rolled down the back of his hand. He looked out to sea and back again to Lucky.

"I'm in love with you, Lucky. You know that. I've been in love with you for years. Making excuses to see you, talk to you. Pretending what I feel—what I say, what I *dream*—telling myself it's all just innocent, just some harmless neighborly flirtation. But you know and I know . . . oh God. If you *only* knew, Lucky. If you only *knew* what a hairsbreadth keeps me from—"

Lucky covered the ground between them so quickly, he didn't have time to set down the drinks. They crashed to the floor when his arms closed around her, when her mouth landed on his. She kissed him as hard as she could, ferocious as a tiger, and when she pulled back, he gasped for air.

"I'm sorry," she whispered. "I shouldn't have done that."

For a second or two, Teddy stared down at her, and for the life of her she couldn't tell what he was thinking. What he meant to do. His eyes were sharp and blue behind his glasses, his lips were pink from the pressure of her kiss. His skin was flushed, too, but maybe that was just the heat.

"You're right," he said at last. "You shouldn't have done that. And I shouldn't do this, either."

Teddy gathered her up and kissed her back, more ferocious than she'd kissed him, and at that precise moment a crash of thunder split apart the sky, and the first raindrops drummed against the tiles above them.

Within seconds, the deluge had begun.

CHAPTER SIXTEEN

Andie

Newport, Rhode Island
September 2019

THE DIAMOND-PANED WINDOWS in the library shook as the sky shouted with thunder and the leaden clouds unleashed a deluge. I closed my laptop on the desk and put my head in my hands. The unpredictable weather was not only slowing down the production, but seriously messing with my mood. As if I needed reasons other than choosing between losing my livelihood and retaining my personal integrity.

"Hey, did you see this?" Meghan said from behind me.

I lifted my head and blinked, my eyes scratchy and raw from staring at the computer screen for too long. We'd given Luke the excuse of waiting until the rain stopped before going home, and he'd said we could wait in the library. Our main purpose in delaying our departure was to run into Teddy, but apparently the storm was too much even for him. He'd never arrived, and the rain hadn't stopped. At some point we'd have to brave the elements and leave before Luke discovered that we were still there.

We'd spent the time flicking through the thick file of news clippings and watching vintage newsreels on YouTube and from other corners of the internet. At first, I'd only half-heartedly looked for anything relating to the family, scanning through a story quickly, and then dismissing it as irrelevant to the restoration of the house. Anything more would be considered prying and against everything I was. The mere fact that this was what I'd been instructed to do by the producers had me simmering with unexpressed rage.

We'd even tried searching for Joanie Sprague, hoping both that we found nothing, and that we found exactly what we'd need to make our show the most fascinating thing on television since the infamous brawl on one of the housewives shows.

Most of what was online was about Joanie's wild life as a rock star groupie before her marriage and after her divorce, with only brief footnotes about Stuy's mysterious disappearance. I had tried to skip over those, feeling as if I had discovered a hidden diary full of salacious details not meant for public consumption. Not that we had discovered anything more revealing than speculation as to what had really happened. Regardless, we were left with no more information than what Joanie had told me—Stuy had either run off with another woman or had fallen off his boat in a drunken stupor, accidentally or on purpose. It was only after I'd found myself suggesting an on-screen staged fistfight between Meghan and me that I'd given up all hope of rescue.

"Searching for personal information about the Spragues feels icky to me. Kind of like watching *The Crown*. I mean, these are real people, and they have expressly asked us not to talk about the family. This is just . . ." I motioned toward the stack of clippings. "Icky," I repeated, unable to think of a better word.

"Hey, did you hear me?"

I turned to see Meghan pulling a book from a bookshelf. "*Prunella Pratt Schuyler Potts—Cultural Icon and Society Doyenne: Memoirs of a Great American Heroine and Survivor of the* Lusitania." She began thumbing through the pages. "The name sounds vaguely familiar, but I don't know why."

I sighed, happy for a brief distraction from digging up dirt on the

Spragues. "I saw it, too. No clue who she is but considering that's a memoir and not a biography, the title alone tells me all I need to know about Prunella. Besides the unfortunate name that sounds more like a piece of dried fruit than a woman."

"True." Meghan shoved the book back before returning to the chair next to me and opening up the laptop again, her enthusiasm for celebrity gossip impressive if not alarming. "All right. Let's go back a little further. I mean, Stuy's disappearance is great—but with no definitive answers, there's not a lot we can talk about. So maybe going back in history and adding the royal connection might help. Americans always go crazy over tiaras."

"The royal connection?"

"Yep. I was hoping we could find something more current, but this is a possibility I discovered while doing some digging in my free time. It's old history, but it's all we've got right now." She typed something into the browser then turned the laptop so I could see. "Maybelle Sprague married the Italian Prince di Conti in 1899 then moved to Italy. She only returned to the States with her granddaughter, Lucky, at the beginning of the war, in 1939. From what I've gleaned from the little I could find, Maybelle and the prince moved exclusively in aristocratic European society and were great patrons of the opera. There is not a single mention or photograph of Maybelle with any American dignitary or visitor. And no mention of her family ever visiting. I suppose being married to a prince made her completely embrace her husband's country. Still, I thought it odd."

"That's something, at least. Especially if Lucky has a title. That should make the reality TV crowd salivate, right?" I opened up the folder and began flipping through the contents for a small cluster of articles and clipped photographs I vaguely remembered from my disinterested speed-reading, before I'd realized the precariousness of my job. "But who were the Spragues that they could attract an Italian prince?"

Meghan turned back to the laptop and began typing, scrolling through links before clicking. After reading for a moment in silence, she let out a little whoop of excitement and turned the laptop toward me. "Maybelle was a dollar heiress. Just look at this bit from the *Newport Daily Bugle* in March 1899!"

COPPER HEIRESS SPRAGG PURCHASES VAN DUYVIL COTTAGE

Miss Maybelle Spragg of Copperville, Colorado, and New York City has been revealed as the buyer of the handsome Italianate cottage at 603 Bellevue Avenue from the estate of Bayard Van Duyvil, whose recent tragic demise in a house fire in Cold Spring, New York, made necessary the immediate sale of the deceased's real estate holdings. The price of the property has not been revealed to this newspaper, although it is expected to have exceeded one million dollars. Miss Spragg is the daughter and sole heiress of the so-called Copper King, the late Mr. Hiram Spragg, who struck the fabled Spragg Lode near Colorado Springs in 1882, which has so far yielded nearly fifty tons of copper ore of the purest quality. It is believed that the sale was affected through the agency of Miss Spragg's stepbrother and guardian, Mr. John Spragg. Mr. John Spragg may be known to some as the former Mr. John Hardin, who took his stepfather's name shortly before the Copper King's demise in 1897. Mr. Spragg plans to reside with his sister in Newport for the duration of the summer season.

"What's with the different spelling of the last name?" Meghan asked.

"My guess is that John Sprague thought 'Spragg' looked too plebian and changed it. Judging by the changes he made in this house, he seemed to be all about appearances over actual substance."

I turned back to the article to reread it, feeling a nudge of excitement. "This is amazing," I said. "This could be exactly what we're looking for. Where did I put those photographs?"

Meghan slid the pile toward me so I could glance through them. "Here's a photo of Maybelle and the prince on the steps of the opera house in Milan. And here she is at a tea honoring Enrico Caruso." I plucked another from the pile. "She was also a patroness of the local orphanage. This shows her distributing Christmas gifts to the orphans."

Meghan studied the photos thoughtfully, tapping her painted fingernail on the desk.

"What?" I asked.

She frowned. "Do you remember that large portrait of Maybelle that hung on her bedroom wall?"

I nodded. "I asked Devon to move it to the dining room to protect it when we started the reno in the bedroom. What about it?"

"I just find it a little odd that in that portrait and in the two photographs of Maybelle I found in the historical archives, she's wearing a cameo brooch. One of them is from her debut ball, and the other is from the ball here at Sprague Hall to welcome the Prince di Conti."

"Well, if it was her favorite piece of jewelry or had some special meaning, it would make sense that she'd wear it a lot, right?"

"Exactly." Meghan returned her attention back to the photographs of Maybelle in Italy after her marriage. "So why isn't she wearing it in any of these photos?"

I shrugged. "Who knows? People change, tastes change. Maybe the prince wanted her to wear flashier jewelry. It doesn't matter. We need something juicy." I leaned back in my chair, allowing a groan of frustration. "There has got to be more about the Spragues than Stuy's death and the random society function. Except even then there's very little. Like the Tiffany Ball of 1957. Lucky appears in a photo of the organizers here at Sprague Hall in her office, but that's it. Every other mention of the ball is about the Kennedys and the Tiffany Yellow Diamond."

"Well, there are a few wedding photos of Lucky and Stuy. Maybe we have enough. Is it too much to hope that a mere mention of the Kennedys is enough to get the producers salivating?"

Meghan's fingers flew over the keyboard. "Hardly. Unless Jackie got drunk and did a strip dance on top of a table, it's not what passes for reality TV fodder these days."

"That's—"

"Don't blame me. I'm just the messenger. I'd be fine with television going back to the days where married couples still slept in twin beds and one of them always had their foot on the floor. You know, like Lucy and Desi."

I leaned closer. "What are you . . ."

"Your mention of the wedding photos gave me an idea." She leaned forward as she quickly typed something into the search bar. Lightning flashed outside the darkened windows, illuminating the corners of the room, followed quickly by a roll of thunder.

"Found it! It's a news clipping from 1971—Joanie's wedding!" Meghan smiled triumphantly. "I knew there had to be a reason we didn't find a lot on Joanie Sprague. She might have kept her maiden name after her split from rocker Ted Mungo, but the tabloids persisted in calling her Joanie Mungo. Look." She turned the laptop so I could see the long list of hyperlinks sprouting like weeds on the screen.

"Oh my gosh. It's a 1992 episode from *Lifestyles of the Rich and Famous*. 'Champagne wishes and caviar dreams'—remember?"

Like I could forget. My mother had been addicted to watching that show, humming the theme song while setting the table with her thrift market dishes and paper napkins, being meticulous with the correct placement of the silver-plated utensils she'd bought on layaway at Benny's.

Meghan clicked on the link and forced me to watch snippets from the episode. It was mostly about Ted and his rock-and-roll lifestyle, but there were also some pretty incredible shots of a gorgeous and much younger Joanie, including a short clip of footage of toddlers Luke and

Hadley on a Southern California beach. The creepy feeling of reading someone else's diary came over me again as we scrolled through the online photographs, many showing Joanie after her divorce with a long list of A-list actors and musicians.

Meghan began scrolling again, stopping before clicking on the link *Dudley Sprague dead at the age of 68*. "Nope. Saw these already." She moved to close the page.

"Hang on a minute." I peered at the top of the page. It was the same photo we'd seen before, of Stuyvesant and Lucky's wedding, on the steps of Trinity Church in Queen Anne Square. They were looking at each other, both stunningly beautiful, both smiling. Lucky's smile was luminous, the love for her husband broadcasted by her eyes and the turn of her body. The way both hands held on to his arm as if she couldn't believe he was really hers. Stuy's smile was that of a cat that had captured the mouse.

"Scroll down. There's more."

Meghan stopped at the photo of the Tiffany Ball committee. "We've seen this one before, too. I remember because of the artwork. I could swear that's a Titian on the wall behind them, but there are too many heads blocking it."

"Could be, but that's not what . . ." I leaned over and squinted, reading the small print of the caption listing the names of those in the photograph. "Can you make it larger?" I got closer, smiling as I realized I'd been right. "Look," I said, pointing to the back row of committee members standing behind the seated first row where a lone male stood, his face the only one not looking at the camera. "Do you see those glasses?"

Meghan's eyes widened. "Oh my gosh. That's Teddy Winthrop, isn't it? A younger version of him, anyway."

"Exactly. And look." I tapped the screen. "Look who Teddy is admiring. There's no other way I can describe his expression other than of pure adoration."

"And maybe a little lust. That's Lucky, isn't it?"

I nodded, recalling what Joanie had told me about the speculation surrounding her father's disappearance. She thought it was suicide. Yet some thought Teddy might have had a hand in it. And until I'd seen this photo, I'd dismissed the speculation as pure gossip. But now . . .

"This could be exactly what we need, Andie. And whether or not we like it, there is much more to the story we are trying to tell than simply bricks and mortar."

An indecipherable sound, like fingertips brushing against wood, came from the door leading out into the cavernous reception hall. Our eyes met then widened as the more distinctive sound of soft footsteps on marble trickled in our direction. We stood and rushed toward the door. I threw it open, expecting to find the surprised face of a living, breathing person. Instead, only the light from the open door sliced into the dark and deserted room, the sound of the wind and rain outside almost camouflaging the soft snap of a closing door.

"I really think we should call my friend Melanie, in Charleston," Meghan whispered as if there might be someone listening. "This place is definitely haunted. This morning while I was helping set up for filming in the ballroom, my purse disappeared from the spot where I was positive I'd put it. I looked *everywhere* but it was definitely gone and the crew swore up and down that they hadn't seen it, either. And then, right before lunch—it was there. Right where I'd left it."

I rubbed my eyes. "That wasn't a ghost, Meghan. That's one of the crew playing a trick. Probably Devon. Was anything missing inside?"

"No." She looked at me oddly. "But there was . . . sand inside. Like someone with sandy hands had riffled through it."

I stepped back into the room, prepared to pack up and call it a night, when Meghan stopped me. "Hang on—what's this?" She stepped outside the arc of light and picked up something off the floor.

"It's Maybelle's trinket box. The one we found under the floorboard in her room." Our eyes met. "Luke took it from me. Either he left it here as an olive branch, or . . ." I stopped, unable to finish my sentence.

"Or not." Meghan said as another crash of thunder rattled the windows and the sound of dripping water thrummed steadily inside the cavernous hall. We quickly retreated inside the library and slammed the door closed.

WHEN I ARRIVED the next morning—six hours late because I'd had to take Petey to the emergency room to have three raisins removed from his nostril and then got stuck behind a four-car pileup on Route 138 due to the torrential rain—it was to the pungent scent of sage and Joanie leading the film crew on a house tour while waving about a smoking stick-shaped bundle. I was nearly trampled by a frantic Hadley doing her best to either tackle George and his camera, or thrust her hand over her mother's mouth.

Joanie paused in front of one of the bedrooms, her gold bangles jangling as she waved her arm back and forth. "And this was my mother's bedroom. I was still a young girl when my father disappeared, but I was a very good eavesdropper. Believe me, my parents had a very healthy and active sex life!"

"Mother!" Hadley wailed. "Please stop! There is no need . . ."

Joanie settled a gentle glance on her daughter. "But of course there is. We must banish all secrets, and all ghosts of the past from these walls. It is the most important part of any renovation." Reaching into the drawstring pouch at her waist, Joanie pulled out another dark stone almost identical to the hematite crystal she'd given me. The same one that was currently nestled in my jeans pocket, although judging by my day so far it might as well have been a chunk of coal.

Joanie faced the camera. "Did I mention that I have several A-list celebrity clients who hire me to cleanse their new or renovated homes before they even step a foot inside?"

I retreated to Maybelle's bedroom, afraid I'd start laughing at Hadley and her expression of intense mortification and her futile attempts to curtail her mother's soliloquy. I found Meghan sitting on the chaise in the small alcove—now covered with a drop cloth—the trinket box opened in front of her, the lid hanging back on its hinges like a gaping mouth. Pins, chains, a gold locket, and a magnifying glass with an enamel handle were scattered around the box. We'd left it in the library the night before, neither of us willing to bring it home, and Meghan must have retrieved it while I was busy in the ER waiting room trying to entertain an impatient six-year-old.

"What are you doing?" I crouched next to her.

"Trying to be productive while I waited for you and the film crew films the lead singer from ABBA."

"That's not . . ."

"I know. But she looks like the blond one. Anyway, since *someone* left this for us to find, I thought it was my duty to look a little closer inside and see if I might find something juicy for the show."

I sat down on the chaise with a thud. "You really have gone to the dark side, haven't you?"

"I thought you wanted to save your job." Meghan picked up the now empty box and turned it upside down before shaking it. "I do think I found something."

"The cameo?"

"No. I wish. I think there's a false bottom. From the outside, it's a lot deeper than the inside, and there are grooves around the edges that shouldn't be there if it was a regular box. I just can't figure out how to release it."

I took the box from her and stared inside, the faint whiff of lavender brushing past me and disappearing so quickly I thought it might have been my imagination. I recalled another old box, one once used for storing tea and long since delegated to the corner of a dusty attic in an ancient Charleston house where I had been working on a grad school project. Quite by accident, I had discovered its own secret storage place—disappointingly empty—by simultaneously pressing on opposing sides of the box and releasing the bottom.

"Here goes."

Meghan leaned closer at the satisfying *click* as the bottom of the box released and I grasped a corner to remove it, revealing a faded pink-ribbon-tied stack of what appeared to be folded letters.

"May I help you?" Luke stood in the doorway, his eyes almost as frosty as Hadley's.

We both jerked back as if being caught with our hands in the proverbial cookie jar.

Before I could summon air back into my lungs to speak, he stepped forward, pointing at the trinket box. "Where did you get that?"

"It was . . . I thought . . ."

Meghan came to my rescue. "Andie found it outside the library. We thought you'd put it there."

"Why would you think that? It disappeared from my room before I could give it to Lucky. I thought I'd misplaced it."

"Meghan is telling the truth—it was on the floor outside the library door. I assumed you put it there because you took it from me."

Our eyes met as we silently poured over the possibilities, none of which filled the mental slots marked "logical" or "probable."

"All right," Luke said, even though it was obvious that it *wasn't*. "Let's see what you found."

After a brief hesitation, I held up the stack of letters. "The box itself held only little trinkets—the sort of things important to a young girl but not of any real value. But we found a hidden bottom compartment and discovered these."

As a symbol of truce, I slid off the ribbon and handed the first letter to Luke. "These did belong to your great-grandmother so you should see them first."

He uncreased the letter and Meghan and I watched as he read it quickly then reached for the next one and did the same. When I handed him the fourth, he shook his head. "These are all from the same person—a Frank Pratt. Apparently, a man whose love for adjectives doesn't quite compensate for his limited imagination. I believe these are supposed to be love letters to his 'Marvelous, Magnificent, Majestic'—take your pick—Maybelle. They're all so treacly sweet and poorly written that I'm actually feeling a little nauseous. I'd like to think that she kept them for when she needed a good laugh, but the fact that they were tied with a pink ribbon tells me she might have actually had a fondness for this Frank Pratt guy." He tossed the letters on the chaise. "I guess he was no match for a prince."

Meghan sat up. "He was probably Maybelle's true love, but her family wanted the prestige of claiming a prince in the family. You know, like Consuelo Vanderbilt and the Duke of Marlborough—one of the most well-known dollar princesses. Money for title kind of thing. It was very popular in the Gilded Age. Mostly loveless marriages that didn't last, but the weddings were pretty spectacular."

She stood, the letters sliding onto the floor. "Oh my gosh. That's it! That's the hook we've been looking for!"

Luke and I sent her a wary glance.

"The ghost of Maybelle is haunting Sprague Hall because she's looking for her lost lover! Aren't there stories of a lady in white hanging out at the boathouse? Haven't we all experienced stuff missing or being moved during the production of our show?"

"That's ridiculous," Luke said. "I've seen lots of people die, but not a single one has come back to tell me about it."

Before I could question him, Meghan began walking from the room. "I'm going to research what happened to Frank Pratt. But first I'm calling Melanie."

I stood, a letter crumpling under my foot. "Meghan, shouldn't we talk about this first. . . ."

But she was already gone.

"She's kidding, right?" Luke didn't sound as worried as I thought he'd be. Maybe Joanie's belief in unleashing all secrets for the good karma of everyone was starting to get to him.

I faked a smile. "Probably."

Instead of pressing further, he surprised me by saying, "I missed you at yoga this morning. Joanie had a mat for you and some hideous green breakfast smoothie."

This time my smile was real. "Sorry to have missed it. I'm guessing it was a lot more fun than trying to pry raisins from Petey's nose."

He tried to smother a grin. "I'm sorry. Just be glad it was only raisins. I've seen much worse."

"From your time with Doctors Without Borders."

It took him a moment before responding. "Yes."

His response made me even more curious. "So, you're a doctor?"

It took him even longer to answer this time. "Yes." He paused. "I'm taking a break right now."

I noticed again his tanned skin, the expensive watch. The perfect white teeth. The bloodshot eyes. Maybe it was my exhaustion or my frustration over a life I couldn't seem to control, or the precariousness of my career, but I suddenly wasn't seeing Luke anymore. I was seeing dozens of guys just like him. Guys who were given every advantage yet still thought the world owed them something and believed everything was theirs for the taking. Even when it wasn't.

"I wish I could afford to take a break. But someone has to put food on the table."

His face whitened under his tan, and I wished I could call back what I'd said. But it was too late. And because I'd already started I couldn't stop. "So you went to medical school and then were a doctor for a couple of years and then just decided to hang out on boats?"

His lips thinned, but he didn't try to defend himself. Which made me feel even worse.

The sound of a car horn blowing brought Luke to the window. "Teddy's here, right on schedule. But your film crew hasn't left for some reason even though they're supposed to be gone by now." He let the curtain drop. "I guess I'd better get my useless self downstairs to open the door. It's the butler's day off." He strode out of the room, his heels heavy against the wood floors.

"Luke, I'm sorry. . . ."

Meghan stuck her head around the doorway and sent me a meaningful look. "The film crew is on its way. You know what you need to do. Meanwhile, I'm off to dig up anything I can find on Frank Pratt. And the Teddy and Lucky angle. I've already put a call into Melanie Trenholm about the ghost angle. I think we should have enough juicy bits to keep the wolf from the door." She gave me a brief thumbs-up, then slipped away.

I took a deep breath, then turned toward the sound of shuffling feet and Joanie's voice saying something about mental health, and how she'd learned everything she needed to know about sex from listening at her parents' bedroom door. When she and the film crew appeared in Maybelle's bedroom, Joanie was still wafting her sage stick at the front of the group, but Hadley was conspicuously absent. She had either gone for reinforcements or had simply given up trying to curtail the force of nature who was her mother.

As George directed the camera in my direction, I held up the small box full of the memories of a girl long since dead, and then each letter as I talked about the possible scandal and wandering spirit that surrounded them and felt my soul shrivel a little more. Maybelle Sprague had hidden the letters because she hadn't wanted them to be seen by anyone but her. Because there were some secrets meant to remain so, and some ghosts meant to stay dead.

CHAPTER SEVENTEEN

Ellen

Newport, Rhode Island
July 1899

ELLEN'S HAT WAS dead.

There was no getting around it. The flowers were broken, the brim was limp, the color had run. She had hoped that by dint of a bit of dye and some determined buffing she might be able to refashion the felt back into shape, but the cheap material had been no match for seawater and Dudley's vicious little hands.

Ellen regarded the battered material with vexation. She needed *something* to wear on her head. She was meant to be accompanying Maybelle to the Newport Casino, the club on Bellevue Avenue in which the elite of Newport demonstrated their skills at such polite sports as tennis, archery, and gossip. Ellen had been conscripted as attendant, to stand behind Maybelle and hold her wrap.

Perhaps with a bit of wire . . . Ellen gave the brim a tentative tug in the right direction. The material, weakened by the water, tore straight across with a horrible rending sound.

Could one sew the halves of a hat together?

Ellen dropped the hopeless bits of felt, trying not to cry. How ridiculously foolish would it be to cry over a hat, when she had so many more worthy things over which to cry? But she couldn't help it. She could feel the tears threatening. What was she to do? It was such a stupid thing, really, a hat, but she needed one, and she didn't have the money to buy one, not a red cent, and the helplessness of it, her own helplessness, made her want to sink onto the floor and howl.

She had her board—and very opulent board it was, here, in her sapphire velvet jewel box of a room—but Mr. Sprague had yet to pay her a single penny of her promised wages. Paid quarterly, that's what he had said when she had gathered up her nerve to ask. Dependent on her performance.

Dependent on whether Maybelle married the prince, he meant.

That hadn't been part of the job description; none of it had been part of the job description. But what was she to do about it? John Sprague could change the terms of her employment all he liked, could withhold her salary and claim she was only to be paid yearly, could refuse to pay her altogether on the grounds that her performance had been unsatisfactory, and what recourse did she have? She could hardly take him to the courts. Lawyers cost money, even if she knew how to find one. And the sort she'd be likely to find would never be able to contend with what John Sprague could deploy. Not to mention that to appear in public, to make herself notorious in court, would be to sign her own death warrant. She was at Sprague's mercy, all right. Because to be at Sprague's mercy, to be a pauper in his house, was better than being dead.

Or was it? What was this foolish insistence she had on being alive? Maybe she wasn't meant to be alive. Maybe she was meant to have died with her mother and siblings. Maybe that was why she'd been condemned to live this half life, hiding under a name not her own, dependent on the whims of strangers, trying, trying, always trying, but never getting anywhere, never putting away enough coin to make a difference, running and hiding, hiding and scared.

What had she done wrong? Was there something wrong with her? Ellen buried her face in her hands, fighting for composure. Maybe it was because she'd turned a blind eye so long at the Hibernia. Maybe she was being punished. Maybe she was being punished for the things her father had done, after her mother died.

But before then? What about that? What were they being punished for then? Her mother, her sisters—what were they being punished for, that the sickness had taken them? What sort of original sin had tainted them?

She missed them. She missed them so.

She missed having a place, even if that place was only a tenement. It hadn't mattered. It hadn't mattered that they were poor or that there were too many of them crammed into too little space. They'd been together, and that was what had mattered.

Until they weren't.

Ellen forced herself to stoop and pick up the broken pieces of her hat. It was just a hat, only a hat. She'd find something. Maybe there was a castaway she could salvage. Ladies' maids got the pick of their mistresses' leavings, and Maybelle's maid had no fondness for Ellen, but maybe, just maybe, if she asked . . .

She would think of something. Mechanically, Ellen put the ruined bits in the wastebasket. After the storm of emotion, she felt numb, drained. It was only a hat. Just a thing to cover her head. She'd never liked it anyway.

But she'd bought it herself, with her own hard-earned coin. It was a statement of her respectability. Her covered head showed she wasn't reduced to total abandonment; she could maintain the outward semblance of propriety.

Because what happened once one could no longer cover oneself? When one was totally destitute? What then?

Maybelle had to marry the prince.

There was a sick feeling in the pit of Ellen's stomach. It was her only hope and yet—what guarantee had she that Sprague would actually pay her then, and not just turn her out, her purpose accomplished?

She'd had a dream that maybe Maybelle would take her along, find her a place in her retinue, but there was something about that image, accompanying the prince and Maybelle on their bridal journey, that made her feel vaguely sick to her stomach.

Probably the result of not having eaten her breakfast, Ellen told herself briskly.

Ellen's doorknob rattled. "Oi!" came the aggrieved tones of Maybelle's maid Delphine. She didn't bother to be French around staff. "Open up!"

Ellen hadn't even realized she'd locked the door. Her hands shook slightly as she turned the key. Habit. "Yes?"

Delphine shoved the door the rest of the way open with her shoulder, her arms entirely occupied with a giant, round box. "What's the idea of locking up? What you got in there? The crown jewels?"

"No . . . just . . ." How to explain? No one locked doors here. Maids came in and out at will. Everyone knew everything about everyone. "I like to be quiet sometimes."

"Sure, quiet." Delphine dropped the box unceremoniously on the floor, her eyes roving around the room, with particular attention to the bed. And under the bed. "Here. His Highness's man said I was to give this to you."

"To me?"

"And why he couldn't carry it himself, mister high and mighty? Well? Aren't you going to open it?"

"I—" It's not for me, Ellen wanted to say. It can't be for me.

"Oh. It came with this." Delphine thrust a note at her. The paper didn't feel like any paper Ellen had ever seen before. It was foreign, foreign and beautiful, with a crest impressed in wax upon it. The only reason, Ellen suspected, why Delphine hadn't already read it. She cracked the seal, and the folded halves sprung open. Inside, it said only, "An eye for an eye—and a hat for a hat."

It wasn't signed. It didn't have to be.

Delphine was shamelessly reading over Ellen's shoulder. "A hat for a hat?"

Ellen gave her head a little shake, feeling strangely giddy. She knelt by the box, looking up at Delphine as she lifted the lid. "It's . . . I should have realized it was a hatbox. Master Sprague threw my hat into the ocean yesterday. His Excellency felt sorry for—oh."

Her breath caught as she lifted the hat from its protective tissue.

This wasn't just any hat. It was a fantasy of a hat, an indulgence of a hat, all tulle, and flowers, and an enormous cream straw brim caught up in the fashionable leghorn style. It would never wear well . . . one couldn't wear it for winter . . . the pale color would show dirt within the week . . . but it was beautiful.

"I wish he'd feel sorry for me," said Delphine. "Just look at that!"

"It's not very practical, is it?"

Delphine snorted, snatching the hat from Ellen. "Move over to the mirror, will you?"

With the ease of long practice, she maneuvered Ellen squarely in front of the looking glass and set the hat deftly on her head. Whatever her other qualities, Delphine knew her trade; with a quick tuck of hair here and a slight tug on the hat brim there, the hat was firmly on Ellen's head, skewered into place with a mother-of-pearl-headed hatpin that had arrived in the box with the hat.

"Voilà," said Delphine, in her French maid voice, before going back to her normal accent. "There. What do you think now?"

The woman in the mirror wasn't Ellen at all. This was a lady in a portrait, her skin a wonder of cream and rose, her hair a miracle of pale gold. Beneath the wonder of the hat, her features seemed to take on new definition, her face fine-boned, elegant, of a woman who had never known drudgery or want or fear.

"Oh," said Ellen, unable to look away, afraid to blink in case the mirage should disappear. It was a mirage, she knew, but . . . "Oh."

Delphine gave a satisfied sniff and squeezed her shoulders. "See? Didn't I tell you? Who needs practical when you can have that?"

By two o'clock that afternoon, practical was looking rather more appealing. Ellen would happily have traded the wonder on her head for her old black felt toque. It was one thing to be Cinderella, to go to the ball under false pretenses in a borrowed gown. It was quite another to be only half transformed in the full, glaring light of day.

It started the moment they arrived at the casino, the women looking sharply at her, fooled by her hat into thinking she might be one of them, trying to figure out who she was—and then looking down and seeing the plain dark twill that marked her so plainly as a hireling. She was like one of those children's toys, where one had to turn the blocks until the appropriate tops and bottoms matched. Ellen was mismatched, and it was causing far more attention than she liked.

Maybelle, bless her, was entirely oblivious. She wouldn't have noticed if Ellen had worn a rooster on her head.

Ellen sought refuge behind the umbrellas set up to shade the ladies in between sets, standing as far in the shadows as she could with the other lady's maids and attendants, who were there to hold wraps, provide towels, and fix hair, invisible except when needed.

But the hat could not be ignored. After annihilating her opponent on the tennis court, Prunella Schuyler made a beeline for Ellen, or, rather, Ellen's hat.

"Where did you get that hat?" Prunella demanded peremptorily, standing on her tiptoes to peer at Ellen's hat with a complete disregard for the woman beneath it. She poked it with the bottom of her tennis racket. "Is it Maybelle's?"

"No!" Ellen stepped quickly away, appalled at the suggestion of larceny. "It's . . . my own. I would never take anything of Miss Sprague's."

Prunella's Delft blue eyes narrowed. She circled Ellen, examining the hat from every angle. "No, darling Maybelle wouldn't have a Madame Montpensier. She hasn't an ounce of taste. Where did you get it?"

Ellen frowned at the other woman. "A Madame . . ."

"Montpensier. Only the most exclusive milliner in Boston." Prunella glanced swiftly up at her. "You didn't know?"

"I needed a hat," said Ellen weakly, damning the prince and his good works. "It was a gift. My only hat was ruined at the beach."

"It was a wreck to begin with. I'm amazed you could tell the difference." Prunella took a moment to smirk before returning to the matter at hand. "No one gives a hat like that to a servant. Do you know how much a Madame Montpensier costs? The last time I bought one—all, right, the last time I bought five—I really thought my husband was going to need to call for the doctor. Silly man. It's not as though he can't afford it. And it was entirely absurd of him to say one could buy a small country for less. One doesn't buy countries; one invades them."

"I"—Ellen's hands went instinctively to her hat—"I didn't know. If I had, I would never . . ."

She had needed something to put on her head, that was all. It had never occurred to her, she had never imagined, that a bit of straw and tulle could be worth so much, could be so easily recognizable. Certainly, she'd known it was a good hat, a better hat than any she'd ever owned, but she'd had no idea . . .

Ellen's cheeks burned red under her confection of a hat. No wonder Delphine had looked at her like she had.

Prunella Schuyler's sharp eyes caught the blush. Her eyes opened wide before narrowing again, an intensely speculative expression crossing her face. "So it's like that, is it?"

"It's not like anything," said Ellen hastily. She didn't like the way Prunella was looking at her, as if she were a species of butterfly pinned to a wall.

"Oh, my dear, don't be so modest." Prunella smiled a close-lipped smile. She looked like the cat with the cream. "You don't have to tell me who it was. I can guess."

"But it's not . . . it was only . . ."

Prunella tapped Ellen lightly on the cheek. "Aren't you a sly little thing. And right under the nose of your mistress." She sounded genuinely admiring. She leaned forward, so that her face was right under the brim of Ellen's hat. Her nose twitched with interest. "Does she know? She doesn't, does she? She wouldn't, the little darling."

Ellen took a step back. "There's nothing to know. The prince took pity on me. . . ."

"Pity, is it? Is *that* what they're calling it now? Now, now, don't bother protesting." Prunella wafted a hand. Unfortunately, it was the hand holding the tennis racket, which nearly took down an umbrella. Prunella didn't let that bother her. "We're women of the world. Gentlemen will have their diversions. It's such a pity that innocents like Maybelle don't understand that."

Ellen could feel all the color drain from her face. "I swear, I've done nothing—"

"A very expensive nothing. You don't think he gave that to you with no expectation of return? My dear." Prunella gave a tinkling little laugh. "Why fight it? It's rather a romantic thing to be mistress to a prince. Don't they do special things for royal bastards? In any event, you'll have very nice clothes while it lasts."

"But I . . ."

"I shouldn't waste time if I were you. Best enjoy it before he comes to his senses." That sounded more like the Mrs. Schuyler Ellen knew, the poison beneath the sweetness. She let her eyes drift from Ellen's hat to her plain gray dress. "Who knows? You might get a dress out of him to go with the hat."

Waggling her fingers at Ellen, Prunella Schuyler departed with some speed.

To tell Maybelle? No. Maybelle was still on the tennis court. But she would tell her. Ellen had no doubt. Why look like that otherwise? Prunella didn't like Ellen; she thought Ellen was above herself. She was the sort of woman who meddled for the joy of meddling.

And she wanted Maybelle for her cousin, Frank.

The thought hit Ellen like a bucket of cold water. Yes, there she was, dragging her cousin by the arm, tugging him down so she could whisper in his ear. That was what this was all about, spoiling the match with the prince so she could secure Maybelle and her inheritance for Frank Pratt.

Ellen sucked in a breath. Her dress was too tight, the air too humid; she couldn't breathe properly. She resisted the urge to yank out the hatpin, to claw it off. That would only draw more attention. A Madame . . . what had Mrs. Schuyler called it?

She had to return the hat.

Maybelle came off the court, glowing with pride. Mr. Pratt had complimented her backhand. She wasn't terribly good yet, but she would get better, Mr. Pratt said, he said you could tell.

"Miss Sprague," Ellen interrupted. "Miss Sprague. I must explain something. About my hat . . ."

Distracted, Maybelle said, "Oh yes, it's very pretty."

"Dudley threw my only one into the water yesterday, so the prince felt sorry for me and had this sent," Ellen said quickly, before she lost her nerve.

"Did he? That was very kind of him," Maybelle said wonderingly, as though she wouldn't have expected it of him. An expression of distress crossed her face. "Oh, but you ought to have told me. I feel awful I never realized . . . I would have found you a hat."

"Do you have a very old one you wouldn't mind lending? Just until I get my wages and can buy my own." Ellen hated to ask it, but it was better than being presumed the prince's mistress. "I don't like to keep this one. I know His Excellency meant it kindly, but it's far too grand for me."

"It is a bit big around the brim," said Maybelle, misunderstanding entirely. "I'm sure I can find something that will fit you better when we get back. Although I think it's very pretty on you."

"Thank you," said Ellen, giving up the attempt. She supposed she ought to be grateful that Maybelle didn't understand the implications, that, if anything, it appeared to have raised the prince slightly in her esteem.

But if John Sprague were to hear . . .

Ellen could feel the cold sweat prickling along her spine despite the heat of the July day. Her hands felt like ice in her cheap cotton gloves. No, John Sprague wouldn't share Maybelle's sanguine attitude.

She had to get the hat back to the prince and hope the whole, ridiculous debacle never reached the ears of John Sprague. Because if John Sprague were to hear, Ellen would be out on her ear. With one very expensive hat to her name. And a price on her head.

Back in the house, Ellen bundled the hat back into its box, stuffing it into the tissue paper. How could she have been so stupid as to have accepted it? Because it had been a hat. Because she had been seduced by her own image in the mirror, by the momentary fantasy that she could be . . . oh, not one of them, she would never be one of them. But that perhaps their differences weren't so bone-deep after all. That with the right hat she'd look like she belonged in that world, in the center of the drawing room rather than on the side of it, holding Maybelle's wrap.

Insanity. Idiocy. What was she thinking? She didn't even deserve the status she currently claimed. She wasn't a music teacher, a young lady of quality fallen on hard times. She was the pianist from a music hall that served as a front for all manner of criminal activity, the product of the Boston slums. If they knew who and what she was, they'd have her scrubbing dishes in the scullery, not sleeping next to the daughter of the house.

A musician, the prince had called her.

A fraud. That was what she was. And the best way not to be discovered was to fade into the background. Not call attention to oneself with a ridiculous and inappropriate hat.

For a moment, Ellen contemplated selling it. But how? To whom? The society ladies had their hats specially made for them. A pawnshop would give her pennies. And selling it felt worse than keeping it. The only way to make clear that she wasn't what Mrs. Schuyler claimed was to return it, clearly and definitively.

Ellen crept through the halls with her absurd burden in her arms, dropped the hat outside the prince's rooms, and fled.

The note arrived after her dinner tray, shoved under the door of her room.

The ink had been wet when the note was folded and the letters were so blurred as to be practically illegible.

Meet me at the rose arbor. Midnight.

It wasn't a request. It was a command.

Ellen stood holding the note, staring at the blurred words.

She could hear Prunella Schuyler's nasty, twittering voice in her head. *You don't think he gave that to you with no expectation of return.*

But she had. As foolish as it was, she had. He had always seemed . . . honest. Honest in his way. And she had felt—oh, but that was what seducers did, she supposed. They made you feel as if there were a special connection between you, as though they understood you. Look at Frank Pratt and poor little Maybelle. There she had been, pitying Maybelle, worrying over Maybelle, feeling so superior and wise and put upon, and all the while she had been just as gullible, lapping up the prince's compliments in regard to her music as Maybelle basked in Pratt's false praise of her tennis game.

Ellen crumpled the paper between her fingers. This wasn't the beautiful foreign paper of the note with the hat, but a scrap torn off any old thing.

Perhaps he'd grown bored with the game, grown bored with subtlety. No more fairy tale wooing, just a click of the fingers, a *come here, you.*

She shouldn't go.

But if she didn't . . . what might a prince thwarted do? And if there had ever, at all, been even the slightest bit of truth to what she had felt between them, she would rather explain, cleanly and honestly, let him know that she didn't have it in her to live that life, to betray her employer, to be his mistress.

At five to midnight, Ellen slipped out of the house, taking the long way around via the loggia, rehearsing her speech in her head. Frosty but polite. Firm and dignified. She'd say her piece and leave.

The air was thick with the scents of July flowers; the moon silvered the topiary and turned marble pillars to pearl. In the day, the gardens were pretty enough, but decidedly earthbound. This was something else entirely, a fantasy land out of a poet's fevered imagination, a scene from a painting. It was unreal and Ellen felt unreal in it, stealing past the formal parterres down to the wilderness garden, along the winding path that led to the rose arbor—and the man standing within it.

She didn't see him at first. The rose arbor had been designed with the vines trained around two sides, so that the inhabitants would be shielded from the house and the path, an illusion of privacy for confidantes. Or lovers.

But when she rounded the side, there he was, standing in the shadow of the roses, a little away from the two stone benches set at right angles against the trellis. The moonlight stole through the vines in uneven patches, obscuring more than it illuminated. Ellen stopped short at the threshold, unwilling to come closer, not sure, suddenly, what to say, her prepared speech frozen on her lips.

The dark figure by the bench turned slightly but made no move to come toward her. "So," he said. "You did not like your hat."

Ellen squinted into the shadows, wishing she could see his face. "It was too grand for me."

"You do yourself too little credit, *mia bella*."

His beauty. But she wasn't his beauty and couldn't be his beauty.

Ellen clasped her hands in front of her and attempted to remember her speech. "Your Excellency. It was kind of you to—to replace my hat for me, but I would never want you to think . . . I had never meant to make you think, to give any indication—"

"That you might need a hat?"

Ellen looked at him squarely in the moonlight. "That I might be for sale."

The prince grew very still. When he spoke, his voice was clipped. "It was a gift. Not a—how would you say it?—an advance payment."

"That's not how others see it." Ellen swallowed hard. So much for saying her piece and leaving. This wasn't at all what she had expected. But the prince never did do what she expected, did he? Forcing herself to meet his eyes, she said, "I wasn't sure if that was how you saw it."

"And yet you wore the hat today."

"I had nothing else to cover my head." Ellen grimaced, realizing how ridiculous that sounded. "I hadn't realized—it hadn't occurred to me—how it might be perceived. I wouldn't have worn it had I known. It was only after . . ."

"Ah. Persephone and the pomegranate seeds." When Ellen looked blank, the prince explained, "The goddess of spring was kidnapped by Hades. In the depths of his kingdom she ate six seeds of the pomegranate, not realizing that in partaking of his fruit she bound herself to him for six months of each year, down below, in his kingdom of endless night."

A kingdom of endless night. Moonlight dancing on the water and the scent of roses heavy all around them. No one but them and the roses and the moonlight.

"I wore it for only an hour," Ellen said helplessly.

"Are you attempting to work out the tally? How many hours to nights?" As Ellen made an instinctive gesture of negation, the prince dropped his teasing tone. "There is no obligation. I bought the hat because you needed a hat and it was, in some small sort, my fault that yours was lost."

"Thank you," she said, in a very small voice. She wasn't sure whether she ought to feel grateful or disappointed or embarrassed that she had so unfairly leapt to assumptions. Horrible, insulting assumptions.

"And because," said the prince, and he seemed to be speaking almost to himself, in a sort of dream, "it seemed a travesty to me that one who creates such beauty should be surrounded only by coarseness. A hat was a very small token to pay."

A small token to pay for what? One moment he said one thing and the next another and Ellen was thoroughly confused and exhausted, and all she knew was that she had to get this straight, now, even if nothing with the prince was ever straight or clear. He spoke in riddle and innuendo and Ellen was as out of her depth as she would have been trying to swim in the surf below.

"Don't," she said, because that was all she could think to say. "Don't pay me any tokens. If it's meant as a kindness—it's not a kindness to afford me these sorts of attentions. You'll lose me my position. And if it's not meant as a kindness . . . if you expected some return . . ."

"Yes?" The world seemed to shiver to a stop around them; even the moonlight lay quiet. The prince looked at Ellen, one brow raised. Waiting.

For a mad moment, the words stuck in Ellen's throat. Would it be so bad? she wondered wildly. Would it be so bad to be the prince's mistress? What was she, after all? She wasn't a lady to be ruined. She hadn't a family to protect her or honor to defend. She was a woman alone in the world, and if she were to succumb . . . who would there be to care but her conscience?

A kingdom of night. Their kingdom of night. Caresses unimaginable, roses and moonlight and riches hers for the taking.

In secret. For a time. Until he grew bored of her.

And Maybelle. There was Maybelle. She couldn't let herself forget Maybelle.

But it hurt. It hurt to step back, to abandon the promise of the waiting silence between them when she knew, knew down to her bones, that all she needed was to hold out a hand, make a sign, any sign, and the prince's arms would be around her.

There would be no going back. Ever. Ruined was ruined was ruined. She'd seen what happened to women abandoned.

Ellen drew in a deep breath, letting the chill salt air scour her lungs. "Then you should know that you're wasting your time," she said crisply. "I won't be your mistress."

The magic was gone, the bond between them shattered. The prince was a prince again, distant and urbane. "Is that what you summoned me here to say?"

Ellen frowned at him. "I didn't summon you. You summoned me."

The prince's voice changed. "I had a note from you."

"So did I." With a sense of dawning unease, Ellen remembered the cheap scrap of paper, the blurred words, so different from the note that came with the hat, the ink crisp and clear on linen stationery. She looked at the prince in alarm. "You didn't send it, did you?"

And if he hadn't . . .

"No," said the prince, just as footfalls sounded on the path.

Ellen froze, staring in horror at the prince. The only way out was the path, but the second they stepped out, they'd be seen. Seen by whoever had sent those notes.

"Quick," said the prince, and grabbed Ellen's hand, dragging her down into the darkness behind the stone bench as the heavy fragrance of crushed rose petals enveloped them.

CHAPTER EIGHTEEN

Lucky

Newport, Rhode Island
July 1957

A GIGANTIC BOUQUET HAD found its way into Dudley Sprague's hospital room, filling the air with the scent of roses. The sight and smell of those damn flowers reminded Lucky of her wedding day—delicate, joyous pink roses everywhere—and how hopeful she'd felt, how madly in love with her dazzling new husband.

She looked back at her father-in-law's yellow face, his rheumy eyes. "Of course I'm not planning to leave your son," she said. "Why on earth would you imagine such a thing?"

"Let's just say a fairy whispered in my ear. Some artsy-fartsy fellow who calls himself an architect—"

"Teddy? *Teddy* told you?"

"Ha. I was right. And here I thought you didn't have the nerve."

"I don't have the nerve. You're mistaken."

"Well, why shouldn't you dump the moron? Stuy's a lousy husband. Goddamn useless son of a bitch. But if you think that Winthrop fairy's going to make you any happier—"

"Oh, for God's sake—"

"All that goddamn artsy garbage. What a fruitcake. At least my son knows how to give it to a woman."

Lucky reached for the flowers and gently pulled a petal from one of the roses. For some reason, the bluster didn't bother her so much this time. She felt an extraordinary calm, a certainty like you felt in church, right after Communion, except more electric.

Teddy. She was leaving for Italy with Teddy and Joanie and Nonna. Nothing could change that, now. She'd promised him in the teahouse. They had kissed and kissed while the rain thundered against the glass, until Teddy had pulled his lips away and told her they had to stop, right now, and Lucky had looked up at his dear face, his eyes, and knew she couldn't go back.

All right, she'd said. Then we'll run away together.

And this time she wasn't kidding around.

"You can believe what you like," she said to Dudley Sprague, as she tore the rose petal into tiny pieces. "I certainly don't intend to defend myself to you. Let alone make you privy to my personal decisions."

Sprague struggled up on his elbows. "You wouldn't dare!"

Lucky tore another petal from the rose and smiled.

"You little bitch," he whispered. "You think I can't bite, do you? You think I'm helpless, lying here?"

"No. I just don't care anymore, that's all. You don't matter, you're just a mean little toad nobody will mourn for a single second. I don't care what you think or do."

"Well, you *will* care, by God! Once they read out that will, you'll care!"

"Why should I? Do you think I care about money? Stuy can have it. He can have it all, I don't care."

"Ha. There *isn't* any damn money, don't you know that? All gone."

Lucky snatched another petal. "Well, I guess I didn't expect any less from you, did I? That's the thing about you and your son, you're awfully good at spending other people's money, but you—"

"You think you're any different? It's not even yours, you fool. That's right. It was never yours, none of it. Not the house, not the money that came with it. If it weren't for me—I could snap my fingers and—damn it, you're not going to get away with this—leaving my son *penniless*! You'll be penniless, too, just watch—"

He collapsed back on the pillow and shut his eyes. His chest heaved for breath.

Lucky dropped the tiny pieces of rose petal on the floor and picked up her pocketbook. "Goodbye, Dudley. May God forgive you for—"

"The boathouse." His eyes flew open. "I'm going to tell everyone about the boathouse."

"I don't know what you're talking about."

"You will. Everyone will. By the time I'm done, everyone's going to know the truth about you, you goddamn little upstart, you Eye-talian brat, you fraud—"

"*Fraud*?"

"That's exactly what I said! You think I can't ruin you? You think you can have the last word? I'll *show* you the last word, by God! I'll—"

Lucky spun around and left the room, and the rest of his words floated harmlessly into the rose-scented air.

When she returned to Sprague Hall, Lucky took the back stairs in order to avoid the brutal cackle of Louise and Reggie arguing in the sunroom. Angela had already laid out her gown in the dressing room. The hairdresser was supposed to arrive in an hour. But Lucky didn't have the slightest desire to make herself ready for the ball, like some kind of Cinderella. Her serenity had vanished with Dudley Sprague's apoplectic rant.

Under the bed, her suitcases lay hidden, packed and ready to go. She'd packed Joanie's things, too, and a suitcase for her grandmother. This morning, a note had arrived from Teddy—*We start the rest of our lives tomorrow*—along with a small box that contained a gold pendant in the shape of a dove, and the eye of the dove was a tiny diamond. She had strung the pendant on a fine gold chain and wore it now, under her blouse, against her skin. Everything was prepared, her old life folded up into suitcases, her new life bright and shining before her.

So why did she feel this terrible premonition of doom?

Maybe it was the weather. All of Newport hung still under the weight of so much heat—under the heavy air, under the heavy sun drooping toward the horizon. Even the ocean lay tranquilized. Hardly a sail interrupted all that glassy blue, except for the one that edged its laborious way toward shore from the open water on the last hint of breeze. Lucky paused to stare through the window as the boat dipped closer. A man sat at the tiller, golden-haired. He lifted his arm and drank from a large bottle. On the deck a small child lay on her stomach, dangling her arms from the bow.

Lucky swore and ran out of the room, down the stairs, past the astonished Louise and Reggie in the sunroom. On the terrace she stumbled, almost falling. By the time she reached the boathouse, the sailboat had finally gained the little cove, the man had jumped to the rocks and wound a rope around one of the rotting bollards, and the little girl gleefully dove off the stern to swim to shore.

"What on earth do you think you're doing?" Lucky cried.

Stuy looked up and waved. "Well, blow me down. If it isn't my adoring wife!"

"You're *drunk*?"

"Only a little bit."

Lucky scrambled down the slippery rocks to grab Joanie by the hands and haul her in. "It isn't safe, bringing the boat in here!"

"It *is* a boathouse, after all."

"Not a real one! Not for mooring a sailboat! My God, what if you'd crashed into the rocks?"

"For God's sake, nobody's going to crash into the rocks on a day like this!"

"In your condition, he might!"

"Hardly enough wind to bend a blade of grass. Was there, princess?" Stuy hoisted the dripping Joanie into the air. She squealed with laughter and flung her arms around his neck.

"Daddy let me take the tiller!" she said.

"Oh, Stuy! You didn't!"

"Sure I did. She's a good little sailor, aren't you, Joanie-belle? Make your daddy proud."

"Put her down before you both end up in the water. Stuy, show some sense. She's too young to handle a sailboat by herself, you know that."

"Yes, I can!" Joanie exclaimed.

"Aw, you're just coddling her. Why, at her age, I was out on the ocean all day in my little dinghy, never mind the weather—"

"Well, you're lucky to be alive, that's all. Anyway, you're drunk, it's too dangerous, you'll—"

"Mommy! Look at me!"

Lucky turned just in time to see Joanie leap from the rocks to the sailboat deck and turn a pirouette on the polished teak. For just an instant, she had to admire her daughter's grace, her long young limbs, her skin turning gold under the falling afternoon sun.

Then she screamed.

"Joanie! You get right back here! What if a wave comes up?"

"There's no waves, Mommy!"

"Stuy, do something!"

Stuy sighed and set down the whisky bottle. "All right, all right. Hold still, princess."

He waded back to the boat and swung her, giggling, to the rocks. Lucky felt a pang of guilt. Maybe she should tell him what she was going to do, give him a chance to say goodbye. But what if he tried to stop her? Tried to take Joanie away? Already she regretted visiting her father-in-law. What a stupid impulse! She'd done it out of remorse, that was all, a stupid sense of duty to a dying man who'd never had a kind word for her. When would she learn? Nobody else around here had a conscience to speak of. Nobody else felt badly about betraying others. She had to stop feeling guilty about her plans and just—for *once*!—do something for herself, something that was right for *her*, and for her daughter, and her grandmother.

Lucky took Joanie's hand.

"Now wave goodbye to Daddy so he can take the sailboat back to the yacht club and come home in time to dress for the ball," she said. "If he can still sail straight, that is."

DURING THE SHORT drive to Marble House, Lucky thought about apologizing. Decided against it. She was too hot, the silence between them too frosty. She wore her beautiful gown of pink chiffon, her pink satin sandals, her necklace of South Sea pearls, her pearl-and-diamond earrings. Sweat crawled down the small of her back, down her cleavage. In the back seat, Louise and Reggie kept up a giddy patter of conversation, something about a house party at some castle in the north of England and this chap who had turned up to dinner drunk as a skunk—that was the phrase Reggie used, *drunk as a skunk*—wearing plus fours. *Plus fours!* Reggie roared with laughter. Louise giggled. She wore a turquoise ball gown of somewhat avant-garde design, featuring a stuffed bird on one shoulder, and smoked two cigarettes in the time it took for them to bounce down the long, uneven Sprague drive, turn left into the line of cars, and crawl down Bellevue Avenue a hundred yards or so to the Marble House gates.

As they rumbled up the carriage drive, a premonition of doom crept over Lucky. Stuy slammed the brakes angrily, bringing the car to an instant stop. The valet jumped out to open Lucky's door. Out popped Stuy from the driver's seat to toss the keys in the valet's general direction. He'd cleaned up, at least—rakishly handsome, gold hair gleaming, gold skin glowing against his sharp white collar, black jacket, black silk bow tie. Lucky stood stiffly by the car until he turned back and offered her an ironic arm. Louise adjusted the bird on her shoulder and crooked her neck back to take in the sight of Marble House, ground floor windows all alight.

"Why, it's just like the old days, isn't it?" she exclaimed. "Newport the way it's *supposed* to be."

Inside the magnificent entry hall, the roses overwhelmed Lucky. She tightened her grip on her husband's arm and turned toward him. "Stuy, I need to tell you—"

But Stuy had already slung an arm over Reggie's shoulder and pulled away from her, in the direction of the bar.

TEDDY'S FACE LIT up when Lucky entered the Gothic room, where the committee members had gathered for a celebratory toast before the official start of the ball. He extricated himself from a conversation with Mrs. Whitehouse and wove between the bodies to reach her.

"Devastating," he said, kissing her cheek. "Simply devastating."

"Thank you. You're not so bad yourself."

"Everything all right?"

"Oh, just fine. You know, the usual."

He fixed a serious look on her. "You're not having second thoughts, are you?"

"No! Of course not. I just—"

"*Theodore!* There you are."

Lucky looked over Teddy's shoulder to the woman behind him, who tapped his shoulder with a single white-gloved finger.

"Mrs. Potts," he said. "Can I help you? If you're looking for Stinky, I just—"

Prunella Potts waved away the idea of her husband. She leaned forward and spoke in a confidential whisper. "I noticed you were speaking with Mrs. Whitehouse a moment ago. I want your honest opinion, now. What do you think of those Tiffany people giving *her* the diamond?"

"They haven't *given* it to her, Mrs. Potts," said Lucky. "It's only a loan for the evening."

"A *loan*. Hmph. In *my* day we didn't *borrow* jewelry."

"Times have changed, Mrs. Potts. That was such a *very long* time ago."

"Well, I wouldn't be surprised if she keeps it. Really, I don't know *what* those Tiffany people were thinking, draping their diamond on a bosom like *that*. It would have been so much more *becoming* on a lady of substance and breeding."

Lucky turned back to Mrs. Whitehouse, who chatted with elegant animation to an admiring circle near the fireplace. The gigantic yellow diamond licked and flared in its setting. "I think it looks wonderful on her," she said.

Teddy cleared his throat. "You know, I've always loved this room. I think it's my favorite in the entire place."

"Really? I thought you went in for more classical designs," Lucky said.

"It's the sheer audacity of it. The rest of the house evokes all that baroque European grandeur, and then you walk in here and it's like you've stepped into some kind of medieval museum."

"A *new* medieval museum," Lucky murmured.

"True. No chipped stonework or worn flagstones around here, that's for sure." Teddy nodded to one of the glass cabinets. "Of course, the artifacts are astonishing."

"I've always wanted to spend an afternoon just looking around, but I've never had the nerve to ask."

"I remember when Marlborough proposed to dear Consuelo in this very room," said Mrs. Potts. "Right there by the fireplace."

"You were there?"

"No, but she told me all about it afterward. Oh, we were great chums, Connie and me. *Bosom* friends. I was heartbroken when she left for England, *heartbroken*. Of course, she invited me to stay at her palace, but I never could find the time to visit."

"You don't say," said Teddy.

"And yet they weren't in love at all," said Lucky. "It's really sort of tragic, when you think about it."

"Of course they weren't in love. The idea! Love is for the middle classes, Mrs. Sprague. We married for *duty* in my day. Like your grandmother. Poor old Maybelle, renouncing her passion for my dear cousin. She had her title, but she never—"

The tinkling of crystal ran over the rest of her sentence. Everybody turned to the monumental fireplace, which dwarfed the regal Mrs. Sheldon Whitehouse in her long white gloves and silk gown, canary diamond flashing on her bosom, diamond earrings dangling from her ears. A pair of silent waiters materialized, bearing trays of champagne. Mrs. Whitehouse lifted a glass in which the wine fizzed gleefully, the exact same color as the diamond.

"Ladies and gentlemen," she said. "To Newport."

LUCKY KNEW SHE was probably drinking more champagne than she should, but she didn't care. She drifted from room to splendid room, too nervy to settle down and make small talk with anybody. Small talk at a time like this! All those months of excitement—planning for this ball, this glittering night, and now all that glitter was eclipsed by the gold that was to come. Tomorrow she'd leave Newport behind for good. Tomorrow she'd be flying down the highway next to Teddy, Joanie and Nonna in the seat behind, suitcases stuffed in the trunk. It didn't seem real, it couldn't be real. Too good to be true, and yet it *was* true.

It *had* to be true—she would *make* it true!

Through a doorway, Lucky glimpsed Louise standing a few inches too close to the well-ironed chest of a tall, handsome, blue-eyed, thick-haired man Lucky recognized as Jack Kennedy, the junior senator from Massachusetts, who'd married one of her old Miss Porter's classmates in a spectacularly tasteful wedding right here in Newport a few years ago. Nearby, Stuy stood with cocktail glass in hand, speaking to an elegant brunette with large, wide-set eyes—Jackie Bouvier, now Jaqueline Kennedy, the senator's wife, wearing an expression of weary tolerance bordering on distaste. Stuy's hand seemed to be reaching for her waist; Jackie angled her face away.

Lucky drew a deep breath and swooped in, like an angel of mercy.

"Why, *Jacqueline*!" she exclaimed. "I was hoping to find you. My goodness, what a lovely dress."

They exchanged kisses in the air next to their cheeks. Jackie spoke in her breathless voice. "Lucky, how lovely to see you. It's been absolutely *ages*. Your husband was just telling me how hard you've been working, putting this lovely night together."

"Oh, it's just another day in the salt mines! Stuy, would you mind awfully if I borrow Jackie for a moment? There's somebody who's absolutely *dying* to be introduced."

"Knock yourselves out," Stuy said coldly, and turned away.

"If you don't mind," Jackie said, more breathless than usual, "could we perhaps sit down a moment instead? I've been feeling a little delicate, you know."

Lucky's gaze dropped briefly to Jackie's middle. "Oh! Of course, how silly of me. I'll find your husband."

"Oh no! That's not necessary. Let's go outside, shall we?"

Out on the terrace, the Lester Lanin Orchestra was finishing up the last happy notes of "I'm Gonna Wash That Man Right Outa My Hair." Lucky steered Jackie toward one of the tables. "It's so awfully hot, too," she said, urging Jackie into a chair.

"You're so sweet. Jack's been bustling around, meeting everybody. Absolutely exhausting! But I did *so* want to come tonight and support the cause. I do worship all these splendid mansions, don't you?"

Lucky laughed. "I certainly wouldn't be here if I didn't! A party like this is really not my kind of thing at all."

"It's such a shame, you know." Jackie's gaze traveled wistfully over the acres of marble. "All these palaces crumbling away for want of money and families to bring them to life. They had a single perfect moment in history, and then the hour was past. Nobody wants them anymore. Isn't that sad?"

"Well, who knows? Maybe they'll have a second heyday."

"I don't know. I don't know if you can ever get such a thing back once it's gone." Jackie looked at Lucky and smiled. "Oh, listen to me. Getting all sentimental on a beautiful night like this! How hard you've all worked! And everything's just wonderful, simply wonderful. They'll be talking about this ball for years."

A flicker of movement from the side of the terrace caught Lucky's attention. She replied, "I certainly hope so. We're raising piles of money for the preservation society. Mrs. Whitehouse thinks we should . . . we should . . ."

Jackie peered at her face. "Why, what's the matter?"

Lucky stood up. "I'm so awfully sorry, could you excuse me a moment?"

LIKE MOST DRUNKS of his class, Stuy kept up appearances. Everybody drank, after all, and a lot of people drank a lot of booze, so how did you tell the difference? Lucky herself looked forward to tossing back champagne and martinis and gin and tonics—my God, how else did you survive all the boredom, all the sneaking suspicion that you were some kind of fraud, living in a house like this in a town like this, such that ordinary people gawped at you like a tourist attraction or something?

Anyway, Lucky first worked out that Stuy might actually have some kind of drinking problem about a year or two into her marriage, when she got a call from the yacht club at two in the morning. The manager was awfully apologetic, but could she maybe come by to pick up her husband? He was lying on the dock in a puddle of his own vomit, not quite unconscious but not exactly coherent, either. So Lucky changed into a housedress and climbed into the car and drove down to the yacht club. She cleaned up Stuy with a wet towel from the bar, and the manager kindly helped her drag him into the car for the drive home. She'd left him in the driveway—well, she couldn't exactly haul him up the stairs to bed by herself, could she?—and the next day the car was empty and her bedroom was full of flowers. Eventually he stopped giving her flowers for every episode of drunkenness, though, and she stopped expecting them.

Now here he was, trying to start a fistfight with Teddy Winthrop on the terrace steps, even if he couldn't quite stand up straight long enough to throw an actual punch.

"Stand still, why don't you!" he yelled at Teddy. "Stand still so I can sock you one!"

"Nobody's socking anybody," said Teddy.

"Like hell!"

Lucky grabbed her husband's arm just in time. "Stop it, Stuy! My God! What on earth are you doing? Everybody's staring!"

"Well, we can't have that, can we? God forbid the whole world should see me knock the lights outta my wife's lover!"

"You're not going to knock anybody's lights out! Not in your condition!"

Stuy shrugged off her hand. "Stay out of this, all right?"

"Oh, *where's* Reggie when you need him? Teddy, help me get him into the garden or something."

Teddy stepped forward, but Stuy held up his hand with exaggerated dignity. "We'll go into the garden, all right, but I don't need any help from you."

He lifted his hand, which held a bottle of some kind—whisky, from the look of it—my God, how had Stuy got his hands on an entire bottle of whisky? Before Lucky could snatch it away, he lifted the neck to his mouth and slugged down.

"Stuy, I think you've had enough," Teddy said.

"You think so?"

Teddy reached for the bottle and yanked it out of Stuy's hand. "I do. Now let's just step out of everybody's way here—"

"Mrs. Sprague?"

Lucky spun around to find a white-faced man in a dark suit staring at her in alarm. His gaze shifted back and forth between her and Stuy. "I'm so sorry," she said breathlessly. "I'll just take him home—"

"No, sweetheart. Go enjoy the ball. Don't worry, I'll handle this," said Teddy.

"*Sweetheart?*" roared Stuy. "Did you just call my wife your *sweetheart?*"

"Don't make a *scene*, Stuy—"

The man in the suit reached for Lucky's arms. "Mrs. Sprague, I'm terribly sorry—"

"Oh, not you, too—"

"Sprague, so help me, if you lay one hand on her—"

"—call from the hospital—"

"You'll *what*, Winthrop? Go on, say it!"

"—tragically—"

Lucky spun around to face Teddy and Stuy. "Will you two *just shut up*!"

The two men stared at her, stunned. She turned back to the man in the suit. By now a discreet crowd had materialized, not exactly watching them but doing a terrible job of pretending *not* to watch. Lucky tilted her chin and said, "I beg your pardon. Please proceed."

The man took a deep breath. "The hospital just called. I'm grieved to say that Mr. Sprague's father passed away half an hour ago."

A peculiar noise came from Stuy's throat, like he was choking on a chicken bone, like he couldn't breathe. Teddy lunged forward just in time. Stuy's eyes rolled back, his body toppled to the flagstones, his stomach heaved out pretty much everything he'd had to drink that evening, and more.

"CARDIAC ARREST," SAID Dr. Goldberg. "He was dead by the time the nurse arrived in the room."

Lucky put her hand to her mouth. "My God. It wasn't even his liver."

"The liver disease was a contributing factor, of course. But the rest of him wasn't in the best of condition, either. A lifetime of drink, rich food, and sedentary habits will catch up with the heartiest constitution, I'm afraid."

"You should tell that to my husband, when he wakes up from his alcoholic stupor," Lucky said.

It was nearly midnight, and the hospital corridor was deserted, except for the head nurse at her station. Everything seemed eerily normal. The usual smells of antiseptic and chicken broth filled the air; the hum of machines made a veil of sound that hung over them in the sallow fluorescent light. Dr. Goldberg looked weary and annoyed, like Dudley Sprague's death had caused him considerable inconvenience.

Dudley Sprague's death.

He was *dead,* Lucky thought. Dead!

The thought was too big, too impossible. Something fluttered in her chest, like a butterfly trying to escape. Oh God! She curled her fist against her mouth, willing the joy to remain trapped inside. Willing her face to remain fixed in sorrow before Dr. Goldberg's stern appraisal. The squeak of wheels caused them both to turn their heads in the direction of Sprague's room, where two orderlies pushed out a gurney draped in white cloth.

"My God, is that him?" Lucky said.

Dr. Goldberg turned back to her. "I'd offer my condolences, but I suspect congratulations are more in order."

Lucky stared into the doctor's eyes, which hadn't changed expression an iota—if Dr. Goldberg could even be said to wear something so trivial as a human expression. For an instant, though, she could have sworn she spotted a twitch at one side of his mouth.

"Why, you're on my side, aren't you?" she whispered.

He slid his hand into the pocket of his lab coat and drew it out again, holding an envelope. "I found this on his bedside table when I went in to pronounce him dead. I trust you'll ensure it reaches the intended recipient?"

Lucky took the envelope and turned it over. It was addressed to the firm in New York that handled Dudley Sprague's legal affairs.

"Of course I will," she said.

"Yes," Dr. Goldberg said solemnly. "That's what I thought."

Once the gurney had passed by, and Dr. Goldberg had walked off down the hall in the opposite direction, Lucky slipped into her father-in-law's room and opened the envelope with her fingernail. Inside, she found a single piece of plain white paper, no letterhead or anything, folded into thirds. Already the lamps had been turned off, the room shrouded respectfully in darkness, so she had to tilt the folded paper with her cold, trembling hand to catch the light from the corridor.

Sprague's handwritten scrawl came into focus, almost illegible, sprawling downward across the page in a few furious lines. Lucky squinted at the words. Her heart hammered, her lips moved as she read, as if that would help to decipher them. To make some rational meaning out of Dudley Sprague's final confession.

When she was finished, she pressed the paper against her chest and stared in shock across the room, at the shadowy bouquet of roses still giving off their suffocating scent.

Then she turned and raced toward the elevator in her ball gown of pink chiffon, her satin shoes, her pearls, where she rang bang into Louise Pelham-Mayhew, dress askew, lipstick smeared, mascara streaked down her cheeks.

"I've just heard the news!" she cried. "Where have they put my daddy?"

CHAPTER NINETEEN

Andie

Newport, Rhode Island
September 2019

"SO SHE HAD all of Daddy's money. Must be nice," Meghan said.

Meghan and I stood together in the dining room—standing our only option since the table and the twenty-five Louis XIV–style gilded bronze chairs had long since been sold—and examined the full-length portrait leaning against the bare wall between the now chipped gold-painted columns. In other Newport cottages, the columns would have been covered with gold leaf, but the Spragues had been a rarity during the Gilded Age. Instead of the familiar Vanderbilt or Astor motto of the era, Only the Best, the Spragues had adhered to the Good Enough philosophy as soon as they'd acquired the property.

Weak light struggled to peer through heavy clouds and the salt-crusted windows. Despite the constant rain, the weather forecast said that we'd have a break around three o'clock. I'd told George to go ahead and set up the equipment in the rose arbor so they could squeeze in some outside shots during the final hour of our workday. I was supposed to be out with them to pretend to have seen a woman in white floating across the yard toward the boathouse. I was hiding in the dining room now to avoid it, planning a voice-over so I wouldn't have to stare into the camera and lie directly to my audience. I was hoping that

George would give up on waiting for me and pack up and come inside, but so far we seemed to be in a standoff.

What little scrap of self-respect I still clung to beneath my pink construction hat had shrunk even more when Marc had called the previous evening with instructions from Christiana including a personal request to add more footage regarding the presence of ghosts and even to film in places where we'd had ghost sightings. When I protested that we hadn't seen anything, I was told in very frank terms that it didn't matter. Which was why I was now in the dining room studying a portrait instead of outside in the rose arbor with the film crew jettisoning the last of my professional integrity.

"She looks kind of sweet," Meghan said, her head tilted as she regarded the painting.

The girl in the portrait stared out at us with a slightly startled expression, her pink gown festooned with so much lace and ruffles that the flounces had flounces. Satin dancing slippers of a matching hue peeked out beneath her hem, making it seem as if she'd been captured on canvas dressing up in her mother's clothes. Her fair hair, despite obvious attempts to constrain it into a smooth coil at the back of her head, had defied instructions and instead presented a fuzz of curls around her forehead that, along with her pink cheeks and round, innocent eyes, reminded me of the cherubic angels appearing in Renaissance artwork. Only the appearance of a generous bosom informed the viewer that the subject was past adolescence with one foot already firmly planted into womanhood.

"More like a lamb to slaughter. Poor Maybelle," I said. "Sold to the highest bidder into a loveless marriage."

"Don't be so cynical." Meghan leaned closer to examine the brushstrokes. "She married a prince and moved to Italy. For all we know, she fell in love with her Prince Charming and it really was a fairy tale. From those photos we saw online, they did look happy together, and Maybelle was able to pursue her interests in music and helping orphans. Not to mention having access to gorgeous clothes. I'm actually a little jealous. Being set up by your family seems a lot better than using Tinder, that's for sure."

"Meghan," I said, using my Petey voice.

"Well, it's true. Not that you'd know. You haven't been on a date since, well, for a long time. It's a shark tank out there, trust me. I'm considering the convent."

"Well, you do look good in black and white." I grinned. "Have you had a chance to dig for info on Frank Pratt?"

"I did, and there's not too much out there, but what I did find was pretty telling. I don't think he was too broken up about being jilted for a prince because he married some heiress three months after Maybelle left for Italy. Kind of sad, if you think about it. Especially if her ghost is supposed to still be looking for her one true love. And those letters Frank wrote to Maybelle. What a con artist."

"We should probably not mention that fact if we're going to be forced to go with the ghost angle. Makes it much less romantic. Anything else we can use?"

"Not really. But you might find this interesting. Remember that memoir in the library about the self-proclaimed American heroine?"

I scrunched up my nose, trying to recall the name. "Putrid or Purina? Or some kind of dried fruit, right?"

"Prunella. Prunella Schuyler Potts. Frank was her cousin. Nothing that we can use, I just found it random yet interesting."

"Definitely random." I pointed at the brooch tucked inside the voluminous pink ruffles at Maybelle's neck. "There's the cameo. I wish I knew where it was. *That's* the sort of thing I want in this series. Pieces of the past that tie the decades together. Not fabricated ghost stories or titillating rumors. Streaming services and cable networks are already full of that stuff. Why can't *Makeover Mansion* be the lone bright and shining light?"

"Because that's not what they're paying you for?"

The sound of tires rolling over gravel brought our attention toward the French doors overlooking the loggia and the side of the house where a sleek Bugatti was making its way up the drive.

I glanced at my watch. "Oh no. It's almost four thirty and Teddy's here. Luke will blow a gasket when he finds out I haven't left yet."

Meghan had moved to another set of French doors, pushing back dusty panels of what might have once been crimson velvet but had since faded to a pale raspberry. "That's the least of your worries. The film crew is still outside waiting for you."

I might have said one of those words my mother would have labeled unladylike and low-class. I started toward the door but stopped. "You know . . . ," I began.

"Yep," Meghan said. Knowing what the other was thinking was one of the bonuses of having been friends for so long. "Since you're already in trouble, might as well go ahead and meet Teddy and ask for an introduction to Lucky. Luke can't get any *more* mad, right?"

Without giving myself time to really think of the appropriate answer, I headed toward the door and into the cavernous great hall just as Luke was letting the famous Theodore Winthrop inside.

The older man removed his hat and smiled, looking at us through thick glasses as we approached. Despite his age-diminished stature and the lion-head cane, he still possessed the swagger and presence of an Indiana Jones, complete with tweed jacket and elbow patches, and well-worn leather loafers that had probably seen more of the world than I had. All that was missing was his whip.

Turning to Luke, he said, "If I'd known you were entertaining, I would have worn my dinner jacket. But what a lovely surprise."

"I'm not . . . ," Luke began through gritted teeth.

Ignoring Luke and his simmering anger radiating heat that could singe unprotected skin, I held out my hand to Teddy. "Dr. Winthrop. I can't tell you what an absolute honor this is. My name is Andrea Figuero, Andie to my friends." I smiled warmly, so he'd know I already considered him a friend. "You have been my icon ever since I became interested in historic preservation. I've read all of your books, but your *Reclaiming the Beauty of the Past* has a permanent position on my bedside table for constant referencing. And when I was a young girl and dreamed of one day visiting Italy, my mother and I would watch your PBS series about your yearly research visits to Tuscany for your books on in-depth examinations of the architecture and art of the region." I blushed, realized I was probably gushing yet unable to stop myself. "I own every single one of your books." I didn't mention how I'd scrimped and saved to buy his first three books for my mother one year for Christmas. They were the only things from the house she'd taken with her when she left.

Teddy took my hand in both of his and squeezed them gently. His grip was strong, and I recalled that he had been an avid rower. I imagined he still was. "Ah yes. What a glorious time that was. We always had such lovely summers together."

I wondered at the word "we," knowing that his wife had been dead since long before his PBS series. I opened my mouth to ask, but he continued.

He lifted his cane. "But now . . ." He shrugged. "What a pleasure meeting you, Andie. And thank you for your kind words. What a compliment—I'll have to make sure my head doesn't grow so big my hat won't fit anymore!" He chuckled, the sound as warm and inviting as a crackling fire. "Did you and your mother ever make it to Italy?"

I managed to hang on to my smile. "I haven't, not yet. But my mother . . ." I shrugged, trying to pretend that it didn't matter. "I believe she might have gone with her second husband once or twice. We don't really stay in touch."

Teddy squeezed my hands again before letting go. "Her loss. Fortunately, you're young. And I feel quite certain a trip to Italy is in your future." He actually winked, the movement magnified by his thick glasses.

Luke stepped between us. "Andie is here to film a reality series involving renovating several rooms in the house. Lucky might have mentioned it. She and her crew should have been out of the house twenty minutes ago according to our contract, so I'm sure she was just leaving. Let's . . ."

Doing my best to ignore him, I turned toward Meghan, who was almost hopping from foot to foot in her excitement at meeting her idol and preservation icon. "Dr. Winthrop, may I introduce my good friend and fellow preservationist, Meghan Black? She is a huge fan and—"

Meghan didn't allow me to finish, unable to hold back her enthusiasm or fangirling for another minute. She took Teddy's hand and began pumping it up and down like an old-fashioned water spigot, causing me to worry about the elderly man's shoulder and elbow joints. "I can't tell you what an honor this is." Her Southern accent marched uncontrolled out of her mouth like wayward soldiers as it always did when she was excited. "I wrote my thesis on you and your work. You are an absolute icon for everything I believe in."

"Well, thank you, young lady. I'm truly humbled. I'm also quite convinced I will need a new hat to contain my swollen head."

Luke glowered from behind Theodore. "Teddy, Lucky is waiting."

As if Luke hadn't spoken, the older man said, "So tell me about this television series you're working on. If it has anything to do with my field of expertise, I'd be more than happy to make a guest appearance. If you think it might be helpful. I don't want to impose."

I thought Meghan might self-implode as her head nodded rapidly like a bobblehead doll on the dashboard of a getaway car.

"Thank you, Dr. Winthrop," I managed to say calmly. Taking a leap of faith that Marc would get behind me and support me, I said, "I think we might take you up on that. *Makeover Mansion* has taken a turn away from the serious restoration show I'd originally envisioned, but an appearance by you will definitely put it back on track. Not only do you have fans in the preservation world, but also fans from your PBS series. I'm seriously flattered that you would even consider it."

"Ah yes. *Makeover Mansion*. Lucky has mentioned it. She's looking forward to seeing the final product. So, of course I'd like to be a part of it—no matter how small. I'd be honored."

With a glaring look at me, Luke said, "Teddy, you know how Lucky hates to be kept waiting. And Andie was just leaving . . ."

Imagining the hot breath of the producers on my neck and thinking about the emergency room bill for the raisins in Petey's nose, I blurted, "I would love to meet Lucky."

"There you all are!" Joanie approached us, gliding down the wide staircase, her long skirt billowing around her and making her appear to be floating. The sound of jingling bangles heralded her descent. "I was wondering where everybody was and here you are starting the party without me. It's cocktail hour, and we all know how much Lucky expects her martini dry and on time."

"Andie and Meghan were on their way out," Luke said. "The rules say that the film people need to be out of the house by four thirty. No exceptions."

"Really, Luke," Joanie said, already digging into the pouch hanging from her waist. The look in Luke's eyes made her pause before drawing out a stone. "You're starting to sound like Hadley. Rules are made to be broken, I say. Besides, this isn't film people. This is Andie." She peered behind my shoulder and spotted Meghan and smiled. "And her research assistant. I can't believe that they haven't met Lucky yet."

Remembering what Meghan had said about it not being possible for Luke to be *more* mad than he already was, I said, "That's because your son won't let us."

"Well, that's just ridiculous." Joanie drew her arm through mine. "Besides, I think Lucky would love to meet Andie. I believe they are of like minds regarding this house." Leading me toward the stairs, she called over her shoulder, "Lukie, please be a dear and make the martinis and bring them up?"

"Joanie." Luke's voice held more panic than warning. "I think it would be better if I stay with you. . . ."

"Actually," Meghan spoke up. "When I was in grad school, I worked at a fabulous bar called the Gin Joint. I can make a mean martini."

"Wonderful." Joanie's bangles jangled in agreement as she brought her hands together. "Dry with two olives. Bring six glasses, if you would. Everything you need including a tray is on the kitchen table, unless Hadley drank all the gin out of spite."

"Got it." Meghan raised her eyebrows at me before hurrying toward the back hall and kitchen, while I headed up the stairs with Joanie, my arm firmly trapped against her side. Luke and Teddy followed behind, accompanied by the firm snap of a cane against marble. I was the only one winded by the time we reached the third floor, confirming my suspicions that Dr. Winthrop was still an avid rower. And I was hopelessly out of shape.

Joanie tapped on the door. "Mother, I've brought guests. I hope you're decent." Without waiting for a response, she opened the door.

I stood in the doorway, blinking as my eyes adjusted from the dim corridors to the light from the sparkling clean windows bouncing off the white eggshell walls of the large room. What had most likely once been a mouse maze of corridors and small rooms for servants had been merged to create a large living space with high ceilings, the windows, unencumbered by any form of covering, welcoming in light despite the dismal sky outside.

I stood still for a long moment as I tried to reconcile the space with the untouched wreck of the first two floors, which more closely resembled a haunted house, to this penthouse suite that would have been at home in any upscale Manhattan high-rise. The clean, sparse lines of mid-century modern furniture blended neatly with the high-tech gadgetry in the sitting room area. A sleek glass-topped desk sat on four simple light-wood legs. An Apple iMac placed on top showed a rotating screen saver display of Italian scenery.

A large flat-screen television hung from the wall, displaying a Wii tennis game frozen in midplay, a shelf full of gaming equipment below it. Built-in ceiling speakers were playing a familiar aria from an opera I couldn't name because my brain was too busy trying to take in the sheer unexpectedness of everything I was seeing. Instead of the anticipated thick gilt, heavy brocade, and dark wood, this third floor was an oasis of light, an intriguing hint about the personality of the woman I was about to meet. I opened my mouth to ask where Lucky was when my eyes were drawn to the one spot of color on the otherwise bare walls. Above the bed with tapered legs and a low headboard hung a familiar work of art.

It was the painting Meghan and I had seen in the photograph of Lucky and Teddy and the rest of the organizers of the Tiffany Ball. The photo had been taken in Lucky's office here in Sprague Hall. I had assumed that it, along with the furniture and other valuables, had long since been sold to keep the house and its occupants from complete ruin. I moved closer to examine it.

"It's real." A movement from one of a pair of neon-green egg chairs—straight out of the *Mad Men* set—drew my attention to where a slim elderly woman with a model's bone structure and the poise of a watchful swan sat with a game controller in her hands. Her thick white hair was piled on top of her head, her bloodred silk blouse opened at the neck to reveal olive skin. At one of her wrists a diamond tennis bracelet twinkled as she moved to place the controller on a side table. She watched me with eyes that seemed almost black. "It's a Titian, although I'm sure you already knew that, right, Andie?"

It took me a moment to respond. "Um, yes. How . . . ?"

She smiled. "I may be old, but I miss nothing."

Teddy approached her chair. "Don't be alarmed, Andie. She means to say that she knows how to Google." He leaned down and kissed

Lucky's cheek, his lips lingering longer than I imagined a platonic relationship might warrant. "Hello, darling. Sorry I'm late. I was having the most delightful conversation with Andie and her friend, Meghan. Your martini will be up shortly."

Their eyes met for a long beat before Lucky turned her attention to me. "Come sit by me, Andie, so we can have a chat."

Luke shook his head, but Joanie took my hand and led me to the other egg chair. I sat, finding the ridiculous-looking chair rather comfortable. "Thank you, Mrs. Sprague. I've been hoping to get a chance to talk with you."

"Lucky, please. Everyone calls me Lucky. Only people I don't like have to call me Mrs. Sprague. And I like you. So far. Believe me, you'd do well to keep it that way."

Joanie, Luke, and Teddy sat down on the adjacent low-slung leather couch, the latter leaning heavily on his cane and Luke's arm to lower himself onto the cushion. Joanie let out a low, deep laugh. "Now, Mother, no need to scare her."

"I'm not trying to, but why not? I'm still fierce. It's possible to be fierce and old, you know." She turned her gaze toward the window, her voice softening. "Unlike some people."

"Do you mean your grandmother?" The words escaped me before I could talk myself out of saying them. But I was glad I'd spoken. I knew my time with Lucky was limited, and I was afraid I wouldn't get a second chance.

"Andie." Luke's voice carried a warning.

Ignoring him, I said, "Maybelle Sprague. I was just admiring her portrait. She was your grandmother, yes?"

Lucky regarded me with those dark eyes again. "Yes. She was. I suppose I shouldn't be comparing myself to her. She had a . . . difficult life, full of loss. In her later years when she wasn't of right mind, I'd like to think that she might have escaped to the past inside her head to give her some comfort."

Meghan appeared at the open door with a tray of martinis, a bottle of gin and vermouth, a shaker, and torn paper towels in lieu of cocktail napkins. As she handed everyone a glass and paper scrap, she said, "We've heard that Maybelle's ghost still wanders Sprague Hall—especially around the boathouse. Is that why we're not allowed to film there?"

Lucky took a large sip of her martini, closing her eyes as she let the liquid slip down her throat. "No. Of course not. There aren't any ghosts." She looked at me again. "From what I've been told, anyway. It's just that the boathouse isn't sound and is quite dangerous. We don't have enough insurance to protect us from personal injury, which is why it's forbidden."

I took a sip from my own drink, nearly choking. I sent Meghan a glance but she just shrugged. "We found Maybelle's trinket box. Nothing valuable was in it, just a stack of ribbon-tied love letters from a Frank Pratt. Did she ever mention him to you?"

Luke slammed down his glass. "Really, Andie. What has that got to do with the renovation? Interviews are off-limits, remember?"

Lucky sent her grandson a gentle smile. "I rather like the direction Andie is taking. The entire Gilded Age angle is long before my time or that of anyone still alive so there's no damage done, really. I've never heard of Frank Pratt and I think the letters are rather romantic. Perfect fodder for today's television. And if you add that her ghost is looking for her long-lost love, how can viewers stay away? More edifying than watching the Kardashians, surely."

I remembered Meghan saying the same thing and wondered if Lucky might have overheard her. Maybe she'd become an expert at eavesdropping as her world had receded into a single—albeit large and beautiful—room on the third floor of her once opulent home. It would certainly explain the mysterious appearance of the trinket box outside the library door, among other things that kept disappearing and reappearing. And the stealthy footsteps I continued to hear even when I thought I was alone.

I sat back, my gaze locking with Lucky's. She might be old, but she was certainly still fierce. "Just so you know," I said, "I joined this production because I saw an opportunity to do a different take on restoring old houses. My goal was to focus on preservation and history, all tied together by the personal stories of the people who once lived in these houses. Not to sensationalize, but to make the history of place come alive for a generation of viewers who see history as a dead thing." Lucky nodded, giving me the courage to continue, to tell her something I'd never shared before. "It's my lifelong dream to host a show about the stories of families told from the point of view of the house—the witnesses of time and change."

"How marvelous." Joanie clasped her hands together amid a jingling of gold bracelets.

"That it is," Lucky agreed. "And I applaud your ambitions, which, considering your background and your current handicaps, makes them even more admirable."

I sat up, quickly understanding that eavesdropping wasn't the worst of Lucky's sins. I held up my glass to Meghan, suddenly needing another drink. "I don't really think . . ."

"What do you mean?" Joanie asked, her expression full of real sympathy. I half expected her to pull out another crystal from her pouch.

Before I could redirect or leave or accidentally throw my glass against the wall, Lucky spoke. "Andie has had a difficult time since her mother abandoned the family, struggling to keep them afloat and trying to make a better life for all of them." Lucky spoke without malice, making me wonder what her point was in calling me out. She regarded me coolly, waiting for me to speak. She lifted her martini glass to her mouth, the diamonds in her bracelet winking in the light from the windows.

I kept my gaze focused on my fingers as they clutched the stem of my glass, feeling Luke's eyes on me. "I don't . . . I mean . . . none of that . . ." I stopped. "That's not what I wanted to talk about when I met you. But now I realize how uncomfortable personal questions can make someone, so I'm doubting that what I wanted to ask you would be appropriate, even if it would make good screen time on *Makeover Mansion*. And make the producers very happy."

"But not you." It wasn't a question.

"No. But what makes me happy has nothing to do with making this show a success."

Lucky flicked her manicured hand in my direction. "Oh, don't be so old-fashioned, Andie. When you get to be my age you can stop worrying about other people's feelings and just get the job done. In other words, go ahead and ask me. Ask me what happened to my husband the night he disappeared."

A window-rattling crack of thunder jerked me out of my seat, almost making me spill the last of my martini. Heavy rain pelted the glass and the roof, the sound like approaching cavalry. "Oh no." I chugged the rest of my drink, slamming the empty glass onto the tray. "All the film equipment is outside. Come on, Meghan, we've got to go."

With a quick wave goodbye and without meeting anyone's eyes, I raced toward the door, Meghan's footsteps pounding behind me, her repeated litany of *holy crap, holy crap, holy crap* following me until I'd flung the kitchen door open and run out into the deluge.

CHAPTER TWENTY

Ellen

Newport, Rhode Island
July 1899

"Oh bother, and now it's starting to rain." Prunella Schuyler's petulant tones cut through stone and bramble, all the way to Ellen's hiding place behind the bench, as Prunella swept into the rose arbor. "They were supposed to be here by now."

Ellen crouched down farther behind the bench, trying to make herself as small as possible, wishing she could fold herself up like a letter. The thorns of the roses poked through the fabric of her dress, like the prick of a million tiny pitchforks, pinning her into place for whatever torments were to come. She could feel the prince beside her, still and watchful. Only the stone of the bench sat between them and Prunella Schuyler and ruination.

Surely she'd find them? Surely she'd see? How could she not notice two grown people hunched behind a bench? But it was dark, Ellen thought wildly. Whatever moon there was lay hidden behind the gathering clouds.

"Maybe they didn't get the notes." Frank Pratt slouched in after his cousin.

"The horrible girl swore she'd delivered them." Prunella gave an aggravated swish of her skirts as she paced the perimeter of the enclosure, her flounces brushing the edge of Ellen's bench. "I suppose we'll just have to wait."

"It's raining harder," Frank Pratt complained, rubbing at the back of his neck. And so it was. Ellen could feel the drops seeping through the thick matting of vines, making cold spots on her back. She rested her forehead against the rough stone back of the bench, letting the misery seep into her bones like the rainwater.

"It's barely drizzling," said Prunella impatiently. "What's a bit of rain to a fortune? Once little Maybelle sees her prince is dallying with her music teacher . . ."

"And how is she meant to see that?" Frank Pratt loomed over his cousin. "You told me you'd get them here. You told me you'd fix it for me."

Despite being half his size, Prunella wasn't the tiniest bit daunted. She poked him in the chest. "Well, I tried! Maybe they didn't want to come out in the rain."

Pratt stuck out his lip. "Maybe you didn't do a good enough job with the notes."

"Don't be a boor, Frank." Prunella tilted her head, stylishly adorned with a hat Ellen now knew to be a Madame Montpensier, and said sweetly, "We're not all as good at forgery as you."

Pratt stiffened. "That was only one check."

"And you're just lucky I covered for you! If I'd told my husband . . ."

"What? He would have cut off your allowance? The allowance you've already spent? You need the money as much as I do." Pratt gave an ugly laugh. "My creditors aren't going to be patient much longer. And neither are yours. I need to marry her soon."

Prunella put a hand on his arm. "I'll see to it, Frank. Trust me."

Pratt shook her hand off. "If you don't, I'll have to deal with it myself."

"Don't. Let me fix it for you." Ellen could hear the genuine alarm in Prunella's voice. "You'll go too far, you know you will."

"What is that supposed to mean?" Pratt demanded.

"You do have a way of breaking your toys, Frank."

Something about the way Prunella said it made Ellen go cold. Colder than she was already. He was playing with Maybelle's reputation. Worse, with her heart. There was something so fragile about Maybelle. So breakable.

Pratt glowered at his cousin. "You're not still holding that doll against me! I was eight!"

"And you still smash things," said Prunella bluntly. She turned to go, secure in having achieved the last word. "I'll arrange things for you, Frank, but you must let me do it in my own way."

"Because that's worked so well so far," Frank groused, but he followed his cousin out of the rose arbor.

"One little plan gone awry." Prunella's heels clicked against the stones of the path, her voice dimmed with rain. "And what did you lose by it?"

"One very nice jacket," groused Pratt. "I'll never get the water stains out."

"Don't be such a baby."

"We don't all have rich husbands to buy us things."

"No, but I'm getting you a rich wife, aren't I?"

Their voices grew fainter with their footsteps, but still Ellen stayed crouched behind her bench, not wanting to move until she was quite, quite sure they were gone, that this wasn't just a ruse to flush out their prey. She didn't think it was. She didn't think they would have spoken so openly about their plans had they known there was an audience . . . but she couldn't be sure. There was more to Prunella Schuyler than met the eye. The woman had a horrible, animal sort of cunning.

And a taste for expensive hats. A taste she meant to fund with Maybelle's dowry.

Was it worse than the prince using Maybelle's dowry to restore his roof? Yes, Ellen decided fiercely. Yes. At least the prince was honest in his ambitions. He'd never pretended to more than he felt. He'd made a point of it.

"Do you mean to stay down there much longer?" The prince had extricated himself, quietly, efficiently. "They're gone. You may emerge."

"I'm not sure I can," said Ellen honestly. Her knees felt frozen into place, her back pinned to the trellis by a thousand thorns. "I may stay like this forever."

"Grown into the roses like a woman cursed by the gods? Picturesque, but not, I think, practical."

The prince reached out a hand. Without thinking, Ellen put her hand in his. His ungloved fingers closed around hers, warm where she was cold, thawing her frozen limbs. The prince pulled her smoothly to her feet. But he didn't let go.

Ellen snatched her hand away, scrubbing it against her skirt. Bits of torn petals lay against the stone of the bench like ghosts.

"We've hurt the roses," she said, in a voice that didn't sound like her own.

"The roses hurt us." The prince regarded a long scratch on his wrist with a jaded eye. "It was just retribution."

"It wasn't their fault we had to hide behind the bench," said Ellen. She wasn't sure why she felt she had to be fair to the foliage. Maybe it was because everything else didn't bear thinking about. Not what Prunella Schuyler and Frank Pratt had planned for Maybelle. Not the way the prince's hand had felt, holding hers.

"No, it wasn't their fault, was it?" The prince looked in the direction Prunella and Pratt had gone. "That we may lay at the door of the two most blundering schemers since the marriage of Figaro."

"They very nearly succeeded."

"Despite themselves," said the prince, and even in the dark, Ellen could catch the shadow of his grin.

Ellen thought of the sheer, physical menace of Frank Pratt, the man who broke his toys. She wrapped her arms around herself. "It's not funny."

It was raining harder now, the drops fighting their way through the chinks in the trellis, damping her dress, causing her hair to straggle out of its pins and hang limply around her neck.

"*Mia bella,* of course it is. It's less Machiavelli and more Molière." The prince reached out, gently tucking a wet strand of hair behind her ear. "Their strategy is pure farce, lurking behind curtains, sending fake notes. It's barely credible on the stage. In the world as it is . . . what harm can they do to you, to us?"

Ellen looked up at the prince, all the fear and anguish she worked so hard to hide pouring out of her. "They can stop you from marrying Maybelle. They can lose me my position. You can make fun of them all you like. They fooled us with the notes, didn't they?"

"Yes. That was a mistake." The amusement was gone from the prince's voice. "I ought to have known."

"Known what?"

He looked down at her, his eyes dark in the shadow that was his face. "That a summons from you was too good to be true."

She should look away, she knew. But Ellen couldn't seem to make herself do it. The rain dripped unhindered from her hair, making damp trails down her cheeks, but she couldn't find the will to lift her hands to wipe the wet away.

The prince did it for her. He brushed his thumbs across her cheekbones, smoothing the raindrops away. The wind off the sea battered the roses, smelling of salt and blossoms, but inside the arbor there was nothing but Ellen's hurried breath and the prince's fingers gentle on her cheeks, sliding down to cup her face as she, not letting herself think, not able to think, let herself sway toward him, let the rain and the wind and the roses swallow her as his lips brushed hers, soft as his touch on her face, and then more urgently, the thrumming in her veins resonating with the crashing of the waves against the rocks below, as if they were part of nature and nature part of them, part of the storm, inevitable and unshakable.

Her dress was soaked through; she could feel the prince's hands burning against her back, the one warm spot in a cold world. Ellen twisted her arms around his neck, pressing herself closer, closer, giving herself up to the moment, to the storm.

Until the lighting forked across the sky, a brief, horrible moment of illumination that lit the sea below and startled Ellen out of the prince's arms, the following thunder booming in her ears like a reproach from above.

Ellen pulled back, yanking at her sodden dress, trying to make herself respectable. Her hair had come down, her lips were swollen with kisses that rightly belonged to another. "This . . . we shouldn't."

"But we did." The prince's voice was mild, but she could hear the jagged breath beneath it, a sign that he was as affected as she.

"Yes, but . . ." What defense did she have? She had been wanton, abandoned. Ellen curled her hands into fists at her sides, not trusting herself not to touch him. "It was wrong."

The prince touched a finger gently to her lips. "I know. You won't be my mistress."

It was such a simple gesture, almost innocent, but the feeling of his finger against her swollen lips made Ellen shiver with longing. "Mrs. Schuyler thinks I already am. Or ought to be."

"That one judges all women by herself." Ellen couldn't see the prince's face, but she could hear his scorn. "Call herself what she will, she is no more than a courtesan under cover of matrimony. She trades affection for hats. But you . . ."

"Also have a hat," said Ellen helplessly.

A hat that might as well have been a brand. Everyone took it for what it was. The prince's mark. Claiming her.

"That was a gift freely given. Did you think I imagined you had promised me anything in return?" The imperious voice softened, taking on a wry note that tore at Ellen's heart. "Nothing but the courtesy of your company and that only on sufferance."

"There was not . . . there was not so much suffering in it." There was too little suffering in it. She ought never to have taken—to take—such enjoyment in the attentions of her mistress's intended. "I shouldn't have. We ought never, no matter how innocent it all was. You're not mine."

"Aren't I? Don't you know by now?"

Ellen shoved her wet hair back behind her ears. "You're—you're like the hat. You're too grand for me, not for workaday use."

"Nor are you, no matter how you've been used in the past." As the lightning briefly lit their little enclosure, Ellen caught a glimpse of his face. The way he was looking at her, the tenderness of it, was dizzying. "Ever since I saw you last month in that loggia, I knew there was something fine about you. Something fine and true."

"No, not fine. Anything but fine." Ellen's throat felt clogged. The Hibernia. Dermot. The blood and fear. The thunder growled in agreement. "You don't know who I am. Who I really am."

"Don't I? You are yourself and none other. Most people, they are chameleons. They play to those in power, angling for advantage. I have never seen you be anything but what you are."

Which she wasn't.

"I'm a fraud," Ellen blurted out. "Nothing I've told you is true. My real name isn't Ellen Daniels. It's Eileen O'Donnell. I never knew the Van Duyvils. I only read about them in the papers. I lied. I lied about all of it."

The prince failed to react with the proper horror. "There are lies and lies. Do you think any of that matters? Ellen, Eileen. It doesn't change who you are in your heart. In your soul. It's all one."

"But it's *not*. I'm not poor but honest. I'm—" What was she? Ellen didn't even know anymore.

The prince took her hand, drawing her down onto the stone bench. "Tell me."

The bench was wet, but so was Ellen. Her dress clung damply to her legs. She plucked at it. "My mother and sisters died of the typhoid. My father started working for a man named Dermot. Dermot O'Shea. I don't know what my father did for him. I didn't want to know. He delivered messages, that's what he told me. But those messages—"

"Were more than just messages?"

"I don't know. I think so." She hated to think of it, hated to think of her father doing anything of the sort. But her father had been a different man after her mother had gone. The one constant had been his love for Ellen. She pushed on, determined to make a clean breast of what she did know. "Dermot owned—owns—a music hall called the Hibernia. He employed me as pianist there. After my father died. That's how I found out about the job here. One of the chorus girls was John Sprague's fancy woman. I was never onstage. I always sat behind a screen—but I was there."

The prince shrugged. She could feel the movement next to her, smell the bruised flowers as his arm brushed them. "You had to live. There are worse ways to earn one's keep for a woman alone."

Ellen drew in a ragged breath, every word stabbing like she was chewing nails. "You don't understand. The Hibernia—it wasn't just a music hall. And Dermot's business—it wasn't just the Hibernia. There were always people sneaking in the back way, bringing money. And upstairs . . . I—I tried not to see. I sat behind my screen and pretended that was all there was, just the dancing and the music. Because I didn't want to know."

The prince leaned forward, unable to help himself. "*Mia cara*. That was nothing to do with you."

"But it was. I took Dermot's money. I ate his bread. And then, one day . . ." Ellen could feel her throat close around the words. Just remembering made her sweat, even in her cold dress soaked with rain. "I'd forgotten my music. When I went back, I heard . . . there was a man. They'd tied him. To a chair. He was pleading, begging for his life."

She could smell the urine and sweat, the stench of fear, see the man sagging against the ropes that bound him, babbling, begging, pleading for mercy, offering anything, anything, saying it had all been a mistake, just let him go, he'd do better next time, just let him live.

And Ellen had stood there, frozen, not wanting to see it, not wanting to know, but knowing, knowing deep down, that this was what it had been all along, this was what she had been hiding from, this was what happened after she retired to her boardinghouse at night. And she'd done nothing. She'd stood there while Dermot's man—a boxer, or he had been once—looked at Dermot.

And Dermot had nodded. Just the smallest inclination of his head.

And that's when the man started screaming, screaming and trying to scramble away, chair and all.

"*Mia bella?*" The prince's arm curled around her shoulders, his breath warm against her ear. "*Mia bella*, tell me."

"They killed him," said Ellen flatly. She looked at the prince, waiting for him to hate her. "And I did nothing to stop it. I stood there and watched them kill him."

Just saying it, she felt like lightning should hit her and strike her dead, the ground should open and swallow her, waves should engulf her and drag her to the bottom of the ocean.

She had let a man die. She had stood there and let them kill him.

"What were you meant to do?"

"Something! Anything. I went to the police." It sounded so painfully inadequate. "I've been hiding ever since. That's why I became Ellen Daniels. That's why I came here. They were after me. They can't let it stand, you see. It's—it's bad for discipline."

The kind of discipline that left a man dead in a back room, hanging limp against the ropes that had held him.

"If others heard I'd told . . . Dermot was kind to me, in his way. My father was one of his own, so he took care of me for my father's sake. And I betrayed him. But I couldn't—"

"No, you couldn't. Not you." The prince put a finger under Ellen's chin, tilting her face toward his so he could look into her eyes. "Didn't I tell you what you were? Not a person in a thousand would have done what you did."

"Anyone with a conscience would have spoken sooner. You don't understand. I *knew*. I knew they were making people pay them for protection. I knew they were—were hurting people. And I ignored it. I pretended it wasn't happening."

Because Dermot had taken her in, given her a job. She was a part of his family now, that's what he had told her. He looked after his own, he said. She'd tried to convince herself whatever he was doing couldn't be so very bad.

"Most people would have gone on ignoring it," said the prince.

"But what about before? What about all those months and months? I condoned it—I condoned it with my silence. I'm to blame for that man's death, as much as anyone."

"Am I to blame for all the men my ancestors slew? I hold my lands, my title, through the deaths of countless men, some won honestly, some by treachery. We were what we were through force of arms. Time has cleansed my name. But make no mistake. The oldest, noblest families have their origins in the pain of others." The prince grinned at her, a rogue's grin. "Five hundred years from now the great-great-grandson of your Dermot will be marrying an heiress to fix the chinks in his roof."

"That doesn't make it right," Ellen said stubbornly. "It doesn't make any of it right. If I'd said something then, if I'd intervened—"

"You'd be dead, too. Or given a lesson to keep you in line." The prince's hands were on her shoulders, warm and comforting. "You did what was needed. There was no saving that man. But by going to the police, you might have saved others."

It was a comforting thought, but she couldn't lie to him, not anymore. Ellen shook her head helplessly, fighting the tears that pricked the backs of her eyes. "It wasn't any use. The police were in Dermot's pay. It was all for nothing."

The prince's hands moved soothingly up and down her arms. "Not for nothing. It brought you here."

"To Maybelle?"

"To me."

He folded her into his arms, close against his chest. Ellen hunched herself up, feeling like she didn't deserve this, didn't deserve this comfort.

"Shhhh," he said, as though she were a child, and Ellen felt herself relaxing into him, her head settling into the hollow above his collarbone. The tears ran silently down her cheeks, mingling with the raindrops. Tears for that nameless man, for the months of doubt and fear, for having finally shared her burden.

They sat like that for a very long time. Ellen rubbed her nose against his waistcoat, smelling his own particular scent of orange blossom and bergamot. She was soaked through, but she didn't care, not now. The rain could fall, the thunder could crash, but none of it could touch her here. It was like the stories her mother used to tell her about fairy feasts. How people would think they were banqueting on succulent meats and choice pastries and come to themselves again to find their mouths full of mud and dried leaves. She knew, in the not so very distant future, she would come to herself to realize she was sitting cold and bedraggled, exposed to the elements, her fingers frozen and her lips turned blue.

But while the illusion lasted—oh, it was beautiful.

The prince rested his cheek against her hair. "There is a legend," he said, "that once all people were complete in themselves. It made them too strong. It threatened the gods. So Zeus, with his lightning, split us in two. And, ever since, we have been left weak and wanting, searching for our other half to make us whole."

Ellen lay against his chest, feeling his breath go in and out in time to hers, their hearts beating the same rhythm. As if they were the two halves made whole again, one person in two bodies.

"Your roof needs fixing," said Ellen quietly, not moving from her warm nest.

"So it does." The prince pressed his lips to the top of Ellen's head. "There are times when I think it would be a fine thing to let it all crumble and be done with it. Let the fortress fall, block by block. Let the stones sink into the sea. To be just a man and not the errand boy of my ancestors."

She stirred, looking up at him, at his chin and the underside of his nose. "What would you do then?"

"I would marry the woman I love." Gently, he loosened his embrace, holding her out at arm's length. "You're shivering. It's time to get you inside."

The world was very cold without him. Ellen felt as if a piece of her had been ripped away. Which was ridiculous. She'd known him only a little over a month. They were from different countries, different worlds.

But when she'd rested against his chest, she'd felt she'd found her place, like a piece in a puzzle, finally turned the right way around.

The woman I love, he'd said.

"Yes, you're right." Ellen clasped her cold fingers together, grasping at the practicalities. "We'd best go separately. They might still be watching."

The prince helped her to her feet, his hand closing briefly around hers. "You go first. I want you safe inside. And warm."

The concern in his voice made Ellen feel like crying. How long since someone had worried over her? How long since someone had cared if she caught a chill?

She knew she shouldn't, but she couldn't help herself. Instead of drawing her hand away, she looked up at the prince, and asked, in a voice that trembled, "Love?"

"Isn't that what I've been saying?" With all the reverence due to a noblewoman, a lady of his own world, the prince lifted her hand and kissed it. "Go now. I will keep watch."

WHEN ELLEN WOKE, the storm had passed and the morning was bright and clear.

Too bright. The sky was alarmingly blue, a pugnacious blue that hurt the eyes. The birds were chirping as though their future employment depended on it. And the clock told Ellen that it was nearly ten, well past when she ought to have been awake and about her duties.

Ellen burrowed back into her pillow, not wanting to trade the rain for the sun, wanting to go back to last night, to the rush of the sea and the pelting of the rain and the scent of wet roses. To the darkness that let them say things they might not otherwise say.

Had it been real? Had it happened? Ellen rubbed her sleep-dulled eyes then raked her fingers through the tangled mass of her hair. She'd fallen into bed without braiding it. And, yes, there, over a chair hung her sodden dress, only half-dry even now. And there by the door were her boots, water-stained, and caked with bits of leaves and petals.

Ellen swung her feet out of bed, feeling curiously light. It was real. She had sat there, last night, in the arbor with the prince, and felt all the fears and guilt of the past year lifting, blown away with the wind.

She had felt—she had believed—all this while that she was being punished, and justly, for her omissions. But maybe the crimes weren't hers after all. Maybe she didn't deserve to suffer. Maybe that man's death wasn't her fault.

Ellen had no hat; she'd sent back the prince's gift and her own was beyond repair. So she went down without one. It ought to have made her feel bare, to have quaked with the impropriety of it, but it didn't.

She had to stop herself from looking into every mirror she passed, to check if she were still the same Ellen she had been yesterday. She didn't think she was. This woman stood straighter, held her head higher.

Whatever happened, wherever she went, whether the prince married Maybelle or not, he had given her that gift, a glimpse of the woman she could be. Not a piece of trash, the flotsam of the world, to be kicked into the gutter, but a woman with principles, with value. And she knew, deep in her bones, that whatever happened, she would never let herself be treated as nothing again. She might be poor, she might work for her living, but she was herself, and that mattered. It was something.

It was such a strange thing, feeling like she had value. That she had something in her, something intangible and entirely her own, worthy of respect. Worthy of love.

He would marry Maybelle, she knew. He had to. But when she remembered the night before, the brush of his lips against her hair, his arms around her, warming her, comforting her, sustaining her, it was hard not to daydream of that other world he had spoken of, the world in which he was just another man and she another woman, and there were no practicalities to separate them, no roofs to mend.

Two halves of a whole.

Ellen headed to the music room, to prepare for the daily lesson with Maybelle. Italian arias, John Sprague had demanded, and Italian arias Ellen had been teaching, phrase by careful phrase. The house was tranquil, most of the guests still sleeping.

But when Ellen arrived at the music room, the door was shut fast and a curious sight greeted her: the fashionably draped bottom of Prunella Schuyler jutting up into the air as she leaned over nearly double to press her ear against the keyhole.

"Mrs. Schuyler?"

Prunella started, banging her forehead on the elaborate doorknob. "What are you doing sneaking up on people?" she demanded, as if she hadn't herself been trying to sneak up on Ellen the night before.

"I wasn't sneaking," said Ellen warily. With everything else, she'd nearly forgotten Prunella's plots and plans. Last night, with the prince, it had felt almost as silly as he said it was. But it made her nervous to find Prunella lurking by the music room, for what nefarious purpose, goodness only knew. "I was going to the music room. Where I teach music."

"Oh, that," said Prunella irritably. She narrowed her eyes at Ellen. "You forgot your hat."

"I gave it back," said Ellen. "If you'll excuse me, I must—"

Prunella moved to block her before Ellen could reach the door. "The prince is in there with Maybelle. He demanded an audience." Prunella fizzled with nervous energy. "They've been in there for *ages*."

Ellen felt as though a hand had closed around her heart and squeezed. "Is he—"

"I don't know! They're speaking too softly." Prunella glowered at the door, thoroughly put out by the inconsideration of people who refused to conduct their private affairs at a volume sufficient for other people to hear. She shot a long look at Ellen under her lashes. "It sounded like Maybelle was crying."

Ellen felt a shameful rush of something that felt very much like hope, quickly followed by guilt. She stepped back from the door, clasping her hands behind her back. "We shouldn't be listening."

Prunella eyed Ellen with open dislike. "Because you have no interest in the matter."

"I do." Ellen fought to find her better nature, to think of Maybelle rather than herself. "I have an interest in Miss Sprague's happiness."

"Ha," said Prunella, and would have put her ear to the keyhole again, but the door burst open, nearly knocking her off her feet, as Maybelle ran past in a confusion of flounces. She flung herself up the stairs, tripping on her own skirts in her haste, her face a mask of distress.

"Maybelle?" Prunella took off after her in what for any other woman might have been termed a sprint. "Maybelle, what's happened? It's meeeeeeeee. Surely you'll tell *me*!"

Ellen hesitated, not sure whether to follow Maybelle or go into the music room. To find her lover, who had said something to Maybelle that had sent her fleeing pell-mell through the house.

Had he told her he didn't mean to marry her, not even for the sake of his roof?

It was horrible to hope that. She shouldn't hope that.

Making her decision, Ellen hurried to the back stairs. She couldn't leave Maybelle to Prunella. If the prince had thrown her over—*if,* Ellen reminded herself—then Prunella would do all she could to press Frank's suit, and Ellen couldn't, wouldn't, let that happen. Maybelle deserved better.

Ignoring Prunella in the corridor, Ellen slipped into her own room.

"Maybelle?" Ellen tried the connecting door between their rooms, but it was locked fast. She couldn't remember Maybelle ever locking it before. "Maybelle? It's Ellen."

No answer.

Outside, Prunella was carrying on a one-sided conversation with Maybelle's door. John Sprague came barreling red-faced down the hall. He grabbed Ellen by the shoulder. "Is it true?" he barked. "They said the prince asked to speak to Maybelle? Is it true?"

"That brute distressed my poor darling," said Prunella, putting her hands on her hips. "Goodness only knows what indignities he attempted to perpetrate."

"Matrimony, hopefully," said Sprague shortly. Pushing past Prunella, he banged peremptorily on the door. "Maybelle. Open up."

The door opened. John Sprague went inside, slamming it shut behind him, right in Prunella's indignant face.

"Well! Just see if he's invited to my box at the opera after this! Ouch!" Prunella jerked around as something hit her in her well-padded posterior.

"Ha! Got you!" crowed Dudley, waving his slingshot triumphantly.

"Horrible brat," retorted Prunella, and retreated in high dudgeon, her skirts swishing around her.

"Dudley!" Ellen exclaimed. Between Dudley and Prunella, she wasn't sure which she liked least, but she did know she couldn't let Dudley go around lobbing projectiles at guests.

Dudley put out his tongue at her. "That's *Master* Dudley to you."

"Respect is earned," said Ellen firmly. "Give me that slingshot. You can't go around shooting people."

Dudley smirked at her, drawing back the cup of his slingshot. "You're not people. You're a *servant*."

Ellen snatched the device out of his hand. "You treat people like that, you're going to get what's coming to you someday."

Dudley lunged for the slingshot. "You can't take that! I'm telling my father."

"Telling me what?" Sprague blundered out of Maybelle's room. He looked dazed, his mouth half-open, his eyes not quite focused.

"Papa." Dudley tugged at his arm. "Papa, this *servant* . . ."

"What?" Sprague came back to earth, his eyes focusing on Ellen. He bristled with sudden energy. "*You*. I need you to organize a musical entertainment much grander than what I had in mind before. Something tasteful, but impressive. Maybe fireworks."

"Fireworks?" Ellen looked at him in bewilderment.

"Surely you've heard of them. Big sparkly things in the sky. See to them." Having got that arranged, Sprague turned to his offspring, his face blazing with triumph. "Your aunt is going to be a princess, what do you think about that?"

Dudley shot a considering look at Ellen. "Does that make me a prince?"

Sprague clapped his son on the shoulder, overcome with bonhomie and goodwill toward men. "Close enough. Close enough. You'll have everything. All the best. The Spragues will be a dynasty to be reckoned with. No more telling us we're not good enough for their clubs, oh no. That Vanderbilt woman, she's only got a duchess for her daughter. But us? We got a prince, a goddamn prince!"

Ellen looked at the closed door and then back at Mr. Sprague. "She's accepted him?"

She had known—of course, she had known—that even with all that had been said between them in the arbor there was no hope to it. A prince might love a milkmaid, but he didn't marry her. Not in real life.

"Of course she's accepted him, what do you think? Never mind. I don't pay you to think."

So far, he hadn't paid her at all. He didn't have to. She had no clout, no voice. She was no one, no one at all. Just another disposable menial.

But the prince—the prince had shown her she was more.

And then he had gone and proposed to Maybelle.

Ellen wanted to growl. She wanted to snap and snarl and scratch the smug expression from John Sprague's face. At the moment, she wasn't sure whether she loved the prince or hated him. Or merely wished she had never met him.

No, none of that. He'd only done what he had to do. She knew that. Then why did it hurt so much?

"You! Music teacher." Sprague snapped his fingers in front of Ellen's face to get her attention. "See to the engagement celebration."

Ellen wrapped her hands in her skirt to hide their trembling. "Yes, Mr. Sprague."

"Spare no expense." Sprague rubbed his hands together, dripping sweat and satisfaction. "I want to make it an event that Newport will remember forever."

CHAPTER TWENTY-ONE

Lucky

Newport, Rhode Island
July 1957

Marble House still dazzled with lights and music and laughter—with the frenetic, radiant glow of a party that wanted to go on forever. Lucky slowed the car and gaped at the ghostly white walls, the golden windows, the glittering figures shifting inside. Only an hour had passed since she hurried out those enormous doors and down the curving porte cochere on her way to the hospital. So why did the ball seem to belong to another lifetime?

She sped on, up the last hundred yards of Bellevue Avenue before the narrow Sprague Hall drive spilled its gravel from the right. The car skidded as she whipped around the corner. The house emerged from behind the trees, lit by a few forlorn lamps. Overdesigned and underbuilt, shabby and garish and pretentious—still, it was *her* tasteless mansion, wasn't it? Her home. The one thing that actually belonged to her and Nonna, which nobody could take away.

Or so she'd always thought.

At the top of the drive, right in front of the garage, Lucky slammed the brakes. The car shuddered to a stop. Stuy's beloved car, his little red convertible. She turned off the engine and threw open the door. Her feet tangled up in her ball gown as she tried to leap out, and she thudded to her hands and knees in the gravel. She stared at her raw palms and swore.

Nonna. Joanie. What was she going to tell them?

Teddy.

Lucky clambered to her feet. Her skirt was torn, her knees bloody. She started for the columns that flanked the front entrance of Sprague Hall—*her* damn columns—and turned back. Reached into the passenger seat and pulled out the small, sequined evening bag and slung it over her arm.

The front door was unlocked, the hall light burned dimly. Lucky limped over the threshold and hurried across the cavernous foyer to the stairs—upstairs, she had to go upstairs, she had to find Nonna! She almost didn't hear her name called across the stagnant air. Not until the voice called again, more loudly, did she whirl around and clutch the pocketbook to her chest.

Teddy stepped from the shadows.

"Good Lord, are you all right?" he asked.

"I fell," she whispered.

He strode forward and caught her against his chest. "Everything's all right," he said. "It's going to be all right."

"He's dead. Sprague's dead."

"I know. I was there, remember? When they gave you the message from the hospital."

"Yes, but it's *true*. He's *dead*, he's really dead."

Teddy pulled back. "What's the matter? You're shaking. Has something happened? Did Reggie and Louise get there all right? I called them a taxi, but they both seemed a little worse for wear—"

Lucky heard herself laugh, a touch hysterical. Just a *touch*. Must keep one's composure, remember? Must—oh God. She forced out some words. "Has something *happened*? He's *dead*, Teddy! He's gone, he's—oh, never mind. Let me go. I need to speak to my grandmother."

She drew away, turned back to the stairs. Teddy caught her arm.

"Wait a moment, darling. Before you go up."

"What is it?"

"I don't want you to worry—everything's fine—"

"Why, what's the matter? *Stuy!* Did he hurt himself?"

"No, no. Not old Stuy. Still passed out. I got him upstairs with the help of a footman—Mrs. Prince was very understanding. He's tucked up in one of the guest bedrooms."

Lucky clutched his arm. "Then what? What is it?"

"It's Joanie," he said.

Lucky only half heard the explanation as she raced up the stairs, cuts and scrapes forgotten, her heart hammering against her ribs. How Teddy had walked to Sprague Hall, after settling Stuy upstairs at Marble House, after rooting out Reggie and Louise from disreputable corners and putting them in a taxi for the hospital. How he'd taken the back way along the cliff path, had spotted a pale figure flitting around the boathouse.

Nonna? Lucky gasped, at the top of the stairs.

"Yes. She was wringing her hands, said someone was out in the boat or something. I looked out and saw the dinghy. Just in time, too—"

Lucky whirled. "Oh my God! *Joanie!*"

"She's all right! Lucky, she's all right!"

But Lucky was already racing down the hall, around the corner, throwing open the door to Joanie's bedroom. The room was dark; a woman sat on a stool beside the bed. She looked up as Lucky rushed across the floor to her daughter, still and quiet under the blankets.

"I'm so sorry," Nonna whispered. "I tried to help her."

Joanie stirred and opened her eyes. "Mama?"

"I'm here, darling. I'm here. Thank God, thank God."

"I was just trying to take the sailboat back to the club . . . Daddy forgot—"

"Oh, darling, *no*! All by *yourself*?"

"I didn't want you to be mad at him."

Lucky sat on the bed and scooped her daughter to her chest. The tears ran and ran down her cheeks, without so much as a sob to propel them. Just long, unstoppable tracks of salt water. Joanie's body was warm and firm against her ribs; her hair was still damp against Lucky's cheek, against her lips, which couldn't seem to stop kissing Joanie's small, round head.

"Sweet girl," she gasped. "Sweet girl. Oh God."

Next to her, Nonna murmured, "I'm so sorry, I never meant it to happen. Her skirts were so heavy. So heavy. They dragged her under, I couldn't pull her out, I couldn't—"

"Shh, it's all right. She's fine, she's alive. Thank God for Teddy."

"It's all my fault. Sweet girl, she never deserved it. She deserved . . . she deserved . . ."

Slowly Lucky's arms loosened around her daughter. She turned her head and picked out the soft, ghostly shape of her grandmother on the stool nearby—hands folded in her white lap, hair loose, eyes staring. Everything tasted of salt. Joanie's hair, her own tears. Her head seemed to be full of brine, the taste of grief.

"Nonna?" she said.

"Poor thing," Nonna whispered. "She never stood a chance."

WITH TEDDY'S HELP, Lucky settled Nonna in her own bed, tucked Joanie back to sleep. Once her daughter's eyes had closed, her chest stirring in a reassuring rhythm, Lucky turned to face him. His eyes were grave behind his glasses, his mouth worried. He grasped her shoulders gently and kissed her forehead.

"Everything's going to be all right, darling," he said. "Don't you see? The old bastard's finally dead. You're free now, free to choose whatever path—"

"Free?" Lucky pulled away and started to laugh. "Free? Are you kidding?"

"Lucky, what's wrong? I don't understand. He's gone. Gone at last. He can't do anything to hurt you."

Lucky couldn't hold back the laughter. *Laughter!* What was *wrong* with her? She was turning into some kind of hysteric. She hurried out of Joanie's room and sank against the wall, a fist against her mouth, trying to hold it all in, the panic and grief and *everything,* her whole world crumbling to tiny pieces around her, the damned reek of salt in her head. She felt Teddy gather her up, rub her back, murmur things in her ear that weren't true, ludicrous words like *Everything's all right, he's gone, he's dead*. She choked on a final giggle that had turned into a sob against Teddy's shirt. Teddy's beautiful, handmade formal shirt, still damp from rescuing Joanie from the sea—saving her daughter—oh God! Now all that fine, pintucked cotton was ruined, drying stiff, reeking of salt water like everything else, this stupid ocean that washed all the world's troubles onto her shore.

"Come with me," she gasped.

"Come with you? Where?"

She lifted her head from Teddy's chest.

"To the boathouse."

A BLURRED GIBBOUS moon hung from the night sky, illuminating their way down the lawn. The grass was slick with dew and soaked Lucky's darling pink satin slippers with the slender kitten heels—oh well. Just another thing ruined this evening, just another shipwreck. The air streamed past her cheeks, warm and muggy. Teddy's breath made foggy puffs beside her. Ahead, the boathouse roof glinted silver against the shimmering water.

"What are we looking for?" Teddy said.

"I don't know!"

"Then what in hell are we doing out here?"

Teddy grabbed her hand and stopped them both. They'd just reached the Cliff Walk. The boathouse perched on the other side of the path, atop the scrap of shore below. Lucky had always thought it was a ridiculous place for a boathouse, practically unusable for launching boats to begin with, exposed to weather and tide and surf, separated from the grounds of Sprague Hall by a public footpath. Why on earth would anybody build such a thing, in such a place?

She turned to Teddy and looked up at his worried frown. He lifted his hand to cup her chin. The moon flashed from the surface of his glasses. From behind her came the faint noise of orchestra music and a few hundred voices having a good time at Marble House, a couple hundred yards and a world away, where her husband lay, passed out drunk.

"You can tell me, Lucky," Teddy said. "I'm on your side, remember?"

Lucky drew some breath into her lungs. "My father-in-law. My good old father-in-law, a real doll. Just before he died, he wrote something down, a note of some kind. He was going to send it to his lawyers."

"I see. But now you've got this note instead?"

"It's in my pocketbook."

"Well? What did it say?"

Lucky closed her eyes. "*I hereby testify that my aunt, Maybelle Sprague, is not the rightful heir of Hiram Sprague, and therefore the fortune she obtained by fraud is instead the property of Hiram Sprague's nearest relative, the evidence of which may be found inside the Sprague Hall boathouse. Sworn by the undersigned, Dudley Sprague, the thirteenth of July, nineteen fifty-seven.*"

"*What?*"

"Or something like that, I didn't exactly memorize it."

"But that doesn't make any sense! What does he mean, *fraud*? Your grandmother wouldn't hurt a flea!"

"I know that! But what if—I don't know—well, he was lying, of *course* he was lying—but what if *he* did something, something terrible that could be twisted around—"

"Lucky, stop. Listen to yourself. We're talking about Dudley

Sprague, not some criminal mastermind. He would've been just a kid back then, when your grandparents were married. Whatever trouble he meant by that note, he made it all up. He made it up because he was desperate, because he knew you meant to divorce Stuy as soon as he was gone. Kick him out without a penny."

"Yes, but—oh, I can't help it, Teddy. If there's even a *chance* he knew about something awful, some terrible secret . . . oh, it would *kill* her—poor Nonna—it would kill her, she's so fragile already!"

"Then rip up the damn note! He didn't *send* it, did he?"

"No."

"So nobody knows but you."

"But he said there was evidence in the boathouse!"

"Evidence of what? What *kind* of evidence?"

"I don't know! That's what I'm here to find out!" She gripped his shirt. "Teddy, I'm scared to death! I can't explain it. Nonna's been acting so strange. There's something there, I know it!"

Teddy took her hands and detached them from his shirt. "Lucky. Lucky. It's nothing. Nonna's just—well, she's getting older, she's not all there. You know that, we both know that. She's in a dream world or something. It's not real."

"I *know* it's not real. But something's bothering her, and it has to do with the boathouse, and now this note, this stupid note from Dudley Sprague. I have a bad feeling, I can't help it."

"All right. Fair enough. I understand." Teddy squinted down at her, stroked her fingers with his thumbs. "Look, I'll come into the boathouse with you. We'll have a look around. Then you'll come back to the house, rip up that note, and forget all about it, okay? Dudley Sprague was a troublemaker. He just wanted to make you fret. It's nothing."

Lucky stared into Teddy's eyes. "It's nothing," she repeated.

"Nothing." He tugged her hand. "Come on. We'll have a quick look around, set your mind at ease. There's nothing there, I promise."

"Promise?"

He lifted her hand and kissed her knuckles. "Promise."

Yet there *was* something inside the boathouse. Lucky felt it as soon as they stepped through the door, hand in hand, her fingers tucked firmly inside the shelter of Teddy's fingers. She couldn't put a name to what she sensed. Something in the air—some vibrating energy, some fine pitch of anticipation, like a note of music beyond the reach of human hearing. The air was warm and dark. The moon came ghostlike through the small windows, one on each wall, illuminating the air just enough so you could make out the shapes around you—the leaky old rowboat on its horse, the coils of rope, the buckets and the fishing rods on their hooks. This was Stuy's domain—Stuy, who loved to sail, who was always happiest and most *himself* on the water, away from his father. Unlike the rest of his world, the boathouse he kept in perfect order.

Maybe that was why Lucky had always avoided this place. She'd felt like an intruder. An eavesdropper on some life that wasn't hers.

Teddy released her hand and shrugged off his tuxedo jacket, which he laid over the rowboat. He wandered to the shelves on the wall. "Is there a flashlight or something?"

"Probably. Stuy's the least organized guy in the world, except when it comes to his sailing. Try the top shelf."

"Ah. Here we are."

A beam of garish light shot from Teddy's hand and traveled along the wooden boards, the walls, the floor, the roof. Everything spare and tidy, not a single useless item. Even the air smelled clean, just brine and summertime. Above them, a small loft stretched halfway across the peaked attic roof, reached by a solid seaman's ladder. Stuy sometimes slept off his drunks there, on a pile of old blankets.

Teddy started toward the ladder. "What's up here?" he asked.

"I don't know. I haven't been up in years. Careful!"

But Teddy was already halfway up the ladder, climbing nimbly, flashlight tucked into the waistband of his dress trousers, moonlight catching the white of his shirt. When he reached the top rung, he pulled out the flashlight, turned it on, and swept it along the walls.

"There's not much," he called down. "Old sofa, pile of blankets, kind of a chest or a footlocker or something, some magazines stacked on top."

"Dare I ask what kind of magazines?"

A slight pause. "Well, they're not about sailing. Shall I look inside the chest?"

"That's probably where he keeps his booze."

Teddy set the flashlight on the floor and hoisted himself up. Lucky craned her neck to watch him cross the floor, bend over, lift the magazines from the top of the locker. He rattled the lid. "It's locked," he said.

"Do you see a key anywhere?"

The flashlight meandered around. "No."

"Well, that's funny. I don't know why he'd keep it locked. Nobody else goes up there."

"Lock's kind of rusted. Doesn't look like it's been opened in a while."

A funny feeling stirred Lucky's belly, as if that peculiar vibration she'd felt in the air had somehow penetrated her skin. She moved to the ladder and kicked off her slippers. Hitched up her skirt.

"What are you doing?" Teddy demanded.

"I want to have a look."

"You can't climb up a ladder in that dress!"

Lucky paused with her fingers on the rungs. "You're right," she said.

She reached behind her back and found the zipper, nestled into the pink satin bodice. She yanked it down. Heard something rip, so what. The gown was ruined anyway, dirty and bloodstained, torn at the knees. So much expense, so many fittings. She stepped out of it and kicked it aside. Unfastened her torn, bloody stockings from the girdle. The silk stuck a little to the scrapes on her knees. Ruthlessly she peeled them down her legs, bracing herself on the ladder rungs, and tossed them on top of the dress.

"Ready," she said.

"Lucky . . ." Teddy sounded as if he meant to admonish her, but his voice kind of choked on her name and died as she climbed the ladder with the confidence of a child, dressed in her brassiere and satin slip, her girdle and silk underpants beneath. She sprang from the top rung and joined him in front of the chest. It was larger than she imagined, about six feet long, solid-looking. More of a footlocker, like Teddy said. She kicked it with her bare toe.

"Ouch!"

"I'll say. What happened to your knees?"

"I fell in the driveway. Tripped on my dress."

"You should—" He swallowed. "You should put something on those cuts."

"I should."

Lucky ran her hand along the top of the locker. The latch was secured with a formidable Yale lock. She jiggled it a little. "You're right, it's stuck fast," she said.

"Heavy, too. It's not going anywhere."

"If you had a gun or something, we could maybe shoot the lock apart."

"I've got one back at the house. But it's all locked up, because of—well."

"Because of your wife?"

Teddy didn't reply, just stood next to her with one hand braced on his hip, the other hand holding the flashlight. She felt the motion of his breathing, the beat of his heart almost. The flashlight moved across the top of the locker. He'd dumped the magazines on the floor, but Lucky glimpsed the covers anyway.

"They're awfully pretty," she said.

"What's pretty?"

"The girls on the covers of those magazines."

Teddy snorted. "Not as pretty as you."

"But more alluring. I'm an ice queen, remember? The ice queen he married, poor man."

"You're not an ice queen. Not at all."

Lucky folded her arms across her chest and stared down at the locker. "Whatever it is, it's not booze."

"Probably just some old sailing gear or something."

"Probably."

Teddy turned, keeping his eyes fixed studiously on her eyes. Not the smooth, bare flesh lower down. "I'll open it, if you want me to. Might take some doing."

"Do you think it's worth it?"

He shrugged. "You're the one who wanted to search the place."

"Because I was afraid. I was afraid of what might be hidden here."

"And now? You're not afraid anymore?"

"A little, I guess. But maybe you're right. Maybe it doesn't matter, anyway. He's dead, after all. Nobody knows about that note but me. And you."

"Well, *I'm* certainly not telling anybody."

"So there. Maybe we just let it lie."

"If that's what you want."

They stood facing each other. Teddy's features gained weight under the lurid glow from the flashlight. She felt his breath on her face, the warmth of his eyes. Her skin prickled, but it wasn't the quivering in the air, the inhuman music that hummed around them. Or maybe it was. Maybe this peculiar atmosphere wasn't so otherworldly after all. Maybe this was what you felt when you were alone with somebody you loved, somebody who made your every nerve vibrate at a treble pitch.

Maybe *this* was why she'd come here with Teddy. Not some old, rambling threats from a dead man.

Lucky reached down and pulled the flashlight from Teddy's hand.

"*This* is what I want," she said, and she flicked the light off.

CHAPTER TWENTY-TWO

Andie

Newport, Rhode Island
September 2019

THE SINGLE BULB on the port-cochere ceiling fixture flickered off just as I staggered through the rear door with two tripods, the final pieces of filming equipment to be brought inside. Since it had been my fault that the crew had been stranded outside after hours and in the sudden storm, I'd sent them and Meghan home as soon as the most vulnerable pieces had been secured, promising I'd do the rest on my own, regardless of the plummeting temperature and the teeming rain that stubbornly refused to stop.

My phone vibrated in my rear pocket. I tried to find a dry spot on my clothing to wipe my hands, but soon gave up as I whipped out my phone, grateful to see it still worked despite having been essentially dunked in the ocean for the better part of an hour. I felt a stab of panic as my dad's name appeared on the screen. It took two swipes before my thumb was able to open my phone. "Is everything okay? Is Petey all right?"

"Yeah, yeah—we're fine. Everything is good here. It's you I'm worried about. Have you left Newport yet?"

"No. I'm still here. Sorry, I meant to call you to say I'd be late but . . ."

"Good. The Newport Bridge is closed, and a bunch of roads are washed out. It's much too dangerous for you to try and make it home. Can you stay there?"

"Stay here? I mean, I guess I could try and find a hotel. . . ."

"Just as long as you don't have to get in a car. Promise you won't so I don't have to worry about you."

A drop of water from the ceiling landed on my head, making me look up to see a swollen plaster teat full of rain leaking from the roof. I stepped to the side, making a mental note to find a bucket to protect the marble tiles. "But what about Petey? And who's going to cook dinner?"

"Don't worry about a thing. I'll hold down the fort here. I'm letting Petey have cereal for dinner, and after his bath we'll watch the Red Sox annihilate the Braves until his bedtime. I'll take care of him in the morning so you don't have to worry. We'll be fine. Just stay safe."

Petey started yelling something in the background. "Sorry, gotta go. We're in the middle of a game of Go Fish and it's my turn. Call me in the morning, okay?"

"But doesn't Petey want to talk . . ." I let my voice drift away when I realized I was speaking to empty air.

I shivered in my wet clothes, the cold air inside the cavernous house more biting than it was outside. A loud slap of rain hit the door, and the wind finding its way through the gaps in the stone wall and door surround made my teeth chatter. Yet still I stood there, not sure what to do. Even if I could find a hotel room, I doubted my car could get me out of the flooded driveway. Not to mention that I'd promised my dad I wouldn't. A puddle had begun to surround me on the marble floor, like I was an overwatered plant. My teeth were chattering so loudly now that it was impossible to think clearly or figure out how I was going to find a towel to clean up the puddle, much less solve the problem of where I was supposed to sleep.

To add to my abject humiliation, warm tears slipped down my

cheeks and mixed with the icy rainwater. I hated crying ever since the day my mother had left us and I'd seen how truly pointless my tears were. It was the first time I'd ever seen my father cry, and even the tears of a grown man and two young daughters hadn't been enough to turn her car around.

"Andie?"

I jerked my head in the direction of Luke's voice, my humiliation complete. "I'm . . . s-s-sorry," I chattered. "I'll . . . c-c-clean . . . the . . . f-f-floor. . . ."

His quick steps approached, his gaze remaining on my face and not down at the mess I was making. "You're freezing. Let's get you warm and into some dry clothes."

He gently took hold of my arm, but I resisted. "I'm f-f-f-ine. I j-j-just need a t-t-towel. . . ."

"This isn't the time to be stubborn, Andie. Here, take this." He slid his sweater over his head and placed it over mine, gently guiding my shaking arms through the holes. I was too grateful for the warmth of it to resist or complain that it smelled of him. Or that it felt like cashmere and I was probably ruining it and couldn't afford to replace it.

He took my elbow and gently pulled me forward. "Come on. You can fuss later. But you really do need to get out of your wet clothes and warm up. Doctor's orders."

I wanted to argue or make some comment about him being a doctor of convenience, but I really was too cold. And exhausted. And my stomach growled because I hadn't eaten since breakfast.

As we headed up the stairs, my chattering had subsided enough that I could speak almost normally. "I'm sorry I'm still here. The roads are washed out and I can't get home. If I can just borrow a blanket, I can sleep in my car."

Luke stopped walking, making me stop, too, since he still held my elbow. The look in his eyes was unreadable. "Don't be ridiculous. Even you can't be *that* stubborn. We've got thirty bedrooms, some of them even habitable." He put his foot on the next step, then paused. "Unless you're too afraid to stay. Because, you know, the ghost of the lady in white."

"Honestly," I said as I resumed the climb. "You could have Vlad the Impaler lurking in the halls and I wouldn't care as long as I was warm and dry."

He may have laughed, but it was drowned out by the sound of a dozen bangle bracelets clattering as Joanie appeared at the top of the stairs. "Andie! You poor thing!"

"The roads are too bad for her to travel," Luke explained, "so she needs to stay overnight. I was thinking that the bedroom at the end of the hall . . ."

Joanie floated down the stairs to slip her arm through my free one. "Don't be silly. Hadley's room has fresh sheets on the bed and clean towels in the en suite since I was hoping she'd stay. No matter—her loss. And it's right next to your room so if she needs anything you're close by."

"Joanie—" Luke began.

She cut him off. "She can wear that soft bathrobe I gave you last Christmas. The blue one, remember?" To me, she said, "While you take a nice hot shower, I'll whip something up for us to eat for dinner, all right?"

I nodded, too grateful to protest that I was fine and didn't want to intrude. Besides, Joanie seemed almost eager to have me there. "Will Lucky be joining us?" We hadn't finished our conversation, in which she'd told me to ask her what had happened to Stuy. I told myself I wanted to know for curiosity's sake. But I couldn't completely ignore the fact that just that one detail could be all I needed to put me in the good graces of the producers.

"No. She and Teddy like to eat early. It will be just the three of us. Won't that be fun?"

That was certainly one word for it, but not necessarily the one

I might have used. I smiled and nodded, then turned in surprise as Joanie began to float back down the stairs, leaving behind a scent of cedarwood and bergamot, and her signature clinking of bangles.

"I guess she wants me to get you settled." Luke reached ahead of me and turned a door handle before leading me through to the room beyond. "The bathroom door is hidden on the far right wall—just push to open it. You'll see the hinges. My bedroom is on the left. I'll go grab the blue bathrobe and be right back. I'm sorry it's not fresh out of the dryer. I've used it a couple of times after a shower, so it's still relatively clean."

It was such an intimate thing, to share his robe, and I wanted to decline but my attention was quickly refocused on the large sheepskin rug in the middle of the room, strategically placed in front of the fire and completely at odds with the traditional dark wood tester bed and towering armoire.

Following my gaze, Luke said, "Oh, that's one of Joanie's 'treasures' she brought with her from California. She thought it might help Hadley relax. I don't think it worked. Or she never tried it because my sister's as uptight as she's always been. You should try it—it's very comfortable against bare skin." And at that, Luke left, presumably to go fetch the bathrobe he'd worn and would undoubtedly smell like him. I couldn't decide why that didn't bother me quite as much as I thought it should.

By the time I made it downstairs and into the kitchen, wearing nothing but Luke's incredibly comfortable robe and my feet inside a pair of fluffy lambswool slippers, I was happily warm but ravenously hungry.

Luke was opening a bottle of wine—presumably from a private collection kept out of sight from the crew and construction people—while Joanie stood at the one-burner temporary stove, stirring something in a large pot.

"Good," Joanie said. "You found the slippers. I thought we might be about the same size. I didn't want you back in your wet shoes or going barefoot. You'd get frostbite on these drafty floors!"

She took a taste from a wooden spoon, then resumed stirring. "This is the perfect warming soup—mushroom, spinach, cinnamon and coriander. It's delicious and nutritious—and vegan. I hope you're hungry, because I've made a whole pot."

"Thank you. I'm so hungry I could probably eat the pot."

"You might need to," Luke said. "If it stops raining, I could go get us burgers." He placed a cut-crystal glass containing a healthy pour of red wine in front of me. "At least we have this."

"Won't you join us, Joanie?" I asked. It felt awkward to be waited upon, to say nothing of being completely naked beneath the bathrobe. Joanie had taken all of my clothes to be washed and dried somewhere in the house, and hadn't seemed to have a problem leaving me with nothing but the robe.

"You're so sweet, Andie, but I'm going to stick with my special herbal tea. This house always congests my sinuses and my aura, so I try to stick to a clean diet while visiting." She began ladling the soup into three stoneware bowls. "But Lucky sent down the wine for you and Luke to enjoy."

"That's very kind of her," I said as Luke placed three linen napkins on the table, along with heavy sterling silverware, the handles embellished with a florid engraved capital *S*. "Where did these come from?" I asked, genuinely surprised that anything had survived the pillaging of paintings and furniture in the desperate attempts to pay the bills.

Joanie placed a bowl of soup in front of me. "Lucky is quite a genius at squirreling things away in her hidey-holes throughout the house. I think it's a skill she acquired as a child. She doesn't talk about it very much, but I know her stepcousin and his children made her feel as if she were a visitor in her own house, and helped themselves to much of the valuable jewelry she and her grandmother brought with them when they escaped from Italy."

Luke brought over the remaining two bowls and he and his mother joined me at the table. "So why . . . ," I began.

Joanie propped her elbows on the table, resting her chin on her folded arms. "Let's talk about you, Andie. I feel as if I've known you forever—and perhaps our souls have a shared past—but I know very little about your current life except that you are a single mother. I was a single mom, too, after my divorce. It's incredibly difficult being on duty all the time, isn't it? And having to be mother, provider, and disciplinarian simultaneously. I had no idea how to do any of it. Frankly, I'm surprised my children didn't end up as serial killers."

"I think the verdict's still out on Hadley," Luke said as he took a sip of his soup.

I pushed my spoon through the soup that, despite the heavy fragrance, was surprisingly tasteless. It needed salt—lots of it—but I didn't want to hurt Joanie's feelings and there were no salt or pepper shakers on the table. Instead, I took a healthy gulp of my wine.

"Petey isn't my son. He's my nephew," I clarified, earning a look of surprise from Luke. "My sister, Melissa, was never part of his life and I'm the only mother he's ever known. When he started calling me Mommy, I didn't correct him. And it's sort of stuck."

Luke poured more wine into my empty glass before topping off his own.

"Happily, my father is very involved in Petey's life. He used to own his own business designing and building boats, but after Mom left us he seemed to founder a bit and ended up losing the business." I took another sip of wine, the alcohol and the warmth of it bolstering my mood. And my need to share just how awful things had been, but how we'd managed to get beyond it. "He now works for other builders because he's got a great reputation as a dependable and talented craftsman, and it gives him a bit of an income while also allowing him the time to help watch Petey while I'm working."

Joanie reached over and squeezed my hand. "Believe me, I understand. It looks like you inherited your remarkable eye for design and craftsmanship from your dad."

"Yes, definitely. Maybe even from my mother, too." I took a long sip, enjoying the soothing warmth that settled inside me. There was something in Joanie's inviting smile and kind eyes that encouraged sharing things I rarely told anyone. Or maybe it was the wine and the growing feeling of frustration at how my life was turning out despite years of working hard to make it better than my mother had ever thought I could. "I haven't seen or spoken to my mother in a very long time."

Joanie squeezed my hand again while continuing to gaze at me with sympathetic eyes. It was like an invitation to continue unloading all of my pent-up feelings. Melissa, not long before she disappeared from our lives for good, had called me Fort Knox. And I'd yelled at her, telling her one of us had to be to keep everything from falling apart.

Feeling emboldened by Joanie's compassion and understanding, I blurted out, "I never planned to be a single mother. I mean, I'd love to have kids some day, but only when I have a partner to share the parenting. I'm exhausted all the time. I'm expected to work like I don't have a kid at home, yet his teacher and the mothers of his classmates act as if my job were secondary to getting the right treats sent on snack day and not to help keep a roof over our heads."

Joanie slid my glass closer to me. "I understand completely. You poor dear." She patted my hand before sitting back in her chair. "But Luke tells me you're a wonderful mother, and that's what's important. The jury is still out on Hadley, although I do know she tries very hard, but Luke would have made a wonderful father." She paused and looked at her son. "And Daphne a wonderful mother." Luke's hand tightened almost imperceptibly on the stem of his glass. "I'm sorry," Joanie continued. "I know you don't like to talk about it. But that's part of what has poisoned this family. Too many things we don't talk about."

Joanie slid her chair back and began to bring dishes over to the sink that still clung to the wall, its counter and cabinet having been removed. "I don't think there are enough chakras and healing crystals in the world to work through our family tree. We're like graphite, we Spragues. Layers sealed together with all of our secrets and untold stories. I still haven't given up hoping that one day we might manage to create a single, beautiful diamond from all of the pain and loss."

I could almost feel Marc prodding me on the shoulder, could almost smell the bourbon on his breath, reminding me of that awful moment when my beloved mentor had slid off his barstool in an apt tableaux of the current state of our lives and careers. All of it reminded me of what I was supposed to be doing. Which wasn't what I wanted to do at all.

"Joanie, do you remember anything from the night your father disappeared?"

She split the remainder of the wine between my glass and Luke's, her bangles clinking against the bottle. "I do. I was very small, but there are some things that imprint on one's memory, you know?"

I nodded, my mind flashing to the back of the taxi while I stared after it, hoping that my mother would look back just once. She didn't.

Joanie sat back down and stared straight ahead as if she were peering into the past. "There was a big party. Lucky was wearing a shiny dress and she let me pat her face with the big powder puff. Lucky always said that she wasn't completely dressed until I'd done that." She smiled to herself. "The housekeeper put me to bed—my nanny had been let go—but I couldn't sleep. Lucky would always check on me when she came home and if I were awake she would tell me all about the party. I remember not being sleepy at all. And then Nonna . . ." Joanie blinked, tilted her head. "I can't recall exactly, but she came into my room and was saying something that didn't make sense, something about not being able to save someone and I thought she was talking about Lucky.

"When she ran out of my room, I followed her, down to the boathouse. There was a bright moon—just like tonight—and Nonna was talking the whole time, saying things that didn't make sense, or maybe they did but I was too little to understand. But that's when I saw my daddy's boat and knew Lucky would be angry with him for leaving it there. They had been fighting so much, and I didn't want them to fight anymore so I thought I could sail it all by myself back to the marina."

She gave a small laugh and looked down at her hands, where I saw for the first time the smooth black stone she was rolling between her fingers. "It was Teddy who saved me. I don't remember much else besides him pulling me from the water and my mother kissing me over and over once I'd been dried off and put back to bed."

"Was your father there?" I asked, my voice soft.

Joanie met my gaze. "No. No, he wasn't. I remember the police asking me that the next day, after he went missing. But he wasn't. Just Teddy." She stopped, and smiled uncertainly.

"What else?" I prompted.

"No more secrets, right?" She straightened her shoulders. "Lucky told me not to mention to the police that Teddy was there. And . . ."

Joanie looked at Luke. "And what, Joanie?"

"And there was something else I remember. It had nothing to do with my daddy missing or anything else, but now I'm wondering if maybe it could have. But I've never told a soul."

I held my breath, wanting to know at the same time as being reluctant to hear something I would be compelled to share in a tabloid television show that didn't care about the pain of a missing father and a traumatized child.

Luke spoke first, taking the decision from me. "What, Joanie? What was it?"

"Nonna. She said something to me that didn't make sense then, and still doesn't. She was very confused at the end of her life, and I knew that even back then. But sometimes the truth can be disguised in the incoherent ramblings of an old woman. That's what my grandpa Dudley always told me."

I shared a glance with Luke while Joanie placed her hands palms down on the table, the stone beneath them. For the first time, she met my gaze. "Nonna kept repeating the same thing, over and over." She pressed her hands together over the stone. "She said, 'She's in there.'"

"In where?" Luke asked.

"She kept pointing at the boathouse. She looked like a ghost because she was wearing her long white nightgown, but then she started talking to me, saying that she was sorry and then over and over 'She's in there.' When I couldn't get her to tell me who, I went to get the sailboat."

"And you have no idea what she meant?"

Joanie pressed her lips together. "No. She died soon after. I never had a chance to find out. But I told Lucky. That's when she made the boathouse off-limits and said it wasn't safe anymore. I always thought she'd get it fixed, but maybe it's too painful because it was Daddy's favorite place and it might be too hard to be reminded of it. Or, more than likely, she didn't want to spend the money. There's a lot of competition here as to which part of the leaking roof or missing tile gets replaced first. I guess you'll have to ask Lucky."

She grinned then stood again, tucking the stone into the pouch at her waist as she moved to look outside the glass door. "Well, that's certainly a good sign. The rain's finally stopped, and a full moon is beaming from between the clouds." She turned to face us. "The large window in Hadley's room is perfect for seeing it. I remember lying down with Hadley there many times when she couldn't sleep. Lucky would tell the children the lady in white stories to keep them away from the boathouse. Didn't bother Luke, but Hadley wouldn't sleep." Joanie shrugged. "Just put some pillows on the rug and lie down there and it will be like you're on the beach outside—except warmer and drier. Why don't you two go on up and I'll take care of the dishes? And if you decide to watch a movie or put on some music, don't mind me. I'm headed to bed soon and I'm a very heavy sleeper."

I'm fairly certain she may have winked before hugging us each good night and shooing us out of the room.

"I guess we should go look at the moon," Luke said.

"Joanie seems so pliable and sweet." I snuggled deeper into my robe as we passed through the foyer to the main stairs, a veritable crosswind blowing through it.

"And she is, for the most part. But it's a pretty good disguise for the steel rod that runs through her core."

We paused in the upstairs hallway outside our rooms, staring awkwardly at each other. "You don't have to keep me company, you know. I promise not to tell Joanie."

"Maybe I like watching the moon. I haven't done it in a long time." He smiled and I noticed for the first time a small crescent-shaped scar on his eyebrow.

He caught my glance. "I can blame Hadley for that. She slipped on the cliff path and when I tried to hoist her, she kicked me in the face. She claims it was an accident but I'm not so sure." Luke shrugged. "She broke her arm and I immobilized it with a stick and my T-shirt."

"And that's why you wanted to be a doctor."

He didn't answer right away. "No. I always wanted to be a doctor."

Our eyes met as I waited for him to say more, to explain why he wasn't one any longer. Instead, he reached behind me and turned the doorknob to my bedroom. "The moon awaits." He raised an eyebrow in question.

"I doubt the moon waits for anyone." I walked past him to pull two throw pillows from the bed—hideous faux-tapestry things with fringes of gold tassels—while he shut the door.

Luke arranged the pillows at one end of the sheepskin rug. "I've done this a few times before. Back when Hadley was bearable and still afraid of the dark I'd sleep here on the floor so she wouldn't be alone."

I pictured the much younger Luke and Hadley that I'd seen in photos on the internet, and him comforting his twin because she was scared of the dark. I don't know why I hadn't seen this side of him before. Maybe because I simply hadn't bothered to look.

"I'm surprised," I said.

"What, that I'd sleep on the floor?"

"No. That Hadley was once bearable."

I situated myself and the pillows on the sheepskin rug. From this vantage point, the view of the sky through the diamond-shaped window mullions brought the moon and the night sky into the room. Luke turned off the overhead light, then lay down next to me. Maybe it was the lulling warmth of my long shower, the soup and the wine, or maybe there was something about Luke Sprague and his solid presence that made the situation much less awkward than it should have been. I felt an odd sense of security, something I hadn't felt since I was a girl in my childhood bed, safe in the knowledge that my entire family slept under the same roof and all was right in my world.

We lay side by side without speaking, bathed in the milky light of the moon and listening to the sounds of our breathing and the cracks and pops of the old house. I wanted to tell Joanie that we had found our aura of peace and contentment within our cocoon of light. But that could wait. I snuggled deeper into the robe, nestling into its warmth yet still finding it lacking.

"You must be freezing," Luke said. "I think we might have a stash of firewood in the old coal room behind the kitchen if you'd like me to start a fire in the fireplace."

I shook my head, finding the thought of his absence suddenly unbearable. "Don't leave. But would it be all right if I moved closer?"

Without hesitation, he placed his arm around my shoulder and slid me against his side. His chest was the only logical place to rest my head, and Luke didn't complain so I left it there, grateful for the warmth and the lulling beat of his heart beneath my ear.

The nearness emboldened me, encouraging me to ask the question that had been haunting the periphery of my thoughts since our conversation with Joanie. "Who's Daphne?"

"My wife." He paused. "My late wife."

"I'm sorry."

"Me too."

"You must still love her."

I felt him nod. "It's been five years, and there's a part of me that will always love her. But in the part of my heart where I keep the love for people and things from my past, like a trunk in the attic to be revisited every once in a while instead of taking up space in my living room." He gave a small laugh. "Joanie's the one who taught me to do that. And she was right, as usual."

I smiled at the moon. "I imagine she usually is."

"Remember how I said that I'd always wanted to be a doctor? It was Daphne's death that made me stop."

I sat up on my elbow so I could look into his face. "But why?"

"Because I couldn't save her. She had a malignant and fast-growing type of skin cancer, and I didn't see it until it was far too late. I was a doctor and her husband and that shouldn't have happened. But it did."

I placed my head back on his chest, then wrapped my arm around him in a futile gesture of comfort. "I'm sorry," I said. "But not just for the loss of your wife. I'm sorry for all the other people you couldn't save because you stopped being a doctor."

His body tensed beneath me. We remained silent, staring out at the night sky as his muscles slowly relaxed. "Was it suddenly becoming a mother that made you so smart?"

"Pretty much. Nothing like a crash course in taking care of an infant and a grieving father, paying bills, and going to school to jump-start adulthood. Not to mention searching for my sister. She sort of went AWOL when Petey was born. Not that I really blame her."

"Is the father not in the picture?"

I gave a short laugh. "Even if she knew his name, I doubt he'd be interested in helping out. He completely derailed Melissa's life, while he's blissfully unaware of any responsibilities as he works for his daddy on Wall Street and spends his spare time on a sailboat."

Luke sucked in his breath. "I'm starting to understand your instant dislike when we first met."

"Yeah, well, that's not your fault. I do lump all you sailor boys into the same category because it's easy to do. Melissa was a freshman at

Brown on a full ride when she made the mistake of going to a frat party and drinking too much. She found herself in a room with a bunch of guys who look a lot like you. She says she blacked out and didn't remember what happened. She didn't even tell me about it until she knew she was in her second trimester, her baby bump hidden because she was starving herself, thinking she was just gaining weight. Our mother had always taught us that the biggest sin was being fat."

His arm tightened around me. "That's a lot of baggage to carry around."

"Yep. It was her decision to keep the baby, and her decision to split after he was born. She'd show up sometimes asking for money—she was heavy into drugs at that point—and I'd give it to her because she was so pathetic and I'd make her promise to get clean. She never did, and she stopped showing up. I have no idea where she is now. Or if she's even alive."

The clearing sky winked at us with rising stars, the moon glowing fiercely as if to prove it had survived the storm. I sighed. "I wish we'd met at a different place and time. Because I have a feeling that you and I might have become a permanent thing."

Luke lifted up on his elbow, and my head slid gently down to the pillow. "Might have? I disagree."

I tried to pull back, our confessions leaving me with no energy to argue. "Never mind. . . ."

He put a finger on my lips. "I disagree because I think we can become a permanent thing. Or at least we should definitely try." His face was in shadow with the moonglow behind him, but I could hear the smile in his voice. "And my mother already approves."

Luke lowered his head, his lips brushing mine. My skin was suddenly on fire. I wrapped my arms around his neck and pulled him closer. "You're right. We should definitely try."

And we did for the rest of the night until the sun replaced the moon, and the stars slipped from the sky.

CHAPTER TWENTY-THREE

Ellen

Newport, Rhode Island
July 1899

MAYBELLE'S ROOM WAS a patch of night in the midst of day, all the curtains drawn shut, and Maybelle herself on her favorite chaise longue in the alcove, curled up in a ball like a hedgehog.

"Maybelle?" As Ellen ventured closer, she could see Maybelle was hugging her trinket box, cradling it close to her chest. "I hear congratulations are in order."

"I suppose so." Maybelle's voice was very small in the large room. "People seem to think so."

"Isn't it every girl's dream, to marry a prince?"

"Not mine." Maybelle ducked her head over her trinket box, her long blond curls screening her face. "I never asked for a prince."

To be just a man, the prince had said last night. Oh, if only he were just a man. But he wasn't, and there was no point in wishing he were. The man and the prince were inextricable. The man might want Ellen, but the prince needed an heiress. He needed Maybelle.

"Think what it will be like to live in Italy. You'll be surrounded by art and music." Ellen had no idea, really. But it sounded good. And she couldn't imagine the prince not surrounded by such things. "Italy is the birthplace of opera. Think of the singers you'll hear!"

"I'm not like you." Maybelle shook her curls. "I don't need any of that. I just wanted . . . a quiet sort of life."

With Frank Pratt? Ellen doubted life with Frank Pratt would be quiet. More likely filled with people banging on the door demanding their debts be paid.

"When you're a princess, you can live however you like," she said soothingly.

Maybelle lifted her head, looking at Ellen straight on. "You don't really believe that."

Taken by surprise, Ellen said honestly, "No. I don't. I don't know anything about Italy or what will be expected of you. All I know about princesses comes out of old storybooks. But I do know that the prince is a good man. A decent man."

"He's so cold," said Maybelle despairingly. "And old."

He hadn't been cold last night. Ellen was grateful for the artificial gloom that hid the flare of color in her cheeks. "Not that old. He's still in the prime of life."

Maybelle pulled her knees up to her chest. "He makes me feel about five years old. I never know what to say to him."

Ellen sat down tentatively on the edge of the chaise longue. "Talk to him about the things that interest *you*. About books and poetry. He might surprise you."

Maybelle twisted away from her. "I tried. I did. He says things that make no sense. He quotes poems I don't know as if he expects me to understand."

"Or maybe he just likes saying them. Maybe he says them for himself." Half the time, Ellen had no clue what he was talking about, but she liked the cadence of his voice, the play of thought across his face. "When you don't understand, tell him."

"It's no use." Looking up at Ellen, Maybelle whispered, "Why do I have to marry him?"

You don't, Ellen was tempted to say. But then she remembered

Frank Pratt. And all the other Frank Pratts out there. Men who would be quick to take advantage of an heiress as sweet-natured and naive as Maybelle. Men who would woo her until her money was in their hands and then delight in mocking her. Whatever else the prince was, he was a man of honor. He would stand by his word. He might not pretend to love Maybelle, but he would treat her courteously.

In the marriage bed?

Ellen decided she didn't want to think about that. "You have to marry him because you're an heiress."

"And he needs my money." Maybelle's round face was bleak in the dim light.

"And you need the protection of his name." Ellen spoke more sharply than she intended.

Maybelle looked at her with wide, startled eyes. "But I don't . . . I haven't—"

It took Ellen a moment to realize what she was saying. And to remember that Maybelle hadn't always been as sheltered as she was now. One tended to forget. Hildie had told Ellen that Maybelle's stepmother, John Sprague's mother, had run the sort of boardinghouse that rented rooms by the hour. "I didn't mean that! I just meant that there will be men out there who will want you for your money, who could take advantage of you, ruin you. Once you're married to the prince, you don't have to worry about any of that. You'll be safe."

Maybelle's shoulders hunched. In a very small voice, she said, "Is it so strange to think someone might want me for something other than my money?"

"No! Not strange at all." Impulsively, Ellen took Maybelle's hands. They were very soft, those hands, and clammy with nervous sweat. "But there are a lot of fortune hunters out there."

Maybelle shot her a veiled look. "Like the prince."

How on earth had she gotten herself into this, trying to persuade Maybelle to marry the one man in the world she wanted for herself?

"Like the prince. But he's never made any pretense about it. You know what you're getting with him. It's an honest bargain. Your money for his name."

Maybelle yanked her hands away, shaking them in distress. "But what if I wanted something more? What if I wanted something more than a name?"

Love, he had said. But in his world—in Maybelle's world—love and marriage didn't always keep company. He could love Ellen and marry Maybelle and see no dishonor in it.

"I think," said Ellen, very carefully, "that in the circles in which the prince moves—in the circles in which you'll move—it might be possible, eventually, to have his name and also something more."

"You mean he'll grow to love me?" said Maybelle dully. That wasn't what Ellen had meant at all, but she didn't want to correct her. "That's what John keeps telling me. But Prunella says—"

"What does Mrs. Schuyler say?"

"Nothing." Maybelle drew back, curling back in on herself. "I think—I think I need to be alone for a bit."

"I'm just next door if you need me," said Ellen, but Maybelle only shook her bowed head and didn't meet her eyes.

"It won't be so bad," said Ellen helplessly.

Maybelle didn't reply.

The music lessons continued. It was to be part of the celebration: Maybelle singing for her prince. It was all part of the charming story John Sprague had concocted and fed to an eager press, the American heiress whose song had won the heart of a prince. Never mind that hearts weren't any part of the transaction and everyone involved knew it. It made a beautiful feature for the shopgirls and downstairs maids who snatched up the cheap papers with a drawing of Maybelle in it, Maybelle and the prince in paired ovals. Neither looked anything like themselves.

The real Maybelle went about her life by rote. Music lessons with

Ellen in the morning, dress fittings in the afternoon. She insisted that Mrs. Schuyler be with her for the latter, and while Ellen didn't like it, she had no say in the matter. John Sprague, enjoying all the benefits of Maybelle's engagement, was inclined to be magnanimous. Whatever Maybelle wanted, Maybelle might have—so long as it was no impediment to her speedy induction into holy matrimony.

Not that it could be that speedy. There were legal documents to be drawn up—Ellen had no part in those, but she had seen Maybelle called into Mr. Sprague's study, papers shoved at her for her signature, no, no need to read them, just sign—and instruction in the Catholic faith, so that a civil ceremony in the States (John Sprague was taking no chances) might be followed in due course by a solemn ritual in the Vatican presided over by none other than Pope Leo XIII, who, of course, was related to the Prince di Conti in a complicated tangle of coronets, quarterings, and blood of so deep a blue as to be nearly indigo.

Maybelle drifted like a sleepwalker through her various obligations, a pretty china doll blinking her eyes when moved.

As for the prince . . .

It wasn't proper, he said, to remain under the same roof as his intended. He removed himself to hired rooms at the Ocean House, returning every afternoon to take Maybelle for a ritual drive down Bellevue Avenue as was right and proper. Ellen did not accompany Maybelle for those drives. But she did notice that Maybelle began to return from them in better spirits, with something less of the air of the gallows about her. She couldn't be called cheerful, but she was calm.

The prince, when he wanted to, could be very charming indeed.

That was the end of it, Ellen told herself. Perhaps he'd write her a reference that would earn her a place in a household in New York, with another hopeful heiress, well away from Dermot and his henchmen.

Eileen O'Donnell would disappear forever, replaced by the music teacher Ellen Daniels, building her new identity reference by reference, job by job, until her hair grayed and memory faded and no one remembered there had been such a woman as Eileen or a place called the Hibernia. And little princelings with Maybelle's golden hair and the prince's green eyes would stage mock battles in a palace somewhere in Italy, secure in both their lineage and their fortune.

It was really a very happy outcome for everyone, Ellen told herself firmly.

Except, perhaps, for Frank Pratt. Ellen was making her way from her room to the back stairs when she saw him outside his cousin's bedroom door. She would have passed quietly by, hoping they didn't see her, but for three words. "This man O'Shea . . ."

Ellen stopped, caught up short.

Frank had clearly been lurking outside his cousin's door, lying in wait for her to come out. The door was half open, Prunella neither in nor out. "You don't know what these men are like. Do you want me to wind up floating in Boston Harbor?"

Prunella shook him off, waving a hand laden with precious stones. "Don't be so dramatic. Just tell them you need to find another heiress."

"I don't have time to find another heiress, Prunella!" Pratt's voice was urgent.

Like another man Ellen had once heard, another man who had fallen afoul of Dermot O'Shea. But that had been something different, Ellen told herself hastily. That had been one of Dermot's own. They wouldn't hurt a society man. Why kill the goose that laid the compound interest?

"Just give me one of your rings. A bracelet! You've got enough of them—you'll never miss them. If they can't take it out of my pocket, they'll take it out of my skin."

Prunella drew her rings prudently out of Frank's reach. "They're hardly going to come bother you in *Newport*. The whole point of Newport is to keep those sorts of people out."

And didn't Ellen hope she was right. If Dermot were to turn up here . . . but no. He wouldn't. He couldn't. Besides, he'd never come himself. He'd send a minion.

But would his minions recognize her? How many had looked closely at the little pianist behind the screen?

No. Ellen flexed her cold hands, feeling the blood rush through them. No one recognized the pianist. No one was thinking about her. Hopefully.

Pratt tried wheedling. "Prunella, you promised me you were going to fix it."

"You can't rely on me to do everything for you, Frank."

"Don't I know it." Pratt turned on his heel, nearly bumping into Ellen in the process. "Never mind. I've decided to take care of matters myself."

Prunella bustled after him, the jet embroidery of her dress jangling. "What do you mean by that? Frank! Frank? You're not going to do anything stupid, are you?" She stopped short and glared at Ellen. "You! What are you doing here?"

"Just going down to the music room," said Ellen, and paused, wondering if she should warn Prunella that her cousin might be telling nothing more than the truth.

"Well go, then," said Prunella impatiently, and shoved past her, following Frank.

Ellen looked after her, and then turned and went toward the back stairs. To say anything would be to expose herself. Unlike the prince, Prunella would never keep her secret. Ellen would be out on her ear, and no good done by it.

Besides, there was no more time. Maybelle's engagement party was upon them. The celebration was to be rapidly followed by a civil ceremony to cement the union in the eyes of the state—and prevent either party from changing their minds.

Ellen had, as instructed, arranged for fireworks.

For once, John Sprague had begrudged no expense. He spent his stepsister's money with abandon. Liveried footmen. Hired chefs. Flowers of every color and description ordered from John Hodgson, who supplied all the best flowers for all the best parties. Musicians to play the guests in, to play for dancing, to trill the appropriate fanfares as the great wheels of color exploded in the sky.

And, of course, a grand confection of a dress for Maybelle, embroidered with real pearls, thousands of them, in whirls and scallops and bows, so that her dress was less a dress and more a walking jewelry box. There were rubies and diamonds at her throat and her ears and her wrists, on top of her long gloves; a matching tiara had been set carefully on her perfectly coiffed curls.

She looked, thought Ellen, with a pang, like a princess.

There was even some matching color in her cheeks, an echoing sparkle in her eyes. Whatever Frank Pratt might have been to her, thought Ellen wryly, there was no denying the excitement of marrying a prince. And perhaps she had, in the end, realized she'd got the better man.

"You look beautiful," Ellen said, stopping by, just for a moment, on her way to her own room. She'd meant to see if Maybelle needed encouragement, some gentle bucking up, but this new, glowing Maybelle was another matter entirely. This Maybelle looked like any young girl before her betrothal ball, rather than a reluctant bride shoved to the altar. "The tiara suits you."

"Does it?" Maybelle put her hand to her head, looking more like the old Maybelle again.

Ellen realized, with a shock, that this was the end of it. No more pausing in the door between rooms. No more Maybelle on the chaise longue. No more music lessons in the morning. No more Maybelle.

No more prince.

Ellen did her best to smile. "Are you ready for your song tonight?"

"As ready as anyone could make me." Maybelle walked lightly in her pearl-studded silk slippers to where Ellen stood, then kissed her gently on the cheek. "Thank you for everything. I couldn't have survived these past few weeks without you."

"You're welcome," said Ellen, surprised and touched. She squeezed Maybelle's hands. "I truly hope you'll be happy."

Maybelle bit her lip, looking down shyly, her tiara scintillating in the lamplight. "Oh, I think I will."

Ellen fought an unexpected stab of pain. If she couldn't have the prince herself—and she couldn't, she knew she couldn't—she would rather Maybelle have him than anyone else. It was a bittersweet thought.

"Will you write to me from Italy and let me know how you get on?"

"Y-yes." Maybelle looked like a rabbit caught out of cover.

So that was how it was. Ellen told herself she should have expected it. "You don't have to. I would understand if you didn't."

"No," said Maybelle, more firmly. She fingered the modest cameo hidden beneath her grand parure of diamonds and rubies. "If there's anyone I would want to tell . . . I will. I will write you."

And then she gave Ellen a quick, crushing hug before running back to Delphine, who was impatiently waving a scrap of lace at her.

Ellen could hear Delphine scolding Maybelle for disarranging herself as Ellen went through the connecting door to make her own, far less intricate toilette.

There was no grand ball gown for Ellen, no jewels. Ellen's dress was dark blue, and she wore her fair hair coiled neatly at the back of her neck. She wouldn't have been at the party at all but for Maybelle insisting she needed her own accustomed accompanist if she were to sing. Ellen's instructions were clear. There was to be no hanging about. She was to play and leave.

The piano had been dragged out of the music room onto the verandah at the back, so that the singing might be followed immediately by the fireworks. Torchieres had been lit on either side, so that Maybelle would stand with the flames sparkling off her jewels as she sang. Ellen's piano had been put to one side, angled so that she could see the singer and the singer could see her, but the guests would see only her dark back melding with the night, just a part of the piano.

Which was quite all right with her.

As Ellen slipped onto the verandah, she looked to see if she could find the prince in the throng. She'd wondered how it would feel to see him again, for the first time since that night in the rose arbor, when they had been wet and disheveled and stripped down to their souls. As she set her music on the stand, she casually glanced into the crowd, as one might poke a sore tooth with one's tongue, testing for weakness.

Yes, there he was, being jostled into a place of honor. John Sprague had arranged for a sort of throne, so that the prince might sit in state to hear his bride sing. The representatives of no fewer than forty major newspapers stood, with pens poised, to record his reactions.

He wore a uniform of some sort, the chest bright with orders of this and that. He looked like what he was: foreign. Remote.

It should feel like a relief, Ellen told herself. It should. He was not for her and she was not for him. They were chance met, and she should take their brief moment together for what it was, an odd sort of gift, a curio to put in a box, to be taken out and looked at every now and again, but not for daily use.

Maybelle sang and sang prettily, her voice all but lost in the vast space, in the shifting feet and people hushing one another even as they whispered over one another. It didn't matter. She looked lovely; she might have been braying like a donkey and it would have been accounted charming.

Ellen nodded her approval to her pupil, and would have risen, but John Sprague's heavy hand pressed her back onto the piano bench.

"We have one more performance," he hissed, and she could smell the drink on his breath, not champagne but something stronger. He stank of whisky and cigars; he'd been celebrating seeing his sister off and couldn't wait to do it properly.

Raising his voice to a shout to be heard over the crowd, Sprague bellowed, "And now the prince has a song for his bride."

That quieted the crowd. Maybelle singing for her betrothed—well, yes, that was very pretty, that was to be expected—but no one had known the prince himself was to sing. Men didn't, generally. This was a novelty. The correspondents perked up and licked their pencils. And the prince stepped to the piano next to Ellen.

Orange flower and bergamot. So much for a curio to be put in a box. Memory shook her, making her weak. His proximity unnerved her.

"Shall I accompany you?" Ellen asked briskly, as though they had never kissed and exchanged confidences in a welter of wind and roses. As though she hadn't buried her head in his waistcoat, smelling that cologne and the salt of his skin.

The prince looked at her, the torchlight doing strange things to his features, flickering along the bones of his face, lighting his eyes with fire. "I should like nothing better."

She knew, down to her bones, it wasn't the piano he was talking about.

"What shall I play?" she asked in a strangled voice.

The prince drew a roll of music from his evening jacket. "Donizetti's 'Una furtiva lagrima.' A song of love requited."

Ellen took the music. "'With one fugitive tear'?"

"I didn't think you spoke Italian."

"I've been helping Maybelle." Never mind that it was less about Maybelle and more because it made her feel closer to him. Ellen bent her head over the sheet music, making a show of studying the notes. "She'll need it when she goes with you to Italy. Are you ready? Shall I begin?"

"We began weeks ago," said the prince tenderly, and stepped back between the torches to sing.

Ellen played by rote, her fingers moving with little conscious direction from her brain, as the prince sang for her, only for her.

To the audience, it might look as though he sang for his bride, his bride who stood awkwardly next to her brother at the front of the crowd, a blur of diamond, ruby, and pearl. His voice, trained, trained better than Ellen had been trained, rose and soared over the crowd.

"*Che più cercando io vo?*" the prince sang, his eyes never leaving Ellen's. *What more need I seek?* "*Che più cercando io vo?*"

She oughtn't, she knew. But she couldn't help it. Her eyes locked with his, seeking—and finding. Finding everything she had both hoped and feared to find. The music boiled up around her, her notes, his voice, two halves made one.

"*M'ama!*" *She loves me.* The words rang out triumphant. "*Sì, m'ama, lo vedo, lo vedo.*"

It wasn't fair, it wasn't right, not on his engagement night. Thank goodness her back was to the assemblage. Thank goodness no one could see her, see her heart was being torn out of her chest note by note, as the prince sang the words that sounded like they were for Maybelle, that ought to have been for Maybelle, but she knew, with every beat of her heart, with every syllable that fell from the prince's lips, were for her, only for her.

She loves me! Yes, she loves me, I see it, I see it.

She felt as though she were being stripped bare. Did the other guests see, did they know? No, they were all deep in their own thoughts, some gossiping in corners, others feigning expressions of interest while thinking of this love affair or that new dress. They wouldn't care. She wasn't a person to them. Only to him. To him and to Maybelle, who trusted her.

The song ended, the guests clapped. A fanfare blared and color rent the sky, the first fusillade of fireworks.

The prince paused by the piano on his way to his betrothed.

"*Lo vedo,*" he said. *I see it.*

Ellen gathered up his music, shuffling the sheets back into order, then rolling them tightly together, as if she could pack it all away again, the emotion, the pain. The love requited. "You shouldn't have done that."

"Done what?"

"You know exactly what." Ellen handed him the roll of music, trying to keep her voice flat and calm, to keep the anguish she was feeling from showing in her eyes. "You'll go off to Italy with Maybelle, but I'll still be here. My reputation is all I have."

Another burst of fireworks, an entwined *M* and *C*. Maybelle and Conti. "Come with us," said the prince.

"To Italy?" Colored lights sparkled at the edges of Ellen's eyes, red and green and gold. Italy. For a wild moment, she could picture it, a carriage, winding through the mountains. Foreign guards, foreign servants, foreign foods.

And Maybelle. His wife.

"There's room enough in the castle."

Ellen forced herself to lift her head, to look him in the eye. "Room enough for a wife *and* a mistress?"

"There is always room for a friend," he said quietly.

It would never be just that. They both knew it. "And betray your wife—my friend—under her own roof? No. Without me there, you might make something of this, the two of you."

"Not like what we have." More red and gold lights exploded over the prince's head.

"I can't repair your roof," said Ellen. She forced herself to look at him, one last time, drinking in the features of his face, illuminated by the torchlight. "Be happy. Make Maybelle happy."

She didn't wait for him to reply. She didn't think she could bear it. Turning, she blundered back into the house—through a side entrance, as befit a servant. Somewhere, out there, the band was playing, the fireworks soaring. Maybelle and her betrothed would be standing beneath that canopy of glowing sparks, accepting the congratulations of their guests.

It meant something, Ellen told herself fiercely. It meant something that she had kept her dignity. That she hadn't betrayed Maybelle.

To have gone to Italy with them . . .

No. No second thoughts. Maybe he would heed her. Maybe he would do what she'd asked and try to make Maybelle happy. Maybelle so desperately needed someone to make her happy.

Even if it meant that Ellen didn't have anyone at all.

Making a face at herself, Ellen let herself back into her room and set about lighting the lamps, making the velvet and silk of the upholstery glow. So much richness, she thought, and for what? There was no one in this house who was truly happy or truly kind. Her family had had more in a three-room tenement than John Sprague did in his eighty-room mansion.

She had just reached up to unpin her collar when something caught her eye, something that shouldn't have been there, a bit of white against the sapphire brocade of her coverlet. It was a note, propped against her pillows.

Ellen felt a sudden, sick lurch of excitement, followed by disgust at herself. Of course it wasn't from the prince. Someone had written *Ellen* across the front in a loopy, ornate script. She knew that stationery and she knew that hand.

It was probably a thank-you note, Maybelle feeling guilty for leaving Ellen as she went off to her new life. It was, thought Ellen fondly, so like Maybelle. Although it wasn't like Maybelle to write at such a jagged angle, or to let her pen spatter ink across the page. This had been written in haste. Maybelle must have slipped it into Ellen's room just before she went downstairs.

But how? Ellen reached for the note, caught by that simple question. Maybelle had gone downstairs before Ellen. Hadn't she?

Opening the note, she scanned the short, hastily written lines—and bolted for the door.

CHAPTER TWENTY-FOUR

Lucky

Newport, Rhode Island
July 1957

THE OLD PALAZZO di Conti might have been crumbling into graceful ruin by the time Mussolini came to power, but still the gardens had bloomed abundant, year after year. Nonno used to pour his heart into them—heart and sweat and blood, right alongside the two remaining gardeners, a father and son whose ancestors had kept the di Conti grounds for centuries. Over the winter he would plan out the beds, what to keep and what to replace, when to trim and fertilize and all those things. A garden is like a lover, he would say. You have to cultivate it every day to make it blossom.

"He said this to you?" Teddy asked.

"All the time."

"And you were *how* old?"

Lucky punched his shoulder. "Italians aren't so puritanical as you New Englanders. Anyway, I knew he meant Nonna. He only had eyes for her."

"Yes," said Teddy, kissing the top of her head.

She rolled onto his chest and stacked her fingers under her chin. "They're probably all overgrown now, without anyone to tend them."

"What's overgrown?"

"The di Conti gardens."

Teddy pulled one hand from beneath her chin and kissed each fingertip. "Maybe I could have a stab at them. I've always had a bit of a passion for gardening."

"Hmm."

"You don't think so?"

"Oh, I'm sure you know all about making things bloom. I just wonder whether your wife minds your tending another woman's garden."

Teddy tucked her fingers inside his palm and lost the teasing expression. "Alice has given us her blessing. She wants us both to be happy."

"She said that?"

"We had a long talk yesterday. She said she should have set me free long ago."

"Free. Are you sure about that?"

"Do you think I'd be lying here with you otherwise? We're free, Lucky. Believe it. Right now, right here, it's the start of our brand-new lives together."

Lucky laid her cheek against his chest and listened to his heart, communicating through bone and skin and cartilage into some thirsty part of her soul. At each thump, she expected it to stop. This couldn't go on—it was simply too good to be true, to have sprawled on some old cushions and blankets on the floor of the boathouse loft and made love to Teddy Winthrop, to lie in his arms afterward and feel as necessary to him as the air in his lungs. No, each thump was surely the last. The signal to wake from this dream and return to her old life, her old husband, her old house.

But his heart thumped on and on.

"Do you want to know something funny?" she whispered. "You're the only man I've slept with, other than Stuy."

"Is that so?"

Lucky opened her mouth to tell him another funny thing—that Stuy had seduced her at this exact spot, almost, and at about this time of year—but she caught herself just in time. What a stupid thing to say! Why confuse it all with memories of her husband? All the ghosts of her old mistakes? This was *different*. She was a different woman than the little green virgin who'd fallen in love with her handsome stepcousin, and Teddy was an entirely different man than Stuyvesant Sprague. Then, she'd been trapped. Now?

She was setting herself free.

So she swallowed back those words and lifted her head to face him. "And you know something else? I have a feeling you'll be the last."

In the moonlight, the grin flashed from his teeth. He rolled her over onto her back and kissed the tip of her nose. "Well, now. I like the sound of *that*."

The second time was even better than the first—slow and tender at the beginning, not an inch of skin left unexamined, until at some point things got feverish, forceful, each stroke like the ringing of a bell. She loved the ropey texture of his arms, the lemony taste of his skin—some kind of soap, she guessed—the way he watched her as they clasped and strained, as if each tiny expression fascinated him. At the end, he said her name almost like a prayer: *Lucia*. They lay together without a sound, joined everywhere, breathing softly into each other's skin, so it was funny that neither of them heard any particular noise emerge from the distant cacophony at Marble House to approach them, step-by-step.

Not until the boathouse door swung open and banged against the wall.

"Lucky?" roared a familiar voice.

Teddy's arms stiffened around her. *Don't move*, he whispered in her ear, not that he needed to. Lucky couldn't have moved if she tried. A terrible paralysis struck her, sheer terror.

"*Lucky!*" Stuy roared again. "Come down here, both of you! I know you're there!"

Teddy sighed and pressed his forehead against hers. *Don't*, she whispered. He shook his head. She tightened her arms around him, but carefully he reached back and loosened her grip. Kissed her fingers and set her arms by her sides.

"Winthrop! You son of a bitch. Yellow bastard, hiding up there with my wife! Come on down so I can—I can take a swing at you, give you the goddamn licking you deserve. Swear to God I'll kill you for this—"

"Stuy!" Lucky exclaimed.

"Lucky, it's all right," Teddy said, yanking his trousers on. "Just stay here, I'll take care of it."

"Teddy, don't! He's drunk, he's mad, it's not worth it—"

Stuy's voice drifted up again, silky. "Now, wait a second. What the hell do we have here? Is this your *dress*, Lucky? Your damn ball gown? Your *stockings*? Here on the floor? On the night my *father* dies?"

Teddy found Lucky's satin slip on the floor and tossed it to her. "Stay here," he growled, and started for the ladder.

"Teddy, wait! Your glasses!"

Stuy's voice rose from the floor below. "So that's how you celebrate, is it? My dad kicks off and you hop right in bed with Teddy-boy—"

"Now, you leave her alone, Sprague!"

"—because now you're free, right? You think you can just run off with some other fella—"

"Leave her alone, I said!"

"Oh, I'm coming up, all right. Gotta have a word with my wife about respect for the dead—"

"You're dead drunk, Stuy. You'll kill yourself."

"—maybe explain she's not so free as she thinks she is. My old dad told me a thing or two, see. A few interesting facts, you might say."

Lucky couldn't get the straps straight, couldn't get her slip over her head. Her arms shook. She couldn't hold a single thought, except fear. Stuy's voice filled her with terror. Those calm, slurred words! All his petulance and anger had hardened into some kind of awful, drunken, ice-cold resolve. She'd never imagined him like this. She tried to shout something, to warn Teddy, but her throat was so tight with terror, the words came out in a strangled squeak.

Watch out, Teddy!

Teddy's voice rang out right over hers. "Stuy! I said stay where you are! I'm coming down. We'll talk this out, man to man."

"Is that so? Well, I'm coming up, so something's got to give."

Finally Lucky got the slip over her head. In the darkness, she saw Teddy's moonlit head disappear over the edge of the ladder. She called out and started toward him.

"I said, *get down*!" Stuy yelled.

Lucky heard a cry, a thump, a grunt. She scrambled to the ladder and looked down. Teddy picked himself up from the floor at the bottom of the ladder. Stuy stood braced next to him, fists curled.

"Stop it, you two!" she screamed.

"Lucky, stay where you are!" Teddy called back. He wasn't wearing his glasses. He took a wild swing; Stuy ducked and laughed and punched him in the gut. Teddy fell back and landed hard on the floor.

Quick as a cat, Stuy turned and made for the ladder.

"Don't you dare!" Lucky yelled. She reached for something—anything—the pile of magazines. She threw them over the edge of the loft, above the ladder. Stuy swore and swung out of the way, hanging on by one hand. The magazines tumbled down the rungs and landed in a heap of splayed pages at the bottom. Stuy laughed and resumed his climb. His white shirt glowed in the moonlight, almost phosphorescent. Lucky scrambled back and grabbed the lamp on the little camp table—an old brass candlestick lamp, purloined from the main house long ago. She yanked the cord out of the wall just as Stuy appeared over the edge of the floor, grinning wildly, blond hair askew. Then his expression changed. His head jerked down, bobbed back up.

"Let go, you bastard!" he yelled.

Teddy's voice barked up. "Leave her alone, dammit! Come down here and hit me like a man!"

Stuy's body whipped hard. Lucky heard a curse, a thump. She rushed to the edge of the loft and saw Teddy through the railing, landing with another terrible thump at the bottom of the ladder. Stuy heaved himself up to land like a fish on the loft.

Lucky brandished the lamp above her head. "Don't you dare!"

"Did you see him, Lucky? Did you see my father's dead body? Laugh over his corpse, maybe—"

"Of course not!"

"—left him all alone—"

"Of course I didn't! Louise is there, Reggie's there—"

"—and then ran straight home to jump in bed with your lover, good old Teddy-boy—"

"You just stop right there, Stuy! Don't you dare come any closer, or I'll—"

"You'll what, honey? Bash my brains out? Hell, why not? You've already torn my guts out—"

"You did that to yourself! All that drinking and running around—"

"I wouldn't've had to if I had a real wife, a wife who loved *me* instead of her damn house! And now you want to take that away, too. Don't you? You want to take away my home and my daughter. Leave me with nothing."

Stuy took another step, a little unsteady, and as he came closer Lucky saw how disheveled he was, how unkempt and miserable, eyes wild, full of agony. She lowered the lamp a few inches.

"Stuy, please."

"He was a rat, all right? I know that. My dad was a rat. But he was my *dad*. You could've shown a little respect."

"Stuy—"

"Straight from the hospital to bed with Teddy-boy—"

"That's not how it happened."

"Well, I've got a surprise for you, sweetheart. It's not yours. The house, the property, everything. Dad told me."

Lucky lifted the lamp. "That's ridiculous. You're drunk, you're not making sense."

"Put that damn thing down, darling."

"Not until you go right back down that ladder and go to bed to sleep it off."

Stuy shook his head slowly. "'Fraid I can't do that."

"Yes, you can."

"See, I figure I owe it to Dad. I figure *someone* has to stick up for him tonight, the night he—what's the thing—mortal coil . . ."

Stuy started to sway. Behind him, a shadow rose from the ladder and heaved itself onto the loft floor.

"Teddy, help!" she called.

Teddy rose to his feet. "Back off, Sprague. I mean it."

"This is between me and my wife, Teddy-boy. We gotta clear the air."

Lucky never was sure exactly what happened then. She remembered Stuy staggered forward, that she lifted the heavy brass lamp. Did she actually hit him with it? Who knew? At the same instant, Teddy launched himself at Stuy. The two men crashed to the floor, fists flying. Lucky fell backward—maybe they knocked her off her feet, she didn't remember—and the next thing she heard was the most terrific crash, wood splintering. She lifted her head and saw Teddy on his knees next to the broken railing. She screamed and looked over the edge at Stuy's body sprawled on the floor below—leg horribly broken, neck tilted at a funny angle, blood creeping from beneath his head, absolutely motionless.

"HE'S DEAD," TEDDY said quietly. He set Stuy's wrist gently back on the floor.

Lucky cradled the blood-soaked head. "Oh my God. Oh no. Oh, Stuy."

"Poor fellow. Poor old Stuy."

"It's my fault. I killed him."

"No you didn't! Lucky, no. None of this is your fault."

"Yes, it is. I hit him with the lamp, I'm sure of it." She raised her hand and stared at the bloody fingers. "I did this."

"No you didn't. He fell on the boat hook, Lucky!" Teddy took her by the shoulders. "Lucky, look at me! You didn't hit him, you didn't push him over the edge. If anything, it's my fault. I should have kept him from going up that ladder in his condition."

Lucky shook her head. "No. He came up because he knew we were together. He was absolutely right, I shouldn't have done it. Slept with you *tonight*, of all nights! His *father* just died!"

Teddy sat next to her and drew her head to his chest. "Shh. Stop. It's all right."

"No it's not! What do we do? He's dead! We have to call the police or something—"

"The police?"

"I'll take the blame. It's my fault. I'll tell them I did it, I was fighting him off—"

"The hell you will! You're not going to jail for *his* sake, that's for sure."

"Neither are you! I won't allow it!"

Teddy ran a hand through his hair. "Well, someone's got to take the blame. He's dead, we can't hide the fact."

A firm, gentle voice came from the doorway. "Yes, we can."

Lucky gasped and scrambled to her feet. "Nonna?"

A white figure stepped into a patch of moonlight from the window. Nonna's face was remarkably calm, her eyes bright and lucid. She looked down at Stuy's body with pity. "Poor man. I suppose he never stood a chance."

"A chance against what?" Lucky whispered.

"Fate. No, not fate. That's the wrong word." Nonna frowned and rubbed her thumb against her forehead. "Retribution, maybe? It runs through families, you see. The sins of the fathers."

"The sins of the *fathers*? What on earth?"

"Never mind. We've got a body to hide."

Teddy stood up. "*Hide?* Hide the *body*? What kind of crazy idea is that? How in God's name are we going to hide Stuyvesant Sprague's dead body from the world?"

Nonna turned to him and smiled like a saint. The moon gleamed in her hair, gathered in a smooth knot at the base of her neck. Her pale nightgown billowed around her. She looked like she'd stepped out from another age.

"Don't worry, dear. I've done this before."

CHAPTER TWENTY-FIVE

Andie

Newport, Rhode Island
September 2019

Bright sun from the window warmed my face, and the slightly fuzzy and hard body of Luke Sprague warmed the rest of me, nudging me from sound sleep. The lulling sound of a gardener with a hedge trimmer buzzed somewhere below the window, letting me know that at least the rain had stopped. For now. I sat up abruptly, blinked, then spotted the blue robe draped over the fireplace andirons, reminding me of how it got there. Blood rushed to my face. "I've never done this before."

Luke chuckled, pulling me back down to his chest. "You could have fooled me."

"I meant"—I fluttered my hand at the blue bathrobe—"that. I'm not in the habit of falling into bed with the first sailor boy who drags me in from the cold."

"I didn't think you hung out with sailor boys."

"I don't, but I'm beginning to think that I might like to hang out with only one." I placed a kiss on his neck, just below his ear, where I'd learned that he liked. "You sure know how to hang your lanyard, captain."

He was still laughing as he rolled me over so I was between him and the sheepskin—which, as I'd discovered, was very nice on bare skin—our grins fading as our gazes locked. "You know, if we do it again tonight and tomorrow night, we can't call it a one-night stand."

I lightly touched my lips to his. "For a sailor boy, you're not as dumb as you look."

"And for a historic preservationist, you sure know how to make it last longer."

We woke up again a few hours later, the sun gone from a now leaden sky, my phone rumbling against the floor nearby. At some point Luke had pulled the blankets from the bed and piled them on top of us, so I had to scramble to find the source of the vibration.

"Here," Luke said, reaching under his pillow and handing it to me.

I slid my thumb across the screen and held it to my ear. "Dad? Is everything all right?" I made the mistake of looking at the mantel clock and saw that it was almost ten thirty.

"Everything's fine here. I just wanted to let you know that Petey threw up four times last night so I put him back in bed."

"What? What happened? Does he have a fever?" I began frantically scouting for my clothes before remembering that Joanie had taken them. I found one slipper then hopped on one foot with the phone pressed between my chin and shoulder while I searched for the other one.

"No, no fever. He's absolutely fine right now. I think it might have been the bag of Doritos and orange sodas I let him have last night. And we split a box of Twinkies, too. As a matter of fact, I'm not feeling all that great myself. Anyway, the school says that the kids have to be twenty-four hours vomit-free before returning to class and I've got that big job repairing the helm of a schooner starting today and the money's real good so I need to be there. I figured I could drop him off with you on my way."

"Wait—now? You're coming now? What about the closed bridge and washed-out roads?"

"I've lived here all of my life, Andie. There's not a backroad I don't know, and I've got a truck. Don't worry about us."

I limped over to the fireplace to retrieve my robe, watching out of the corner of my eye as Luke rose and strode naked to the bedroom door and opened it. I refocused on the conversation. Trying to sound casual, I said, "Okay. When should I expect you?"

"We'll be there in about fifteen minutes. I tried calling you earlier but you didn't pick up. I figured you must have been exhausted from working all day and I didn't want to wake you before I had to. Didn't you get my voicemail?"

"I . . . uh . . ." I watched as Luke retrieved a pile of neatly folded clothes from outside the door and brought it in. "I forgot to look. But sure, fifteen minutes is fine. I'll be waiting outside. I'm sure I can find something for him to do that doesn't involve gorging on junk food."

"I'm packing saltines just in case. See you soon."

I hit End on my phone, noticing other unread voicemails and the low battery warning and having no idea where my charger was. "I've got to jump in the shower. My dad's bringing Petey. Apparently, he threw up last night and is back in bed right now." Despite Luke's efforts to embrace me, I pulled away and raced around the room, remaking the bed and tidying the sheepskin rug. "I just . . . I'm sure he'll be fine. I can't take a day off, and I can't afford another ER visit."

Luke grabbed hold of my arms and held me still. "Don't worry, Andie. He'll be fine."

I pulled away. "How do you know? He's not your kid." I slapped my hand over my mouth. "I'm so sorry. I didn't mean . . ."

He put his arms around me. "I know. Do you think I've never seen a worried parent before? I get it. And if it makes you feel any better, I'll take a look at Petey just to be sure it's nothing we need to worry about. I'm a doctor, remember?"

"Right." I managed a smile. "Thank you." I kissed him briefly, wishing we had more time for a longer goodbye, then headed to the shower.

I reminded myself that I should be upset that I was late for work and that Petey would be crashing the set again today when we were already so far behind, but I couldn't stop myself from singing as I showered. Or humming as I finished straightening the room before leaving to meander through the hallways to the great staircase, then sashay down the stairs, imagining I was the beautiful Maybelle from the portrait, on her way to meet her handsome prince. It was only when I reached the turn of the landing that the soundtrack came to a screeching halt of snapped violin strings and out-of-tune wind instruments.

A crack of thunder outside explained why the film crew was all inside milling about. After checking the weather radar the previous day, I had decided to start the renovation in the ballroom because of the forecast, but had neglected to do my job and inform George and Devon of my plan because I had been otherwise engaged. Granted, I hadn't planned to be stranded at the house and had forgotten my usual routine and prep for the following day. But I had.

For the first moment since I'd slid Luke's sweater over my head, I began to have regrets, not all of them centered around my failure to do my job. I'd also neglected to keep my goals in front of me, the one thing that had guided most of my adult life, born out of necessity and the need for survival. It had taken one warm sweater and the offer of comfort to bring me down to where my mother had been when she'd made the decision to throw everything away, including her two daughters and husband, for the stability and ease of another life. Despite my shower, I suddenly felt dirty.

George spotted me first and headed in my direction. He was usually so easygoing that his expression caught me off guard. "Where in the hell have you been? I've been calling and calling you." I recalled the unread voicemails and the low battery on my phone, but he didn't look to be in the kind of mood to listen to excuses.

"I'm sorry," was all I said. "What's going on?"

"What's *not* going on is more like it. Despite our rush to get the equipment inside, the portable audio digital recorder and video switcher aren't working and neither is my camera. We can't figure out why except that moisture might have gotten inside and shorted something. We called Marc, asking for quick replacements, but I don't know how long it's going to take. Marc . . . well, he didn't sound like himself, if you know what I mean."

I closed my eyes and nodded, knowing exactly what he meant. "Maybe I can jump in my car and pick up what we need to expedite things. I'm sure the roads are better this morning." Despite the bright sun from an hour earlier, the darkening light and thunder were enough to tell me that another storm had rolled in and my car had about zero percent chance of making it out of the driveway. But I had to try. If I had any hope of making the series a success, I didn't have a choice.

George shook his head. "Half the crew didn't show up today because so many roads are washed out and bridges closed." He shrugged. "I think we should wait."

Devon crossed the foyer toward us, his hair dripping water on the scarred floors. "Well, glad you finally showed up. I can't find any of the equipment you brought in by yourself last night. I was hoping we might be able to piece together enough to get something recorded today. Any idea where it might be?"

I looked across the foyer, catching sight of an older man and his cane slowly tapping his way to the door, sticking close to the edge of the room to remain inconspicuous. Teddy Winthrop lifted his hat and winked at me before letting himself out the door, only pulling on it twice to make it wide enough to pass through.

Returning my attention to Devon, I said, "I put it in the alcove inside the door by the back hallway. Did you look there?"

"I did. I've looked everywhere. It's not here."

Before I could offer an opinion, Mike Brantley, the muscles behind the scenes, approached, holding a pink construction hat and matching tool belt. "I found these shoved inside the maid's closet. Not sure how they got there, but I thought you'd want them."

"Great. Thanks. I swear I didn't put them there, but I would like to thank the person who did."

"Maybe it was the ghost of the white lady," Devon said, his eyes round.

"Maybe." I had a good idea who the responsible person or persons were, but I let it slide. If my show had to be a caricature of what I'd once hoped it could be, we might as well add a mischievous ghost to the mix.

I heard my name shouted, and I turned my head toward the library to find Meghan walking quickly in my direction, her red boots matching the bow on her black sweater dress. She clutched her phone as her widened eyes conveyed a dire situation.

"Where have you been? That was Marc. I guess your phone is dead? He said he has news from Christiana so he's coming over now."

"Now? But the roads . . ."

"He said he slept in his car last night in a shopping center parking lot on Bellevue so he's close by." She looked down, as if ashamed to have had to say that out loud.

"He couldn't tell you over the phone?"

She shook her head. "I suggested that, but he said what he needs to say has to be said face-to-face. I don't think it's good news."

For a day that had started so perfectly, it was quickly going to hell in a handbasket, to borrow one of Meghan's favorite phrases. "Wonderful," I said. "I've got to go wait for Petey. My dad's dropping him off."

"He's in the kitchen with Luke. I'll come with you. I found an awesome photograph on the internet and I'm dying to show it to you. It's really old, but it's from the Newport Historical Society collection. It's a sketch that appeared in the newspaper and shows Maybelle Sprague singing to her prince. I think it said it was their engagement party or something like that."

I paused, actually interested. "Really?"

"Yes! But what's really fascinating is that the artist conveyed each of them looking at someone else instead of each other. According to the article, the song Maybelle sang was some romantic Italian opera aria—so she should have been looking at her intended, right? It's probably just a random thing, or the artist had been asked by the editor to make a bigger story, but we could certainly *expand* on it for the show, right? Because that's what they're looking for."

I sighed and kept walking, dropping my pink ensemble along the way. "Sadly, yes."

"Anyway," Meghan continued, "it's given me an amazing idea that will involve my psychic Realtor friend in Charleston."

"Oh boy," I said, heading toward the kitchen, only half listening as Meghan said something about the possibility of her friend Melanie doing a guest appearance on the show.

I pushed open the kitchen door. "I don't think guest appearances are in the budget, Meghan."

"Maybe she'll do it for free, though. I mean, surely Christiana could spring for a plane ticket, right?"

I didn't answer, my attention drawn to Joanie wafting a sage stick in the corners of the kitchen, and Petey sitting on the table holding the toy sailboat, giggling while Luke looked in his ear with an otoscope. "Yep—just like I suspected. I can see all the way to Disney World. And, wait—is that . . . ? It sure is. Donald Duck is waving hello."

"Let me call her," Meghan said from behind me. "Maybe she doesn't need to be here in person."

"Well, hello, Andie," Joanie said, with more meaning in her voice than for just those few words. "You must be famished." She smiled, her eyes sparkling. "Your skin is positively glowing. Isn't it, Lukie?"

Petey and Luke both looked up, and I wasn't sure whose smile I was happier to see.

"Yes," Luke said. "It certainly is. You have to tell me your secret sometime." He grinned as he settled Petey onto the floor and patted his head. "He's back to fighting form. Just a case of junkfooditis. Keep his diet pretty bland today and he'll be ready to go back to school tomorrow."

"Mommy!" Petey ran to me and threw his arms around my neck before stepping back to show me the little wooden boat. "Look what Luke fixed for me! He said if it was all right with you, I can keep it. He doesn't need a toy sailboat anymore because he has a real one."

"Isn't that nice of him?" I said, my eyes meeting Luke's over Petey's head. Luke replaced the otoscope inside a worn leather doctor's bag on one of the chairs. "If you're very careful with it, I think it's all right for you to keep it."

Petey let out a huge whoop and began racing around the kitchen with the boat, moving it up and down on invisible but very treacherous waves. Joanie took hold of his shoulders, stopping him with a hug. "Have you ever played on a Wii before?"

He nodded with teeth-shattering enthusiasm. "Yes! My best friend Connor has one and we play it all the time when I have a playdate. Mommy says I can't have one because they're too expensive, but if I did I'd play all the time with my grandpa because he'd let me stay up."

"Well, we don't have a grandpa here, but we do have Luke's grandmother, Lucky, and guess what? She has a Wii! And she's upstairs now looking for someone to play with her. Can you think of anyone who might enjoy that?"

He let out another whoop and began jumping up and down, his hand pointing straight up in the air. "Me! Me! Me!"

Joanie laughed. "Well, then, if it's okay with your mother, I'll take you upstairs and introduce you to Lucky."

"Please, Mommy. *Please?*" Petey threw his arms around me again, ensuring that there could be only one answer.

"If Joanie is sure that Lucky won't mind." I looked at Joanie, whose eyes were twinkling with ulterior motives.

"I'm absolutely positive. I'll make chicken soup for him for lunch, and make sure he has a lot of saltines with it. And I'll deliver him personally to you when he and Lucky have exhausted themselves, although I warn you it could take a while."

"No worries—really. I've got quite a bit of catch-up work to do here, and I'm waiting for my boss to stop by, so if you can keep Petey occupied even for a little bit, I'd be grateful."

"Great. It's all set. You ready, Petey?" Joanie extended her hand to the little boy, who immediately grabbed it and began leading Joanie out of the room. "Do you know where you're going?" Joanie asked, laughing.

"No, so you'd better hurry up before I get lost."

Joanie was dragged out of the room, jogging to keep up with Petey.

I turned to Luke but was interrupted by Meghan talking loudly into her phone. "What do you mean it doesn't work that way? You can talk to dead people, right? So why can't you do it on FaceTime? It's the same thing!"

I made a shooing motion with my hand to let her know she needed to take her conversation elsewhere. As soon as she left, her voice trailing back to us down the long corridor, I turned to Luke and took a deep breath. "Thank you. For taking care of Petey. I appreciate it."

If I thought there might be awkwardness between us, I'd have been wrong. He opened his arms and I walked into them, feeling as if it were the most natural thing in the world.

"I was happy to do it. You carry way too much on your shoulders. I'm glad I was here to help, even in a small way."

I tilted my head up to him, but as he lowered his lips to mine, the door to the outside crashed open and Marc stumbled inside the kitchen, staggering enough that he had to brace himself on the opened door so as not to fall over. He brought in the smell of rain and wet tweed and very expensive bourbon. Despite the misbuttoned jacked and wild hair and the knowledge that he had slept in his car, the fact that he still drank good bourbon made me believe—however irrationally—that all was not lost.

Luke pulled out a chair before helping Marc into it while I poured him a large glass of water. He tried to push it away, but I handed it back to him. "Drink this. You're probably dehydrated and this will help. I'll go get you some coffee. . . ."

"Don't bother," he said. "It doesn't matter. Nothing matters. We've failed."

Hot fear bolted through me. I pulled out the chair next to him and sat. "What do you mean, Marc? The equipment is replaceable. And we can still record some of the audio voice-overs while we wait for—"

"They've canceled the show. They're pulling the plug as of today and cutting their losses. They've found a more commercial show that will bring in more viewers. Some Beverly Hills housewife doing a home-flip while undergoing a gender transition. They already have confirmed sponsors, including the biggest home improvement retailer. They want everything packed up and out of here by end of day."

He put his forehead down on the table and after a moment his shoulders began to shake with silent sobs.

I sat motionless, unable to move, unable to put a consoling hand on Marc's shoulder, unable to utter my own sobs that had congealed in my throat, making breathing almost impossible. It took me a moment to realize that Luke had put his hand on my shoulders and was squeezing gently.

"It's going to be all right. This is just a setback. Not the end."

I wanted to believe him. He'd suffered through something many people found unsurvivable. But he had survived. He was still trying to find a place in life to drop anchor, but he hadn't stopped searching. Yet I couldn't be so optimistic. I still had school loans and grocery bills and a six-year-old whose education I was determined would lead him to Brown on a full ride to fulfill his mother's lost ambitions. I opened my mouth to speak or cry or scream, but only empty, useless air emerged.

I didn't look up when the back door opened again, convinced nothing good was going to come through it.

"Mr. Sprague? Do you have a moment?"

It was one of the two gardeners—down from a previous total of twelve—left to maintain the acres of lawns and gardens of the estate. Which explained the patchy condition of the grass and the weed-choked gardens.

Luke walked toward the door. "Sure, what is it?"

The older man—I think his name was Joe—pulled off his John Deere hat and wiped his forehead with the sleeve of his fleece jacket. "Well, it looks like we got ourselves a mudslide. Greg—that's my nephew—says it looks like the entire hill washed over the cliff and into the cove. He says the boathouse has seen better days."

At the mention of the boathouse, I stood. "How bad is it?"

He shook his head. "Don't know. My bones can't handle a slip and fall. Greg's still down there, though, if you want to talk to him. The boy's a good carpenter, too. Probably could help rebuild it, ya know?"

"Thanks, Joe. We'll go check it out."

I warmed at the word "we'll." It was the single bright spot of a dismal morning so far and I clung to it as I stood to follow Luke outside.

I looked at Marc, who had at least stopped sobbing and was sitting up and sipping his water, his eyes glassy. "Will you be okay here? I'll be right back and I promise to get you that coffee, all right? And then we can inform the crew together."

He gave me a wooden nod, which I hoped meant that he would be there when I returned. I slid on a short rain jacket and pair of rainboots left by the door—presumably Joanie's so I didn't think she'd mind—and headed outside with Luke, hoping that some rain and mud might distract me from Marc's news.

"Good luck!" Joe said as he followed us out. "Tell Greg I'll be in the gardening shed if he needs me."

A drizzle fell on us, not enough to soak us but wet enough to be annoying as we carefully made our way over the lawn and overgrown path that were now entirely obscured by a river of mud. My feet slipped several times, causing Luke to grab hold of my hand. He nearly lost his balance but somehow managed to keep us both upright. We got halfway down the hill before I stopped. "Luke, it's getting steeper. I don't think we should go any farther."

I took a step backward, but my boot stayed rooted in the mud as my foot floundered in midair, not wanting to land in the muck. To regain my balance, I jerked my hand out of Luke's grasp. That was my first mistake. My second mistake was attempting to remain standing on one booted foot in an oozy puddle of muck as I aimed my other foot into the abandoned boot.

"Andie!" Luke shouted.

But it was too late. I'd already landed on my backside and was slipping quickly down the hill. Backward. Which allowed me to see Luke try to run after me and land on his chest in the mire and follow me down the hill toward the cliff and the water. Fortunately for us, the slope leveled out before the steep drop so we were spared from flying off the cliff like lemmings.

We both lay still, our breaths harsh in the freezing drizzle. Mud caked in every crevice of my face and clothing and when I looked at Luke, I had to assume I was looking in a mirror. A funhouse mirror. Except the white of his teeth were showing because he was laughing—the kind of laughing that was so intense it stayed inside for a bit before erupting.

"I'm glad you find this funny," I said, although I was now smiling and close to laughing myself. I grabbed a handful of mud and slung it at him, pinging him on the shoulder.

Luke glanced at his shoulder then back at me. "That's not what I meant last night when I said to talk dirty to me."

We both began to laugh hysterically, not because it was so funny, but I at least found it a welcome antidote to the disappointment that lurked behind it. We were still laughing when we heard squelching footsteps approach and a younger man than Joe—presumably his nephew, Greg—towered over us.

"Mr. Sprague?" he asked.

Still lying prone on the ground, Luke looked up. "Yes?"

"I think you need to go to the boathouse, sir. There's something you need to see."

CHAPTER TWENTY-SIX

Ellen

Newport, Rhode Island
July 1899

Dear Ellen,

By the time you see this note, I will be on my way to my new life as Mrs. Francis Pratt. Francis loves me and I love him and I want nothing more in the world than to be with him, not even thrones or crowns. Francis has borrowed a boat to sail me away—not for a year and a day like the owl and the pussycat but for always.

I feel terrible leaving you like this. I am truly grateful for all you've done for me. If there's anyone I mind hurting, it's you. I have tried to reconcile myself to marrying the prince, truly I have tried, but how can I marry him when my heart belongs to another? I hope you can find it in yourself to forgive me.

I know it is a great deal to ask, but would you tell my brother and the prince for me?

I hope you will be happy for me when you know how happy I am.

With love,
Maybelle

PS. If we have girls, I hope you will come and teach them music.

Maybelle's room was empty but there were signs of hasty activity.

Fabric protruded through the closed doors of the armoire, as if someone had swung them shut in a hurry, not bothering to shove the clothes properly back inside first. Maybelle's bookcase had telling gaps where her favorite novels had once stood, empty spaces like missing teeth. It gave the shelf a lopsided jack-o'-lantern grin. Her monogrammed silver-backed brush and comb had been taken from her dressing table.

By the time you see this note, she had written.

How long? Ellen ran for the door, wrenching it open, not sure whether to alert the household or try to find Maybelle herself. If the world knew, Maybelle would be ruined. But to let Maybelle elope with Pratt . . . Ellen wasn't sure which was worse. Then she remembered Pratt yesterday, hanging about Mrs. Schuyler's door, begging for money. Pratt, dipping Maybelle in the ocean.

Pratt was worse. Once he married Maybelle he'd have full control of her money and her person.

But how? Where? Sail away, she'd said. With Maybelle, one could never tell if she was being poetical or just stating the unvarnished truth.

It would have to be a boat, wouldn't it? The drive would be clogged with carriages. There'd be no way to make a hasty escape that way—someone would be bound to see them. But to slink off in the other direction, through the gardens, down the cliffside . . . Yes, that they could do with relative ease, mingling with the other guests.

Maybelle had been there while the prince was singing. She wouldn't have dared been elsewhere; there were too many eyes on her. But after . . . oh yes, it would have been easy enough to slip away after, while Ellen was deep in conversation with Maybelle's betrothed and the guests were mingling and jostling, distracted by their own flirtations and dramas. Run up to her room, grab her favorite things . . . That would take, what, five minutes? Ten?

The interlude with the prince had felt like an eternity, but it couldn't have been more than a few minutes in reality. Ellen tried to take comfort in that. Maybelle and Pratt couldn't have gone far. Not yet.

She slipped out a side door, into the loggia—and bumped right into the prince, smoking a cigar in the shadow of the columns.

Just as he'd been the first time she'd met him.

Ellen had never been so glad to see anybody. If there was one person in the world she could trust with this, it was he. "Your Excellency—"

"Sebastiano," he corrected her. He pitched his cigar aside with a quick, decisive movement, clasping her arms in his hands, his face alight with sudden triumph. "You've reconsidered."

"No." Ellen wrenched free. "It's Maybelle. She's eloped."

"Eloped?" He stared at her, the Chinese lanterns draped behind him glinting off the gold of his uniform. "With Pratt?"

"Yes." It was such a relief not to have to explain. "I think—I think they mean to take a boat. But they've only just left. We have time still. We can stop them."

"But do we want to?" The prince touched a finger gently to Ellen's cheek. "Perhaps this is as it was meant to be. Perhaps we should just let them go."

"What?" Ellen gaped at him.

"Why not?" The prince cradled her face in his palms, looking at her so tenderly that it was all Ellen could do not to close her eyes and lean into that touch. "It might be . . . simpler that way. If she wants him that badly, let her have him."

It was like a spell. But she couldn't let herself fall prey to it. "No! I can't leave Maybelle to that parasite. You know what he is. You know what he'll do to her. He's in debt to horrible people." The prince was the one person in the world who would know exactly what she meant. Ellen looked up at him, letting all her fears show in her face. "He's in debt to Dermot."

That gave the prince pause. "Maybelle's money will cancel the debt."

"This time. What happens when he spends it all?" Ellen had seen what happened to the people who couldn't pay. And their families. Dermot was a sentimentalist—to a point. That point ended when there was money owed. She put her hands on his arms, looking up at him pleadingly. "I can't let Maybelle live like that. Please. We have to find her."

"Miss Daniels!" John Sprague grabbed her roughly by the shoulder, whisky thick on his breath, blurring his words, if not his intent. "What are you doing back down here? You're not needed anymore. Thought I made that clear."

"No, sir, but—" Ellen stalled. She could imagine how damning the scene must have been.

"Go away. Didn't hire you to dally with your bettersh. We'll dishcush—*discuss* this tomorrow." Turning his back on her, he squinted at the prince. "Where'sh Maybelle? You're supposed to be opening the dancing together, not hanging about the music teacher."

"Maybelle," said the prince succinctly, "is not here. It appears that your sister has decided to elope with young Mr. Pratt."

"Elope?" John Sprague's face turned an unhealthy shade of crimson.

"I do believe that is the accepted term." The prince inspected an imaginary piece of lint on the gold braid of his sleeve. "The 'music teacher,' as you have termed her, was expressing her concern for your sister's well-being and begging me to aid in getting her back."

"How . . . where . . . ," Sprague blustered.

"She left a note," said Ellen, thrusting it at him even though it was too dark to read it.

Sprague squinted at it and snapped, "Just tell me what it says, damn you."

"Language," said the prince warningly.

"Please." Ellen stepped in between them. Time was wasting. All she could think of was Maybelle, innocent and trusting, going to Pratt like the proverbial lamb to slaughter. "It says they mean to sail away."

"Sail? Away?" Sprague seemed to be having trouble with the concept.

"It's all very romantic," commented the prince. "If rather impractical."

Ellen gave her beloved a quelling look. "We have to find her. Now. They can't have been gone long, but every moment we waste . . ."

"Makes it harder to keep secret," the prince finished for her. "The faster we find her, the less chance of a scandal."

His words had a remarkably sobering effect on John Sprague. "Right. No scandal. Where d'we find 'em?"

That's what Ellen had been wondering. She looked from one man to the other. "The only thing I can think of . . . there's that path down to the water. He wasn't at the party. If she slipped away through the gardens . . . but there's no dock."

"They wouldn't need one. Not for this." The prince was already moving, striding out of the loggia, not toward the garden, but to the working parts of the grounds, the greenhouses and the toolsheds. "There's a metal hook driven into one of the rocks. It's not large. But it would serve to tie up a small boat for the few minutes needed."

Ellen hurried to catch up with him, Sprague puffing along behind her. "That's all they need. A few minutes. Sebastiano—"

She hadn't even realized she'd said his name until it came out.

The prince grabbed her hand in a brief, reassuring clasp. "We'll catch them."

"Damn right we will," slurred John Sprague. Ellen had practically forgotten he was there. "What do you Italian chappies say? Andiamo?"

"I don't," said the prince, and plunged down the steep path, surefooted in the dark.

There were no lanterns here, no torches. Ellen tried to keep up, but it was rough going, these stairs set in the cliff, and she didn't know the terrain nearly as well as the prince. John Sprague was well behind them now, cursing as he staggered and slipped.

But there, there at the water's edge—no, there wasn't a boat, but there was a woman, balanced on the rocks, standing as far out as she dared, the pearls on her dress glimmering in the moonlight.

She looked like something out of legend, like one of the fairy tales Ellen's mother used to tell her about princesses being lured by mermen.

Although, of course, this was nothing of the sort. Ellen felt a giddy surge of relief at seeing Maybelle safe and sound. No mermen, just a handsome scoundrel trying to marry an heiress for her money, not lure her into the depths. And they'd been in time. They'd been in time.

"Maybelle!" she called, and the girl turned, and in turning skidded on the slick rocks, treacherous with algae, catching herself just in time to keep from falling.

She was still, Ellen realized, wearing her impractical pearl-embroidered high-heeled slippers. What a thing to elope by boat in!

"Don't come any closer!" the girl called, her voice wobbling on the words.

"Maybelle, it's me! Ellen! I found your note."

Maybelle shrank back. "But you weren't supposed to. You can't make me go back! I won't. Frank was supposed to be here by now."

"He's not," said the prince, and Ellen could have slapped him for it.

"You told *him*?"

"I had to," Ellen said miserably, edging closer. "Please try to understand. I couldn't let you run away with Pratt."

"Because my brother is paying you?" Maybelle cast Ellen a look of outraged betrayal that cut Ellen to the bone. "I thought you were different. I trusted you."

"I am—" Ellen looked helplessly over her shoulder at the prince, and back at Maybelle, speaking rapidly, trying to make her understand. Two yards of rough shingle and rock separated them. "If it had been anyone but Frank Pratt—I couldn't let you marry him. He doesn't love you, Maybelle. He's only using you."

Maybelle shrunk back as far as she dared. "What would you know about it?"

"I know the men he owes money to." Ellen stood very still, looking her former pupil in the eye. "He's a gambler, Maybelle. He'll gamble your fortune away."

"*They* told you that, didn't they? They're lying. My brother will say anything so long as I'll marry *him*." She pointed accusingly at Sebastiano, nearly oversetting herself in the process. "What did you do to him? What did you do to Frank? He should be here by now."

"Nothing, nothing, I swear!" Ellen edged forward, terrified that Maybelle might fall. She could hear John Sprague behind her, crashing down the path, cursing as he landed heavily. That was all they needed. "Please come back, Maybelle. Please. You don't have to marry the prince."

Sprague muscled up beside her, incoherent with drink and rage. "What do you mean she doesn't—"

Ellen drove an elbow into his side, knocking the wind out of him. She knew there'd be hell to pay, but he'd never intended to give her the money he owed her anyway. And it was Maybelle who mattered.

Keeping her eyes focused on Maybelle, Ellen took a tentative step forward, out onto the shingle. Ahead of her were rocks in a ragged jumble, as though a giant had got bored with his toys and flung them down. "I don't care if you marry the prince or not. And I don't know why Mr. Pratt isn't here—but I do know he's a wastrel and a scoundrel."

Maybelle eyed her suspiciously, hugging her carpetbag to her chest. "Prunella told me you'd say that. She said you'd try to separate us by any means you could. Because *he's* paying you. I thought you cared for me more than that. I thought you'd want me to be happy."

It was the guileless cry of a little girl and it made Ellen's heart ache. "I did! I do. And that's why I'm telling you the truth." There was no going back now. She stayed where she was, on the shingle, the Atlantic at her feet, choppy at midtide. "I lied about who I was, Maybelle. I wasn't Annabelle Van Duyvil's music teacher. I was the pianist at a music hall called the Hibernia."

"What the—" she heard John Sprague bluster behind her. But she didn't care about Sprague right now. She only cared about Maybelle.

"The Hibernia was run by a group of dangerous men. Ruthless

men. These are the men Frank Pratt owes money. That's why he wants you to elope with him. That's why he couldn't wait."

Maybelle shook her head wildly, her ruby-and-diamond tiara askew over her high-piled golden hair. "No. No. He didn't want to wait because he loves me, because he couldn't bear another night without me." She looked desperately over her shoulder, searching for a boat that wasn't there. "Frank! Frank! Where are you?"

The prince stepped forward, beside Ellen. "Let me make this simple," he said, not unkindly. "There is no need for these histrionics. You can marry Pratt or not as you choose. I release you from our betrothal."

Maybelle paused, turning. "You do?" Something like hope showed on her face.

"The devil you will!" snarled John Sprague, horrified. "We had—we have—an arrangement! And don't think I won't hold you to it just because the little bitch is in heat! You—you stupid whore."

He advanced on his sister, who shrank back from him, still clutching her carpetbag close against her chest.

"Mr. Sprague!" Ellen flung herself in front of him, trying to ward him off, but he shoved her aside, sending her stumbling back into the arms of the prince.

"You think you're going to ruin what I took months to build? This isn't about you, my girl." Sprague stalked heavy-footed out onto the shingle. "You get yourself back here and you paste a smile on your face and you tell all those Vanderbilts and Astors just what a lucky girl you are."

"No." Maybelle glared at her brother, tottering on her pearl-embellished heels on her sliver of rock. "I won't. I'm not."

"Oh, won't you?" said Sprague, and lunged for her.

"This is quite enough." The prince grabbed at Sprague, but it was too late. Maybelle scooted instinctively back as her stepbrother grabbed for her, her heels sliding on the rock, and Ellen saw as she lost her balance. Her arms flung into the air, the carpetbag splashing into the water, as Maybelle flailed, her blue eyes wide with shock and fear.

She fell backward, hitting the water with an audible *thwack*.

"Maybelle!" screamed Ellen. "Maybelle!"

But the prince was already there, stripping out of his braided coat, diving down among the rocks. Ellen slid and skidded as far as she dared, crouching by the edge, peering into the water.

"Maybelle, you lousy whore," shouted John Sprague. "Get up! Get out of there!"

The prince surfaced, spat out water, dove again. And again. And all the while, up above, the music played and the guests danced on.

It was, Ellen would hear later, a marvelous party. One for the scrap-books.

But now she was leaning over the water, crying out as she saw something, as the prince surfaced again with his arms full of a sodden burden. It looked like a bundle of damp fabric streaming long trails of seaweed, only that wasn't seaweed, that was hair, Maybelle's hair, dark with seawater.

Half crying, half praying, Ellen leaned over and tried to grab Maybelle beneath the arms, helping the prince to drag her up onto the shingle, apologizing for hurting her all the while. The rocks, the rocks, they were so rough, and her dress was so heavy, so very heavy, weighed down with jewels and soaked in seawater.

"I'm so sorry," Ellen muttered, as they dragged her clumsily, so clumsily. "I'm so sorry. Maybelle? Maybelle?"

But Maybelle was limp and still, her hair not golden anymore but dark with wet, falling starkly around her white face.

"Please," Ellen begged, falling to her knees beside Maybelle. She was soaked, too, and hadn't even noticed it, any more than she'd noticed the tears falling down her face. She chafed her pupil's freezing hand. "Please, Maybelle. Please."

The prince touched Ellen's shoulder. Just that. One hand on her shoulder. "I'm sorry," he said.

"No!" Ellen hunkered down, hugging the other girl close, and for a moment, she wasn't sure if it was Maybelle or her mother, just sleeping, just sleeping, tired with fever, but she wouldn't wake up. "Maybelle."

"Wake her up! Wake her up!" John Sprague shouted, jumping from one foot to the other. "Slap her awake!"

"It's too late for that." The prince's voice was very cold as he faced the man who had wanted to be his brother-in-law. He sounded every inch the prince. "She will not wake again. Not in this life."

"No. You're lying—you're—"

Ellen sat back on her heels, heedless with grief and rage. "*You* did this. You pushed her to it."

John Sprague backed away, blustering, "You can't blame this on me! It was an accident! I didn't even touch her!" He stopped short, a look of pure horror crossing his face. "If she's dead . . . all the money . . . there's a cousin—"

Turning, he retched into the ocean, driven to a depth of emotion by the prospect of the loss of his fortune that mere death couldn't produce.

He was disgusting. He was worse than disgusting. Maybelle had deserved better. From all of them.

Ellen struggled to her feet, insensible with anger and self-loathing. "You might have taken better care of her. You might have listened to her. You'd have your precious money, then. All she wanted was someone to love her."

Sprague snarled at her. "Just like a woman. You're all the same." He paused, a strange expression crossing his face. "You're all the same. You're all the same. What if . . ."

He grabbed Ellen by the arm, so quickly she didn't have time to protest.

"Get your hands off her, Sprague." The prince's arm was between them, his voice low and deadly.

Sprague was too elated to be afraid. "But don't you *see*?" He jabbed a finger at Ellen's hair. "Look at her! Look at the color of her hair. Give it a bit of curl . . . they're almost the same height. Who's to say who's taller if they're not next to each other. Maybelle's a bit plumper . . . nothing some padding wouldn't fix."

Her employer was unhinged; he'd gone around the bend. Ellen yanked away. "I don't understand. I have no idea what you're talking about."

"Don't you?" Sprague rubbed his hands together in glee. "I'll wager *he* does. No flies on the prince over there. Who's to say who fell in the ocean tonight? Why shouldn't Maybelle be alive? One blond chit is much the same as another."

He was practically dancing now, jumping up and down with jubilation as his stepsister's corpse lay limp in the moonlight.

"Maybelle wanted to elope? Let her elope. Only *you'll* be Maybelle. You'll do as well as any," Sprague added, as though it were a matter of supreme indifference.

"What?" Ellen gaped at him, numb with cold and grief.

"Not with Pratt, you ninny. With the prince. Maybelle runs off with her intended on her betrothal night. The papers will lap it up. And why shouldn't we? That way the money stays where it's meant to be. And you get to be a princess, you lucky slut," he added, as an afterthought. "No one in Italy's ever met her. One blond girl is as good as another."

"No," said the prince.

"Whaddya mean, no? It's the perfect solution. Don't think I haven't seen you panting after her. This way you get 'er. And Maybelle's money, too. Unless you didn't really want 'er. But Maybelle's money, that's the price you pay. Same terms as last time. Jus' a diff'rent Maybelle."

Ellen couldn't listen to this. She looked around frantically, up the cliff, at the house alight with merriment. "We need to get help."

"What help? She's *dead*," said John Sprague brutally, moving to cut

Ellen off. "No helping her. But we can help ourselves. Just us three. Keep it in the family."

"It's insane." Ellen looked to the prince for help. "*Insane*. Anyone would know I wasn't Maybelle. Anyone who had ever met her."

"You would never be able to come back," said the prince thoughtfully. "Not to Newport. Not to America. But if you were to come to Italy . . . if you were to live your whole life abroad, an exile . . . who would there be to know?"

"Someone!" said Ellen hysterically. Maybelle's body was lying right there. They were talking about her as if she were nothing, as if the person she had been hadn't mattered at all. "People move about, you know! They take steamers! They visit! You're not—you're not considering this, are you?"

How could he? How could either of them? It made her sick to her stomach. All she wanted to do was turn back the clock and make it yesterday, put Maybelle back on her settee with her apple and her book.

"Ellen." The prince gently slipped an arm around her, moving her away from Sprague. "Ellen. I find that poor excuse for a man as repugnant as you. But for once in his miserable life . . . there is something to what he says."

Something. Something horrifying.

Ellen blinked up at the prince, at her love, feeling utterly adrift. "I couldn't—we couldn't—how could we betray her like that?"

The prince squeezed her hands, warming them. "She's dead. There's no hurting her anymore. As much as I hate to agree with that creature about anything . . . he's not entirely wrong."

"Of course, I'm not wrong," sputtered John Sprague. "If you two lovebirds—"

"Hold your tongue!" the prince snapped. He smoothed the tears off Ellen's cheeks with the pads of his thumbs. "My love. We can have what we never thought we would. We can be together."

Ellen choked on a sob. "Do you need your roof fixed that badly?"

"It's not the money." The prince held her face between his palms, forcing her to meet his eyes. "I can find another heiress. I could find ten. You know that. But I could never find another you. Not in all the wide world. Having found you, I find myself reluctant to lose you."

"This is all very charming," blustered John Sprague, hopping with impatience, "but someone might come along at any moment, and—"

"Shut up," snapped the prince, never taking his eyes from Ellen. His eyes were very bright in the moonlight, green as a cat's. "Tell me you feel otherwise. Tell me you want nothing to do with me. And I'll cry out to the revelers above and release you."

Ellen squeezed her eyes shut hard. See no evil, hear no evil. "It's a snare from the devil. Stealing her life."

"Giving her new life." Ellen opened her eyes and saw the prince looking down at her. Not a prince but a man. A man used to looking at the more unpleasant aspects of life. "My love, she's gone. Whatever happens now, there's no going back."

Ellen felt sick. The worst of it was that it was all true. "She should be buried properly," she said stubbornly. "People should mourn her."

"Who? Prunella Schuyler? Frank Pratt? There was only one person in the world who cared enough about Maybelle Sprague to mourn. And I don't mean that cretin." The prince jerked his thumb back at John Sprague. "You're the only one who truly cared for her. Of all the world, who do you think she would most want to benefit from her fortune?"

Ellen forced herself to look at Maybelle, to really look at her. There was no Maybelle there anymore. Just bones in a ball gown. Maybelle's cameo pinned to a breast that would never stir with breath again. "It's blood money."

"All money is blood money. My family is awash in it." The prince pressed his forehead against hers, so there was nothing but the two of them, his hands cupping her face. "The real question is: Do you want to marry me? You would never be able to go back to America again, never be among your own people."

She thought of her mother, still and cold. Her siblings, one after the other. Her father. "I have no people."

"You have me." He leaned his forehead against hers and for a moment, Ellen let herself lean into him, breathing in the familiar scent of him, orange and bergamot and salt water. "My love, I know these are not the circumstances either of us would have wished. But Fortune works in strange ways. It doesn't do to shun her gifts."

She could feel the tears building again, clogging the back of her throat. Tears for Maybelle, who would never grow up, never love, never marry. For the life Ellen was taking from her. She couldn't believe she was considering this. But she was. "I'm not sure I would call this a gift."

"Call it a chance, then." Stepping back, the prince lifted her hand to his lips, pressing a kiss to the back of it. "Maybelle would want you to be happy."

He was right. Maybelle, of all people, would only have wanted a happy ending. Even if it wasn't her own. Ellen could stay and spend her life hiding from Dermot's men. Or she could go and be with the man she loved. "I hate that it's at the expense of her death."

Sebastiano squeezed her hand. "Let her death mean something, then. Honor her with your living. Live the life she might have lived. With me."

Bored by this display of irrelevant affection, John Sprague knelt down to try to tug a ruby bracelet off Maybelle's wrist.

"Stop! Leave it!" Ellen flew at Sprague, beside herself with guilt and grief. She stopped just short of touching him, her hands curled into fists at her sides, her nails biting into her palms. "Don't you dare take her jewels off her. It's bad enough to steal her life; I won't let you rob her corpse as well."

"You heard her, Sprague," said the prince, and it was his voice Sprague listened to, the voice of hundreds of years of absolute rule.

Sprague cast one last reluctant look at the rubies, but he obeyed all the same, rising slowly to his feet. "Does that mean we have a deal?" he demanded. "I leave the rubies. You take the prince."

One last chance. One last chance to do the right thing, to say no.

Ellen looked from Sprague, to Maybelle, to the prince. "Yes."

CHAPTER TWENTY-SEVEN

Lucky

Newport, Rhode Island
October 1957

It's a raw deal, poor thing.

Lucky sucked fiercely on her cigarette and watched the smoke curl up to dissolve against the blue sky. Around the corner, the two men kept on talking. Women were supposed to be the gossipy sex, but men were just as bad, weren't they? Everybody covets knowledge about his neighbor, whether he admits it or not. It's human nature.

Oh, I don't know, said the other man. *I hear she doesn't mind so much.*

A little chuckle passed between them. Lucky dropped the end of the cigarette on the chipped paving stone and ground it under her heel. A chilly autumn breeze kicked up from the cliff. Lucky wasn't wearing her coat, only her navy tweed jacket and a dark, demure silk scarf around her neck. She wrapped her arms around her chest.

The first man said, *You think he's really dead?*

Father? Or son?

Another chuckle. *Both.*

Who knows. Poor old Stuy. You saw him at the party. Drunk as a bum. You know what I said to Mary that night? It's the damnedest thing. I said, Mary, that fella's not going to live out the year. Drink himself into the grave. And I was right.

A low whistle. *I'll say. Were you ever.*

Lucky levered herself away from the wall, wiped beneath her eyes with the edge of her tweed cuff, and marched around the corner of the building. "Hello, gentlemen," she said. "Enjoying the party?

OF COURSE IT wasn't really a *party,* Dudley Sprague's memorial reception, but since nobody had really liked the man you couldn't quite restrain the buzz of sociable satisfaction. People were a little giddy anyway at the novelty of gathering in Newport in October, seeing each other out of season. Such a good excuse to sip cocktails and trade gossip. And boy, was there gossip to trade! As Lucky wound her way between the bodies, she heard it all. Somebody was absolutely dead certain Stuy had run off to California with some girl. No, he'd been beaten up by the mob and left for dead, on account of owing the wrong people too much money. Don't be silly, he jumped off the cliff and drowned. No, he fell. No, he jumped! Then why didn't they ever find a body? Maybe he was pushed. Maybe he faked his own death.

Oh, she heard it all, all right. Except the truth.

They'd buried old Dudley Sprague in a private ceremony a week after his death—it was July, after all—but you couldn't hold a funeral service while Stuyvesant Sprague remained missing, while the whole town and more than a few curious outsiders combed the cliffs and beaches of Newport and Narragansett Bay for weeks, searching for some sign of his fate. That would be unseemly. Instead Lucky had watched from the window as these strangers looked and looked for something they weren't going to find. She'd answered all the questions from the police, who were extremely polite and not a bit suspicious, so far as she could tell. This was Newport, after all. No, they treated her with deference, with tremendous respect for her grief. You're absolutely sure you didn't see him again, after the party?

No, she hadn't seen him. She'd come straight home from the hospital, where her daughter commanded all her attention. Her daughter had nearly drowned that night, it was awful. (*Stick to the truth as much as possible,* Nonna had advised her, as lucid as could be.) In all the excitement, she hadn't given Stuy another thought, and she'd never forgive herself for that! (Here she dabbed her eyes with a handkerchief, and it wasn't entirely an act.) Not until morning, when he hadn't returned home, and when she phoned Mrs. Prince over at Marble House, he wasn't there either.

So the policemen asked her if she was absolutely sure her husband hadn't arrived back at the house. A couple of guests had seen him wander out to the Chinese teahouse around two in the morning. He never made it home at all?

No, Lucky said firmly. He never entered the house at all.

It was the truth, after all. And they believed her.

Now it was October, and people had resigned themselves to the idea that Stuyvesant Sprague—wherever he was, on earth or in heaven or possibly purgatory, depending on whom you asked—wasn't coming back. It had become unseemly *not* to hold a proper service for Dudley Sprague, so here they were, milling about Sprague Hall, sipping cocktails and nibbling what Lucky and Angela had been able to scrounge out of the kitchen.

Lucky crossed the sunroom, where Louise sat on the wicker sofa in a smart suit of black tweed, dabbing her eyes, flanked by a pair of sympathetic friends. The tears were genuine. Within a week of her bereavement—around the time the state of Dudley Sprague's finances became evident to his heirs—Reggie had left Louise for a wealthy widow in Palm Beach, twenty years his senior.

Lucky made her way through the room, accepting condolences with the same grave expression, the same automatic responses. She was looking for her daughter. Joanie was perfectly convinced that her father would finally surprise them all and return home today—he wouldn't miss his own father's memorial service, not Daddy!—and in all the morass of Lucky's emotions, guilt and terror and more guilt, grief and anger and shock and back to guilt again, always guilt, only one thing remained firm, only one idea withstood the daily churn: *hold Joanie tight*. As tight and as close as she possibly could.

Because nothing in the world could give Joanie back what Lucky had taken from her.

A hand clamped around her forearm. "*Lucky!*"

The word was part rasp, part bark—a couple of urgent syllables, emphasis on the *Luck*. Lucky turned. A pale, parchment face confronted her, a few inches closer than she expected, punctuated with lurid magenta lipstick and a pair of high half-circle eyebrows.

"Mrs. Potts? What can I do for you?"

Lucky found herself gripped by both hands. Mrs. Potts's blue eyes fixed on hers. "*I know,*" she said, in the same intense voice, flavored with gin.

"Know? Know what?"

"How you must feel. Such a *terrible* loss."

Lucky's breath returned. She gave Mrs. Potts's bony fingers a polite little squeeze and drew her hands away. "Thank you. He was sick for so long, it was really a release for him."

"Old Sprague? God no. I mean your husband."

"Stuy! What do you mean? He's . . . there's no evidence . . . we're clinging to hope—"

"Mrs. Sprague, I *saw* him."

"Stuy? Where? When?"

"The night he disappeared! I saw him walk out of the house—stagger, really—and head for the cliff path. I remember thinking he was in no condition to scramble along the cliffs in the middle of the night."

"Why didn't you say anything?"

Mrs. Potts drew herself up. "I thought perhaps he was going to meet an amour. *And I was right.*"

"But that's ridiculous!"

"I'm very sorry to have to tell you this, Mrs. Sprague—of course I'd never breathe a *word* to another living soul—but I think you should know." She lowered her voice to a stage whisper. "I saw him *enter the boathouse*."

"*Our* boathouse?"

"What, is there another one? Such a stupid place for a boathouse, of course, right there on the edge of the cliff, next to the ocean. The water or the weather will get it, sooner or later, you mark my words—"

"But Stuy!" Lucky found herself seizing Mrs. Potts's sharp elbows. "What did you see?"

"That's all. He went into the boathouse. I heard a woman's voice—it doesn't take much imagination to guess what they were up to, Mrs. Sprague. Anyway, I thought you should know. He must have run off with her afterward, that's all there is to it."

Lucky found just enough breath to speak. "My goodness."

"Oh, I wouldn't look so surprised. History has a way of repeating itself, they say."

"What on earth do you mean by that?"

Mrs. Potts waved her hand in the general direction of the ocean. "I mean *this*. A big party, a couple elopes while everybody else is busy having a good time. A broken heart left behind. Poor, poor Frank."

"I beg your pardon. Frank?"

"My cousin. All those years ago. They were so in love, and the prince—just whisking your grandmother off like that—poor Frank. It should have been him. And then none of this would have happened, would it? Sprague Hall would have passed to Frank's children, and of course they would have kept it up to a proper standard." Mrs. Potts flicked an eyebrow at the paint peeling from the moldings around the French doors.

Lucky drew a long, deep breath. "Now that I think about it, Mrs. Potts, you never did say *why* your cousin Frank never made it to his rendezvous with my grandmother. It seems to me that a man so much in love would have moved heaven and earth to keep her from running off with another man."

"Well! I can *assure* you, Mrs. Sprague, were it not for the hand of a terrible fate—fate in the form of a pair of criminal thugs, who *mistook* Frank for some man who owed them money . . . poor Frank, he was beaten almost to death!" Mrs. Potts choked back a sob. "So you see, he *would* have moved heaven and earth, if his thumbs weren't so badly broken."

"His *thumbs*, you say?"

"He was in agony for weeks."

"I see."

Mrs. Potts's gaze turned dreamlike as it traveled around the sunroom and came to rest on the glimmer of blue ocean that floated in the distance, just above the cliff's edge. She said softly, "And were it not for that dreadful mistake, all this would be ours."

"Yours?"

"Well, *his*, of course."

Lucky stared at the side of Mrs. Potts's face, on which a peach-pink circle had been carefully daubed like a setting sun. Her eyes had lost focus somewhere on the horizon, drifting a half century into the past. For an instant, Lucky allowed herself some glimpse of the strange workings of the universe, the fickle breath that had blown *her* into existence and into Sprague Hall, instead of Prunella Potts. How many other tiny, unknown chances had added up to this moment? The two bodies buried beneath the boathouse, the rest of the world carrying on, the secret guilt on the souls of Nonna and Lucky?

Lucky reached out and patted the old woman's arm. "What a terrible shame for you."

SHE FOUND JOANIE upstairs in her room, staring out the window at the ocean. Teddy stood next to her, resting his hand on her shoulder. When Lucky said, in an overbright voice, *There you are, darling*— Joanie didn't even turn her head.

"He's not coming back, is he?" Joanie said dully.

Lucky met Teddy's gaze for a second or two and stepped forward to Joanie's other side. She touched her daughter's shoulder and said, "No, darling. I don't think he is."

The autumn sun flickered on the water. Lucky found Teddy's knuckles and brushed them with her own fingers, light as a feather.

"I hate him!" Joanie burst out.

"Oh, darling, don't say that!"

"It's true! I do! How could he leave us like this?"

"He didn't *want* to leave you, Joanie! Of course he didn't! I think he thought—he *must* have thought—we were better off without him."

"Well, I guess he was right about that, wasn't he? We don't need him, do we? Now you can marry Mr. Winthrop, and we'll be a family together. Won't we? You'll come to live with us here, won't you? Mr. Winthrop? Won't you?"

Lucky stared through the window. On the other side of Joanie, Teddy said, "Well, that all depends on your mother, of course."

"Mommy?"

Lucky swallowed hard and blinked her eyes. She tried to speak, but the first word came out in a strangled croak. Joanie turned to look up at Lucky, eyes swimming.

"Joanie, honey," said Teddy, "why don't you go downstairs to the kitchen and have Angela give you some of those cookies she baked up? Nice cold glass of milk from the icebox?"

"Cookies don't solve anything!"

"No, that's true. But they sure do help."

Joanie's mouth screwed up. She looked at Teddy, then at Lucky. "I guess you're trying to tell me you want to talk about grown-up stuff."

"Say. Speaking of cookies, you're a pretty smart one yourself."

Joanie climbed to her feet. "See if I care," she said, and stomped out of the room.

Teddy let out a low whistle. "Just imagine what she'll be like when she hits her teens."

"Oh, Teddy, stop."

He turned and reached for her, but she stepped away and wiped her eyes with her thumbs. "Lucky, sweetheart! What's the matter?"

"What's the *matter*? How can you even *ask*? No, don't touch me!"

"Why not? Lucky, look at me."

He reached for her again, but this time Lucky moved to the other side of the room, next to Joanie's bed. She picked up a book on the nightstand and set it down again. So many words choking her throat, and she couldn't say any of them. For the past three months, she'd scrupulously avoided this—standing in the same room, alone with Teddy. To be alone with Teddy was to acknowledge what had happened, what they'd *done*, my God, actually *done* in the panic of the moment, the fear and shock—actually *buried* her husband—buried *Stuy*—right underneath the floorboards of the boathouse, in some cavity already occupied by the remains of a young woman she'd never known existed, the real Maybelle, the heiress to whom Sprague Hall rightfully belonged. Or *would* have belonged to, if she'd lived. Mrs. Potts was right—Lucky should never have owned this place, should never even have been born! It was too much to think about, too much to bear. So she *hadn't* borne it. She'd sidestepped it, circled around it, pretended it wasn't there. Pretended Stuy was just missing, like the papers said. Only the expression in Teddy's eyes made it real—this truth they shared between them—so she hadn't allowed herself to look.

Teddy cleared his throat. "I realize you're still in shock. But when your head clears—"

"He deserved better."

"Yes, he did. Every human being deserves some dignity."

"We weren't thinking straight. We should have gone to the police."

"One of us would have gone to jail. Probably both of us."

"Maybe that would have been better."

He crossed the room so quietly, she didn't hear his footsteps until he was right there, just behind her shoulder. He didn't try to touch her, but she felt his warm breath on her ear, stirring the hair on her head.

"We'll go away together, like we planned. The three of us. Italy, the place you were born. We'll leave all this behind and start fresh."

"Leave? Leave Newport?"

"Leave this crumbling old house, these memories—"

"Are you crazy?"

When he didn't reply, she turned to face him.

"I can't leave, Teddy. It's impossible. Don't you see? I'm stuck here now. I can't leave him. I can't leave either of them. It's my penance, to watch over them both. To keep some kind of vigil over them."

Teddy peered at her through his glasses like she was some faulty facade, some flaw of design or symmetry, to be put right by a few strokes of his pencil. He took off his glasses, wiped them with his handkerchief, replaced them on his nose, and sighed.

"Lucky, I know you feel responsible for what happened. But you're not. He brought it on himself. You didn't push him off that ledge. He fell. It was a tragic accident. For God's sake, you didn't mean for him to die!"

"Just because it's an accident doesn't mean I'm not responsible. He was my husband. I was committing adultery in that boathouse, and if I hadn't, he'd still be alive."

Teddy stepped back. "Are you serious? That's how you see it?"

"That's how I see it. I'm not leaving, Teddy. Joanie and Nonna and I, we're staying in this house until they wheel us out of it."

"How? Living on what? It's mortgaged to the nines, don't you know that? You saw Sprague's will. All those mortgages Stuy took out, when his dad ran out of Maybelle's money. You can't possibly pay those back, let alone keep the place up and feed yourselves!"

"I'll find a way."

"Sure you will. Ever heard of a little thing called foreclosure?"

"What am I supposed to do, Teddy? Sell up? Nobody would buy it, nobody's got that kind of money anymore. It'll go to the preservation society, and then what? They'll find those bodies for sure."

Teddy turned away and stuck his hands in his hair. "I don't believe this. What kind of life is that? What about us?"

"I don't know about us. I don't know about anything, just that this—this—" She thrust her hand toward the window, toward the ocean and the boathouse perched on its edge. "This is my penance, Teddy. My burden. This is the price I pay."

"You can't afford it. Don't you see? You're stuck, you're dead broke. There's nothing left but debts."

A voice came clear and lucid from the doorway. "Yes, there is."

Teddy and Lucky turned in the same instant to regard the willowy, white-haired woman who stood in an elegant, old-fashioned dress of cerise silk, spectacularly unsuited to an October funeral.

She closed one eye and crooked her finger. "Children. Come with me."

NONNA HUMMED TO herself as they crossed the damp lawn, cluttered with leaves that rose and swirled and died again in the capricious breeze of early autumn. Beneath a huge blue sky, the ocean played with the toy sailboats scudding across its surface.

For some reason—denial, maybe, or just plain inattention—Lucky didn't realize they were headed to the boathouse until the warped gray shingles came into focus ahead of them. She hadn't returned there since July, had scrupulously avoided going near the building. Sometimes her gaze happened to fall there as she glanced out the window or went about some business in the garden, and that mere fleeting encounter made her heart race, made her breath choke in her throat. Now she looked up and saw the walls and the worn, familiar angles of the roof, this humble structure that had formed part of her world since she was a child, and she knew it was something else—not a boathouse, but a tomb. Her legs went stiff. She stopped in the grass and listened to her heart thundering in her ears, felt the blood rush to her head.

Nonna turned. Her dress was bright red against the blue sky. The breeze made her white hair fly around her head.

"Don't be afraid," she said. "It gets better."

"That's rich, coming from you," Lucky muttered.

"I mean you'll get used to it. The boathouse, it's just an old building."

"So why are we going in there?"

Nonna glanced over her shoulder at the roofline and back again. "Because I have something to show you, darling. Something I've been saving for you."

"Is it alive or dead?"

"For goodness' sake, just come along and see for yourself."

Teddy cupped Lucky's elbow. "Stay here, if you want. I'll go."

She shrugged him off. "I'm going in. It's got to be done, after all, and I might as well do it now."

It surprised Lucky that the boathouse was exactly as she remembered it, exactly as it had always been—dinghy on its horse, ropes and tackle and tools occupying their proper places. You would never guess what had happened here, or what lay buried in the rocks beneath the floorboards. Lucky paused in the doorway. The sun streamed through the western window and the air smelled of damp and tar and salt. Maybe this was a fitting tomb for Stuy, after all. His favorite place, his favorite smells—the one place he could be himself, as he really was.

Nonna marched without pause across the floorboards to the ladder.

"What are you *doing*?" Lucky exclaimed. "You can't go up there!"

But Nonna was already climbing nimbly to the loft. Her feet were bare and curled around the rungs like an orangutan's. Teddy swore and hurried after her. "Nonna, come down! You'll fall!"

"Don't be ridiculous."

She swung herself up to the loft and stood, smoothing her dress. Teddy sprang up behind her, all stiff and formal in his dark funeral suit, hair slicked back. He pushed his eyeglasses into place and looked down at Lucky, one eyebrow raised.

Lucky's throat was dry. She stared up at Nonna, avoiding the telltale floorboards to the left, near the dinghy on its horse. "Nonna," she said, "please come down. This is no time for a lark."

"A *lark*? You think I've come up here for a *lark*?" Nonna made a noise of contempt and turned away. She pulled a chain free from around her neck, hidden underneath her dress, and walked to the opposite side of the loft.

"Nonna, what's up there? What are you doing?"

"You'll see! Come on, Sonny. I'll need a hand."

Lucky called up desperately, "It's *Teddy*! Not *Sonny*!"

"Like the bear," Teddy grumbled. He made a helpless gesture with his shoulders and followed Nonna across the loft. She was humming again, some aria, inserting a few Italian words here and there. Lucky realized she was biting her nails. Nonna now stood in the exact spot where Lucky had kissed Teddy, where they had undressed each other, pulled the cushions and blankets from the old sofa. Where Stuy had lurched forward and fallen—

"Here it is!" Nonna said. She bent over something and made some rattling noises.

"Teddy! What's going on up there?"

"It's the chest," he said. "She's unlocking the chest."

"The chest?"

"You know, that old footlocker against the wall. The one we tried to open up. Come on, Nonna, let me help you with that."

Lucky kicked off her shoes and headed for the ladder. Her silk stockings made her feet slip on the rungs, but her damp hands gripped better. She thrummed with alarm now. Her heart smacked, her blood sang, her brain seemed to pick up every little detail of noise and sight and touch, all at once.

The footlocker, she thought.

Nonna's footlocker.

Some memory flashed across her mind—an old, heavy, odd-shaped chest that sat in their second-class cabin across the Atlantic, and how her quiet, grieved, preoccupied Nonna barked at the steward when he loaded it a little too carelessly on the rack, to be wheeled down to the Brooklyn dock. *For God's sake, be careful!* she'd snapped. *That's priceless!*

Priceless.

Lucky climbed from the ladder to the floor of the loft and stood, regaining her balance. With Teddy's help, Nonna was raising the heavy lid of the locker until they rested it, ever so carefully, against the wooden wall.

Teddy gasped.

"It's lined with lead, to keep out the damp," said Nonna. "Looks like it's done its job."

Teddy lifted his head and turned to Lucky. The blood had drained from his face.

"Darling," he said, "I think you need to see this."

Lucky stepped across the floor and came to stand between Nonna and Teddy, peering over the edge of the locker. Inside, rolls of canvas lay packed together, each tied with a bright red silk ribbon, the exact shade of Nonna's dress.

She lifted one out and untied the ribbon. Carefully she unrolled the section at the bottom to reveal a rich, luminous scene in oil paint.

Lucky put her hand to her throat.

"Good Lord," whispered Teddy. "It's a Caravaggio. It's the Caravaggio from the lost di Conti collection."

"Some are more valuable than others," Nonna said modestly, "but your grandfather didn't want any of them to fall into the hands of the fascists. And *I* didn't want any of them to fall into the hands of the Spragues. So here you are, darling. They're all yours. Your inheritance."

CHAPTER TWENTY-EIGHT

Andie

Newport, Rhode Island
November 2019

I SMOOTHED MY HAND over the brightly painted Vista Alegre porcelain dinner plate, remembering the holidays and birthdays when my mother had still lived with us and she'd allowed us to use the good china. The six place settings and two serving pieces were the only things worth any value brought over by my Portuguese great-grandparents. They were my inheritance. Or had been before I'd found a buyer online who'd offered me enough money for the entire set that would allow me to replace our furnace before winter settled in.

My father stood behind me and placed his large hand on my shoulder. "You don't need to do this, Andie. I'll find more work, and you'll get a new job."

I set the plate on a square of bubble wrap and taped it tightly. "I hope that we will. But I think we've both learned that there are no guarantees in life. The only thing I *do* know is that we will freeze this winter if we don't get a new furnace. We're already sleeping in our sweaters and it's only November."

I put the package next to the felt-wrapped sterling silver coffeepot on which my mother had spent a month's worth of grocery money when we were children. She'd given it pride of place on the scarred sideboard in what she'd called our dining room in her attempt to detract from the shabbiness of the rest of the room, but instead the result had looked like she'd simply put lipstick on a pig. I wished I'd known that expression back then to explain to my mother what we were all thinking, but I hadn't learned it until I met Meghan. The first time I heard it I thought immediately of the coffeepot and what had been the first loose thread pulled from the hem of our unraveling lives.

We listened to the sound of Petey in the next room playing with his toy boat and plastic dinosaur figures, happily absorbed inside his childish fantasy world where everything was possible. I felt that I had failed him, and that I was responsible for shortening a fragile childhood and leaving him with permanent scars just like his mother's.

The sound from the street of car doors shutting was followed by Petey's shouts of "Luke! Lucky!" and then his sneakered feet running across the vinyl tiles toward the front door.

My father and I shared a look as I stood. By the time we reached the door, Petey had already pulled it open—despite the thousands of times we'd told him not to open the door to anyone—and had his arms firmly wrapped around Luke's legs.

"I am so sorry to intrude without warning, but Luke didn't want to wait." Lucky spoke with her deep voice and mid-century prep school accent, and for the first time, I noticed a slight inflection that might have been Italian.

"Come in, come in." My father pulled the door wide and ushered in the visitors along with a cool blast of November wind. "Perfect timing, too. I've just taken a pan of my famous *pastéis de nata* out of the oven and they are waiting to be eaten. Andie, take their coats and show them into the living room and I will bring coffee and plates. Make sure you seat them next to the space heater. Petey, come with me so you can help."

"Ah, Portuguese custard tarts," Lucky said. "I remember them from my childhood in Italy. Our chef had a Portuguese grandmother who'd taught her how to make them, and so she made them for me because I had such the sweet tooth. I adore them."

I briefly met Luke's eyes as I took his jacket, a fissure of electricity passing through me as my fingers brushed his. We hadn't seen each other since the day of the mudslide and the destruction of the boathouse, which had forced the revelation of over a century's worth of Sprague family secrets. I found it ironic that if *Makeover Mansion* had waited one more day before pulling the plug, they would have had front row seats to the biggest social register scandal the country had seen since the outing of the Mayflower Madame.

When he bent to kiss my cheek, I quickly turned away, reaching for Lucky's heavy mink coat. Luke and I had only spoken briefly in the two months since the remains of two bodies had been discovered beneath the boathouse. National attention had suddenly been directed at Sprague Hall in its secluded corner of Sheep Point Cove, with reporters camped outside and police swarming like termites. Local and national newspapers splashed the Spragues' dirty laundry on their front pages, forcing Hadley and her family to decamp for an extended European vacation.

For weeks, the bodies had been the lead story on the evening news, but the first time I'd seen Luke's picture splashed on the screen, I'd flipped off the television. Even my father didn't have the stomach to hear what he referred to as unfounded rumors and speculation.

Luke called once to let me know that he would be staying away, just to make sure that my name wouldn't be dragged through the muck along with his. I'd understood his reasoning, especially because I had Petey to worry about, but that small part of me, that young girl who'd been abandoned by her mother, couldn't quite believe that Luke was telling me the truth even with the evidence of the continued media presence clogging Bellevue Avenue. Our time together had been short, yet I thought I knew the person Luke really was. But it wouldn't be the first time I'd been wrong about someone. So as the days ticked on without any word from him, and the story disappeared from the front pages and the number of media trucks dwindled, I grew more and more certain that once again I'd been left behind.

I ushered our visitors into the TV room, quickly picking up old newspapers and scooping Legos and matchbox cars into a pile. I indicated for Luke and Lucky to sit on the threadbare sofa whose back my dad had thrown knitted doilies over to try to make it look better. It didn't, but he'd felt obliged to accept them from the widows at church who circled him like vultures and had no other place to put them.

"This is charming," Lucky said as she looked around the room, actually sounding like she meant it. She took the heavy ceramic mug, made by Petey in kindergarten, from my dad and took a sip from it as if it were fine Wedgwood. "Everything is so warm and inviting. I especially love the framed sketches of the cliffs. Such artistic insight! Did you do those?"

I shook my head. "My sister, Melissa. She was the one with all the talent in the family."

Lucky reached out and took my hand, her dark eyes staring into mine like a fortune-teller's. "We all have our talents, Andie. You might not be an artist, but you have a rare fighting spirit not seen in ordinary people. It allows you to pursue your dreams against enormous odds while at the same time being generous with your love and time to those who need you. And you have never quit despite the hardships. That is a rare and precious talent."

She squeezed my hand but didn't let go. "In my years on this earth, I have known too many weak people who folded at the first signs of distress, who lost their way because they were too distracted by small disappointments and couldn't see past them to the love and beauty that existed in their lives. Nor did they have a consuming passion that went beyond money and status, a reason for existence. But you have all of that, Andie. And you have never quit."

It was almost as if she could see through me to the packing box in the dining room, her last words sounding like an accusation. I pulled my hand away, grateful for the excuse to help Petey, who was carrying a large plate of *pastéis de nata,* his small arms wobbling as he approached. "Thanks, Petey," I said, taking the plate from him. My heart hurt as I saw that my dad had used a platter from his wedding china, a pile of inexpensive plates and dishes that stayed in a low cupboard in the kitchen and never saw the light of day.

Dad followed Petey into the room with three more mismatched coffee mugs and placed them on the laminate coffee table before sending Petey back to the kitchen to grab the paper napkin holder. I didn't even flinch when he thunked it down on the table and I recognized it as the one that had sat on the kitchen counter since I was a small girl, the wooden holder topped with what had once been a brightly painted rooster but had long since lost its luster and most of its paint.

Dad pulled a folding chair away from the card table where we always kept a puzzle in progress and set it next to Luke before sitting down in his recliner, mercifully covering most of its food stains earned from too many meals eaten while sitting in it and watching television.

Everyone took a napkin and a tart except for me. My stomach had tightened into too many knots from being so close to Luke that I could barely sip my coffee. Because no one seemed to be in a hurry to discuss the reason for their visit, I directed my attention toward Lucky. "I'm so sorry to hear about your husband. And your . . ." I stopped, not quite sure what to call the woman whose remains had been discovered in the collapsed boathouse.

"Maybelle," Luke finished for me.

Lucky took a dainty bite from her tart, swallowing it down with a sip from her mug. "When I first saw the remains, I knew immediately it was her, of course. I recognized the cameo from her portrait. Although, can we really be sure?" She raised an eyebrow. "Thank goodness for modern DNA testing, although it couldn't confirm *who* she was. All that they could say for sure is that she and I—even if she *is* the real Maybelle—are not blood related."

She took another sip of coffee, watching me closely, seemingly able to see the inner workings of my brain as I flipped through what I knew of the Spragues—of Maybelle's elopement with an Italian prince, and Lucky and her grandmother's escape from Italy during the war. I sat up, my eyes widening in surprise as Lucky smiled, watching me reach the conclusion she already knew.

Before I could ask the obvious question, Lucky continued. "Unfortunately, they couldn't find anything more specific regarding cause of death, or how she ended up in the boathouse."

I looked over at Petey, who'd stopped chewing and was listening intently. My dad excused himself to take Petey into the kitchen and after a moment I heard the small portable television turn on to the sound of cartoons.

Lucky continued. "The only damage to the remains was a small crack on the side of the skull, which makes it appear that Maybelle was either hit on the head by someone or sustained the blow by slipping on a rock as she fell into the water and most likely was knocked unconscious. At least long enough for her to have drowned." She looked down at her hands, her fingers long and still slender. "Poor thing. I suppose we will never know exactly what happened. Or who she really is, as there are apparently no living blood relatives to compare with her DNA." She leaned forward, her eyes staring intently into mine. "But I think it's Maybelle. I know the Spragues better than most and understand what they're capable of."

A small shudder trickled down my spine, but I couldn't look away. "If Maybelle never made it to Italy, then who was your grandmother?"

She glanced at Luke with a secret smile. "Who knows?" Before I could question her further, she said, "I've been meaning to thank you for the lovely note and flowers you sent for Stuy's funeral. It was very kind of you, and I sincerely appreciated that the flowers came from your own garden."

"You're very welcome. I wanted to come, but Luke thought it better I keep any media attention away from me until things had settled down." I avoided looking at Luke when I spoke, not wanting to see something in his eyes I didn't want to see. I didn't think I could take one more loss or disappointment.

"Have there been any new developments in his case?" I asked.

Lucky reached into her large Italian leather bag that she'd placed at her feet, but quickly drew out her hand. With an apologetic smile, she said, "I keep forgetting that I gave up cigarettes years ago, yet every once in a while I find myself craving one."

"It's been difficult for my grandmother since they found the bodies, as you can imagine," Luke said, speaking directly to me for the first time since he'd arrived. "Once my grandfather's body was identified, she became the focus of the investigation, which has been very hard on her, even though they found no evidence that implicated her in any way in his death. They did uncover a lot of gambling debts and are speculating that the people to whom he owed the money took care of the debt themselves when he told them he couldn't pay them back."

Luke pulled out a linen handkerchief from his jacket pocket and handed it to his grandmother. "Which is true. The estate was essentially bankrupt at the time of his death. It was only the discovery of the Italian art that gave the estate the necessary infusion of funds to keep it going for decades."

"I can't imagine your relief," I said to Lucky, sensing Luke's eyes on me, and beginning to wonder at the purpose of their visit. People like Lucky and Luke Sprague didn't pay social visits to a town like Cranston, thirty-three miles away from their estate in Newport. After the initial excitement at finding Luke on my doorstep, I concluded that his showing up with his grandmother made it clear that his visit wasn't going to be romantic in nature. I told myself I was fine with that since I had other matters more pressing than my love life. Like feeding my family.

I casually glanced at the rooster mantel clock, worried that I hadn't been on LinkedIn since the previous night, and afraid I might be missing employment opportunities. I caught Luke watching me, a slight grin on his lips.

I turned back to Lucky, aware that she was speaking to me. "Luke and I stopped by today to discuss a business proposal we think you might be interested in."

"Excuse me?"

Luke leaned forward. "I'm sure you can imagine that you're not the only one who has been wondering that if the woman found in the boathouse is the real Maybelle Sprague, then who went to Italy and married the prince? Who is the real Principessa di Conti? Who is Lucky's grandmother and my great-grandmother?"

"True." I drew out the word. "But I'm not sure how that would involve me. I'm not a detective."

"But you are," Lucky said. "Don't you see? Your passion is the history behind old buildings, the stories that happened within their walls that only they can tell. They really are the storytellers of history, aren't they?"

I was speechless, remembering how I had shared my idea with them the day I'd met Lucky up in her rooms, and confided my dreams. "But . . ."

"That was your idea," Luke finished for me. "We know. That's why we also know that you would be the perfect host for our series."

"Your series," I repeated.

Lucky nodded. "Teddy and I want to bankroll a new series idea—either network or streaming—with you as the official host. The first installment could be you digging into the true identity of the Principessa di Conti—find out who she is. Bring her back to me, if you will. You can tell her story through the houses she called her home. Which is what you love best, yes?"

"As much as all of the media attention has been unbearable," Luke added, "the fact that everyone knows who we are and that the skeletal remains of an unknown woman were found in our boathouse—along with those of my grandfather—means this could be something every network will want."

"I—"

Lucky interrupted me. "I'll give you time to consider our offer. But you should know that Luke and I have decided to sell Sprague Hall. A tech billionaire from California thinks it would be a fun—his word—project to restore it to its former glory and has offered us a ridiculous amount of money. I will be happy to share your contact information with him as someone whom I would recommend to help with such an undertaking.

"Luke and I thought that we could use some of the proceeds to build a home and center for single mothers to raise their children in a healthy environment while they get back on their feet. The house has been a millstone around my neck for far too long and it's time to let it go, and allow it to create something positive for a change."

My mind raced with unasked questions, finally settling on the first one I could grasp. "But where will you live? With Hadley?"

Lucky barked out a raucous laugh and continued laughing until she had to wipe the tears from her eyes. "No. I'm offering her a job at the center because she is the queen of organization and getting things done, but I will not be living with her. I treasure my sanity far too much. Nor will I be moving in with Joanie, much for the same reason. But I'm putting Joanie in charge of the center because she's the only one who can control Hadley and she does have a calming presence and so much to offer to struggling women.

"As for where I'll be living, Teddy and I have decided to marry, and we will be moving to Italy. The Palazzo di Conti was abandoned years ago and it is our desire to restore it and live in it for the rest of our days. Together. It's something we should have done years ago. It's time to grab what happiness I can with what's left of my life. And we will allow you full access for research and filming. We believe our idea is network gold, with all the mystery, history, drama, and a castle in

Italy. Not to mention two buried bodies. And with our connections, there are many more stories waiting to be told in future installments, and with you as the longtime host. Like Robin Leach and his *Lifestyles* show, but with more history and depth."

"And a much more charming host with the gravitas of an advanced degree," Luke added.

I placed my hands on either side of my head as if to keep my thoughts from spinning. There was so much to think about—the furnace, and Petey's education. My dreams that I thought I'd put on hold indefinitely. And I thought of Marc, and how he'd recently checked himself into a rehab facility, and my constant worry about what he would do when he got out.

"If I accept, would I have free rein to bring on board my own consultants?"

Lucky smiled. "Of course. It would be your show. You would call the shots, so to speak."

I felt the sting of tears in my eyes, yet I didn't feel the need to hide them.

Petey rushed in from the kitchen, his face smeared with custard. I immediately grabbed a napkin and wiped his face and hands before he could throw his arms around Lucky. "Lucky, ya wanna come play Minecraft with me? I'll let you beat me, but only the first time."

"I would love to, sweetheart." Luke helped Lucky stand. She took both of my hands in hers and held them tightly. "Please think about it, Andie. Then let me know if you will accept. The series can't exist without you. I see it as a way to save us all." She smiled warmly then leaned over to kiss my cheek.

"I will," I said, although I was pretty sure I already had an answer. I'd never once in my life backed down from a challenge and I wasn't about to start now.

She followed Petey to his room, leaving me alone with Luke. I felt him behind me, that heady pull between us that existed whether or not I wanted it to. It just *was*. I didn't turn around, unsure of what I'd see. If this was going to be goodbye. I would have preferred for him to continue ghosting me. As pathetic as I knew it was, at least that would have let me still hold on to some hope, however unrealistic.

"I wanted to thank you in person." His voice came from directly behind me, and I knew if I turned, we'd be close enough to touch.

This is goodbye. I swallowed. I didn't turn, not wanting him to see. "For what?" I managed, hating how my voice was thick with unshed tears. Mostly because I did *not* cry.

"I've decided to go back to being a pediatrician. And I don't think I could have come to that conclusion without you."

My surprise propelled me to face him as his hands came up to gently cup my shoulders. "Because of me?"

"And Petey." His lips briefly lifted in a smile before his face became serious again. "I've missed you."

I met his eyes, loving how they reminded me of an endless horizon. "How much?"

"Like the desert misses the rain."

I smiled. "Did you make that up yourself?"

"No. I heard it in a song. But it's true."

"I like that. I've missed you, too."

He grinned that sailor-boy grin that I had once hated, but now dreamed about in an almost annoying frequency. "I know we're kind of doing this backward, but . . . can I take you out for dinner sometime?"

"You mean like a date?"

"Exactly like a date." He lowered his lips to mine while his arms wrapped around my waist and my hands reached behind his head to pull him closer, not even stopping at the sound of my father clearing his throat or Petey's whooping in the background, content to let it all fade away like old ghosts and forgotten disappointments, and a once grand estate still clinging to the high cliffs of Newport.

EPILOGUE

Ellen

Lombardy, Italy
October 1899

THE PALAZZO DI Conti swaggered over the surrounding countryside, all square towers and brown stone. It wasn't a fairy-tale castle, like the fantasies on Bellevue Avenue with their turrets and mock battlements, but a fortress given a veneer of civility.

"Do you like it?" asked Sebastiano, as their carriage rattled through the village and up to the castle proper, looming against a storm-struck sky.

"Like" wasn't quite the right word. It was solid, that was for certain. Solid and very, very old. But Ellen wasn't sure whether those walls were there to keep her safe or hold her in. Or maybe a bit of both.

It was October already, a misty, damp October that turned the walls of the castle to ochre and turned the landscape into muted daubs, like the Impressionist paintings they had seen in Paris.

Paris. It felt like years ago already. That's where they'd gone first. Not straight to Italy, but to France.

His bride needed a trousseau, Sebastiano had said, and Ellen had been just as glad to agree, to put off going to Italy, because once they got to Italy, once she stepped foot into his home, the deception would be made solid, as solid as the walls in front of her.

They had spent August in Paris—off-season as it was—acquiring Worth gowns and embroidered underthings, walking dresses and driving dresses and day dresses. When Ellen wasn't being poked with pins and turned this way and that, her new husband began the task of easing her into her new world, his world. *Tout Paris* was away, in Baden-Baden and Trouville and Biarritz, but that only made it all the easier to pay a call on a black-clad dowager in the Faubourg Saint-Germain or a monocle-wearing bachelor in his grand apartment on the Boulevard Hausmann.

"So much the better," Sebastiano told her. "Word of you will spread. By the time you're introduced properly, everyone will feel they know you already."

They avoided Americans. The word had been put out. The former Miss Maybelle Sprague, now the Principessa di Conti, had no interest in her compatriots. Snobbery, the American colony called it, and delighted in tearing her to shreds behind her back. Everyone suddenly remembered that she had been a bit cold. Shyness, ha!

Ellen minded doing an injustice to Maybelle's memory.

"My darling," said Sebastiano. "*Mia bella*. They would have done the same regardless. No one likes to be outranked, not even those of supposedly republican sensibilities. Even had Maybelle been Maybelle, they would have found reasons to hate her."

"No one could hate Maybelle," Ellen protested, but her husband had only shaken his head at her and told her she was charming and she was wrong.

She tried very hard to remember Maybelle, the real Maybelle, with her baby-round cheeks and her nervous duck of the head, her pink flounces and her romantic novels, to hold her in her head and her heart.

But, sometimes, all she could see was a body, bones in a ball gown, buried under a makeshift cairn hard by the river walk. Ellen had insisted they bury her. They owed her that much at least. They'd shifted rock and shale to cover her, working together.

He'd build a boathouse over her, John Sprague had said.

For Maybelle, who had wanted to sail away, and would be forever locked in place, there, beneath the stone, hard by the sea.

There were worse monuments, Ellen's new husband said, and took her to Père Lachaise to see the mausoleums, as if the presence of many graves might lessen the pain of the one. Men had died and worms had eaten them, he told her, and women, too. They would be worms themselves someday, and, in the meantime, they should take the gift they'd been given, the gift Maybelle had given them.

There were times when Ellen could make herself believe him. Paris, even an empty Paris, was fascinating and exciting beyond words. Paris on the arm of the man she loved, even better. It was a delight to dine at Maxim's; to discover foods she hadn't known existed; to wander in wonder the grand, vaulted spaces of the Louvre; or to watch her husband watching her be shocked by the dancers at the Moulin Rouge.

"My darling, your face," he said. "You purse your lips so delightfully."

Together, they climbed the seventeen hundred steps to the top of the Eiffel Tower, Sebastiano complaining all the way, but clearly enjoying himself hugely.

There was a post office at the top, so one could send cards out to one's acquaintances from the top of the world.

Ellen looked at the brightly printed postcards and then at her husband. "I haven't anyone to send one to."

"You have me." His lips quirked in a devilish grin. "You could send one to your loving nephew. 'Dearest Dudley . . .'"

"That's not funny."

When he saw she wasn't laughing, he put his hands on her shoulders, drawing her to him. She could never resist him up close, and he knew it. "My darling, you must stop blaming yourself."

All around them, Paris flaunted itself in its glory. The whole world lay in front of Ellen, the whole world, and this magical, charismatic man, who was somehow, unbelievably hers.

Not hers. Maybelle's. Maybelle, who lay buried beneath layers of stone and wood, unmarked, unmourned.

Ellen looked at him, biting her lip hard enough to hurt. "What if I'm discovered? What if someone realizes?"

"They won't," he said, and drew her close, kissing her until her head spun, kissing her to drive out her fears.

Once her wardrobe was ready, a wardrobe fit for a princess, paid for with Maybelle's money, they caught the very end of the season at Trouville. Ellen dipped her toes in the waters of the Atlantic in one of her new bathing costumes, marveling at how different it was from the rough shale and harsh waves of the beach at Newport. It might be the same ocean, but this was its softer guise, turquoise and beige, not gray on gray, and the late summer sun beamed on them like a blessing. In the evenings, Sebastiano decked Ellen in diamonds and taught her to play baccarat at the casino.

In the casino or on the plage, one could meet people in the most casual way: British lordlings and French marquises. There was the odd American, but they weren't the sort Maybelle would have met during her debutante year.

"If any of them had met Maybelle, they would simply say that marriage brought her out of herself," said Sebastiano, adjusting the cuffs his valet had already adjusted. Ellen was only just beginning to be used to the fact that they traveled with an entourage. She herself had a very correct French maid who seemed to be in a constant state of war with her husband's valet.

Her husband.

That was the strangest thing, how easy it was now to say it, to believe it. Her husband. Hers. In their everyday life, she was becoming accustomed to it, starting to take it for granted, just as she was becoming accustomed to turning her back to the maid to undress her, to chatting in French with their new acquaintances and laughing at herself over her American bêtises, to wagering large sums on the turn of a card.

"Don't you think marriage suits you?" Sebastiano turned her so she faced the mirror. "Look at yourself, *mia bella*."

It wasn't Ellen in the mirror, framed in baroque gold curlicues. It was the Principessa di Conti, with her golden hair frizzed in curls around her face and piled high in more curls on the top of her head; carefully applied maquillage heightening the color of her cheeks, turning her eyes to delft blue; sapphires and diamonds circling her neck and wrists. Not rubies, she'd told her husband, remembering a woman lying on the shale, rubies like drops of blood around her neck. Anything but rubies. So he'd bought her emeralds and sapphires, pearls and diamonds. Never pink. Never red. The new principessa wore greens and blues, and people had already begun to notice and to comment, the princess who reflected the shades of the sea, like Venus rising from the waves.

She didn't look like Maybelle, not really, but she didn't look like herself, either. She looked like the other people one met in Trouville. Like the heiress wife of an Italian prince, a woman who belonged to everywhere and nowhere.

They stopped in Monaco, where they dined with the American-born princess, the former Alice Heine, speaking passionately about theater, ballet, the opera. Sebastiano promised the Princess of Monaco that he would bring his wife back during the season and that they would sit together in the royal box at the opera.

"But La Scala first," he decreed, and the princess and Ellen exchanged a look, two American women together with an overbearing European nobleman, and Ellen was amazed at how easy it was, how natural it felt.

From there, it was a house party in a château in the Loire Valley, with British tweeds and French conversation. No one thought it odd that Ellen didn't ride. Or, rather, they thought it just what one would expect from an American copper heiress whose family didn't know better. Not comme il faut, but certainly not too terrible, as American heiresses go. There had been worse. She was young; she could be taught.

But her voice and her playing—yes, they were universally approved, and the word went out that the Prince di Conti could have done worse.

"You see?" Her husband kissed her on the nose in the privacy of her assigned bedchamber in the French castle. His, as befitted their station, was a different room entirely. It was the talk of the household that the prince spent his nights with his own wife. "No one suspects a thing."

"It seems unfair that we have everything and she has nothing." Ellen drew her knees up to her chest, feeling very small in the great baronial bed hung with silk draperies. "I dream of her sometimes."

She dreamed of that night at the edge of the ocean. Of Maybelle, toppling backward into the sea. Sometimes, in Ellen's dreams, Maybelle rose, sodden with seawater, choking, alive, and Ellen woke, not sure whether to be relieved or ashamed.

It was her fault. Her husband claimed it wasn't. He called it fate and made inscrutable pronouncements about fortune's wheel. But Ellen was a pragmatist at heart. And she knew, deep down, that whatever wheels had been set in motion, she was the one who had propelled Maybelle to her death.

She wasn't to have known, of course, that Frank Pratt had been waylaid by Dermot's men. That was what she reminded herself, when the nightmares came. She'd never meant to steal Maybelle's life. She'd meant to save Maybelle—save her from a life of penury and disillusionment with Frank Pratt.

If she hadn't interfered, if she hadn't told John Sprague . . . Maybelle would be alive.

But how was she to have known Frank wouldn't come? How was she to know that Maybelle would have stood there, alone, on the rocks, until she grew cold and slipped back home?

Maybelle would have married the prince. She would, even now, be visiting this castle in the Loire as part of her honeymoon journey. She would be curled in this great bed with her husband, the prince, sitting by her side, smoothing her long hair, freed from its pins, away from her face. This was Maybelle's life, Maybelle's honeymoon, Maybelle's husband. And Ellen had stolen it. She'd stolen it all.

She hadn't meant to. She hadn't planned to. But did that make her any less guilty?

There were times Ellen pretended she was the prince's mistress rather than his wife. That she was Ellen still and living in sin. Was it worse for one's soul to live with a man outside wedlock or within it in another person's life? Was a marriage a marriage if one married under a name not one's own?

"What's in a name?" her husband asked, tickling her cheek with the soft petals of a hothouse rose. The smell brought with it the memory of their first kiss: all sea air and desire. It was hard not to turn her face up to him, kiss him, pull him down to her.

Ellen made a face at him. "A great deal, apparently." There had been a long discussion at supper over whether a bourgeois family had the right to use the same surname as a noble house. "What about the faux Tournelles?"

"Ah, but that's different. That's a question of lineage, of bloodlines." Sebastiano ran the soft petals of the rose along her throat, making her gasp and arch her neck. His lips followed the rose. "Neither you nor Maybelle had any blood, so there's no difference between you."

"Are we interchangeable to you, then?" Ellen gasped, having trouble keeping track of the conversation. "One blond girl much like another?"

Sebastiano raised his head, looking into her eyes. "My darling, you are you and you alone—but it's not for your name I love you, but for your nature, which would be what it is whether you were named Melusine or Martha." He stretched her arms up over her head, lowering his body over hers. "Don't fret."

Ellen fretted. Not all the time. But in the gray hours before dawn, as her husband—contrary to aristocratic fashion—slept beside her. In the gap before supper. Not about discovery—she'd learned that her husband was quite right, and to the bored nobility of Europe, all Americans did look the same—but about Maybelle. About the life she had stolen from her.

There were times, in a gilded salon, a champagne coupe in her hand, diamonds heavy on her wrists, when it would strike her, forcibly, that by rights she shouldn't be here at all. If the world had spun as it ought, she should have been in a narrow brownstone in New York teaching someone's talentless child to play scales. It should be Maybelle tapping the Prince of Wales—the Prince of Wales!—on the shoulder with her fan, Maybelle standing beside a piano rich with gold leaf and singing "Where'er You Walk," now immortalized in the illustrated papers as "the song that won the heart of a prince."

And so it had, in a way. Ellen clung to that, to the knowledge that the prince had loved her before, when she was nothing more than a music teacher.

But he would never have married the music teacher. He would never have brought her back to his ancestral home as his bride.

Here, now, in the October rain, with the Palazzo di Conti before her, the true magnitude of what they had done, the lie they had told, slammed down on Ellen like the iron grating of an oubliette. An oubliette, where one dropped people one wanted to forget. But that was the problem. She couldn't forget. She couldn't forget that she wasn't Maybelle.

And she couldn't pretend, as she had in their flit across Europe, that this was a sort of dream, a magical, temporary time.

The Palazzo di Conti was too solid, too real. Once she stepped out of the carriage, this would be her home. She would be Maybelle, forever and always. And the real Maybelle abandoned. Forgotten.

"There's no going back, is there?" she whispered.

Her husband's hand settled over hers. "My darling, there was never any going back. Not after that night."

Ellen looked up at him, at his familiar, beloved face, knowing that he knew exactly what she was thinking, that he was the one person in the world who knew her for what she was, down to the bone. The one person for whom she didn't have to pretend. "Sometimes I imagine I'm only your mistress. It makes it feel . . . less cruel."

Warmth kindled in the prince's eyes. "You can be my mistress all you like," he said, and lifted her hand to his lips, "but you are also my wife. Ready, *mia bella*?"

She wasn't, not at all, but Ellen stepped down from the carriage. The servants had been lined up in rows to meet their new mistress. The Principessa di Conti. Ellen took a deep breath and smiled and nodded and tried to take heart from the fact that to them, that was all that mattered. She was the American woman their lord had married, and it didn't matter to them whether she were Ellen or Maybelle.

The only person to whom it mattered was a third cousin twice removed who had been defrauded. John Sprague had his annual allowance and the use of the house in Newport, to continue through his lifetime and his son's, per the bargain he had struck with the prince for Maybelle, the real Maybelle.

One blond girl was much like another, so long as the money went where it was meant to go.

Ellen followed her husband into his ancestral home, feeling rather unreal. And perhaps just a little queasy. It occurred to her, vaguely, that some of their activities might have led to their logical conclusion. An heir for the house of di Conti.

Unlike the Sprague house, there was no doubting this was a home. It seemed strange, but there it was. Grand as it was, this was a house that had been lived in, where everything had grown up over the centuries, added to generation by generation, as much for use as for show.

Her husband took her through a room with a high, ribbed ceiling, the parquet floor worn smooth with generations of use, waving a hand at the paintings as they passed, "Caravaggio . . . Tintoretto . . . Rubens. That pug-nosed man with the breastplate is one of my less reputable ancestors. We call him a condottiere, but he was really a bandit. And that lady, with the side curls and the smug expression—that's the Medici bride."

Would someone a hundred years from now walk this gallery and point to Ellen, saying, "That's my ancestress, the American bride?"

"Ah, and here's my favorite." The prince drew to a stop in front of a thoroughly naked woman, water lapping around her thighs. Her long, damp hair trailed over one shoulder, hiding absolutely nothing.

"Another ancestress?" said Ellen, trying to keep her tone light, trying not to show how intimidated and scared and wrong she felt.

Her husband squeezed her hand. "Titian. Venus, rising from the sea." He looked down sideways at her, his face taking on an expression she knew well. "When I met you, I thought of this painting."

Ellen couldn't help it. Even when she felt most guilty, most like she should abandon this deception, she still desired him. She licked her dry lips. "I was rather more clothed."

Sebastiano grinned at her, a rogue's grin. "I was wishing you weren't."

Ellen looked at the painting. This wasn't the stylized Venus on a shell she had seen elsewhere. This Venus had emerged wringing wet from the waves, her skin dappled with water, her fair hair dark and dripping with it. She was twisting the water out of her hair, glancing over her shoulder as though afraid she might be engulfed.

Like Maybelle.

Maybelle pulled up out of the sea.

"You were meant to be marrying Maybelle." Ellen could feel the tears prickling her eyes, all the guilt she'd been trying to hide from surging through her like the surf, threatening to drown her. "You were meant to be showing this to Maybelle. It should be Maybelle in your bed, not me."

"You are Maybelle and Maybelle is you." Her husband turned her to face him, holding her by both hands. Any trace of humor had faded. He was very serious and every inch the prince. "The past is past. It is done. That night, you were reborn out of the sea like Venus, rising from the waves. My Venus. My love. My wife. *Mia bella*."

If she closed her eyes, if he said it just the right way, it blended into one: Maybelle, *mia bella*.

"I feel like I'm losing myself." She had to say it quickly, before she lost her nerve. "I feel like I'm not anyone at all. If you loved—loved Ellen, how can you love what I am now, what I've become?"

"You are still you. What happened on that beach doesn't change that. What happened in front of the priest doesn't change that. What will happen in the future doesn't change that. I loved you before. I love you now. I will love you when you are a terrible dowager terrifying our grandchildren."

"I won't be terrible!" Ellen protested.

"Won't you?" The intensity of his gaze was lightened by a little glint, gold flecks in green eyes. "You don't know your own strength, *mia bella*. But I do. That is what you bring to this family. Not Sprague money. But your own heart. Your strength. Your firmness of purpose."

Ellen took a deep breath, trying to find that strength, that purpose. "There's no going back."

Her lover folded her in his arms. "As long as I am alive, *mia bella*, you will never have to go back."

ACKNOWLEDGMENTS

No book is an island (even if Newport is located on one). Team W would like to offer our sincere thanks to all the people without whom this book would never have happened, starting with Rachel Kahan, Liate Stehlik, Tavia Kowalchuk, Brittani Hilles, and the entire team at William Morrow, who make it possible for us to do what we do, and underwrite our bar bill. This bottle of prosecco is for you!

Thank you to the always awesome A-Team: Alexandra Machinist and Amy Berkower, the A to our W, expert hand-holders, cover critquers, and author-whisperers—who also understand about our bar bill. Cheers, darlings!

There is a nasty rumor going around that Team W picks our book topics based solely on places we wish to take tax-deductible vacations. (Ahem, Paris, ahem.) We have no idea where anyone got that idea . . . (Ahem, book talk, ahem.) But it is true that getting to wander the cottages and cliff walks of Newport was a major incentive. Covid might have delayed us, but it didn't stop us! So many thanks to the charming Gilded hotel in Newport, which provided us the perfect spot to hammer out the revisions to this book (and those delicious breakfast sandwiches), and to the Hotel Viking for a blissful evening of drinks and plotting. A huge thank-you is also due to our fellow author, the charming and brilliant Deborah Goodrich Royce, for putting the perfect cap on our trip with a wonderful evening at the historic (and perfectly glorious) Ocean House hotel in nearby Watch Hill.

We are so grateful to the Preservation Society of Newport County for maintaining these monuments to a bygone era and for the marvelous tours (and app!). Although Newport tends to be synonymous with the late nineteenth century, for this book we needed to know about mid-century and the present day as well. Huge thanks to Lydia Tower and Elijah Duckworth-Schachter for being our window into modern Newport and fielding questions about the intricacies of yachts and yacht clubs. Any mistakes are entirely our own and probably because we were drinking too much prosecco. Thank you to Private Newport, Newport Mansions, and Mansions of the Gilded Age for providing daily inspiration in our Instagram feeds and making us feel like we were back in Newport even after we were dragged away by our more mundane obligations.

For those of you as enchanted by the history of Newport as we were, we strongly recommend a visit to this legendary seaside resort with a knack for reinventing itself over the generations. You can tour many of the locations described in the book, including Marble House (where the Tiffany Ball of 1957 really did take place, diamonds and Kennedys and all) and the Cliff Walk, which leads you past the backsides of many of Newport's most splendid "cottages." (Note: bring sturdy walking shoes for the more rugged portions of the trail!) Sprague Hall itself, of course, is a figment of our fertile imaginations, but as you walk between Rosecliff and Marble House—along the wonderfully-named Sheep Point Cove, which our longtime readers will adore just as much as we do—you can just about imagine Lucky's mansion wedged in there among its pedigreed neighbors. And if you pay close attention, you might just notice a boathouse perched on the cliff between path and sea. We're pretty sure there's nothing scandalous hidden beneath.

Thank you to our families and pets for not having more than the usual number of crises while we were writing this book, and for staying off the Wi-Fi during our marathon FaceTime plotting sessions during early May of 2020, after our dreams of a team retreat in Newport became dust in the wind of a global pandemic. We also owe a big thank-you to Meghan White (the inspiration for Meghan Black) for sharing her knowledge and expertise on historic preservation and explaining the difference between restoration and arrested decay (hint: the latter has nothing to do with skin care).

One of the things we've learned writing this book entirely during the pandemic was that even though everything might be remote, our friends in the book world aren't. So many thanks to our wonderful fellow authors, bloggers, reviewers, bookstagrammers, and readers who kept us going through canceled events, quarantines, thwarted research trips, and all the other ups and downs of the past two years. We're so hoping that by the time these words are on the printed page we'll be with you in person again!

About the authors

About the book

Insights,
Interviews
& More . . .

Meet Beatriz Williams, Lauren Willig, and Karen White

Amanda Suanne Photography

Beatriz Williams, Lauren Willig, and Karen White are the coauthors of the beloved *New York Times* bestselling novels *The Forgotten Room, The Glass Ocean,* and *All the Ways We Said Goodbye.*

Beatriz Williams is the *New York Times* bestselling author of eleven novels, including *A Hundred Summers, The Secret Life of Violet Grant,* and *The Summer Wives.* A native of Seattle, she graduated from Stanford University and earned an MBA in finance from Columbia University, then spent several years in New York and London as a corporate strategy consultant before pursuing her passion for historical fiction. She lives with her husband and four children near the Connecticut shore, where she divides her time between writing and laundry.

Lauren Willig is the *New York Times* and *USA Today* bestselling author of more than twenty novels, including *Band of Sisters, The English Wife,* and *The Ashford Affair,* as well as the RITA Award–winning Pink Carnation series. An alumna of Yale University, she has a graduate degree in history from Harvard and a JD from Harvard Law School. She lives in New York City with her husband, two young children, and vast quantities of coffee.

Karen White is a *New York Times* and *USA Today* bestselling author of twenty-five novels, including *Dreams of Falling* and *The Night the Lights Went Out*. She currently writes what she refers to as "grit lit"—Southern women's fiction—and has also expanded her horizons into writing a mystery series set in Charleston, South Carolina. After spending seven years in London, England, and attending the American School in London, she obtained a BS in management from Tulane University. She has two grown children and currently lives near Atlanta, Georgia, with her husband and a spoiled Havanese dog.

Reading Group Guide

1. Had you ever heard of or visited Newport, Rhode Island, before reading this book?
2. What did you make of Stuyvesant Sprague and his marriage to Lucky? What do you think she meant when she said at the end that Stuy "deserved better?"
3. Was Ellen right to report Dermot to the police despite his personal kindness to her? How does her flight from New York foreshadow the decision that Ellen makes later in the book? Do you agree with her choices?
4. Ellen thinks to herself: "She'd no call to be feeling sorry for an heiress . . . As long as her salary was paid." Did you feel sorry for Maybelle? What kind of different ending would you have written for her?
5. Prince Sebastiano encourages Ellen to take Maybelle's place, saying, "Honor her with your living. Live the life she might have lived." Is that what Ellen does? Would you have been persuaded by that argument?
6. Jackie Kennedy tells Lucky: "All these palaces . . . had a single perfect moment in history, and then the hour was past. . . . I don't know if you can ever get such a thing back once it's gone." Do you agree with her? What do you think the next phase of Sprague Hall's history will be like, once Lucky sells it?
7. Each "Team W" book is written in alternating storylines by Beatriz Williams, Lauren Willig, and Karen White. Can you guess who wrote which storyline?